phoenix's last heist

Love and Other Cosmic Crimes

Book One

lily riley

To the readers who believe space is cold so characters must be hot out of spite.

1

lyra

Watch Your Step While Looting

WHEN THE FLOOR gives way beneath me, I know I've gone too far.

The sharp crack of breaking rock and dull rumble of shifting earth boom through the stone-hewn temple, shattering the silence like blasphemy. My gut drops—hard, sudden—as if my stomach's been ripped out through my throat. The rush of air tears at me and gravity drags me down, faster, deeper. For one wild, unthinking moment, I imagine the sound my body will make when it meets the stone below. The ugly, wet crunch of bone and flesh. Darkness yawns wide beneath me, so absolute that even the full-spectrum lights on my helmet can't cut through it.

My father's words of warning flash through my mind as I flail wildly, grasping for something to save me from plummeting to what promises to be my untimely—but unmourned—death. Pulse roaring in my ears, my sweat-slick hands tangle in the fibrous, rope-like roots of the banthus tree growing through the walls of the ancient ruins. My body jerks to a stop with a violent snap, slamming into the side of the pit and dangling above what sounds like a very, *very* long drop.

Pain detonates through my shoulder as ancient dust floods

my mouth, a loamy note on the copper I already taste on my tongue. Heart battering against my aching ribcage and head spinning, I desperately try to reorient myself.

For a heartbeat, the only sounds are the soft skittering of pebbles and dirt as they rain down from the gaping maw that was the temple's floor. It's like a kiss of salt on my wounds—and my pride. Then, from somewhere deep in memory, my father's voice again:

"If you get to the Chamber of the Second Moon, turn back—you've gone too far."

Too far. Always too far.

"Could've used a bit more of a heads-up there, Dad," I huff to myself, jittery with a heady combination of relief and humiliation. "Something like, 'Oh, watch out for boobytraps and structural integrity issues in the five-thousand-year-old temple, kiddo!'"

My ass and side ache where I slammed into the wall of the pit, but I'm otherwise fine—no major injuries, minus the bruises that will certainly color to a festering blue-black over the next few days. Slithering rivulets of sweat drip down the back of my neck as I pull myself up, gripping the thick roots with my thighs and sliding my hands along the slick bark. My progress is slow, but I don't want to risk slipping back down, so I climb with the cautiousness I should've shown before instead of barreling through the ancient structure with my characteristic impatience and irritation.

Grunting with effort, I haul my body over the edge of the crumbling floor and shimmy away from the lip of the hole, tucking myself between the massive trunk of the banthus and the cool stone walls of the chamber. Bright afternoon light filters in through the open roof and verdant rainforest canopy where lush jungle has reclaimed the once-sacred space. Towering trees —even bigger than the banthus—cast mottled shadows while parasitic vines twist through tiny cracks in the mortar, and strange purple and green mosses cling to every damp surface.

The outside jungle is a riot of competing sounds and smells—a cacophony of strange animals and stranger insects, cloying aromas of flowers and overripe fruits mixed with vegetal decay, but in this massive sanctuary, it fades behind the peacefulness of dripping water and ancient stone.

Although this temple once belonged to a race of alien warriors older than time itself, even they are faint blips in the storied existence of this planet. Nature was here long before them and has continued to thrive after the decline of their civilization.

Despite the dappled shade inside, the heat from the twin suns of this system makes the tropical humidity thick and oppressive, making my brief rest feel anything but rejuvenating. The sultry air and the chemical composition of the atmosphere on this planet make breathing feel more like a chore than anything, and I regret my decision to leave my full life-support suit back on my ship. Not only would the filtration system have been helpful, but the cooling system would have been decidedly welcome. At the time, I'd opted out of the extra gear partly because it's heavy and unwieldy, and partly because I just spent three months on a frozen chunk of stupidity some asshole had the nerve to call a moon. Despite my orders, smuggling contraband glacillite crystals off-world wasn't worth the frostbite that almost claimed my fingers and toes.

A quick romp through a tropical paradise sounded too good to be true, and of course, it is. There's nothing good about this trip, except for the fact that when I get what I've come for, I'll be one step closer to freedom—real freedom, the kind that doesn't come with a leash or a homing beacon. Every assignment, every bruise, every sleepless night is a transaction toward that goal. But the closer I get, the more I feel the walls tightening—the rules and false promises of the grasping hand that still owns me.

Some stars-forsaken species of fat, blood-sucking insect flies over, landing on my sweat-sticky skin and I swat it—the slap echoing off the temple walls.

Paradise, my ass.

A cheery tone dings in my helmet.

Internal body temperature approaching critical levels. Rest and hydration are recommended to avoid heatstroke. Artificial life-support system is advisable for this planet.

"I swear to the stars, Ada—if you hit me with an 'I told you so,' I will rewire you. Again," I grumble.

Acknowledged. That went so well for us last time. If you're interested in the data, having my entire neural network ripped apart and rebuilt at the whim of a frequently inebriated hybrid has decreased our mission success percentage by 66.6%.

I wince. The Advanced Digital Assistant, or ADA, that came installed in the *Aldrin-136* has all the charm of a black hole and about as much warmth. I'd inherited the ship in a haze of grief and regrettably reprogramed the system after one too many jars of illegal Zorium moonshine. When I rebooted her, Ada had come back online with a computer chip on her shoulder and an overactive sarcasm drive. In other words, I'd drunkenly created the galaxy's most irascible AI navigator.

"I'm not heading back to the ship just yet. I'm already inside the Celestial Temple. All I have to do is find the Chamber of the Early Sun and grab the idol of the Solar Mother or whatever, and then—assuming I can successfully duck Brill and his flunkies long enough to decipher the clues—it's back to the Epsilon-6 station for a little R&R," I say, cheered by thoughts of booze-soaked pleasures involving little clothing and even fewer attachments.

What do you mean by R&R? Ada asks, not one to grasp colloquial nuances.

I chuckle. "It means I'll learn what I can from the idol and then unload it before indulging in as much debauchery as I can lay my fingers on," I huff, brushing the dirt from my filthy shorts. "I'm talking gallons of moonshine and some burly alien dude with tentacles in all the right places, if you know what I mean."

Your lack of ambition is disappointing and your extracurricular choices are ill-advised.

Ada's motherly disapproval makes me snort in derision. I take a swig of tepid, metallic-tasting water from my canteen.

"Yeah, well, the water you recycled from the ship tastes like robot piss. So there."

Perhaps you should clean the filtration system, if you are displeased. In fact, all of my systems could benefit from regular cleaning and routine maintenance.

A distant crash and angry shout interrupt the din of rainforest patter and my snarky response to Ada dies on my lips.

"I thought you said this landing site was clear!" I hiss into my helmet, scrambling into a low chamber on my left. The downward sloping room is littered with remains of ancient statuary partially obscuring a small shaft in the back corner. An exit, perhaps? I haul ass toward it.

Accurate. The landing site is clear. But the site of the Celestial Temple is within a protected area.

"A protected area? Dad's journals didn't mention anything about that and I don't remember it on any of our maps. What the fuck does that mean?"

Heavy footsteps thud on the packed earth path outside, and while it only sounds like one set of feet, I don't want to stick around to find out who they belong to. Other looters? Feds? Or worse—Brill's flunkies? I grimace, considering my options.

I do *not* want to go into the small, dark tunnel.

Small, dark tunnels are usually filled with boobytraps, undesirable poisonous critters, and rotting filth that makes the interior of my ship look pristine.

Again, I regret my decision to forgo my full suit. *Fuck.* Maybe fate will throw me a bone and whoever is skulking around outside will just pass on by.

The Celestial Temple is in the center of a Xylothian historical site and protected nature reserve.

"Shit. Fuck. Shit. Okay…what does the law enforcement look

like here? Please tell me it's just some local bullshit and it's not an Interplanetary Federation outpost. I swear to the stars, Ada, if you dumped me next door to the Feds, rewiring will be the least of your worries."

You are in the jurisdiction of the Xylothian Protectorate.

I shut off the lights from my helmet just as metal-soled boots clunk onto the stone floor of the temple's entryway—one room away from where I'm currently crouched. Typical. Of course whoever it was wouldn't just pass on by. That would make my life too easy! I curse every god in every star system I can think of and crouch, preparing myself mentally for what will almost certainly be unpleasant at best.

Silently, I crawl through the tunnel that opens into the darkness.

"Ada!" I hiss as my hands and knees sink into a layer of soft, wet, wriggling sludge. "Can you do a scan down here? Do you detect any life forms? Anything particularly venomous or creepy or crawly?"

Infrared scans detect multiple life forms of varying degrees of danger.

My hands brush against something slimy that hisses and burrows in the opposite direction. Panic-laden nausea rolls through me and I allow myself the tiniest whine.

"Do I want to know what they are?"

The probability is high that you do not.

The tunnel veers sharply left, then right, curving downward beneath the temple. Over the sounds of my limbs squelching through muck, I can hear the faint rush of water. A muggy breeze blows past me from somewhere up ahead, smelling like silt and vegetation. Perhaps the shaft lets out near the river encircling the temple. Assuming I can find my way out of here, I'll head back to my ship and wait until nightfall to come back, find the idol, and then hightail it off this cursed planet.

The tunnel starts to rise upward and, at last, a pinprick of light appears in the blackness ahead. I crawl faster, spurred on by the warm, buoyant relief flooding my body. *Bye bye, creepy tunnel!* Thick greenery blocks much of the view, but the sound of the river grows louder when I near the end, hopefully far enough away from the mystery intruder to make a quick escape, if necessary. I tumble out onto a plush carpet of dark purple moss and scan the area.

It's not the riverbank.

I'm still in the temple complex in some kind of inner courtyard. Towering walls of pitted black rock encircle the overgrown garden and at the center stands a tall, carved figure—some likeness of the warrior monks who built this temple and worshipped the stars.

I take in the long limbs and muscular torso of the alien statue. His face holds a serene expression written in the captivating eyes, high cheekbones, and full lips.

"Don't recall coming across any Xylothians before. He's kind of cute," I murmur. "I'd hit it."

The figure is a Xylothian Protector. A class of warriors known for their devotion to their sky-borne deities, their single-minded focus on training in lethal hand-to-hand combat, and their abstinence from alcohol, frivolity, and intercourse. You would not be compatible, Ada chirps in my helmet.

"Pity," I reply, already moving on. "Now, what's the best way out of here?"

The walls around the courtyard are partially obscured by shoulder-high shrubs studded with hot pink flowers, so it takes me a minute to find the low door tucked into the back wall. As I duck to enter, I turn my helmet lights back on. This chamber is mostly intact—as if the voracious jungle itself has deigned to honor the sanctity of the space.

The vibrant illumination from my helmet lights falls across intricate reliefs carved into the walls and even though I've seen my fair share of otherworldly wonders, I can't help the small gasp that escapes my lips. *Focus, Lyra.* One relic left—*just one*—and you're done.

The carvings shimmer like constellations frozen in stone, a reminder of what's at stake if I screw this up. If I'm caught here, I'm finished. Not just dead—worse—frozen in my own kind of miserable stasis, still tied to the same monster, the same work, the same horrors.

Dust drifts from the ceiling as I move deeper, the beam of my helmet slicing through the dark. Shapes emerge from the gloom —a celestial map, carved so precisely the stars seem to twinkle when I pass my light over them. All around me, the heavens whirl.

I recognize some of the star systems etched into the stone, but many of them are unknown to me. Dad would've killed to see this—to trace the missing constellations no one on Earth's even named. An unwanted flare of loneliness surges, deepening the cracks in my heart that formed long ago. I breathe slowly through the ache, and through the blur of gathering tears I see something sparkling in the darkness.

At the center of the opposite wall stands another statue—a Xylothian priestess, I'm guessing—kneeling before a polished golden sun. In her cupped palms, she holds…

"No fucking way," I murmur, taking a tentative step forward.

The Solar Mother idol. The figurine glitters like gold but is made of a precious metal far rarer—enaurium. Small symbols trail from the top of the idol's head across her breasts and down her legs. My pulse kicks hard. That's it—the key to my way out, sitting in a goddess's hands. I'm eager to get the idol back to my ship so I can copy the writing down and get to work translating it.

My fingers itch to pluck the treasure from the hands of the statue, but I've been down this road before and I know better. One wrong move, and the whole chamber could collapse and bury me six feet under alien stone. The first thing I need to do is survey the area—the Chamber of the Early Sun, if my dad's journals are right—for any traps or ancient security measures. Just because these Xylothians built this monument thousands of years ago doesn't mean they were primitive or foolish. If this mother goddess is the reason for the creation of this entire temple complex, there are bound to be some boobytraps.

"Ada, do a scan of this chamber with particular attention on any load-bearing columns or walls. I'm looking for traps here. I'd love to grab the goods and get out of here without having my hand chopped off."

The floor directly around the feet of the main statue is hollow beneath the tiles. Scans indicate stepping on the floor within a three-meter radius of the base will result in the collapse of the ground beneath you. Again.

"Great. Instant death, Xylothian style. Super helpful," I reply, trying to work out the best way to get to the outstretched hands and my future payday. To the left of the statue stands a long, low rectangular crypt made from the same pitted black rock as the courtyard outside. "Anything weird about the creepy sarcophagus?"

I do not detect any surface abnormalities.

"Good enough for me," I say, jumping on top of the moss-slick surface. I slip when I land, going down hard on my knees. With a curse, I wobble back up and gauge the distance from the edge of the crypt to the statue.

Would you like me to calculate the odds of you achieving a successful landing?

"Never tell me the odds," I grunt, leaping forward and reaching out with both arms. Adrenaline spikes as I consider the amount of noise I'm making and the mystery intruder skulking around nearby. I can't turn back now, though—not when I'm *this* close.

I slam into the shoulder of the statue and hook my arms around its neck, lowering just enough to reach the shimmering idol. Tentatively, I reach out.

It's warm to the touch and emits a faint, vibrating hum. That's unexpected and…slightly alarming. I can't decide if I'm more worried about something supernatural or something toxic.

"Uh, this thing is safe to handle, right? I mean, it's not radioactive or anything."

Radioactivity levels are within the acceptable range for a half-human, half-Velusian hybrid.

"You could just say 'it's fine,' Ada. No need to bring my parents into this," I say, not bothering to hide my bitterness.

It's fine.

"Thank you," I reply sarcastically, pulling the heavy idol from its resting place. I stash it in the open pocket of my thigh holster and climb back up to the head of the statue. Begging the stone priestess's forgiveness, I launch myself back over the crypt, landing with another inelegant crash.

The way out of the chamber is relatively easy this time and when I find myself back in the courtyard, I spot an opening in the wall I must've missed before. Crouching low, I cross through the crumbling gateway, hoping the intruder has already come and gone.

The air hits me like a wet towel to the face, but I can't stop the grin that tugs at my lips. My boots sink into moss as I push through the foliage, lungs burning, heart drumming with the echo of the escape. Every nerve feels lit, raw, alive. Just a few miles east along the river and I'll be back at my ship—almost there, almost done. The thought makes my pulse jump all over again. Then I can stow the cargo, take an actual shower, and finally dig into the secret ration of chocolate my dad smuggled me from his last trip to Earth.

The thought of him catches me off guard—a flicker of warmth that twists before it lands. For a second, the jungle noise dulls, and I swear I can smell the engine grease, dirt, and ozone that always clung to his jacket. My chest tightens, but I shake it off. I can't afford to drown in ghosts right now. It's as good a time as any to break out the good stuff and celebrate. Because for once, I actually pulled it off. No alarms, no guards, no blood— well, very little blood. Just me, the relic, and the open sky ahead. Stars, I might even pop open the bottle of fizzy carbonyl I stole off that Jovian Stormrider last year. He swore it'd taste like lightning. Tonight, I'll find out if freedom does too.

With a bounce in my step, I make for the riverbank, careful to veer away from any poisonous-looking plants. The first sun is setting over the horizon, bathing the jungle in melted golden light and lowering the sweltering temperature to something bordering on bearable. Vibrant birds chirp, fragrant tropical flowers bloom, and the milky teal river burbles over mossy green rocks. For the first time in months, everything feels like it's working out in my favor.

"Hey Ada," I begin, relaxed enough to indulge my curiosity. "You said the Celestial Temple was in the territory of the Xylothian Protectorate. What are they about?"

They are about one and a half meters behind you.

"What the shit?"

I whip around, just in time to catch the butt of a plasma rifle to the temple.

2
orion

The Ancestors Are Not Going to Like This

FUCKING LOOTERS.

Every time I think I've stamped them out, another swarm shows up. The black market for Xylothian relics is booming again—nothing like a good old tragedy to turn history into merchandise. Ever since the *Arkanium* went down, our sacred sites have been stripped bare one artifact at a time.

The name still hits like an electric shock. I drag in a breath that's heavy with sweat-seasoned humidity and press a hand to my chest. The ache's duller now—less sucking chest wound, more phantom ache—but it's still there. Twenty thousand souls, my parents among them, swallowed by the void. And me, left here to play galactic hall monitor in the ruins of our own extinction myth.

I used to report every raid, every desecrated site, begging for backup. The answers always came back the same: *Too risky. Too political. Too remote.* Translation: *Not worth saving.* So now it's just me out here, one ranger to an entire sector, surrounded by jungle thick enough to swallow sound.

Static crackles in my comm. No answer. Figures. The silence ringing in my ears is faithful, predictable, and comfortable enough to be a friend.

I make a note to log another incident report the Feds will ignore. Out here, law enforcement is just a formality—the kind of duty that keeps you busy so you don't think too hard about how little it changes. Most looters end up right back where I found them, pockets heavier, excuses thinner. It's a cycle, and I keep playing my part in it because *someone* has to.

But this looter's new. The body at my feet is filthy, still, and not one I recognize.

Her helmet's display flickers before fading to black. A few strands of hair—brown streaked with pink—stick to her temple, matted with blood and sweat. When I shift, the light filtering through the trees catches her face: soft angles, a sharp jaw, a faint shimmer beneath the dirt that marks her as Velusian.

It's no wonder Velusia is home to the best and most highly sought-after pleasure district in several galaxies. Even unconscious, she looks engineered for charm—beauty as biology's best negotiation tactic. But there's something off here, something too rough around the edges for a Velusian alone.

Her gear's a mess of contradictions: mud-caked hiking boots, black shorts, a filthy white shirt, a thigh holster, and a waist harness stuffed with under-maintained weapons—a small plasma pistol and a serious-looking knife. The only piece of real tech worth a damn is the helmet, and even that didn't save her from me.

I crouch beside her. Red blood seeps from the gash along her hairline, dark against the pale dust. Human, then—or close enough.

I probably shouldn't have hit her so hard. The thought lands heavy, dull, like the echo of the rifle's butt against her helmet. I'm not allowed to kill anyone in Protectorate territory—not just because the Feds will be pissed, but because it's forbidden by my ancestors who built the Celestial Temple.

We're on sacred ground, and I've already committed an act of violence—even if she's just stolen our most revered artifact. The relic's absence thrums in my chest like a second heartbeat.

Grumbling about my recklessness, I hoist the woman up over my shoulder and carry her to my parked swamp buggy. She's heavier than I would've guessed and it's enough to send a heated thrill through my body that makes me recoil. Now is *not* the time, this is *not* the place, and she is *not* the one.

I throw the woman into the back seat, securing her hands and feet. If she comes to and wants to flee, she'll have a hell of a time getting free without my help. Kicking the buggy into gear, I take off through the jungle toward my temporary camp, where I have a first aid kit stashed in the crates inside my tent. I usually camp out here for a few days at a time, especially if I'm tracking looters. I was eating breakfast this morning when I heard her ship fly in and land in the grassy plain just outside the protected territory.

My camp is in a clearing near the river, and I've taken care to avoid any areas on common wildlife trails. This part of the rainforest is protected from any hunting, mining, and agricultural exploitation, which means the ecosystem supports formidable predators. I don't want to tangle with any if I can help it.

By the time I unload my gear, stow my buggy, and dump the unconscious woman onto my cot, the second sun is setting and the heat of the day is finally waning. I stoke a small campfire, light a few lamps to keep curious creatures at bay, and shuffle into my tent to look after my latest mistake.

Dried blood crusts her hair to her face and mats it against her scalp. I wince—I should've seen to it earlier, but I didn't want to wait to get my camp prepped and risk having to set everything up in the dark.

After double checking the knots on her bindings, I pull out my first aid kit to clean the cut on her head. With a few swipes of antiseptic, she lets out a low moan and shakes her head as she comes to. Bleary violet eyes blink up at me, unfocused.

Shit. Did I give her a concussion?

When she sees me, her gaze clears and after a few unsteady heartbeats, she opens her mouth to scream—not in a helpless, distressed sort of way, which I'd expect from a Velusian—but in an enraged, shoot-first-ask-questions-later sort of way, which I'd come to expect from humans.

"Who the fuck are you? Let me go, you asshole! Untie me so I can kick your ass!" she spits in softly accented Kailorian—the universal tongue of galactic tradespeople. It's common among merchants and traders, as well as smugglers and dealers.

I narrow my eyes and hold up the stolen idol.

"Greetings, thief," I return in Kailorian. It isn't my native tongue, but I know it well enough. "I'm afraid you've been found in possession of something that doesn't belong to you. Care to explain how that happened? It'll make it much easier for the report I'm filing with the Interplanetary Federation."

At that, her eyes widen and she clamps her lips together. Ha —got her!

"Ah, so you're familiar with the Feds. I'm guessing this isn't your first run in with them, though it must be your first time on Xylothia. It takes a special kind of ignorance to show up dressed for the jungle like that," I grumble, gesturing at her bare legs and tight shorts. Purpling bruises and angry red insect bites dot her otherwise *very* nice legs, leaving a constellation of discomfort that should give me satisfaction. Looters don't deserve kindness in any form.

So, why does the sight fill me with a cloying sense of protectiveness? There's a faint throb pulsing from my heart down to my cock and I shift, hoping she doesn't notice.

Her nostrils flare delicately and embarrassment colors her cheeks a flattering shade of pink. Stars, she *is* lovely. What a pathetic waste.

She glares at me, seething silently.

"Very well. I don't actually need information from you. It matters little to me who you are and why you're here. You trespassed on Protectorate soil, entered a holy site without permission, and stole an important cultural and religious artifact. Whether you intended to sell it is immaterial—you've already broken the law," I toss out with a nonchalant shrug. "It's too late to travel back to the nearest city tonight, but tomorrow morning I'll take you in and hand you over to the Feds. It'll be up to them what to do with you. I hope for your sake you aren't wanted for any other illicit activities."

She flinches, confirming my suspicion that she has some kind of record. That knowledge gives me pause. If she's a career smuggler or looter, maybe she'll have information I can use. I've long suspected that there are a handful of major buyers trading specifically in Xylothian artifacts, but every time I catch someone, they refuse to talk. The names at the top of the food chain have to be big—and bad. If this new woman can help lead me to them, I can give some names over to the Feds and they'll have to sit up and take notice. Prosecuting low-level criminals might not be worth their time, but stopping the black market trades at their source could be a career-making move for the right Federal agent. The wheels turn in my mind and I decide to adjust my approach.

"If you want to tell me what you were doing with this—who you were stealing it for and who's trying to bankroll all this Xylothian looting—maybe I could convince the Feds to go easy on you. Say you were cooperative," I offer.

Her shoulders slump a little, whether from defeat or the discomfort of being tied up all afternoon, I don't know. Moving slowly, I lean forward to check her bindings to make sure they aren't cutting off her circulation. She narrows her eyes, but doesn't pull away.

"Look," I say, trying for a sincere tone. "I'm sorry about your head. It's my job to take care of the Protectorate territory and I take it pretty seriously. I'm a ranger here—name's Asterth. Orion Asterth."

I hand her a canteen of water, which she eyes suspiciously. I swallow my annoyance that she presumes I'd slip her something. Ignoring the slight to my honor, I assume this isn't the first time she's been captured.

"I didn't drug your water," I said, taking a sip myself. "I already have you tied up. And no offense, lady, but even if you broke out of here, you wouldn't get very far on foot. We're in the thick of the Xylothian rainforest and I'm the only thing that stands between you and a lot of really hungry nocturnal creatures. And let me tell you, even though we have two suns, nighttime here is *long*. Can you at least tell me your name?"

She closes her eyes and leans back on the cot, apparently weighing her options. Finally, she sits back up, snatches the canteen from my outstretched hand and chugs. I'm briefly transfixed by the dribble of water that escapes and traces a path down her neck and through her breasts, but I quickly turn away. I ended things with Sylph well over a year ago, but I'm not about to lust after some criminal who sees my entire cultural heritage as ripe for plunder.

The woman is quiet after she finishes drinking, for long enough that I give up expecting answers to any of my hopeful questions. When I lift the tent flap to head back to the campfire outside, she clears her throat.

"Lyra," she says. "You don't get my last name. But for the water—and for patching my head—you can call me Lyra."

I throw a tentative look back over my shoulder.

"Anything else you want to tell me?" I press.

She meets my gaze with challenge in her eyes.

"Yeah, *Orion*," she says, my name falling from her lips like a curse. "When I get loose, I'm gonna kick your ass."

Fortunately, I leave fast enough to hide my smile.

HOURS LATER, something pulls me from the fog of sleep. I gave Lyra my cot hoping that a decent night's rest would loosen her tongue some more, but my friendly approach is starting to wear on my nerves. Still, the Solar Mother isn't just *any* relic and the fact that she's clearly here for it alone raises a lot of questions. I'm almost certain the information she has is as priceless as the statue she tried to steal.

I open my eyes from my makeshift pallet on the ground and scan the tent, trying to find what woke me up. Lyra is sprawled in my cot, snoring louder than any woman I've ever shared a bed with. One of her wrists is still tied to the bed frame, as is one of her ankles, so I know it isn't the noise of her making a covert escape.

There it is—soft, shuffling steps and harsh whispers filtering in through my tent's woven walls. Four men, it sounds like. They're speaking in a language I don't recognize, which means they aren't from this system. *Not Federation, then.* Could Lyra have a crew that came looking for her when she failed to return to her ship? It seems unlikely. Surely, someone would have gone with her to retrieve the artifact—a lookout, or something.

I consider two equally unpleasant ideas. It could be other looters heading for the temple, but typically looters would avoid a campsite and favor the well-worn trail that cuts straight through the jungle. If it *is* another group of looters, not only will I be outnumbered, but I'll be put in a position of having to protect the woman I arrested *and* keep the Solar Mother safe from all of them. Not ideal for a single ranger miles away from help.

There's a metallic clatter in the distance. From the sound of it, someone is dismantling my swamp buggy. Keeping one eye on Lyra, I creep to my pack where I keep my plasma rifle. I quietly check the charges and flick the safety off.

The other possibility is that these men somehow tracked Lyra. Given her profession and the angry tones emanating from the group rifling through my camp outside, that seems the most likely. I could give her up, of course, but they'll probably make off with both Lyra and the idol, and there's no guarantee they won't kill me, anyway.

Shit.

One I can handle easily—even two. Three would be a challenge. Four is simply out of the question. I only have a couple charged plasma cartridges, so shooting my way out seems futile. Suddenly, Lyra's hand latches onto my wrist and I almost yelp. She continues to snore, but gestures to her bound hand and ankle, and then at the weapons I confiscated.

I shake my head.

Her grip on my wrist tightens and she points at the tent door. When I refuse to budge, she beckons me closer. In between her exaggerated snoring, she whispers, "Void Stalkers."

My blood runs cold. Ruthless, bloodthirsty mercenaries. I've only encountered them once in my life, and I still have nightmares about it.

"Are they here for you?" I whisper back.

She nods once.

"How far are we from the city?" she asks. *Snore.*

"Too far," I reply. "They'd hunt us down and gut us before we ever got out of the jungle."

She shakes her tied wrist at me once more. Reluctantly, I cut the rope binding her hand and her ankle. Watching her get filleted and eaten is not something I'm prepared to do tonight.

"This doesn't mean I'm letting you go," I growl.

She flips me off, and the curiously human gesture makes me smirk against my will.

"My ship is close," she says, rubbing her wrist where the rope rubbed her skin raw. Damn. Too tight.

"How are we going to get past them?"

For the first time since I caught her, Lyra smiles. Though the expression is ominous with mischief, her entire face lights up like a meteor streaking through the early sky. She's stunning.

"Leave that to me," she says. "Give me my helmet. I can get the ship started from here. I'll create a distraction, head north, and then double back once I lose them. Head straight for my ship. Do you know where it is?"

I nod. "I know where it is but I'm not leaving you to deal

with Void Stalkers on your own. They'll cut you up into little pieces and toss you all over the forest."

She makes a derisive snort. "And you'd miss the chance to hand me over to the Feds, who'll surely be more lenient?"

"No," I huff. "But your chopped up carcass would be bad for the wildlife. And it'd be a lot of paperwork for me."

"Well, you don't have much choice. I'm the one they're after, and you'll just fuck things up if I get caught with you."

I watch as she slips her helmet on and slides her knife into her thigh holster, then checks the cartridge on her plasma gun. Ever so slowly, she unzips the front of the tent. When her eyes cut to the idol sitting on top of my pack, I can practically see her plotting. I snatch it and shove it into my pocket.

"Don't even think about it," I warn.

She lifts a shoulder, throws me a glare, and creeps outside. A shrill screech rents the air, followed by outraged snarls and the wet pop of a plasma blast hitting flesh. I suck in a few tense breaths, unsure of who's got the upper hand until I hear her angry roar and manic cackle.

"Fuck you, you fucking fucks!" Lyra yells, then crashes off through the jungle, firing shots as she runs.

Grabbing my pack, I shoulder my plasma rifle and poke my head out of the tent. She hit one of the stalkers in the head—well, it *was* a head. His decapitated body twitches on the ground. Another one lies in the dirt, hissing in pain with Lyra's massive knife jutting from his abdomen. Void Stalkers are ugly on a good day—humanoid monsters with sickly gray skin, oversized fangs, and a ridge of bony spines trailing from their foreheads to their backs. They wear full body armor designed to accentuate their horrible features, making them look like something that crawled out from the depths of the nastiest cave. The fact that Lyra was able to find the small, vulnerable spot in between the armor plates confirms my suspicion that she's had violent altercations with these Void Stalkers before.

Has probably killed their kind before, too.

Black blood burbles through his reptilian lips and nausea rolls through me. As soon as he sees me walking over to him, he reaches for a weapon at his side, but I hoist my rifle first. He stills.

"You," I growl. "You speak Kailorian? What do you want with the woman?"

A rasping laugh issues from his thin, gray lips.

"We might be the only ones in the galaxy that *don't* want the woman," he coughs.

"What's that supposed to mean?" I ask.

The cruel smile returns, but it's clear he isn't going to give me any more information. His fingers twitch for his gun, but I squeeze the trigger on my rifle. The shot takes his head off, and I grimace as I yank Lyra's knife from his gut, clean it on his pants, and pocket it. I'll have to come back to the campsite and burn the bodies as soon as we deal with this mess.

I take off in the direction of Lyra's ship, praying my ancestors will forgive me for desecrating their sacred ground, and kindling a begrudging hope that Lyra is faring well against the two remaining stalkers.

3
lyra

Better the Devil You Know

"ADA, I need you up and running *now!*" I shout, vaulting a fallen tree and ducking a plasma blast perilously close to my head.

The two Void Stalkers tailing me are faster on open ground, but their long tails are more of a hindrance in the thick brush, which gives me the advantage in the trees. I just have to loop back through the forest, get to my ship, and hope that the criminally hot but lawful pain-in-my-ass doesn't put up a fuss when I take off without him.

You were offline, Ada states. *Systems will reboot in eight minutes.*

"I don't have eight minutes! I have two Void Stalkers breathing down my neck and a Xylothian ranger determined to hand me to the Feds if I survive. Boot it into high gear and warm up those guns," I yell.

You were offline, Ada repeats.

My lungs scream for more oxygen as I run and fire blindly behind me. I'm not expecting to hit anything, but am nevertheless disappointed when I don't.

"Do I detect a note of peevishness? Yeah, I was offline. That goody-two-shoes ranger knocked me out and took my helmet. I didn't do it on purpose. I'm still alive and kicking—for now. But I definitely won't be if you don't stoke those fires and get me out of here!" I huff.

Apology accepted. Critical systems can launch at minimum energy capacity. Estimated time to takeoff: four minutes.

"Now that's more like it!" I say, but my relief is short-lived.

Directly ahead is a huge clearing that sprawls out like my doom before me. I veer sharply left, trying to stay beneath the thick foliage. I can hear the soft rush of the river in the distance—not the light babbling of lazy water over smooth stones, but the powerful roar of churning rapids. As the trees thin out closer to the riverbank, I see the source of the sound—I'm standing at the top of a massive waterfall that cascades down over three tiers of incredibly jagged rock. But there, just at the bottom of the first tier, is a small pool that looks clear and deep.

I duck another plasma blast from the screeching Void Stalkers on my heels, and a truly horrible idea takes root in my head.

There's no way I'm going to outrun them long enough to double back through the trees and get to my ship. I might try to stand my ground and fight, but that's ill advised, considering there are two of them and I'm already beyond exhausted. Despair threatens to pull me under—I don't have the idol, I've got a ranger and Void Stalkers on my ass, and my ship might as well be on the other side of the planet.

No. I'm close! I'm closer than I was yesterday! It's not time to give up yet—I have to try to lose these fuckers somehow.

The deadly waterfall looms and my feet sink into the thick mud of the riverbank. Sensing what I'm about to do, the Void Stalkers shout something I interpret to be *very* profane.

"Hold on, Ada—we're going for a swim!" I shout.

Squeezing my eyes shut, I take a deep breath and jump over the first tier of the waterfall, praying to all the stars I miss the rocks and land in the deep center of the pool. For one heart-stopping second, my whirling mind is blessedly silent as I fall, and all I sense is the coolness of the mist dampening my clothes.

I plunge into frigid water, narrowly missing a boulder that manages to scrape my thigh all the way up to my ass. Pain engulfs my leg, made worse by the cold sting of the water. The pounding of the falls pushes me down and I struggle against the current, kicking back toward the cliffside and the jutting rocks that might shield me from the Void Stalkers. If they think I jumped to my death, so much the better. They can spend however long they want searching for my body at the bottom of the falls, and by the time they realize it isn't there, I'll be long gone.

Hope helps buoy me to the surface and I suck in a breath. I can't hear anything above the roar of the water, but I don't think they'd wait long before heading down to the bottom of the falls. I wait for what feels like an eternity, but is probably closer to five minutes. By the time I feel comfortable making a move toward the rocky riverbank on the other side, the freezing water has numbed my limbs and my joints ache in protest. Poking my head cautiously through the brush, I hurry back up the way I came, scrabbling over rocks and trying to keep a low profile in case another group of Void Stalkers shows up as reinforcements.

"Ada, I'm en route. What's your status?" I ask, nearing my landing site.

Standing by.

"Great. Any, uh, Xylothian goody-two-shoes show up yet?"

Negative.

"Hm. Maybe I should go back to his campsite. I wonder if he ran afoul of the Void Stalkers, or if more showed up." Dread skitters up my spine. I certainly don't care about the ranger, despite his eye-popping hotness. *And stars, is he hot!* He fills out that stupid khaki uniform nicely, and something in my gut had fluttered when I came to and stared into those big emerald eyes set off by void-dark lashes. His wavy brown hair shimmers green in the light like a beetle's iridescent shell, and his freckled brown skin darkens to a near purple when he's flustered, reminding me of a cephalopod from Earth displaying its emotions with color-changing chromatophores all over its body. It took incredible strength for me to not rip his clothes off to see if the colorful, flickering passions skate across his skin *everywhere.*

It's too bad he plans to turn me in—he'd be a welcome libidinous distraction on my flight out of here. Still, if the Void Stalkers have gotten to him…I hate to think of them stealing the Solar Mother idol I worked so hard to acquire. The Void Stalkers will hand it over to Brill, and I'll lose my leverage.

On the other hand, if I bail on the score now, maybe the Xylothian boy scout won't feel compelled to chase after me and hand me over to the Feds. *Hmm.* Risk facing the Feds again or miss out on a chance to buy my freedom?

The gentle, comforting hum of Ada's engines makes the decision easy. This Xylothian jungle is a little too hot for me in more ways than one. Besides, I'm sure the ranger will put the statue back inside the temple and I can always come back in the near future and steal it again. If I end up in front of the Feds, it will be hard to plan a return trip from the inside of an interplanetary penitentiary.

"Open the outer bay and lower the ramp for me, will you, Ada? I'm keen on getting out of here post haste," I grunt, dragging my weary limbs into the clearing where she's parked and idling. The second sun is high in the sky now, blanketing the rainforest in oppressive heat once more.

"Lyra Phoenix!"

The guttural hack of a Void Stalker's voice breaches the buzzing chatter of rainforest fauna. I don't need to turn around to know who it is—the filthy, shark-toothed bastard, Kraxis. My hand is immediately on the gun at my hip, but the rasping laugh suggests it won't do me any good.

"I wouldn't do that, if I were you. I'd hate for your carelessness to cost another life," he says. "Turn around—slowly, if you don't mind. Don't try anything hasty."

I do as he asks, anxiety twisting my insides in knots. As I

suspected, Kraxis has a plasma pistol pressed into the temple of the Xylothian ranger. I school my expression in a mask of uncaring dismissal, and while that isn't *too* far from the truth, I'm not a monster. I don't want to see his brains splattered all over the ground.

"What have you found there, Kraxis? A new boyfriend?"

Orion's eyes flash with anger and Kraxis's reptilian lips curl in disgust.

"Your accomplice, Phoenix. Caught in your camp with the bodies of two dead Void Stalkers nearby. Brill won't be happy about that, you know. He'll probably want to add it to the debt you've accrued," Kraxis sneers.

Ah, *two* dead stalkers. So, Orion had the guts to finish one off, after all—not that Kraxis needs to know that. I don't want to entangle myself with the ranger any more than I already have.

"He's a Xylothian ranger, shit-for-brains," I say with a laugh. "He didn't have anything to do with them. He probably stumbled onto my camp after I led your other friends through this stars-forsaken jungle."

Kraxis blinks stupidly. "I thought all the Xylothians were extinct."

"Yeah, well, you've got your gun aimed at one's head, so that's probably incorrect."

"That changes things," Kraxis says, eyeing Orion's massive six-foot-eight frame with interest.

I sigh, not bothering to mask my exasperation and irritation. "Look, it's not my fault if Brill can't manage the details. If he's fencing relics from a not-so-dead race of aliens, that's his problem. My contract is settled as soon as I deliver the Solar Mother idol to him and my slate is wiped clean—you hear? *Clean.* That means you useless fucks stop hounding me every time you think I'm running out on a score or not delivering fast enough."

"Brill knows you were going to betray him, Phoenix. He found out about the buyer on Epsilon-6. You were going to take the idol to someone else, even when you knew it was rightfully his," Kraxis growls, turning his attention from Orion back to me. I can see pure rage igniting in Orion's eyes and I know he's about to argue Brill's alleged ownership of the idol. He opens his mouth to speak, but I cut him off.

"First of all, that's insane. Why would I sell the idol to anyone when all I've been doing is working to get out from under Brill's thumb? I want my freedom as much as that shitbag doesn't want to give it to me." My father always told me the best way to sell a lie was to inject it with some truth.

Kraxis hisses at the disparaging words.

"Secondly," I continue. "The point is moot. The idol isn't even here. I found the temple, all right, but there wasn't anything inside. Just a bunch of dusty ruins and crumbling walls. Brill's information was either outdated, or someone got to it before me."

Orion's eyes widen, but he blessedly keeps his lovely lips shut.

"You lie!" Kraxis shouts.

"Search me all you want, lizard dick. I don't have the statue. Maybe I should just call Brill and tell him someone beat me to it —I'm sure he wants to spend his valuable time looking for a traitor in his midst. I wonder how many of your Void Stalkers he'll immolate while he hunts for the truth."

The threat is unbelievable and improbable, but Kraxis is terrified of his boss and the hold Brill has over his brethren. That fear works in my favor and I can see the wheels turning in his tiny brain.

"No one else knew the location of the idol," Kraxis says slowly.

"Are you sure about that?" I ask, hoping to sow enough doubt to distract him sufficiently. "Look, how many men did you bring with you? If you don't believe me, go and see for yourself. You know where the temple is. I can't leave here empty handed, so I'm not exactly going anywhere."

"This is a trick," Kraxis hisses. His attention flicks back to Orion, whose face appears impassive, but the stormy look in his eyes promises me a world of hurt.

"Maybe it is," I offer with a shrug. "But are you really going to risk it? If I don't return with the idol and you lot don't either, I can't imagine Brill will let it slide so easily. Hell, I don't know. Maybe I missed something back at the temple. I'll wait here with the Xylothian and if you can't find the statue, we can torture him for the location—I'm sure he knows where it is."

The idea of torture appeals to Kraxis just enough to give my words the weight needed. He shouts something in his guttural native tongue and six Void Stalkers melt out of the bushes surrounding the cleaning. I congratulate myself on not launching an all-out attack on Kraxis—I knew he wouldn't have come alone.

"Oglor will stay here with you. If you attempt to escape, he will flay you and lick the blood from your skin," Kraxis says with a cruel smile.

"That's disgusting," I reply, my lip curling. "Can't you just ask nicely? Fuck."

The stalker Oglor licks his lips and gnashes his teeth at me.

"The rest of us will go to the temple. If we cannot find the relic, we will return and torture the Xylothian. Brill will have his prize," Kraxis says. He conveys his instructions to his men and makes his way to the edge of the dense jungle. "And if you are lying to me, Lyra Phoenix, Brill won't be the only one you have to worry about," he says over his shoulder.

"Hey, Oglor," I call when Kraxis is out of sight. "You got any water? My canteen's empty."

The Void Stalker stares at me—clearly not understanding my words in Kailorian. He narrows his beady yellow eyes. I hold up my canteen and mime drinking, then point to the container at his hip.

Scowling, he cautiously walks over to me and holds it out. As soon as his hand is in range, I yank him forward, pulling him off balance and slamming my elbow into his temple. He crumples to his feet, out cold.

"Help me tie him to that tree over there," I instruct Orion, who still regards me with murder in his eyes. "Or he'll come to and contact Kraxis, and we won't get out of here."

Orion folds his muscular arms across his broad chest and glares at me, unmoving. There's something unnerving in the stillness—like he's weighing what I just did, deciding whether I'm a liability or an ally. His eyes are sharp, assessing, and I can almost hear the gears turning behind them: *how far will she go, and what is she hiding?* I get the sense he's less afraid of Kraxis and Oglor than he is of me.

"Uh, hello? Lyra contacting Ranger Orion! Do you *want* to be skinned alive?" I huff, dragging the limp stalker to a nearby banthus trunk.

He still doesn't move.

"Fine! Stay here for all I care. You're welcome, by the way, for saving your ass. Good luck with Kraxis when he gets back here and I'm gone, and he realizes you've had the idol in your pocket the whole time." I don't have any rope, damn it. I rip a strip of fabric off my shirt, then use it to tie Oglor's hands around the base of the banthus tree. I frown. It won't hold him for long, and he'll be *real* pissed when he wakes up, but that won't hold a candle to Kraxis' and Brill's rage. I shudder, not wanting to think about it. That will be a problem for future Lyra.

The ship's ramp is lowered, engines primed, escape practically humming in reach—so why isn't the ranger moving? Why aren't *we* running? I glance back at him, and he's still stone-faced, watching. Suspicion radiates off him, but every second he hesitates, the noose tightens. If he wants to stand here and play moral high ground, fine—but I'm not dying for his conscience.

I turn back to climb my ship's ramp but pause when I hear the unmistakable buzz of a plasma rifle charging up. *Oh no, he didn't.* I whip around to see Orion shouldering Oglor's abandoned weapon, aiming it straight at my head.

"You've got to be fucking kidding me," I mutter.

"I'm sorry, I can't let you leave," he says. "If you're truly wanted by the Feds, I can't just let you fly off."

"Look, you've got your relic—and your life, I might add—and I'm getting out of here. Kraxis could be back any minute and I promise my makeshift handcuffs will *not* keep Oglor contained for very long. And if I were you, I wouldn't want to be around when Kraxis realizes a living Xylothian might be worth more than some silly statue."

"If the Feds find out I let you go, I'll be charged with aiding the escape of a fugitive. I'm not willing to risk my job or my freedom, especially when I'm sure you're going to continue desecrating sacred spaces and stealing—and stars know what else," he says, approaching me slowly.

With every step he takes in my direction, I back one step closer to my ship. My pulse spikes, heat crawling up the back of my neck. He's aiming at me, but it's the calm in his eyes that really scares me. There's no anger there—just duty. Cold, relentless duty…like he's done this before and he's already decided how this ends. I grip the edge of the ramp to keep my hands from shaking. I've bluffed bounty hunters, pirates, and customs officers—but something about Orion's restraint makes my usual tricks feel useless. He's not chasing a payday. He's chasing *justice* —and I have no idea how to outrun that.

"You don't really want to shoot me, do you? I mean, I saved your life. And I know you killed that other Void Stalker, but I'm willing to take responsibility for that. It was probably self-defense, right?"

Orion stills, a flicker of anguish dancing across his face.

"It *was* self-defense, but I regret it, regardless," he says quietly. "I don't relish taking lives, no matter how small or corrupt they are."

I nod, hoping I look sympathetic. "If it's any consolation, he probably would have gutted you and eaten your organs. Void Stalkers have really fucked up appetites. You did the universe a favor. Now he can go on to meet his death god or whatever, and you will have protected countless others who would've been tortured and eaten."

"That's an odd way to excuse yourself for such unforgivable acts," he says with a frown.

I shrug. "Hard to ask for forgiveness if you're dead."

He tilts his head, considering me. "So, it was a matter of survival for you to trespass on a holy site for my people, steal something valuable and important to our heritage, and sell it to one of the most selfish and evil dealers in the galaxy?"

"See, I knew you'd understand. You've obviously heard of Brill." Cold fear spikes in my chest and hollows out my belly, like it always does when I think of Brill. Hard to believe I'm not used to it by now.

The darkness in his eyes confirms my suspicions, or perhaps my sarcastic reply isn't what he wants to hear. The snap of a branch splitting somewhere in the jungle makes me jump, betraying my cool demeanor. Okay, so I'm anxious to get out of here. Orion smirks when he sees the chink in my armor.

"Look," I say hastily. "We can make a deal. You want to know who's trying to profit off the demise of your people, right? Well, it's your lucky day—I've got names, Ranger. Lots of names. Names that make Brill look like a puppy. You let me go, and the names are all yours."

"What is a puppy?" Orion asks, his brows drawing together.

"A puppy! It's an Earth creature. A small, fluffy, baby thing. Like a juvenile lupitian, but cuter. The point is, Brill is the tip of the iceberg. Let me guess: the Feds don't give a shit about chasing down a bunch of smugglers, right? Well, big guy, they're not *bad* enough, you feel me? The Feds would *have* to do something about the looting here if they knew who was involved," I say.

He finally lowers the rifle.

"So, I let you go, and you take me to your dealers," he says.

"Uh, excuse me? That's not what I offered, Ranger. I'm not

going to get us killed when I show up at the doors of some of the most dangerous people in the galaxy. I'm going to *give* you the names, and then you are going to give them to the Feds. I will be long gone by then—hopefully on some sandy beach with a frosty cocktail, a tentacled dreamboat, and plenty of credits in my account."

"No deal. How do I know your information is any good? Am I just supposed to take your word for it? You're a looter, a thief, and a liar—and I'm not an idiot like your buddy Kraxis," he says.

"I'm insulted that you cast such aspersions on my character, but given the circumstances, I'll let it slide. I'll take you to *one* dealer to prove my information is valid, then you can chase down the rest on your own," I reply, folding my arms across my chest. The move draws his gaze for a moment, and I consider it a temporary triumph that he's briefly distracted by my cleavage.

"Three dealers. Take me to three of your dealers, then I'll trust your names," he counters.

"Are you seriously haggling with me right now? I saved your life! One!"

A rasping sound at the edge of the clearing attracts our attention. It seems Oglor is coming to. Anxiety percolates through my limbs, making me jittery.

"Very well. *Two* dealers—and I won't tell the Feds where I got the information," he offers.

Oglor roars back to consciousness, screaming a string of what I can only assume are Void Stalker obscenities. *Shit!* My earlier anxiety was nothing compared to the dump of adrenaline blasting through my veins. I barely register Orion's worried expression as I turn and run up the ramp into my ship.

"Time to go, Ranger!"

He follows me into the outer bay just as Oglor manages to rip through his bindings. The ramp lifts and I haul myself into the captain's seat, throwing the thrusters into overdrive.

"Belt in," I call to Orion. "We've got a long way to go and I'm sticking to the backroads. It's gonna get bumpy!"

Ada lurches forward on a steep incline above the rainforest canopy and Orion falls backward into the rear bunk. I don't even bother to hide my laughter.

4
orion

This Smells Like a Complication

"ADA, chart a course for Minaris. Keep to the lower traffic routes, and scan anything that comes within shooting range. I don't want any Feds to surprise us on our way," Lyra says, piloting us up through Xylothia's atmosphere and away from the two suns I've watched rise and set almost every day of my life.

I stare out the window as the lovely swirls of blue and green grow smaller and smaller, until my home world is nothing more than a distant sparkling speck on a black velvet horizon. Tightness builds in my chest—not just homesickness, but the anxious pull of leaving something unfinished behind.

My father used to say the stars looked different depending on what you'd lost beneath them. I used to think that was poetry. Now, watching Xylothia vanish, I understand it was grief. *Hold formation. Breathe. Don't feel.* That's what he would've told me. I try.

The voice of Lyra's navigational assistant, Ada, chimes over the ship's speakers.

Autopilot engaged. I've set a course for Minaris. Estimated travel time: 16 days, not factoring in a mid-journey stop for refueling and supplies. I recommend the port of Turquin on the moon Amphitreas. They do not honor warrants for Interplanetary Federation fugitives.

"Yeah, no shit, Ada. That place is a haven for bloodthirsty pirates and reprobates," Lyra says, stepping out of the captain's chair and stretching. I try to ignore the way her lithe limbs flex and her torn shirt bares her soft midriff.

You'll fit right in, Ada replies.

I scratch at the stubble on my cheek to cover my grin.

"Behave yourself, Ada. We have a guest on board," Lyra chastises.

She comes to stand at my side and we stare out the window for a few pulses of silence. Melancholy claws at my insides. Xylothia looks so small and fragile from space. Who will be left to miss it when it's gone?

"When was the last time you were off-world?" Lyra asks.

I purse my lips as I recall my family's last trip off-world—the last one we all took together before everything went wrong. Snippets of the vacation filter through my memories—the details blurry and faded behind the intervening years.

"Thirty-seven years ago."

Her brows lift. "You must've been just a kid, then."

I nod. "I was four."

"Family vacation?"

"Something like that."

My throat tightens around the words and my palms feel clammy against my knees.

"You never wanted to travel after that? Must've been some vacation to scare you outta the stars," she jokes.

Not wanting to go down that particularly painful road, I remain silent. I focus on the hum of the engines instead of her voice. She says something else, but it's just sound until I realize she's waiting for an answer. *Too late.* The silence between us stretches taut, and I let it hold, suddenly too exhausted to engage.

"Well, I'm sure you'll want to get cleaned up. I can show you where you'll be bunking. Ada's right—I'll have to make a supply run in a few days, but we should motor out of here as fast as we can to get ahead of the Void Stalkers. Until then, we'll have enough to get by."

Her ship is a bit beaten up, but functional. The wall panels are mismatched, some scorched, others patched with dull metal plates. The place smells faintly of oil, singed electronics, and dust—a strange mix of survival and care. It would benefit from a thorough cleaning, but I'm not one to talk. My living quarters on Xylothia aren't exactly square, especially with Sylph moving out. These days I spend more nights in a tent in the jungle than in my drab, lonely apartment.

Lyra points out a bathroom, several other berths—including hers, which she instructs me to avoid at all costs unless I want a stupendously painful death—a kitchen, a small but well-equipped gym, and a combined office/laboratory.

"And here's your room. I'll clean it up a bit while you shower, and I think I have some spare clothes in a locker down-stairs that might fit you," Lyra says, showing me into a small berth off the ship's main corridor. The room is covered in a layer of grime an inch thick and half-empty crates are strewn about, each one containing some random assortment of expired food supplies, old computer parts, greasy rags, and yellowed paper-back romance novels from Earth. Still, the accommodations are far nicer than I'd imagined they would be.

"Given the reluctance with which you agreed to our bargain, I'm surprised that I'm not stuck in some filthy, dark hold below decks," I say, absentmindedly picking up one of the ancient paperbacks and smirking.

She snatches the book from my hands and glares at me.

"The filthy, dark hold is available if you continue to piss me off," she barks, cradling the book to her chest.

"I didn't mean to offend you," I say, turning my attention toward the rumpled, dust-covered bunk. Tugging the dirty blanket off the bed, I uncover a set of garments that resembles underwear, but has four leg holes. I hold it up between my thumb and forefinger, raising a questioning brow at her. She dives for it and shoves the item in the pocket of her mud-caked shorts.

"Space is lonely," she snaps, cheeks flushing. "And I like human romance novels. Happy?" Her voice is sharp enough to cut through the air, but there's something brittle under it—a crack she doesn't want me to see.

Sensing I'd made more than a flirtatious misstep, I raise my hands in surrender and take a seat on the edge of the bed. "I was only curious why you're suddenly being so accommodating, given you promised to kick my ass less than a day ago. You don't seem particularly put out by the fact that I have every right and reason to turn you into the Feds at any time, and now you're being forced to take me to your dealers."

"We made a bargain," she says simply. "Despite whatever misconceptions you're laboring under regarding who I am, I don't go back on my word. And call me crazy, but I get the sense you don't, either."

"I do not."

"Well, there you have it. We can play nicely until our business is at an end. I'm more than a little flexible," she says, tossing her long braid of pink-streaked hair over her shoulder.

Whether she intends the words to be taken at face value or laced with libidinous intent, blood rushes to every inconvenient extremity. My heart thuds in my ribcage and my gaze reflexively caresses her body. *How flexible...*my traitorous thoughts start to venture.

"Yeah, you'll have to deal with that, by the way," she says in a singsong tone. "We're going to be handling some serious shit on this fun little adventure, and I can't have you getting all hot and bothered every time we're in some cramped space together. This is a small spaceship, you know."

"Wha...what?" I stammer, trying to shake the wave of intense lust from my mind.

Heat floods my neck and ears, my synesfores pulsing with awareness. I drag a hand through my hair, suddenly aware of how close she's standing—and how easily she reads me. Stars, she's enjoying this. I force myself to look anywhere but at her mouth. She smiles at me, but there's an unnerving edge to it.

"My mother is—was—Velusian. One of the last full-blooded heads of the pleasure houses. Surely you're familiar with the stories…I mean, just because you haven't been off-world in decades doesn't mean you're that ignorant, right?"

I struggle to focus amid the haze of desire—*Stars, her breasts are perfection*—and the rising ire at her insults. She casts a pitying look in my direction and sighs.

"Velusians have been bred for pleasure since the universe was mostly clouds of dust and little baby protoplanets. Desire is their stock and trade. The closer you get to one, especially in an enclosed space, the more you can scent their *vellia*. It's a kind of one-size-fits-all pheromone meant to drive anyone wild with— how can I put it politely?—overwhelming horniness. The more anxious, stressed or fearful we get, the more we exude—like a built-in chemical weapon against violence. Sometimes it kicks in when we're aroused, but it's more of a defense thing. It's hard to kill something you want to fuck so badly." A flicker of pain crosses her face. "Though it does happen."

I suspect pressing her for more information on that particular topic would earn me a knee in my groin, so I leave the interrogation alone for now.

She slides the room's metal door closed and takes a step toward me. Closing her eyes, she places her hands on my chest, as if she's waiting for something.

I lean away from her, caught between the worry about her bizarre abilities and the magnetic pull I feel for her. Panic starts to build in me. I don't *want* to want her this way.

"There's no need for you to…" I begin. But then, it hits me like an asteroid slamming into the ground, devastating everything for miles around.

The wanting. No, it isn't *want.* It's *need.* Stars, I need her. I need to wrap her pink chocolate hair around my knuckles and slide my aching cock into her pretty petal lips. To rest seated on her tongue before sliding down her throat…no, that won't be enough. I need her bent in front of me on all fours, spread open like a feast for my eyes, hands, lips, and tongue. I'll give her such pleasure, she'll buckle beneath me, thread her fingers through my chest and around my heart, until the boundaries separating our bodies evaporate into the pure energy of love. Yes. *Yes.* I love her, that's all there is to it. I love her and I would kill for her. I would die for her.

I can't help myself. I reach for her, sliding my hands up the back of her neck, intent on pulling her lips to mine. I have to claim her—my very soul depends on it.

She flinches at my touch, and I freeze, hovering above her lips, ready to detonate with a kiss like a world-ending bomb.

"Ada, ventilate the rooms in the living quarters, pod 3," she murmurs, stepping back.

The low whir of fans and soft breeze clears the stale air from the room, and after a few heart-pounding moments, helps to dissipate some of the chaotic desire that has taken hold of my body. Horror grips me at how out of control I felt, how close I was to sinking to my knees and begging to worship her—how willing I'd been in courting my own destruction in the face of keen sexual need.

She notes the anger and disgust on my face and nods, satisfied.

"Good. You get it. I can keep a lid on it most of the time," she says. "It's worse from a full-blooded Velusian, so you can thank my reprobate human father for the diluted blood. Also, it's not *completely* universal. Some species are totally immune to it—including Void Stalkers. Actually, I don't think they desire much beyond torment and death, so trying to use sex as a weapon against them is pointless."

"Pointless," I echo thickly. It's taking too long for my head to clear—I need to get away from her. I shift to leave, but she holds out her hand.

"No need to run, I'm outta here. I just wanted you to understand. You and I have struck a bargain—nothing more. As soon as I take you to the second dealer, I'll drop you back on Xylothia and we're done for good. I go on my merry way and you keep your mouth shut to the Feds. That was the deal. Anything you think you might feel for me is a lie, thanks to my overbearing mother's obnoxious genetics. Don't trust it."

I frown, feeling exposed and vulnerable after losing control of my senses. I don't know what to do with the anger I feel at the violation, despite the fact that nothing happened between us. I clench my fists, wanting to smash something. Before I can gather enough words to rage at her, she tosses a towel at me and makes for the door.

"You can shower first. Sometimes that helps after getting a full blast of *vellia*. I'll be on the bridge. Ada can help you with whatever you need—just ask," she offers nonchalantly, as if she's oblivious to the storm raging inside me.

Before I can help myself, I call after her.

"What's it like?" I ask, gripping the towel so hard, my knuckles turn white. "For you, I mean. What do you feel when you're giving it off? Do you sense what it does to others?"

If she has any indication of the intensity of my feelings, I might as well leap out the outer door and die in the frozen vacuum of space.

She stops a few steps down the hallway, but doesn't turn around.

"No," she replies. "I don't feel anything." Then, finally throwing a glance over her shoulder, she grins. "But even if I did, you don't have anything to worry about. You're not my type."

I don't want to smile at her teasing—not after what happened. Sour words fall from my lips as she disappears down the corridor.

"Undoubtedly," I call out. "I'm not a lying, cheating, thieving criminal!"

"Nah," she shouts back. "That's not it. You don't have enough tentacles to interest me."

It's easier for me to seize the relief I feel at that fact than it is to acknowledge the sliver of disappointment cutting through my wild emotions.

SHE'S RIGHT—THE shower helps. I grimace at the thought of putting on my filthy uniform again, and I curse myself for leaving without my pack or any supplies of my own. Then again, Lyra mentioned she might have some clothes for me to wear.

Ignoring the discomfort I feel speaking into the silence of the bathroom, I clear my throat.

"Ada?"

Ranger Asterth. How may I be of assistance?

"Oh. You can call me Orion, I guess," I mumble awkwardly.

Very well, Orion. How may I be of assistance? Ada asks again.

"Lyra said something about clean clothes. Can you direct me to the lockers she mentioned?" I ask, wiping the fogged mirror with the edge of my towel.

I'm afraid the lower decks are off limits to Lyra's visitors. It would be better for you to wait in your living quarters. I will inform Lyra that you require fresh attire.

Despite the politeness of Ada's words and her virtual nature, her tone brooks no refusal.

"Thank you," I reply, wrapping the towel tightly around my waist and padding down the corridor to my temporary room.

The door opens automatically and I take in Lyra's feeble attempt at tidying. The bunk has been stripped of sheets and the clean bedding lies in a pile beneath a dingy pillow. Most of the dust and grime still remains on the furniture and the floor, but at least the boxes of junk have been moved—minus a stray paperback romance that has escaped notice and found a spare corner of floor to inhabit. As soon as I get some clean clothes, I'll fix up the place myself. Not that I'm going to hide in here…I'm not *afraid* of Lyra, exactly, but…If it's going to be two weeks until we make it to Minaris, that is two weeks too long to be around someone whose very presence can make me climb out of my skin with barely restrained lust. And two weeks too long to be around that same someone who thinks my people are a resource to be exploited, and sees me as an inconvenient means to an unsatisfying end.

No. Despite the lingering effects of desire that continue to burrow through my veins—even after pleasuring myself *twice* in the shower—tangling with Lyra Phoenix more than absolutely necessary is the quickest way to find myself facing a supernova of destructive forces.

My ancestors were stalwart, single-minded, celibate warrior monks and I'll simply have to inhabit the same kind of mastery over my senses and needs. She's just another woman, after all, and an obnoxious one at that. Her half-Velusian blood works against me, but it's purely chemical. She told me herself—*anything you think you might feel for me is a lie. Don't trust it.*

I won't trust my feelings for her any more than I trust her, and when all is said and done, I can still hand her over to the Feds if things get messy.

The door *whooshes* again, and Lyra storms in, bundle of garments in her arms and an annoyed expression on her face.

"Look, Ranger…" She begins, freezing in the doorway. Her eyes rove down my body, devouring my towel-clad form with what I can only describe as *hunger.* I smirk at first, smug in the knowledge that she isn't as immune to lust as she'd made out earlier. The realization is quickly followed by an even more disturbing one: if she feels romantic stirrings for me, it's obvious there is little I could do to prevent her from using her abilities to take advantage of me at will. It'll be a dangerous balancing act to ensure she doesn't turn me into a puddle of desire, drop me off on the nearest moon, and take off with the idol. That thought leaves me as cold as the rivulets of water dripping off my hair down my shoulders.

"Thank you for the clothes," I say, hoping to get her out of my room and with any luck, far away on the other side of the ship.

"Yes, clothes," she repeats, her pouty lips hanging open in a soft *o* shape. "I have some for you."

She holds them out, but her gaze doesn't stray from my bare chest. The heat sparking in her violet eyes stirs my blood again and I can't resist the onslaught of images that race through my brain—her legs hooked over my shoulders, grinding her sex against my tongue. I lean forward, drawn to her like a heavenly body finding a new orbit.

Fuck.

"Ada," I grit out. "Ventilate the rooms in the living quarters, pod 3."

Lyra blinks, the haze of desire clearing and a slow smile spreading across her face. The fans whir to life, and Lyra throws back her head and laughs.

"Damn," she chuckles. "This is going to be a huge fucking shitshow."

For once, I know she's telling the truth.

5
lyra

Something About This Was Inevitable

AFTER SIX DAYS of avoiding each other as much as possible in the cramped corridors of my ship, I know I've got a major problem.

I want to sleep with the stars-damned, goody-two-shoes ranger. Even worse is the fact that I can tell he's attracted to me, too, but clearly doesn't want to be. *Son of a bitch.* Nothing like a man scoping out your ass and looking like he'd rather punch himself in the face than give it a grab. Talk about going from *sizzle* to *fizzle*.

I've done everything in my power to distract myself and to avoid running into him around the ship as he occupies himself with small, menial tasks. Without a word, he set about cleaning his berth and the common areas, organizing my books on a newly dusted shelf, scrubbing out the water filtration system and the kitchen cupboards. It's *almost* been enough to keep us away from each other.

Today, however, I'm taking stock of our meager supplies in the hold when Ada pings me, informing me that our illustrious guest requested my presence in my abandoned laboratory—one of the few rooms on my ship I'm happy to avoid. The depressing lab is more of a junk repository for me these days, despite it being equipped with state-of-the art tech that can analyze and study just about anything, as well as a long fallow biosphere where crops can be grown on long distance voyages. My dad was a bit of a science nut in his spare time, and when he wasn't teaching me how to sneak, steal, and survive, he taught me everything he knew about Earth sciences and space travel. The only piece of him I kept close to me is his tattered old journal, filled with notes on desirable treasures across galaxies and haphazard daily logs detailing his adventures. I'm still working my way through the crinkled, yellowing pages. I let everything else fall to ruin—too cowardly to confront the disordered mess of both his legacy and my emotions. I haven't had the heart to clear out his gear after he died and left the *Aldrin-136* to me.

"I'm not going in there just because he *summoned* me," I snap. "Tell him I'm busy."

Orion politely requests your presence, all the same.

"He is so obnoxious! First, he complains about the food, and then when I finally relent and dig through the supplies in the hold, he starts pestering me to drop what I'm doing to go attend to him for stars-know-what reason. I'm sorry I don't have a gourmet kitchen and an epicurean cook to whip up something fresh whenever His Highness's tummy growls. And anyway, what's wrong with protein pills and carbo shakes? I mean, what the hell else do Xylothians eat?" I rant.

Is this an opportunity for a joke? Ada replies.

I wince at that. Perhaps it was unfair of me to unleash a wave of *vellia* on him last week when we were both exhausted, hungry, filthy, and sore from our messy getaway. He needs to understand, though; we can't afford to let any false horniness derail our deal. I did him a favor, really, by being so honest. At least that's what I told myself after I saw the look of disgusted betrayal in his eyes in the wake of my little demonstration.

Not many can withstand the onslaught of desire my mother's blood can summon, though it affects every species differently. I've never seen anyone react the way Orion did—with the fire that promises to consume us both, if we ever give it the chance to burn.

Not something I'm particularly keen on, at this point. I still don't trust him not to turn me over to the Feds at the first opportunity. Those kinds of upstanding, holier-than-thou heroes always throw you over for the good of the universe in the end. It should be more of a relief to me that he's particularly susceptible to my *vellia* in case I need an edge, but for the first time ever, thinking about using it on him again just makes me...*sad.* Ugh. Not something I'm interested in examining too closely at present.

Ranger Asterth has been working on something to improve this ship, and by extension, your existence. Rather than continuing to hide from him, perhaps you should see what he's been doing.

"I'm not hiding from him," I grumble, but brush off my dusty pants and head to the second deck and the lab.

I start to knock but catch myself. This is my ship, after all—I can go where I damn well please without anyone's permission.

"You rang, Ranger?" I call out, startling him as the metal door slides open.

I stop in my tracks, taking in the space that used to be a disaster and now looks like it's been restored to clean, organized, functional perfection. The last time it looked like this was before my father died. Tears prick at the corners of my eyes and I swallow around a lump in my throat, embarrassed by the unbidden grief.

"I didn't hear you knock," Orion grumbles with his back to me. "And I didn't actually expect you to come."

Grateful that my irritation masks my sadness, I'm able to shrug into that well-worn cloak of perpetual annoyance before he can see how this room affects me.

"It's my ship," I argue. "I don't have to knock."

He bristles and turns to face me, his lips drawn in a tight line. He's wearing another borrowed outfit—a thin, white, too-small tank top that stretches across his broad chest, and soft gray sweatpants that do more than hint at his endowments. *Stars save me.* I can't remember who left them on my ship, but I curse them with the fire of a thousand suns for leaving me with clothes that barely hide Orion's god-like physique.

Despite my affinity for tentacled partners, that doesn't seem to matter to my raging libido when I take in his powerful body, cut with lean muscle and flushed pink, either from the tepid warmth of the laboratory or his frustration with me. His bronzed shoulders are dusted with dark purplish brown freckles, dotting his skin like flickering constellations. Briefly, I fantasize about tracing shapes in those stars with my tongue and fingertips.

But the way he glares at me makes me think he's more irritated than interested, which is probably better for both of us. He takes a step back and crosses to the other side of the center worktable, folding his arms across his chest. My attention snags on the way his muscles bunch and flex with the movement.

"If you're done ogling me," he quips sharply. "I can show you what I've been doing in here."

"I'm not ogling." I am, though. "I'm assessing."

"Assessing," he repeats, arching a brow. "Assessing me for, what, weaknesses? Are you still planning to—how did you put it —kick my ass?"

"Yeah," I say, my mouth dry. The purplish freckles on his skin darken with his exasperation and I'm momentarily transfixed. The longer I stare, the darker they get. He clears his throat and I pull my gaze back to his face with great effort. The look he wears is very *disapproving professor* and right now, I want nothing more than to be his naughty student.

"Well?" he prompts.

I look around the room and nod with approval.

"You cleaned," I say simply.

He rolls his eyes. "Yes, I know that's a foreign concept to you, but I wasn't referring to the cleanliness."

"What'd you do with all my stuff?" I ask, refusing to clarify that it's actually *my dad's* stuff. The accompanying grief is a sucker punch straight to the chest and almost renders me breathless. "I had some important things in there, you know. And maybe there were some private things in there that you shouldn't have been digging through."

"They're in the storage lockers off the main hallway," he replies.

I gape. "I have storage lockers?"

The corners of his lips quirk at that, but he swallows the smile before it can take its full, blinding shape. *Stars-damn those dimples.*

"I just asked you in here so I could show you the biosphere," he says. "Do you know how it works? It looks like it hasn't been used in a few years."

"I know how it works," I cut in, glaring at him, already pushing back against the unwanted memories of afternoons spent in here with my father. "I just didn't have time to get it set up in between runs."

His brow furrows at that. "Thefts, you mean."

I shrug.

He sighs. "Well, you actually had most of what you needed to get a healthy garden going. Everything was in cold storage—the seeds, soil amendments, and fertilizer. I planted a variety of fruits and vegetables from a couple different planets, at least the ones that I'm familiar with, and programmed their care into the system. Ada helped. In a few weeks, we'll be able to eat something other than that dehydrated, processed garbage you seem to love."

I want to rail at him—to yell at him for coming into my ship and messing up my stuff. I hate that I haven't had a fresh fruit or vegetable from the lab since my dad died and that it's *Orion* bringing them back. I hate how the sight of the lab pokes at the ulcers of my grief, and that it's made worse because it's stupid *Orion* who keeps sneaking through my carefully crafted emotional defenses. Not that he knows, of course. I'd rather swallow a Uranian slug than open up to him. But...he worked hard, and beneath the grief—loath as I am to admit it—is a kind of hopeful nostalgia at seeing the small plants erupting from the little pods of soil.

"It's…" I struggle to wrangle my emotions and find an appropriate response. "You did good."

He lifts a shoulder in forced nonchalance, but there's a flash of pride on his face that lights up his eyes and makes his freckles flicker.

"Thanks. It was nice to have something to do," he says. "I think I'm a bit stir-crazy being cooped up in a metal box without any nature nearby."

"I take it all Xylothians have a green thumb," I hedge.

"Green thumb?"

"Another Earth phrase. It means you're good with plants."

"Oh. Well, yes. But anything can grow, if you give it what it needs," he says.

We stand for a beat, the awkward silence thickening between us.

I turn to leave and catch sight of the Solar Mother idol locked in one of the stasis cabinets. Even through the thick crystalline compartment, I can still sense it vibrating with the same energetic intensity as it did in the temple. I'm dying to get my hands on it again and see if I can translate the markings—see if they'll lead me to the next clue in my doomed treasure hunt. It's right there—the last piece between me and the only kind of freedom I'll ever get. Everything I've done, every sin I've stacked, has been for this. And yet, every time I reach for it, it feels like the universe moves it an inch farther away. Orion sees where my attention landed and sighs.

"What do you actually know about it?" he asks, crossing to the cabinet and unlocking the door.

"Not much," I answer, fighting through my distraction in order to lie properly. "It's a relic—a figure of the Solar Mother entity that the Xylothian Protectorate worshipped thousands of years ago, and it's made of pure enaurium. It might be the largest sample of the metal in existence for all anyone knows. Other than that, it's worth about two million credits to my buyer on Epsilon-6. Or I can hand it over to Brill, which will buy my freedom from him, though I can't say I expect him to honor that bargain once he has the idol in his greedy, nubby little hands."

I don't add that according to my father's journals, it's also the key to unlocking the location of the Dark Star—the only thing in this universe that has power over life and death. That part's mine, and some things you don't say out loud in case the universe decides to listen.

"Two million credits is pathetic," Orion says, trailing off and shaking his head. "You don't even know what you have." He runs a hand through his shimmering green and brown hair.

"That's all I need to know. If I needed to read a library of knowledge for every item I acquired and sold, I'd never get anything done. Besides, I'm not just talking about two million credits. I'm talking about my freedom."

For the first time since I'd entered the lab, his expression gentles and his eyes shine with some unnamed emotion. *That better not be pity.*

"This isn't just a chunk of metal for some payday," he insists, hefting the idol and holding it in front of me.

The glow catches in his eyes, painting him in soft gold. For one awful moment, I see what he sees—something sacred, something worth protecting. I hate how beautiful that makes it look.

"If you say so, Ranger," I reply with a shrug.

He stares at me for one heated moment, worrying his bottom lip with his teeth.

"I wish I could help you understand its importance," he says.

"Well, we've got time. Maybe you can convince me that your golden doll is worth more than what I could get from it," I answer sarcastically. I keep my tone light, but my pulse is racing. He doesn't realize how close he's getting to the truth—what does *he* know about the Dark Star? "But go ahead—shoot your shot."

After a pause, he nods and clears his throat.

"Before the dawn of the universe—before stars and planets and life, nothing existed except Father Darkness…"

As he starts, I roll my eyes—then stop. His voice changes, low and reverent, and I can't quite bring myself to interrupt. I fold my arms fold across my chest and keep my mouth shut.

"In the void of black space, he shivered with cold loneliness, staring at an eternity that sprawled before him and stretched behind him with the kind of hollowness that aches. Eventually, his shivering generated enough warmth that something new sprang from the energy, the first thing to exist that wasn't icy darkness. The Solar Mother. She was the first thing of beauty that Father Darkness beheld—bright and warm and golden and glowing."

Orion's words weave a tapestry of beautiful imagery, and I lean against the door frame, momentarily content to listen to his story.

"Their first coupling produced the stars and suns, their second coupling brought forth rocky planets, meteors, and asteroids, and their third coupling—which they'd had after a particularly nasty argument—gave rise to ice worlds and gas giants. The Solar Mother was overjoyed with her children and lavished attention on them, beaming down on the worlds with warmth and weaving patterns of life everywhere she could. But Father Darkness grew jealous and angry. He wanted the Solar Mother all to himself. He longed to feel her heat when she was away, caring for her children. His resentment soon grew too weighty and became the first black hole."

Orion stares at the idol in the palm of his hand. I'd swear it starts to glow.

"One day, while the Solar Mother was tending our green world of Xylothia, Father Darkness snuck up on her and wrapped his arms around her, pulling her away from her children and holding her tightly against him. The tighter he held her, the more his darkness crushed her, pressing her light and warmth in on itself. Knowing that his love would be her destruction, the Solar Mother flung out her brilliant energy, sending it to help power her children and allow her universe to grow without her nurturing care."

I blink and let out a shaky breath, hoping Orion can't see the emotion in my eyes. Yeah, a parent sacrificing themselves in the hope that their kid might live a better life? Why would something like *that* upset me?

"This creation story is seriously messed up," I say, and he offers me the slightest of smiles.

"Well, when Father Darkness saw what he'd done, his grief tore him apart—literally. Rather than face eternity without her, he stretched himself out as far has he could—the omnipresent darkness of space, rarely allowing himself to come so close and snuff out one of the Solar Mother's precious children," he explains.

"So, your people have worshipped a martyr and a murderer since the dawn of time," I say wryly. "And they made a sparkly little doll to celebrate her."

He frowns, straightening. "Our ancestors gathered the most coveted resource on our planet—in our star system, really—and crafted this statue. The painstaking gathering of enaurium speck after enaurium speck took hundreds of years alone. This idol is a labor of love, faith, devotion, and sacrifice. Legends say that if the statue ever leaves the temple, Xylothia will crumble to dust, taking her people with her."

He places the statue back inside the stasis cabinet and the glowing dims a bit. When he turns back to face me, his eyes have gone cold. Guilt—hot and sharp—slices through me, but I shove it down. If I let myself feel it, I'll start to wonder if I really am the villain in his story—and I can't afford that kind of self-reflection. Not now.

"That's what you stole," he says matter-of-factly. "Not just something to be fenced to the highest bidder. You plucked one of the last beacons of hope from my people—from me. If you're going to use it to barter your freedom, you should at least know the cost."

"The *cost*," I echo. I stare at him, tamping down my guilt to focus on the white hot rage building in my chest. Because if I don't get angry, I'll start to feel small. And small gets you leashed, arrested, or killed.

Stepping around the work table to stand in front of him, I jab a finger in his chest. "Get one thing straight, Ranger. Your ancestors' bedtime story is touching and all, but I will pay any price—every price—to get out from under Brill. Freedom is a fine abstract idea for people who have it. For those of us who don't, the pursuit of it is all consuming."

He isn't intimidated by my anger. He doesn't flinch. Doesn't look away. Just watches me with that maddening calm that says he sees more than I want him to. He merely raises a brow and folds his arms across his chest in that disapproving manner again.

"And then what? When you have your freedom—what's next? Back to pickpocketing your way across the galaxy in a shiny new ship, soaked in alcohol and half-sated by some *vellia* slave with tentacles?" he sneers.

The words hit something raw. For a heartbeat, I picture it—the silence after the chase, the empty bed, the next job that never ends. The thought terrifies me more than Brill ever could.

I bristle. "Maybe! How is it any of your business?"

"Are you really so shallow and predictable?"

"Baby, you have *no* idea," I snap. I almost laugh—too sharp, too brittle—and let him think he's right. It's easier that way. If he wants to believe there's nothing underneath, I'll hand him the shovel. "Judge me all you want—I don't give a fuck. As soon as this stars-forsaken trip is over, you can go masturbate to your own righteousness all you want."

Rather than rise to the bait, he studies me from beneath his drawn and judgmental brows.

"What's your deal with Brill, anyway?" he asks.

For the briefest of seconds, I worry he might see the marks Brill has left on my soul. I tense and stare him down, anxiety twisting my gut. I won't be explaining *that* any time soon.

"You seem pretty free to me," he continues. "Free enough to come and go across the galaxy at will. Free enough to have your own ship, which you use to plunder precious artifacts from desperate people and leave a haphazard mess the rest of the time."

My frustration unleashes my temper and I snarl at him. If he knew how thin that illusion of freedom really is—how every planet I land on has Brill's shadow stretching over it—he'd pity me again, and that's worse than any insult.

"You don't know anything about me or my situation. You don't know what I had to do to earn my way to the end of Brill's leash. You've known me for all of a week and in that time you've seen fit to judge me plenty and never even bothered to ask a single question about me that didn't twist your face in disgust. Don't forget that *I* saved *your* life," I yell, getting in his face.

Orion's eyes dilate and his lips part on an intake of breath. *Shit.* My *vellia* is out of control. I try to calm my mind and slow my racing heart, but my anger makes it nearly impossible. My pulse thrums in my throat; I drag air in through my teeth, counting—one, two, three—but the heat crawling under my skin isn't listening. How dare he judge me when he has no idea what I've been through. Maybe if I was born in some tropical paradise with normal tree-hugging parents, my life would be simpler and I could be all high and mighty about everyone else, too. *What an asshole!*

"I caught you stealing one of the most important holy relics from my culture," he accuses, crowding me back against the worktable. "What am I supposed to think? You're dealing with the galaxy's most violent criminals, you're being hunted by Void Stalkers, and you killed two beings in a single day. My people respect life, honesty, honor, and sacrifice. I may not know you that well, but I can already tell you're the absolute antithesis of all those values."

I squint up at him, annoyed but impossibly aware of the heat radiating off his body.

"If you're so certain, why are you on my ship?" I shoot back. "Why are you trusting me to take you to my dealers?"

His jaw tightens. That restrained control, that almost dangerous patience, it makes my blood hum in ways I shouldn't be thinking about right now.

His gaze darkens with desire, but the muscle working in his jaw suggests he's fighting his body's response to it. The solid warmth of him against me—shoulders, chest, and that damn firm line of his stomach—makes me want to shove him away and pull him closer in exactly the same heartbeat.

"Because I'll turn you in to the Feds if you don't," he grits out, pressing his body into mine. "We'll work together, or you'll go to prison. Now get the hell away from me."

"Gladly," I snap, pushing at his muscled chest. It's like trying to move a mountain. The tiniest thrill sings through my over-heated blood and my fingers twitch. A traitorous part of me wonders what it would feel like if I didn't resist. "All I've wanted to do since we met was keep away from you!"

"Good," he rumbles, his gaze dipping to my mouth.

The hard length of his erection pressing against my stomach sends a bolt of desire to my core that nearly takes my knees out from under me. Seemingly of its own volition, one of his hands comes to rest on my hip, his long fingers digging into my flesh in a not-unpleasant way. Excitement, irritation, and lust surges through my body, tightening my nipples and coiling like a snake in my gut. Even with my *vellia*, I've never experienced such a response from another being, which has alarm bells pealing in my head.

He catches his lip between his teeth and I try to stifle my whimper, but fail. I have to get out of here. If we don't cool down, we'll end up doing something we both regret.

"Ada..." But before I can issue the command to ventilate the room, Orion's other hand shoots up the back of my neck, threading through my hair. With a desperate growl, he pulls my lips to his.

Oh, fuck.

It's electric like a live wire. Messy in the way only weeks of simmering tension could make it. All my thoughts, all my rage, all my self-righteous indignation…evaporate. I want to push him away, I want to throttle him, but my hands are already clawing at him. There's nothing tender or sweet between us—it's the culmination of days of heated anger and irritation and volatile lust, resulting in clashing teeth and tongues and lips as we fight each other in a battle of passion. Part of me knows I'm using this as a distraction—because if I let myself feel anything beyond the pleasure of this, I'll collapse under the intensity.

Fisting my hair in a firm tug, he tips my head back to open my mouth more to him and I groan, mindlessly slipping a hand down his pants to grip his hard cock. *No tentacles—but some very promising attributes.* The bold move might be too much in any other situation, but the noise of anguish that rises from his throat makes me nearly feral with want.

Stars, how long has it been since I wanted another like this? I pride myself on being able to control my *vellia* and my desires, but suddenly I'm blind to everything but the thrall of this new, keen need. Why must it be like this? Why *him*?

His lips stray from mine to drop kisses along my jaw and neck, alternating with small, claiming nips from his teeth. With each movement, I tighten my grip on his length, prompting him to thrust into my hand. His fingers release my hip, slipping beneath my pants and sliding south, trailing fire and electricity in their wake. When they arrive at their final destination and one fingertip starts to stroke my needy sex, I almost scream.

"I thought you didn't feel anything," Orion whispers, panting in my ear, dipping another torturous finger in my wetness and using it to slick the path back to my clit.

"I don't," I lie, bucking against his hand, chasing the orgasm that's already tantalizingly close. "But, stars…don't stop, anyway." My heart is hammering, lungs burning, every nerve on fire. I know I should stop, push him away, make him relent—but the truth? I don't want to. I'm scared of how much I want it, and him, and the chaos of it all.

"I hate you for this," he grunts, the despair in his voice burning me with shame and guilt. "For being who you are, what you are. For what it does to me. But if I don't touch you…something in me will break."

My heart twists, a sharp pang of loneliness and heartbreak threading through the coil of desire. Even as my body hunts for the pleasure he ignites, I feel the bitter taste of it—every moan, every shiver, tinged with sadness. This is what it's always like: exhilarating, consuming, but somehow tainted.

Not enough to make me stop, though.

"Oh, shut up," I cry, fumbling with the buttons on my pants. I need to feel him inside me—need it like I need my next breath. "Don't talk to me unless your words are filthy ones."

An alarm shatters the soft, slick sounds of the laboratory, shaking us both from our foolish, frustrated pursuit of sexual release. I shout a long string of obscenities at the interruption, and the pleasure that vaporizes before either one of us can climax.

"Shit! Ada, ventilate the laboratory on the second deck. What the hell is the siren all about?"

Orion pulls away like he's been stung, then glowers at me as if the whole thing is my fault. Considering how out of control my emotions are, perhaps it is.

I thought you'd want to know, we've arrived at Amphitreas, Ada replies. *Port authorities from Turquin are requesting landing codes and they seem rather impatient about it.*

6
orion

The Best Laid Plans

STARS, I hate her.

What I don't say out loud—what I can't quite admit—is worse: I don't think I *actually* hate her at all, and realizing that makes my chest tighten with frustration. This is not good.

All week I managed to avoid her by holing up in the dilapidated excuse for a laboratory, but even digging my fingers into the dirt pods of the dusty biosphere hasn't managed to quell the heat prickling beneath my skin every time we pass each other in the corridor. I can't stop noticing how her presence makes me alert, uncomfortable, and strangely aware of every little detail about her. After our third day together, I started to wonder if I'd bitten off more than I could chew. I've never had to hide from anyone before, and here I am, cowering like some damn adolescent half embarrassed by the attention my body insists on giving her.

Now that my fears have been proven valid, I feel a grim sense of resignation. She obviously isn't above using her abilities to manipulate me to get what she wants—but I'm not sure if that's the Solar Mother idol, amnesty from the Feds, or her freedom from Brill.

I ignore the emptiness of my arms, the tingling in my lips,

and the slickness of her desire still coating my fingers. *Don't trust it*, she said. Easier to believe when my heart isn't pounding a tattoo of heady lust in my veins.

Where are my ancestors' voices now? I need them whispering in my ears, reminding me that this woman is a criminal with a built-in biological weapon and she'll throw me to a pack of hungry lupitians at the first opportunity. But instead there's only this uneasy curiosity, a quiet fascination that I can't fully name. She's not someone I want to consider jumping into bed with, especially when all evidence points to the frequent and forgettable nature of her partners. I'm better than a one night stand. *But what a night it would be…*

"Ha! *Landing codes*? Funny way of saying 'bribe' if you ask me," Lyra grumbles, taking a step back and straightening the mess of her hair—the mess *I* made of her hair. *My mess.* I desperately try to ignore the primal satisfaction that ignites at that sight.

"Okay, well, it's too bad my *last* job left me with more bruises than credits to spare. Ada, do we have anything we could give them?"

She straightens her pants and flicks a nervous glance at me. It's the first time I've seen something like regret and shame on her face, which cuts me more than I want to admit.

"You don't have enough for a bribe?" I ask, my voice still rough. A pang of guilt twists in my chest as I watch her try to sweet-talk her way out of this.

Lyra's brows lift. "Now, how would a backwater boy scout know about such things?"

"I don't know what a 'boy scout' is, so I'll assume it's another Earth thing. As to the backwater comment, I'll have you know Xylothia is renowned for its forests and for the storied history of my ancestors. The Xylothian Protectorate—"

"Bo-ring," Lyra says, rolling her eyes. "I don't care about your grandaddy monks." I can see the tension in her shoulders, the silent calculation as she searches for another angle.

"Well, if you'd stop interrupting me, I could explain that I've come across my fair share of feckless pirates and they're always after a bribe," I snap.

"Sure, something you're much too upstanding to even consider," she chuckles, turning to go.

"If you mean I'm too honorable to take money for the sale of my principles, you're correct," I say, following her from the lab, which has grown hot and uncomfortable after our ill-advised kiss. Guilt starts to flare, and I can't stop thinking about how my interference has put her in this awkward, exposed position, forcing her to improvise with nothing to offer.

Lyra stomps down the corridor and throws herself into the captain's chair in the cockpit, mumbling the entire time. I hover behind her, noting the tension in her jaw, the flicker of panic in her eyes as Ada beeps warnings about the harbor's sensors.

"Ada, patch them through. Dig through your hard drive for some old landing codes we could try to pass off instead. Better that than nothing," Lyra says. Her fingers hover over the controls, betraying her worry—she has nothing, nothing to smooth over this situation.

Static crackles for a moment, then a garbled voice echoes through the ship's speakers.

"This is Turquin Harbor Patrol," the voice says. "State your business and provide your landing codes."

"This is the passenger transport *Aldrin-136* requesting permission to land to refuel and resupply," Lyra tries. Her hands fidget on the console as if she could conjure the credits she doesn't have, and I catch myself tightening my fists at the reminder that I'm the reason she doesn't have credits to spare.

"Landing codes?" the harbor patrol repeats.

Lyra chews on her bottom lip and I swallow, my mouth suddenly dry.

"So, how important are those landing codes?" she asks.

"You can't dock here without valid landing codes," the harbor patrol cuts in.

"Since when does Turquin play by the rules?" Lyra gripes. Her fingers drum against the console as she searches for anything—old codes, a bribe, a loophole. Nothing.

"I repeat—you cannot dock here without valid landing codes," the harbor patrol radios. "If you don't have them, you'll have to resupply somewhere else."

"Listen, you filthy…" Lyra starts to growl.

I take a step forward, my voice firm but measured, trying to reclaim some control.

"Two hundred credits," I interrupt. "We'll transmit two hundred credits to you to forget about the landing codes and strike our ship from your arrival register."

Her eyes widen slightly, the relief barely visible, and I can't help but feel the sting of guilt again, but at least now I can help undo some of that mess. The silence stretches for a few seconds, but the static-coated reply finally comes through.

"Transmit the credits, then dock in bay nineteen."

Lyra cuts the transmission and glares at me.

"I hope you don't expect me to pay you back, Ranger," she says. "Since it's your fault I'm currently broke, anyway."

"Sure," I say with a satisfied smile. The pressure in my chest has eased some, leaving my only discomfort throbbing between my legs. "If it means we can get some food other than pills, powders, and expired carbo shakes, I'll happily foot the two hundred to get us to civilization."

I toss her my identity chip so she can pull the funds from my account. My compliance only seems to annoy her further, so I rise from the navigator's chair and head back to my berth. I won't risk her irritation sending out a spike of *vellia* again now that I've gotten control of myself. I can't decide who's more at fault—Lyra for her damned genetics or me for goading her. On the way back to my room, I pepper Ada with questions about Turquin and Amphitreas, intent on distracting myself from the ever-present ache in my groin that accompanies every encounter with Lyra.

"What's the environment like down on Turquin, Ada?" I survey my clothing options with disappointment. Everything Lyra has let me borrow is too small, has too many appendages, or is made from some uncomfortable material. Once we get into port, I'll purchase something clean and functional that actually fits.

The equatorial port city of Turquin sits in the Great Sea of Amphitreas. The environment could be compared to tropics on other terrestrial planets, but Amphitreas has no available land mass and is entirely covered by water. Manmade floats make up every habitable surface. Due to the planet's oblong orbit, Turquin resides in a warm, tropical zone averaging roughly 299.8 Kelvin for thirteen months out of their annual twenty. For the remaining seven months, Turquin freezes over completely for the Amphitrean winter, with temperatures averaging 184 Kelvin.

"How do people survive the winters?" I wonder.

Most residents leave when the planet starts to cool. A small population of Charonites are employed to maintain the structures during the freezing season. Charonites hail from the Plutonian moon Charon and thrive in temperatures that are otherwise uninhabitable for most species.

"Thank you, Ada," I say, pulling on my uniform. My stomach drops as the ship descends into the Amphitrean atmosphere and I stumble backward during Lyra's turbulent landing. When things still and the hum of the engines quiets, I breathe a sigh of relief.

"Look alive, Ranger!" Lyra shouts from the main corridor. She strides into my room, freezing when she sees me.

"No way. Absolutely not," she says. "We are *not* strolling around a pirate-infested port with you wearing a freaking uniform."

"These are the only clothes that fit. Do you have a better suggestion?"

"I don't care if you have to walk around naked—you're not wearing that," she insists. "If you think the Void Stalkers' threats of violence were bad, you don't want to know what will happen to a cop in a city of criminals."

"I'm a Xylothian Ranger. I'm not a Fed. I protect wildlife and ancient historical sites."

"Oh! Silly me! There will definitely be time for you to make that distinction when we're dealing a whole lot of shoot first, *then* ask questions types. Besides, how many looters and smugglers have you turned into the Feds, anyway? I'm betting we'll probably run into at least a few of your biggest fans here," Lyra says darkly.

I fold my arms across my chest. "Well, then what do you suggest?"

She considers me for a moment. "Maybe you should just wait on the ship until I get back."

"Absolutely not. I don't trust you enough to let you out of my sight. You could hire some goon to come in here and kill me," I point out, giving voice to one of the anxieties I've kept tucked away over the last several days. Why hasn't she killed me, or intentionally unleashed her *vellia* on me? It's not sitting right with my image of her, which only makes me more unsettled.

Lyra barks a laugh. "I wouldn't need to hire anyone to kill you, Ranger. I could do it just as easily myself. Especially when you're being so damn infuriating!"

Ada's familiar chime rings through our argument.

If I may offer a suggestion…

"No!" Lyra shouts.

"Yes, please," I say at the same time.

Ada continues. *Lyra is correct that a disguise might be advisable. Whether Ranger Asterth has run afoul of anyone in Turquin, it's safe to say a Xylothian Ranger would be a memorable sight. If our goal is to resupply and make our way to Minaris as stealthily as possible, drawing attention is inadvisable. Even if Amphitreas is free from extradition, there may be parties happy to sell information as to your whereabouts to the first person who comes asking.*

Lyra smirks. "See? Even Ada agrees with me, which, truthfully doesn't happen that often."

I agree with you when it is logical to do so.

Ignoring the dig, Lyra sizes me up, her concern evident in the crease between her brows. Then, like a bolt of lightning, her face lights up with inspiration.

"I've got it!" she says, dashing from my room. "I'll be right back."

I frown. "I have a feeling I'm not going to like this."

The probability is high that you will not, Ada chirps.

IT TAKES twenty minutes for Lyra to convince me to wear the artfully arranged bedsheet looped over me like an elaborate cloak. She insists the disguise is perfect—a High Lord of Thelaous, a man so rich and politically powerful that no one would dare question his business on Minaris.

"People like that don't get hassled," she says, looping a gold clasp at my shoulder.

Her explanation for the disguise makes sense, but her cover story is thin enough to make me nervous—anyone with half a brain would see through it. Still, the confidence in her delivery makes it sound almost plausible, and that might be enough.

On top of that, she's opened the aft windows and the saline humidity of the sea has already permeated the ship, making the cloak stick to my skin. The air is thick with salt and heat, and every step feels like I'm sweating through my dignity. The fabric itches like guilt.

My outward discomfort is only exacerbated by the fact that Lyra tells me she'll be wearing the traditional garb of a Velusian pleasure house—her mother's house, she informs me—and when she appears, I forget how to breathe.

She's draped in a whisper of pink gauze, the fabric so sheer it seems to hover over her golden skin instead of covering it. The twist of material crosses her chest, ties at her waist, and falls in soft folds down her legs, catching every light in the room. The outfit doesn't just reveal; it commands. She moves like someone raised in a place where beauty is power and attention is a weapon.

I catch myself wondering how many eyes she's had to hold, how many hands she's had to outmaneuver just to survive in fabric like that. Her soft chocolate and pink hair has been tied in an elaborate updo, which she assures me disguises a small dagger, if I think about teasing her.

Oh, I want to tease her, all right. Just not in the way *she* thinks. Fortunately, the thought curdles fast. The more she jokes, the more I see the 'don't-mess-with-me' under it—the self-defense built into every soft curve…and I hate that part of me wants her, anyway.

"Tell me again," she demands. "Where are you from?"

"I'm a High Lord from Thelaous," I say with a sigh. "I'm called Pater Xandar."

"Good," she nods. "And who am I?"

I swallow around the fluttering in my chest, my mouth suddenly dry.

"You are my *serikka*, Luxura of Velusia," I choke out, desperate to ignore the dark shadows of her nipples beneath her top and the gentle swell of her hips—the way the delicate fabric caresses them just so.

"And why are we here?" she continues, blustering through my misery.

"We're here to resupply on our trip to Theta-9, where I have a diplomatic conference," I grumble.

"Good boy," she says, patting my arm. "Now, take my tether and let's go shopping."

My eyes widen when she hands me a finely-wrought gold chain that connects to a matching gold collar around her neck.

"No way! I'm not going to walk around with you on a leash like some kind of animal," I bite out. "That's completely degrading." The heat rising in my chest has nothing to do with embarrassment this time. I've spent my life hunting those who've treated others like property, and now she's asking me to play one.

She cocks a brow at me. "We don't have a lot of time to get into the finer points of *serikka* tradition. This is how it works on Velusia. If I don't have one, everyone will get suspicious."

"Well, I'll just tell them I trust you," I say. "I'll tell them you're too in love with me to run off."

Lyra laughs again and looks at me with something like pity in her eyes.

"Stars, you *are* ignorant. This isn't about love—Velusians are forbidden to love, Ranger. We serve our houses, we are respected and sought after as bodyguards, assassins, advisors, and occasionally as pleasure workers. It depends on the Velusian, and the terms of the contract. The tether isn't degrading. The tether is a bond," she says.

She must see the confusion written across my face, because she sighs.

"It represents the bond of trust between the patron and the Velusian. Realistically, a dinky gold chain can't protect you from what a Velusian can do with their *vellia*. Have you ever seen someone go mad from an irrepressible surge of hormonal lust? It's not pretty. The chain is a promise—your patron will honor and respect you, and you won't use your *vellia* to control them." She delivers this information in a bored sort of tone, as if she's heard the explanation a thousand times in her life. Perhaps she has.

"Still," I say, distaste rolling off my tongue. "Don't those relationships ever sour? Or go wrong?"

"Partnerships—not relationships. And yes, they do." Something flickers across her face then—quick and sharp, gone before I can read it. Not fear, exactly, or sorrow. Recognition, maybe. The kind of expression that comes from remembering something you wish you could forget.

"Is that why you're no longer on Velusia?" I ask.

She winces, then glares at me, thrusting the end of her tether into my hand.

"Here endeth the lesson. We have work to do. Just…try not to talk too much. Keep your hood up and your face covered. I doubt we'll find any other Thelaousian High Lords here, but we don't want anyone to get suspicious, okay?"

I nod, mulling over everything she's told me as we make our way to the outer bay doors and down the ramp onto the dock. The port city sprawls before us like a floating, ramshackle village, gently bobbing atop the cerulean waves. Most of the small cottages and shops are constructed from recycled shipping containers and corrugated titanium stripped from wrecked vessels, giving Turquin the appearance of a somewhat charming garbage heap set adrift in an aquamarine paradise. About twenty docks lie on either side of us, each with a different ship anchored in. I recognize Jovian windjammers, deep space cruisers, even a few pleasure yachts from Cerin. It's hard to take in everything—so much life and variety in one small place. I've never seen so many different kinds of people all at once.

Lyra urges me forward, pausing at the end of the long dock that stretches toward the bustling knot in the center of the floating town.

"Stop gawking," she hisses under her breath. "You're supposed to be an immortal High Lord from a planet overflowing with wealth. Look bored, for fuck's sake!"

I try to do as she asks, schooling my features in an expression of jaded disdain.

"That's better," she whispers. "Ready?"

As we walk down the dock, a few looks fall on Lyra—her hips swaying seductively, the ocean breeze tugging at the panels of her skirt, a knowing tilt to her full lips. For a heartbeat, I'm worried her beauty and sensuality will draw too much attention, but she was right. Gazes seem to slide over her like water off a liotha leaf.

I begin to find the rhythm of our ruse, throwing back my shoulders and casting bored looks on everyone we pass.

"It's not all bad," she says quietly. "Velusia, I mean."

"I didn't say it was bad," I reply. "It's just different from how we experience desire and matehood on Xylothia." I choose my tone carefully—neutral, curious. On Xylothia, devotion is sacred and private. On Velusia, it's currency. And yet, the more she speaks, the less transactional it sounds.

"People sometimes think we're sorcerers, or evil, for trafficking in pleasure. For courting wealth and protection and power. But that's not what Velusians are all about, you know. They just find beauty in desire. Desire is something every species has in common, whether it's sexual in nature or otherwise. Everyone *desires* something, which is how Velusians believe everything is connected. They worship the power that it has and they devote their lives to it." Lyra's violet eyes focus on some distant point far beyond the horizon.

"Devotion to that kind of ideal must come with a heavy price," I reply. I mean it with respect, but the thought lodges like a stone in my chest. To devote yourself to desire is to give yourself to something that never stops hungering. I wonder what it costs her—to know how to wield that kind of power and still be at its mercy. I don't ask. She wouldn't answer, and I'm not sure I could stand to hear it.

She tilts her head, considering. "Devotion to *anything* is costly. It's not my chosen path, but I don't look down on them for it. It's just that at the end of the day, I don't want to have to trust anyone with my tether."

The bitterness in her tone nearly stops me in my tracks. The word *trust* lands heavier than *tether*. Is that why she's running from Brill? Is *he* her patron? The thought sends a wave of nausea rolling through my insides. It's not jealousy—at least, that's what I tell myself. It's the idea of her belonging to anyone that twists in my gut. An alien feeling of possessiveness and anger rises in me, but I let it go as quickly as it comes. It's just from playing this part—from physically holding the tether of someone I'm supposed to honor and protect. There can't—there won't—be anything else to it.

Before I know it, we're standing at the edge of a long, flat barge that has been converted into a kind of market. There are stinking rows of rotting fish and some other aquatic creatures I don't recognize, a few still twitching in the midday sun. Boxes of desiccated fruits and wilted vegetables, along with crates of bug-infested dried goods stand along the back, tucked behind half a dozen barrels with suspicious-smelling yellow liquid bubbling inside. Lyra sees the disgust on my face and chuckles.

"Don't worry, my lord. We'll be getting our consumable goods from a different shop."

I suppress a shiver at how the honorific affects me. Blood rushes to my cock, and an alarming tightness throbs in base of my spine. *No...there's no way she's my...no. We're just playing our parts.*

Lyra sashays to the back stall and begins haggling with the shopkeeper over the price of fuel. The insect-like alien's huge compound eyes keep flicking in my direction, adding to my nervousness. Reminding myself to act the part, I glower at him. Lyra catches the look and arches a brow in amusement.

"Would you rather negotiate with my lord?" she asks with acid-laced sweetness. "Only I wouldn't recommend it. He has a habit of removing limbs when he feels he's being cheated."

The shopkeeper swallows and shakes his head. I have to fight to keep from laughing.

Over the next hour, Lyra manages to bargain for enough goods to fill the ship's hold and then some. She even finds a couple of replacement parts for the water filtration system so Ada will stop pestering her. Finding spare clothing for me is proving to be more of a challenge, partly because the selection is limited.

"Stop complaining," Lyra calls to me from outside the

makeshift dressing room. "Turquin isn't exactly a fashion hotspot."

"I'm not looking for fashion," I mutter. "I'm just looking for something that fits!"

Lyra's hand appears over the curtain, clutching a moss green tunic and a pair of soft brown pants. As soon as I grab them from her, her hand reappears with a piping hot pie wrapped in brown paper.

"What's this?" I grunt, my mouth already watering with the smell of buttery pastry and fragrant, spicy filling.

"Don't get your knickers in a twist," she says in between mouthfuls of her own food. "I got you the veggie one."

"You…what?"

"You don't eat meat, right?" she asks. "Ada told me it's forbidden for your people. Taboo, or whatever."

"That's correct," I reply, taken aback by the fact that she'd cared enough to ask. She waves the pie over the curtain enticingly.

"Are you going to eat it, or not? It smells amazing. I'll happily have yours if you're going to be all weird about it."

I pluck it from her hand and bite into it, unable to contain my moan of pleasure. After a full week of pills, powders, and bland bars that hardly qualify as "food" beyond their ability to meet basic nutritional requirements, sinking my teeth into the flaky, golden crust and zesty, creamy vegetable filling makes me almost weep with relief.

After I demolish the remaining lunch, I turn my attention back to the pile of garments Lyra has instructed the shop owner to supply.

"Hurry up and pick some stuff out," she whines, her mouth still full. I'm light years more tolerant of her attitude after eating, so I comply by tugging on the tunic and trousers she's just handed me. They fit me adequately, though the tunic is made to hang to one's knees and only comes to mid-thigh on me. I shuck the outfit and try on another one—an Earth-style suit of smooth black fabric.

"This is too…formal," I say. "I'll just take the green shirt and brown pants."

"You need the suit for Minaris," Lyra says, her mouth full of food again. "We're going to be in disguise there, too, but more so for my sake than for yours. I'm less than welcome on that planet."

I feel a flare of guilt at endangering her, all so I can get some names to hand over to the Feds—especially when there's no guarantee they'll do anything with them.

"Is it unsafe?" I ask quietly.

She chuckles. "This whole mission is unsafe, *my lord*." The last words drip with sarcasm since we're alone in the shop. "I did warn you about that back on Xylothia."

I open my mouth to reply, but the wet sounds of her licking crumbs from her fingers kindles the desire in my blood like a forest fire in the dry season. My cock hardens in the black silk trousers and I bite my lip to fight for control again. I don't trust it. It's not real. We're playing parts, which would make her more anxious, so maybe this is just a spike of *vellia*. Or maybe…maybe it's worse than that. Maybe she's trying to drive me into mindless want so I'll let her go without the names of her buyers and without informing the Feds. The pounding of blood in my veins goading me with the feral need to claim her seems to be answer enough. Every lesson I've ever learned about restraint is collapsing, one heartbeat at a time.

But no. She wouldn't do that, would she? We're supposed to be working together here.

Logic is the barest whisper in my mind, but it's quickly drowned out by the steady drumbeat of my pulse, which throbs in time to the salacious fantasies of pumping into her in some sacred, doomed, perfect rhythm. Her musical voice cuts through my attempts at concentration.

"If you hurry up with the shopping, I'll let you have dessert."

7

lyra

Never Trust a Space Pirate

I ALMOST DROP the second pastry when Orion flings the curtain back and pins me with a scorching glare. The black trousers cling to his thick thighs and the jacket hangs perfectly across his shoulders, but he isn't wearing anything underneath. His dark freckles flicker down his muscular torso, trailing low down the line of exposed skin showing between the jacket lapels.

I choke on the pie, breathing in the flaky crumbs and sweet gnuberry filling. He takes a slow, deliberate step forward, his eyes never straying from mine.

"You're supposed to wear a shirt under that suit. The white one with the buttons down the front."

"What are you doing?" he grits out, jaw tight, eyes narrowed, vibrating with anger.

"What are you talking about? Did you hit your head in there or something? We're getting you clothes so we can sneak our way onto Minaris. And so you'll stop complaining," I reply, taking an involuntary step back. The look in his eyes heats me from the inside out and my knees are starting to feel wobbly.

"Cut it out," he growls, grabbing my wrist. "I know you're trying to play me!"

"Okay, what the *actual* fuck are you talking about?" I ask, confusion and lust warring in my brain.

"Your *vellia*! Turn it down, or off, or whatever it is you do to emit it. Just stop it, okay?" He releases my hand, stalks back to the dressing room and whisks the curtain closed again, leaving me standing alone, mouth gaping like a dying fish. I close my eyes and take a deep breath, shaken by his sudden change in demeanor. For once, my *vellia* is subdued—under control, even. I don't understand what he's talking about.

I follow him into the dressing room, anger spurring my movements.

"Excuse me, but you can *not* talk to me like that and then just walk away!" I pull the curtain back and return his scowl. The bell on the shop door chimes and I duck into the cramped room with him to avoid making a scene, whisking the curtain closed behind me. The muffled voices of other shoppers weave through the tension between us, giving me a moment to breathe.

"Get out of here!" he hisses.

"What is your problem?" I whisper back. "My *vellia* is under wraps! Everything was going fine between us until you lost your fucking shit."

"You're lying," he accuses. "You're using it to try and manipulate me—it's not going to work."

"Manipulate you?" I return, my hushed voice turning shrill. "How the hell am I manipulating you? I'm taking you shopping! And I got you lunch! I'm not being nice to manipulate you. We have a deal and I'm holding up my end of it!"

"Oh, and I'm just supposed to believe that you offering me *dessert* doesn't mean anything?" he scoffs, yanking the suit jacket off and tossing it in a heap on the floor. Stars, his shoulders are so gloriously broad, it's hard to focus on my righteous pique.

"Dessert," I repeat. "That's what this is about. You're pissed because I offered you dessert and you think I'm trying to hop into bed with you?"

"Well?" he accuses. "Aren't you? It'd probably be easier to

control me—to get what you want if I'm so desperate to bury myself inside you that I can't tell which way is up. Isn't that how your *vellia* works?"

The heat percolating beneath my skin arrows straight to my core at his deliciously filthy words and I squeeze my legs together to fight the ache building between them. Despite what he obviously thinks about me, I've never used my *vellia* to con another person into bed with me. Most of the time I rarely use it —only when I'm in serious trouble or a tight spot. Orion seems to believe I wield it like a plasma pistol to get whatever I want. I'm almost sorry to disappoint him.

"Dessert," I say again, showing him the fruit pie I procured with the savory ones for lunch. His eyes widen at the sight of the golden pastry oozing with reddish-purple jam. Regret and embarrassment skitters across his face. His cheeks flush almost as red as the jam.

"I'm sorry, I thought..." he starts. But whatever he thinks, I'm not interested. I've had just about enough of Ranger Righteous for one day, so I do what any self-respecting woman would do.

I shove the fruit pie right in his face.

He stands stock still, stunned, as sticky globs of fuchsia jelly ooze down his face and drip onto his bare chest.

"And for your information," I say, turning to leave the dressing room. "I've never used my *vellia* to bed anyone. Truthfully, I've never needed it."

I walk back to the front of the store, pay the shop owner for stupid Orion's new wardrobe, and ask her to bring him a towel.

"My lord got a little overexcited with his lunch," I explain. And then, to Orion, I shout: "I'm heading back to the ship to oversee the loading of our purchased supplies, my lord. I'll attend to you when you're ready to return."

I storm from the clothing shop, not caring that my fury might cast doubts about our cover. We're leaving this port post haste and stars help anyone who comes for me now. By the time I reach the end of the dock, the sun hangs low on the horizon, casting the endless Amphitrean sea in the muted rainbow of dusk. The gentle lap of the waves against the metal floats beneath the dock are oddly soothing, and help to cool my temper.

One by one, crates of food, fuel, spare parts, ammunition, and other dry goods are wheeled down the dock on carts and loaded into the ship's cargo hold. I sit on the edge of the dock, dangling my toes in the warm turquoise sea below, keeping my eye on the dock runners coming in and out of my ship. Schools of small, glittering fish dart around my feet, flashing neon colors in the water.

Idly, I wonder if I've been unfair to Orion. Granted, he's way off base accusing me of manipulating him, but we don't really know each other. What does he know about me? He caught me looting the most sacred site of his people, dealing with space scum, and now he knows about my frustrating genetic quirk. I suppose I can't fault him for jumping to the wrong conclusions, but it smarts nonetheless.

Maybe he's right to keep his distance. If I were him, I wouldn't trust me either. The truth is, trust isn't a luxury I can afford—not with what's on the line.

If he knew what I've done to survive…would he think differently of me? I don't want his pity, but maybe a modicum of understanding. The line between *scoundrel* and *survivor* isn't something most people cared to parse, and Orion has already made his judgments, apparently. It won't matter in the long run — especially once I find a way to leverage the Solar Mother idol. I thought about stealing it, of course, maybe even sneaking back to the ship and taking off if the chance came up, but there's no doubt in my mind he'd send the Feds after me the first chance he got and I'm not about to trade a leash for a prison cell.

The barest whisper of guilt threads through me. Will I still be able to steal the idol after everything? After knowing what it means to him—to his people? I smile ruefully to myself. *Probably.*

It wouldn't be the first time my Sisyphean quest for freedom silenced my feelings of guilt…shame…*regret.*

Assuming we don't end up in bed together, after all. At that, my thoughts turn to all the ways we *might* end up in bed together, and soon it's more than the tropical temperatures and my waning ire heating my blood.

"Well, if it isn't lusty little Lyra!"

The shout has dread climbing up my spine and my stomach turning to stone. That voice shouldn't be here—not this far from the trade routes. *Shit.* It can't be. Turning back toward the booming voice, I force a smile.

"Iathos," I drawl, laying eyes on the sexiest space pirate I've ever met and the second biggest mistake of my life. Ugh, could this day get any worse?

Iathos grins mischievously as he approaches and sits down next to me, his pale blue skin and thick, backwards curving horns almost glowing in the golden light of sunset.

"I can't say I'm shocked to run into you here, but I am surprised to see you in the garb of your mother's house. What *can* you be up to, I wonder?" he says, showing off his pearly white fangs.

I stiffen and my pulse skips. He knows too much—or at least enough to be dangerous.

"Oh, I don't know, maybe I'm here trying to recover what you stole from me."

Iathos chuckles and tugs his boots off, dipping his toes into the water next to mine.

"Now, now. I only stole what *you* stole. Besides, I had every intention of splitting the profits with you. It's just that I knew my buyer would pay more for that box than Brill ever would," he says in a low voice that still gives me goosebumps.

I cut him a searing look. "You stole my chance at freedom. Thanks to you, it took me another six months to earn Brill's trust enough to go after the next score. You have a lot of audacity for someone who owes me thousands of credits *and* an explanation about tipping Brill off." The air between us thickens. My chest tightens, the old betrayal scraping raw again. He'd sold me out once—what's stopping him from doing it again?

"In fact, you're pretty lucky to be sitting here with all of your appendages intact—underwhelming as they are."

"I only told Brill what was common knowledge in our seedy little circles, love." Iathos smirks.

"I'm not your love!" I snap. "And what—exactly—did you tell him that you think is such common knowledge?"

"Mm, just that you've been using your contracts as a smoke-screen for what you're really after."

My stomach flips. He can't mean—no, he wouldn't know. Still, the fact that he's even close sends panic skittering up my spine.

I snort. "Oh? And what do you think I'm really after?"

"Revenge, darling. It's painfully obvious."

Revenge. The word lodges in my throat like a shard of glass. For a moment, I can't breathe. If he's guessed even part of it—if he tells Brill—I'm finished. My panic cuts through my irritation, but I school my features in a sarcastic smirk.

"Revenge?" I scoff. "Against you, maybe. Other than that, I don't have any scores to settle."

"*Tsk.* Give me more credit than that, I beg. The fact that you haven't simply killed Brill is the only thing that's surprising in the whole mess." Iathos says with a devious grin. "Tell me, Lyra love, why haven't you? Unravel this intricate scheme for me, would you?"

Because I've tried running. Because I've failed *so* many times. Because killing him wouldn't be enough—but he doesn't get to know that. My temper flares and I feel my *vellia* prickle beneath my skin.

My palms tingle, the familiar charge building beneath my skin. Just a flicker of it would send him running—along with everyone else on this dock. Still, the temptation isn't easy to ignore.

"You're full of shit, Iathos, and you better stop trying to rile me up because I'm about to unleash a full blast of *vellia* on you." Finally, his bravado dims a touch. Even the great lover Iathos fears becoming a mindless, rutting beast. "Brill doesn't give a fuck about me except for what he thinks I can deliver, and I'm not the only thief in his orbit. So, why don't you be a good little boy and tell me what, exactly, you've been dancing around? And I'd hurry it up, by the way. This conversation is making me feel…rather flustered."

"Keep it under control, Lyra," Iathos warns, but there's a note of anxiety that fills me with satisfaction. "Brill thinks your father knew the location of the Dark Star."

The words hit like a plasma blast to the chest. My breath catches. My vision narrows.

Brill knows. How can he know? My father's journals are my only remaining secret and there's no way anyone else found them. Iathos watches me closely—too closely—so I school my features in disbelief.

"The Dark Star?" I laugh.

My laugh sounds too high, too forced. My pulse thunders against my ribs, the heat from earlier curdling into dread.

"You've got to be kidding me. That's a fucking myth cooked up by hallucinating colonists in a starvation haze."

Iathos lifts one shoulder in forced nonchalance. "Regardless, Brill is certain your father knew where to find it, and I promise you, Lyra, love, Brill won't let you go until you do. Even then"— he eyes my body appraisingly— "I'd bet he'll find other reasons to keep you. I know I would."

Sweat beads at my temples, my body going rigid before my brain can catch up. There it is—the trap snapping shut.

Still, I try to deny the veracity of his words.

"Dark Star or not, if I buy my way out of my contract, I'm as good as gone. Brill respects a deal." Even as I say it, the words taste bitter with desperate hope. Brill doesn't respect anything but ownership. And right now, he still owns me.

"Mm, true, but Brill isn't known to give up his treasures without a fight. And you are quite the treasure."

He trails a finger across my thigh, but the touch repulses me.

"I should gut you like the low-life worm you are and toss you into this sea. I wonder what manner of creature will come up from the depths to nibble at your black heart."

Iathos *tsks* again. "Such violence! That's not the Lyra I remember." He slides a foot up the swell of my calf beneath the water. "Except in bed."

True, Iathos and I enjoyed a fair bit of extracurricular intimacy, but now the thought turns my stomach. I pull away, my fingers itching to throttle him.

"What do you want, Iathos?"

"I should think that was obvious, love," he drawls again.

Unease snakes through me as my suspicions take shape. He's not here by accident. Brill sent him, which means our ticking clock just sped up.

"No, I mean, why are you here? This can't be a chance meeting. Did Brill hire you? There's no way you just *happened* to be on Amphitreas the day I arrived. Out with it, Iathos!"

Something dark flashes in Iathos's black eyes and I silently curse myself. *Stupid, Lyra! Of course this isn't a chance meeting.*

I start to back away, but Iathos jumps up and latches onto my arm with brute strength and simmering violence. His charm falls away like the mask I knew it was.

"Listen to me, Lyra…" But whatever he's about to say dies on his lips as a shadow falls over us both.

"Excuse me, am I interrupting something?" Orion approaches us warily, no doubt taking in my anger and Iathos's grip on my arm.

"Who are *you*?" Iathos sneers, glancing between Orion and I.

"I'm her owner," Orion says.

"No, Orion, not *owner—patron*. And no, Iathos, he's my partner."

"Owner?" Iathos repeats, incredulously, sizing up Orion's

massive frame. "Does Brill know?" A laugh bubbles up in his chest. "Owner? Get real. Some dumb tower of meat like you *owning* Lyra Phoenix."

Every muscle in me coils, ready to strike. He's drawing attention. He's putting everything I've worked for in danger. If anyone down this dock hears my name in the same breath as Brill's, we're cooked.

His laughter grows louder, until it carries far enough down the dock to draw attention. The last of the crates has been loaded and the cargo has been stowed, and I've had just about enough *fun* for one day. I grit my teeth.

I can feel my freedom slipping between my fingers like sand. I need control—over Iathos, over Orion, over the narrative.

"Orion, go wait in the ship," I order. "Iathos, you owe me some answers."

"No," they both say at once.

Perfect. Two men, one ego contest, and me—the only one with something real to lose. I groan, frustration building to volcanic proportions.

"Lyra, love, I think we need to chat," Iathos says, tugging at my arm painfully.

I wince. "Orion, *go wait in the ship.*"

"Hey, take your hands off her!" Orion growls.

"Yeah, *Orion,*" Iathos pantomimes. "Do as she says and go wait in the ship. This doesn't concern you!"

That's it. I'm going to call forth my *vellia* and get some damn answers from Iathos. If Orion is too much of a stubborn fool to get out of the blast radius, so be it. I close my eyes and block out the sounds of the two men arguing, summoning as much desire as I can. I feel it rise through my blood, finding form beneath my skin. But before I can let it go, the pressure of Iathos's hand on my arm is gone, and I hear a large splash.

When my eyes fly open, Orion stands next to me, his arms crossed in front of his chest. Iathos is in the water—quite a fair distance from the dock, and extremely pissed off about it. Stunned, I turn to Orion.

"What the fuck?" I ask. "Did you just…throw him in?"

"Yes," he replies matter-of-factly. "He seemed to need some cooling off."

Iathos swears a blue streak and screams at us, side stroking his way back to the dock.

"Well, I don't really want to be here when he gets back to the dock. He's probably armed," I say.

"Probably," Orion agrees. I see the impish glint in his eyes and his stalwart determination not to smirk, and try to ignore the funny things they do to my insides.

I shake my head. "Let's get the hell out of here."

"Good idea," Orion replies.

As we make our way up the gangplank to the ship's outer bay, Orion draws a feather-light touch across the angry red mark on my arm, left from Ianthos's grip.

"Lyra, about earlier…" he begins, but I wave him off.

"It's fine, Ranger. I know you don't have any reason to trust me. But I still want you to know, I don't use my *vellia* willy-nilly. I only use it when I'm really in trouble. I never, *ever* use it to manipulate or steal. I mean, I do those things, but I don't use my *vellia* for them, and I just…need you to know that," I say.

He nods and reaches behind his back, producing a small plant in a pot about the size of my palm.

"I'm sorry," he says. "For earlier. I was a jerk. I know you don't have much of a reason to trust me, either, but I'm hoping we can at least call a temporary truce. No *vellia*, no threats of Federal incarceration until this is over. Deal?"

"Deal," I agree. "So, um, this is…?" I point to the odd specimen in his hand. The plant has black thorns and a gaping, garishly red maw dripping with some kind of clear, viscous fluid. It looks like something that'll creep into your room and bite you if you don't water it regularly.

"I've been reading your books. Your Earth romances. I understand human women like to receive flowers after they've been wronged," he says.

"This isn't a flower," I say slowly, so overwhelmed by a simple, stupid gesture of kindness all I can do is state the obvious. "It's a carnivorous plant."

"The options in a port run by pirates are limited," he replies, chagrined. "But I can get rid of it if you want."

"No, no! I like it," I say, offering him a small smile. I'm dizzy with the effort of trying to remember the last time anyone's given me anything without an agenda attached. Brill's gifts were always more painful than pleasant. My lovers only ever took. My parents, maybe? Surely there were birthday presents when I was young, but...strangely, nothing comes to mind. Pressure builds in my chest, warm and fulfilling—akin to indigestion but...pleasant. *Nice.* "'Thank you' is what I meant to say. I love it. Apology accepted."

His expression warms at that and I seal the doors to prepare for takeoff.

Rather than hide in his berth, Orion chooses to sit next to me in the navigator seat. I turn over the engines and engage the thrusters, setting my new little plant in a cupholder on the center console.

"Ada, we're up and running! Let's make it a quick trip to Minaris," I say, trying to muster some enthusiasm for leaving the port city behind, but it's difficult.

Iathos's words play over and over in my head—an endless, looping record of the selfsame doubts and fears I've harbored for years. *Brill won't let you go.* Freedom's the kind of promise men like Brill sell to girls like me. And stars help me, I keep buying it.

I knew it was only a matter of time before Brill sent me after the Dark Star, but I thought I'd kept my father's connection to it and pursuit of it well guarded. How would he know what my father only confided in the margins of his journals?

I can't think about that now. I just have to deal with whatever challenge lies in front of me at the moment. And getting to

Minaris—getting Orion safely in front of the Triumvirate there… well, that's the next challenge.

"So…your friend back there. Iathos." Orion makes a show of staring at the hologram chart in the cockpit that shows our route to Minaris. He studiously avoids my eyes.

"Tread carefully, Ranger," I warn.

He rubs a hand over the stubble sprouting on his chiseled jawline. "He mentioned Brill. Should we be worried?"

A bitter chuckle trips from my lips. "I'm always worried about Brill. Whether *you* have the good sense to be worried about him is up to you and your gods. As to the 'we'? Well, I guess you can be glad our arrangement has an expiration date."

The gravity of his frustration pulls his brows and his lips down.

"You know what I mean, Lyra."

"I'm sure Kraxis has already told Brill we left Xylothia together and I'm sure Brill has figured out we have the idol on us. He probably thinks we're trying to sell it, so I'm betting he'll send someone to Epsilon-6 since he knows I was negotiating with another interested party. Iathos is a lying, cheating, thieving, selfish fuck but he's not a lackey like Kraxis. He'll only offer Brill information if the price is right or if he's sufficiently pissed off to want more than a revenge fuck," I utter darkly.

Orion's head snaps up at that. "A revenge fuck? You slept with him?"

"Hey, I told you—space can get pretty lonely," I reply, strangely defensive. "Was it my finest moment? No. Did it end up costing me more than I ever would have paid for a few hours of pleasure? Big time." The truth cuts sharper than I mean it to. I can still see the blue of his skin in the starlight, the curve of his grin right before he walked out with my payday—and my future. I'd thought he wanted me. Turns out he wanted what I'd stolen.

I don't tell Orion that part. I don't tell him that Iathos knew things about my father no one should've known—or that maybe that's why he was really on Amphitreas. Not for me, but for the Dark Star. If I admit that, I'd have to admit how close I came to trusting him, how stupid that makes me, and how scared I am that Brill knows more than I do.

"Will I do it again? I don't know. We run in the same circles and we both like to drink until we don't feel sad, which takes an extraordinary amount of alcohol. As Ada would say, *the probability is high.*"

"He hurt you," Orion insists, his temper rising. "But you would let him touch you again?"

I shrug. Because what else can I do? If Iathos is mixed up with Brill or the hunt for the Dark Star, then he's not just a threat —he's a lead. And if sleeping with him will get me closer to freedom, well…maybe I'm not done making bad decisions.

"I'm certainly not keen on any drunken booty calls right now, no. I'm just saying, we all make mistakes. Haven't you ever sent a late-night message to an ex? Or had a little too much to drink and screwed someone you shouldn't? Oh, who am I kidding, of course you haven't. You probably have one true love back on Xylothia and your people probably mate for life and you all have worshipful, sexually fulfilling partnerships that never go stale."

"Not exactly, but Xylothian men aren't often in a habit of bruising their women," he grits out, his gaze landing on the mark on my arm that's darkening to a bluish purple. "And you forget, Lyra, my people aren't exactly thriving. We mate for life, but it doesn't happen often. Regardless of binding matehood, women are honored and respected."

"Of course they are," I huff, not at all surprised that the *honorable* ranger comes from such *honorable* people. "But I'll tell you, Xylothians are in the minority there. I've met a lot of different species and genders and I can tell you one thing: it is a cruel quirk of fate for Velusians to have desire and pleasure in their veins like a born addiction, and to end up using sex as currency in the pursuit of power. Because power always comes with violence."

Finally, Orion's eyes meet mine in the dim light of the cockpit —with only the glittering stars and the vastness of space sprawling before us. I set our course and engage Ada's autopilot, and now I need a long shower, something to eat, and to find my comfiest pair of clean sweatpants. I rise from the captain's chair and Orion follows the movement.

"Power can come from many places, Lyra," he said softly. "Too often, violence is an expression of weakness, not strength."

"Oh, really?" I tease. "So, throwing Iathos into the Amphitrean sea was a show of weakness for you?"

He crosses over to me, his expression serious. Slowly— impossibly slowly—he lifts a hand to the bedraggled updo on top of my head and unpins the clip fastening it together. My long hair falls over my shoulders and he lifts a lock of it, rubbing the silken strands between his fingers.

The small, deliberate motion steals the air from my lungs. I know why he's doing it—it's not dominance or possession. It's curiosity. Reverence, maybe. His fingers graze my scalp and my whole body goes still, heat blooming low and fierce. He smells like gnuberry pie and spices, a trace of saltwater from Amphitreas still clinging to him. I can feel the warmth of his chest just inches away, the thrum of restrained energy radiating off him like a live current. He's too close. I should step back, but…I don't.

My heart can't decide if it wants to beat out of my chest or stop beating altogether.

Eyes gone dark, he utters one word that turns my insides topsy-turvy.

"Yes."

8
orion

Who Thought a Drinking Game Was a Good
Idea?

LYRA STARES AT ME, unable to hide the flash of panic in her eyes. It's quick—a heartbeat's worth of naked fear before her mask slides back into place. But I see it. The sharp inhale. The tremor that isn't quite a step backward. For all her bravado, she's terrified of what this could mean—of me, or maybe of herself. Regret slices through me at my admission. Rousing herself from the awkward moment, she clears her throat.

"I need a drink," she says.

I drop the lock of hair and step back, embarrassed. What had I been thinking—closing the space between us like that, baring the truth behind my temper? Why had I thought to be honest with her about my moment of weakness back on Amphitreas? Not the throw itself, but the impulse behind it. That flash of possessive rage I can't explain, not even to myself. It's not my place to protect her or to fight for her honor. She certainly didn't ask for it and I highly doubt she'd welcome it.

I turn to head back to my berth. It's been a long day, and my emotions are still a tangled web I need to parse—the unspent lust from the lab and the clothes shop, the wild fury at seeing another man grab her arm and the swell of violence that followed. Throwing Iathos into the sea had been a mercy, because what I had wanted to do was rip his arms from their sockets and beat him to death with them.

Not just because he hurt her, but because he'd *touched* her. Because the thought of his hands on her skin sent something ancient and ugly roaring through me. And then the miserable revelation that not only did he touch her, but he's touched her in all the ways my body longs to. Pair that with the disturbing realization that it isn't just her *vellia* drawing me to her, but something else. Something *more*. Something coming entirely from within me. It feels dangerous, this pull—like standing too close to a dying star and pretending you won't get vaporized.

Suddenly, being trapped on this ship with her—even with our fools' bargain—seems to herald catastrophic self-destruction. I don't think I can keep denying my growing feelings for her, but I still don't trust her enough to lay those feelings at her feet. Doing so would make me too vulnerable when we both have so much to lose. And yet, as I turn to go, the scent of her hair still clings to my hands—a silent betrayal I can't wash off. The guiding voices of my ancestors are conspicuously quiet, which makes the reverberating echoes of my loneliness that much louder.

"I'll leave you to it, then," I say.

"Let me guess," she says, one corner of her mouth tugging up into a smirk. "Xylothians don't drink. Or if they do, it's all ceremonial wine in ritual goblets saved for sacred devotion to your gods."

I bristle, taking the bait. "Hardly. Not only do we indulge, but we do so with alacrity. And still, we manage to hold our alcohol—likely better than both humans and Velusians."

"Well, now, if you're challenging me to a drinking contest, no need to skirt the issue. I'll meet you in the kitchen in a few," she replies.

"I look forward to reminding you that you asked for this," I say.

But the challenge in her expression makes me wonder if I'd be the one to regret it.

TWENTY MINUTES LATER, after I've changed out of my absurd bedsheet costume and into the green tunic and brown pants we purchased, I sit across from Lyra with my arms crossed over my chest. She's removed her Velusian garments—thank the stars—but she's just as stunning in her soft gray sweatpants and thin white t-shirt.

"I assumed there would be more skill to this," I say after she explains the rules of the game.

She rattles the dice in the wooden cup and grins mischievously.

"The skill isn't in the ability to roll a certain way or manipulate the dice," she says. "It's in your ability to handle your alcohol. I'll even allow you the honor of the first roll. Do you have any questions before we begin?"

"Let me get this straight. All I have to do is roll the dice and if I roll a seven, eleven, or a double, you drink. If I roll none of those, I simply pass the dice to you and you try, and we go back and forth until someone calls it quits," I answer.

"That's about it," she says.

"Seems pretty dull," I reply. "I never enjoyed games of chance."

"Well, if you want to spice it up, we can," she laughs.

My cock hardens and I grit my teeth. "What did you have in mind?"

"Easy, Ranger. I told you I'm not trying to seduce you. I figured since you were so keen on interrogating me back on Xylothia, you'd relish the opportunity to ask some pointed questions. How's this: when we have to take a drink, we can abstain if we answer a question. The question can be anything, but it has to be answered honestly."

"It's not my honesty I doubt," I mumble. The idea of asking her anything and receiving an honest response seems almost laughable given her ability to lie and deflect. Yet, it might prove incredibly valuable in my pursuit of the truth and the end of the Xylothian smuggling ring.

"I don't usually back out of a drinking contest, but I swear on my father's grave, if I choose to answer a question, I'll do so honestly," she says, holding up her hand.

"Fine," I agree. "Let's begin."

I shake the cup of dice and let them fall on the table between us—a five and a six. I grin. Lyra picks up the shot glass of Zorium moonshine and downs it. She shudders a breath and gestures for the dice.

She rolls a double, two twos. Smirking, she slides a shot glass of moonshine in front of me. I lift it to my lips, recoiling momentarily when the powerful reek of spirits hit my nostrils. Grimacing, I tip my head back and let the horrid, burning liquid slide down my throat. Lyra laughs when I cough and sputter.

"Yeah, it's best not to let it touch your tongue," she says.

"That stuff is vile," I says. "Don't you have anything better?"

She shrugs. "Nope! But you could always offer me a truthful answer instead. Maybe it won't be so bad—spilling all your secrets to me. Probably better than a belly full of Zorium's finest."

"Just give me the dice," I grumble. She hands the cup back to me and I curse when I roll an eight, and Lyra's answering turn—a seven—has me choking down another swallow of the pungent booze.

So it goes for the next hour, the only sounds in the kitchen the rattle of dice in the cup, followed by our curses and steadily growing laughter. I have to hand it to Lyra—she's been handling her drink well so far, but her giggles are coming too often now and her dice rolls feel a little looser.

Her nose wrinkles at the two fours I roll and I grin in triumph.

"Okay, I'll be the brave one first. Hit me with your best question," she groans.

I sit straighter, willing my brain into some semblance of sobriety. Now's my chance to find out about the smuggling ring and Lyra's resumé of criminal activities. But the words that fall from my lips aren't about either of those things.

"Why are you working for Brill?" I ask.

She winces. I wait.

"Can I change my mind?" she grumbles. "I'd much rather face tomorrow's hangover."

"Hey, you set these rules," I say. "Honest answers only."

She glares at me, then sits back in her chair, crossing her arms across her chest. Her breasts squeeze together beneath her shirt and I fight through the pounding of need in my head.

"I don't work for him," she bites out, the words sounding like acid. "Brill is my patron. He bid for me when I came of age at seventeen."

"Your patron?" I ask, suddenly sick with more than just head-spinning moonshine. The word lands heavy and my stomach knots. I can already picture the gleaming collar, the transaction that made her his. I'd suspected, of course—she'd as good as told me back on Amphitreas—but there's a difference between knowing and feeling it like this, with her eyes blazing across from me.

"I thought you left Velusia."

"I did. Brill took me back to his home planet, Ooneryx," she replies.

"That's not quite the same thing as leaving of your own free will," I say.

She pulls a face in derision. "What part of my situation gave you the impression I had access to my own free will? You think I lie, cheat, steal, and smuggle for fun?"

Her words shouldn't hit as hard as they do. I've hunted enough criminals to know deflection when I hear it—but this isn't that. There's no performance in her voice, no laughter-coated coyness. It's just bitterness worn thin. The jealousy in me twists into something else—grief and rage at Brill. Or anger at myself for caring at all.

She tugs the cup from my hand and rolls. Nine. She swears.

I roll again, grinning smugly at the eleven dots on the dice below. Lyra flips me off and downs her drink. Her next roll is a double, and while I could stomach the drink, I don't want to annoy her enough to stop playing. I just have to focus on getting some real information from her.

"Ask your question," I say.

Her eyes light up and she taps her chin in thought.

"What happened to your parents?" she asks.

"Straight for the throat, I see," I reply, already regretting my peace offering. "They died on the *Arkanium*."

The question hits a hollow I keep carefully barricaded. My chest tightens. There's a buzzing behind my ribs, a low hum of remembered grief. I stare at the dice like they might rescue me from the answer I've already begun to feel rising in my throat.

Lyra stills, the mirth gone from her eyes. "They were on the colony ship?"

"You know of it?"

"Everyone knows about it. It's only the biggest interstellar tragedy in our time," she says, placing a hand atop mine. Her touch is warm and my skin tingles beneath her hand. "I'm sorry, Orion."

Her hand shouldn't undo me like this. The touch is soft, tentative—and somehow it reaches deeper than any sympathy I've ever received. My pulse stumbles. The restless ache that's lived dormant inside me for years begins to stir, raw and uncontained.

"My father was a well-known Xylothian historian. My mother was an accomplished doctor. When they were offered places on the colony ship, they felt duty-bound to go. But the ship ran off course and no one knows what happened next—all we heard about was the crash. There were no survivors, and little more than small pieces of twisted wreckage left floating in the void of space," I say, the lump in my throat tightening with the horrible memories. The words scrape out of me—every syllable feels like reopening an old wound.

Night after night, I'd tried to make sense of it—the silence from them, the silence from the gods. The way my bond with Sylph splintered when I failed her, when the rage took over and I became someone she didn't recognize. I chased oblivion through the bottle and through the hunt, punishing criminals harder than necessary just to feel something that resembled control. The shame still clings to me like smoke. And now, with Lyra sitting across from me, her hand still resting over mine, I realize how long it's been since anyone has simply… *stayed*.

And somehow, against all logic, she's here—bruised, infuriating, impossible—and I can't tell if she's my salvation or my undoing. Both, in all likelihood.

Sensing the shift in the air, Lyra pushes the dice into my hand. When I roll a one and a five, she reaches out to flip the one to a two, offering me an encouraging smile.

"Ask away," she says quietly.

"Tell me about your parents," I murmur.

She can't disguise the pain in her face, though she tries. Her eyes turn glassy and she pours herself another shot of moonshine. After drinking it, she blows out a breath.

"My father was human. He showed up on Velusia one day looking for a good time, and ended up falling head over heels for my mother. He sold her all kinds of lies to win her over—that he was some long-lost Earth prince with vast wealth at his disposal, that he was the universe's greatest lover, that he was an honorable man and a skilled warrior who would protect her for all his days," she says, the ghost of a smile playing about her lips.

"Your mother believed him?" I wonder aloud. "He must've been quite the con man."

"Oh, he was. One of the best in the business. Con man, smuggler, and good-for-nothing rogue," she says wistfully. "We had a complicated relationship, but stars, I loved him. I was always more like him than my mother. Anyway, in an unsurprising twist, their relationship got rockier over time. My mother was pregnant with me when my father left, but he swore he'd come back for me because he didn't want me being sold off to the highest bidder."

She pours herself another glass, but holds it in her fingers for a long while before drinking it.

"Still, my mother trained me as a Velusian. She told me I'd bring great honor to our house because of my mixed blood, even if it lessened the power of my *vellia*. She was…she might have loved me, I think. But Velusians aren't known for their parenting skills. She was distant on a good day, and cold on most other days. But, true to his word, my father came back when I was twelve. I still remember their argument word for word. I never thought my mother would relent—she was so stubborn—but he finally wore her down."

"I take it your father taught you in the criminal arts?" I say, pouring myself a shot.

She smiles again, sending a bolt of pleasure through me.

"He did. This is his ship, you know. Modified to his exact specifications." Something dark passes across her face. "We had five great years together—running amok all across the galaxy. But then we got word that my mother died. It was hard for me, sure, but my dad…my dad just went to pieces. He refused to go back to Velusia for her funerary rites."

The pain evident on her face is so agonizing, I find myself unable to draw breath. She soldiers on between the gathering tears in her eyes, continuing as if we're drawing poison from a wound.

"He got really obsessive about certain things; forgetful of others. He was slipping, and despite all my pleading, he wouldn't relent or take time off to settle down for a bit. And then, the last score got the best of us. Someone tipped off the

Feds and they shot him during our escape. I barely managed to get away, but it didn't do me any good. They caught up to me in the long run and gave me the choice of prison or going back to Velusia. Kind of a rock-and-a-hard-place situation, but I wanted the chance to pay my respects to my mom's shrine. Of course, while I was there on Velusia, I was required to participate in the patronage. I figured it wouldn't be so bad, you know?" She laughs bitterly, and it makes me want to shatter the bottle, because I sense where this is heading.

"If I'd known where I would end up, I probably would've chosen prison. Within a month, my contract was sold to a patron in an arrangement that financially surpassed the previous seven generations of my mother's household."

"Brill," I utter in a low voice. Some unnamed emotion—jealousy, maybe—rips through me and makes my vision burn red.

"Got it in one," she says, tossing back her glass. "Still. The bastard let me keep my ship."

"Which he uses for his own nefarious financial gain," I mutter.

"Well, he's not having me hunt down treasures to gift to the poor," she says sarcastically. "I've been on his tether for fourteen years now, which is longer than most Velusian arrangements. Typically, they max out at five and then you return to Velusia to find a new patron or enter into civil service. It's not a bad deal, actually. You can teach, or work in one of Velusia's libraries."

Before I can help myself, visions of taking Lyra up against a wall of bookshelves assaults my brain and my libido—her legs wrapped around my waist, hands digging into my ass as I thrust into her, all while stifling moans of pleasure in the quiet space. I bite the inside of my cheek to keep from groaning. The worrying, telltale tingle at the base of my spine has built to a burn, despite my attempts to ignore what it signifies.

"Over the last three years, he's been dangling my freedom in front of me like a carrot on a stick—if I only bring him *this* artifact or *this* relic, he'll release me. Every time, it's fallen through my grasp. Lately with Iathos, and now with you and the idol."

The dull knife of guilt slashes at my insides. I suspected she was beholden to Brill somehow based on her behavior and the scant details she's revealed over the last week, but the confirmation of her situation makes me see red.

"Why can't you just leave him?" I ask. "You have the ship and the skills to take care of yourself."

"Been there, done that. I've tried to leave before, and he always finds me and drags me back to his hellish planet."

"In all this time, you haven't tried to kill him?" I ask, surprising both of us with my bloodlust. "Meet with him under some false pretense and cut his throat. Or poison him. Whatever it takes."

Her brows lift. "That's pretty bold talk for a vegetarian pacifist, Ranger. Don't you think I've thought about it? Brill is powerful and wealthy, with insane resources at his disposal. It's not as easy as walking in with a blade hidden in my hair. Besides, I don't want a life on the run," she scoffs. "Brill's Void Stalkers would find me and do stars-know-what to me. They'd certainly bring me back to Brill and let's just say I hate being on his bad side."

Briefly, I glimpse the nightmares in her eyes. Her gaze shutters almost immediately and I start to feel sick with anger and protectiveness again. I struggle to square this new knowledge with what I've believed about her—her selfishness and disregard for others. How she didn't hesitate to kill when the Void Stalkers came for her. No doubt about it, Lyra is a killer. But she certainly isn't a murderer.

Lyra sighs, eyeing the almost empty bottle between us and the cup of forgotten dice.

"Of course I dream of revenge," she says darkly. "Death, and then some. I want to take everything from him. I want his money, his power…I want him to be isolated from everything propping him up. I want him devastated, in pain, and unable to claw his way back to anything. I want him to feel the abyss of grief and the void of loneliness—loss of hope—utter despair. I want him to wish for death. I want him to feel everything he's made me feel."

I'm nearly choking on my surging temper. Stars, I want to make him suffer.

"I'm so sorry, Lyra. I know the words don't help, but I can empathize with a lot of what you felt. The darkness. The loneliness. The…isolation." *Let me help you. Let me make him suffer.*

She nods, unfocused as she's lost in her memories.

"What happened to your mother?" I ask.

"I don't know, exactly. My dad and I just heard that she'd died and when I returned to Velusia, no one would tell me what happened. I missed her funeral, and the Feds wouldn't let me have one for my dad." Her eyes well with tears, and this time she lets them spill down her cheeks.

"Bastards," I growl, temper surging. "I can't imagine not having a way to channel your grief. I'm so sorry, Lyra. We didn't have a funeral for the *Arkanium* victims because there wasn't anything to recover and bury, but we did have a sort of memorial service. We were lucky to have that."

She shrugs, the heavy movement bearing the weight of her grief. Lyra runs a hand over her face, wiping the tears from her cheeks. I rise somewhat unsteadily to cross to her side of the table. Slowly—giving her every chance to refuse—I pull her into my arms and hold her while she cries. When she relents and wraps her arms around my waist, snuggling into my chest, my pulse thunders with a rush of possessiveness I have no right to. I know she'll chalk this moment of vulnerability up to the alcohol and I soothe her as best as I can, rubbing slow circles on her back and holding my tongue. She doesn't need the placating words that make light of the sorrow accompanying the loss of a loved one.

I'm not sure how long we sit like that, but eventually she pulls away. The sight of her tear-stained cheeks and puffy red eyes shatters something in me that's hardened over the last five years, leaving me feeling like a raw nerve. The irritating tingle at the base of my spine pulses now, but not unpleasantly.

Lyra sniffs and pours half of what remains in the bottle into the shot glass and hands it to me. She raises the bottle and we toast each other.

"To family," she warbles.

"To family," I echo. "As flawed as they were, we love them all the same."

A twinge of regret twists her features.

"What's wrong?" I ask, recognizing the look as something other than the pain of dusty memories.

"There's something else," she says, staring down at the empty bottle. "The reason I was after the Solar Mother idol. You're going to think I'm crazy, or that my father was crazy, but…"

"I'm too drunk to judge," I say, joking. "And we're trapped on this ship for the near future. That idol isn't going anywhere."

"I probably shouldn't tell you…" she trails off, gathering herself. "But if all of this goes wrong and something happens to us…you can't let Brill get his hands on the idol. Based on what Iathos said…"

I raise a brow at her, swallowing the anger I feel hearing Iathos's name.

"What did he say?" I ask.

She sighs, leaning her head on her hand and looking up at me with a watery smile, as if she barely believes it.

"The Dark Star. Iathos said Brill wants the Dark Star."

I freeze, panic spearing through my haze of drunkenness.

"That's impossible," I whisper. How could he know?

She lifts a shoulder in a casual shrug. "My dad wrote about it in his journals. He was obsessed with the idea that it could somehow bring my mom back. I don't know. Whether it can or not, if someone like Brill gets his hands on it…well, those kinds of thoughts keep me up at night. I told Iathos that the Dark Star is the stuff of bedtime stories. Sure, my dad wrote about it in his journal, but he was always chasing myths and legends. I've never heard any whispers of it being a real, tangible thing until today."

"Right," I reply, hoping my nervous chuckle doesn't ring quite so forced. Anxiety curdles the foul alcohol and my thoughts turn desperate. *Please don't ask me about it. Don't make me choose between betraying my honesty and betraying my heritage.*

"It's probably just some fancy rock, anyway. I mean, a gemstone with power over life and death? I've seen some pretty incredible things in my life but that's just not possible. It's scientifically improbable," she says, her words slurring a little.

"Definitely. It's got to be some kind of trick. Maybe Brill is just trying to give you unachievable tasks so he can justify keeping you around. He seems reprehensible enough to try it," I say with a frown.

"Yeah, you're probably right," she agrees. "Still, if ever there was a bargaining chip for freedom, the Dark Star would be hard to refuse."

"Too bad it's just a story. You deserve your freedom, Lyra," I say, meaning it.

She chuckles. "Nah, I probably don't. I'd just end up going back to a life of crime, anyway. It's in my blood. Just like being an upstanding, honorable, unbearably hot pain-in-the-ass is in yours."

I throw my head back and laugh. "Oh, so you find me unbearably hot?"

Her cheeks color pink, and she reaches out to shove my shoulder playfully.

"Shut up, you know you are. They say Velusians are bred for pleasure, but with a body like yours, I wonder if Xylothians are, too," she replies, her voice dipping low and husky. Her hand slides down from my shoulder to my bicep, squeezing gently. I can't help but flex beneath her appraising touch.

The air between us thickens. Every heartbeat feels like a dare.

I should pull away—should say something dry and sensible—but my body's already betraying me, leaning into her touch as if it's gravity itself.

I want to kiss her. Even with the threat of artificially manipulated feelings brought on by her *vellia* and through the fog of alcohol, I know the truth in it. I want to kiss her passionately, possessively, desperately—until she begs me to make love to her. Forgetting everything—including all of the reasons not to—I lean forward slightly, my gaze pinned to her full, pink lips.

Her eyes drop to my mouth and her tongue darts out, licking her bottom lip. Every muscle in me goes still, bracing for the impact of what I already know I'll regret and still crave. She tilts her head slightly and I angle in, only intent on claiming what I've wanted since I first laid eyes on her.

Suddenly, she stops. The glaze of desire in her eyes melts into regret and she pulls back.

No. No no no no. The word ricochets through my skull, frantic, disbelieving. The growing space between us feels too cold and distant. I can still feel her warmth against my skin, a ghost of a touch already fading. I want to reach out, to pull her back, to tell her I need her to kiss me—but the words die in my throat.

She shakes her head, as if clearing the potential mistake from her thoughts, then stands from the table and sways unsteadily toward the door. Even the power of the Zorium moonshine does little to my erection at the sight of her mesmerizing hips and perfectly round ass. She's leaving, and I'm left with the taste of what almost was—an ache that feels too big for one body. My hands are still shaking when I realize I'm clutching nothing.

"Goodnight, Ranger," Lyra calls over her shoulder. "Get some sleep. We've got a few long days ahead of us."

9
lyra

Hangovers and Heists

THIS IS what death feels like—I'm sure of it. The throbbing headache builds between my eyes and the swirling nausea roils in my gut, launching me up and out of bed hours before I would have normally woken. I hurtle to the bathroom as fast as possible, crashing into the walls of the corridor in an effort to make it to the toilet before I vomit all over the floor.

I heave, spilling everything I ate and drank yesterday into the shining metal toilet bowl. *Huh.* My toilet isn't usually so clean. I look around and take in the pristine state of the bathroom, down to the clean, folded towels and—is that an *orchid* on the counter?

Orion. Bless that precious, infuriating, sexy tree hugger. Orion has kept my ship cleaner than it was when I first inherited her. It's too bad he's made such a decent partner on this ill-fated trip. It makes stealing from him and dumping his unhappy ass back on Xylothia slightly more complicated than I originally planned.

Another wave of nausea rises and I grip the edge of the bowl. Ada's chime echoes through the bathroom, sounding impossibly loud to my sensitive ears.

Do you require medical care or is this another hangover after exceeding your limits with Zorium moonshine?

"Shh! Stars, Ada, turn down the volume," I moan, clutching my head. After flushing the toilet, I glare at my reflection in the mirror. I've definitely looked better. Dark circles ring my eyes and my left cheek sports ink stains from where I passed out on top of my father's journal and drooled all over the pages. *Gross.* I left Orion in the kitchen after our apocalyptic drinking game, too emotional and horny to be near him any longer. Instead, I stumbled to my berth and dug out Dad's old books to see everything he's written about the Dark Star. Unfortunately, the moonshine caught up to me before I could find anything. *Or maybe Iathos is full of shit and just likes to see me squirm.*

I wash my face and brush my teeth, then trudge back to my room. I desperately want to go back to sleep, but through the mist of stale alcohol still whirling in my brain, I remember everything I divulged to Orion the night before.

"Oh no," I groan from beneath my covers. "Ada, is Orion awake?"

Yes.

"Shit. Where is he?" The last thing I want is to run into him when I look like…well, like I'd just hurled my very soul into the plumbing.

Orion is training in the gym, where he spends every morning.

"What? Every morning?" I ask, incredulous. "You're telling me he gets up at this ungodly hour every morning to exercise?"

Yes. You would also benefit greatly from more training.

"Hard pass. Mom taught me the blade, Dad taught me how to shoot, and that's plenty. Besides, I take back every kind thought I had about Orion this morning. The man is clearly a freak, and not in the good, tie-you-to-the-bed kind of way," I grumble.

Stars, my head aches. I grab some clean clothes and make my way to the shower, hoping the steaming hot water will help erase at least part of my hangover. The rest can be cured with a couple painkillers, a bucket of coffee, and something fried for breakfast.

I feel somewhat better after my shower, but not good enough to brave combing out the tangles in my hair, so I dump it into a messy bun on top of my head and pad on bare feet to the kitchen. Coffee is pivotal to existence this morning.

Halfway through my second cup, Orion strides in, his shirtless torso gleaming with sweat.

"Oh! I, uh, didn't expect to see you up this early," he says, draping a towel around his neck. I stare at a lone drop of sweat trailing down the deep valleys between his muscles, unable to tear my gaze away.

"Before you hit me with an 'I told you not to challenge me,' you should know that I'm wildly hungover and will only be grumpier if you tell me you woke up feeling completely fine after last night," I bite out, laying my head against the cool metal of the kitchen table.

Orion chuckles and pours himself a cup of coffee, then slides into the seat across from me.

"Of course not," he says. "I wasn't *fine.* I woke up feeling kind of thirsty."

I groan loudly and flip him off.

"Well, if you think you can stomach some food, I can make you something that's sure to help you feel better," he says, sipping his coffee.

"Oh, he cooks!" I drawl, rolling my eyes—and immediately regretting it as the symphony of pain in my head returns. "Ugh, I deserved that. Fine, Ranger, ply me with your vegetarian witchcraft."

"I'll make you breakfast on one condition," he says, getting up to pull a host of ingredients from the pantry and small refrigeration unit below the counter. He pulls out two large kitchen knives and sharpens them deftly while prepping the space.

"I'm afraid to ask," I reply. "But I think I'm too hungry to refuse."

"You have to tell me about the buyer we're going to visit on

Minaris." He pulls a few fresh vegetables out and begins to chop them up while I consider the best way to answer him.

"Do you know anything of Minaris?" I ask, swirling the dregs of my coffee around the bottom of my cup. Without missing a beat, Orion grabs the pot and comes over to refill it.

"I know it's one of the most populous metropolitan cities on the planet Mallorus, and as such, they struggle with a lot of crime. The Feds have a strong presence there, but everyone knows they're dealing with their own corruption," he says.

"Have you heard of the Triumvirate?"

The knife pauses mid-air and he looks up at me, concern clouding the deep green of his eyes.

"Everyone knows about the Triumvirate," he says. "Three ancient Senterion families who have held onto power through the darker dealings in Minaris. They control the drug trade, run protection rackets, hoard information for blackmail and control, and have their fingers in every dirty deal this side of the galaxy."

"I hope you don't know any of them personally," I say, wincing, knowing he's already going to be pissed about this half-cocked plan.

"Why?" he asks.

"Well, let's just say I'm no longer welcome on Mallorus," I grumble. "So you'll be going in for me."

Orion arches a brow. "They banned you from the *entire planet*? Stars, Lyra, what did you do?"

I see the warning bells pealing in Orion's head as his expression darkens. He continues to cook, dumping the vegetables into a hot pan and shaking an unholy amount of dried spices over them. The fragrant heat makes my mouth water almost as much as Orion's lean muscles and dark freckles.

I sigh, knowing he isn't going to like what I have to say.

"A couple years ago, Brill sent me to Minaris to bargain for some ancient book that was being auctioned off by one of the Triumvirate families. The auction took place in the back room of one of their swanky casinos—the Red Sands, owned by the worst of the lot of them, Fobos. Have you heard of him?"

Orion shakes his head, stirring the food in the pan with slow, rhythmic circles. I'd be willing to bet a considerable sum on him being an infuriatingly patient lover who displays the same kind of deliberate attention to his partner's body. *How annoying these lusty thoughts are becoming.* My nipples tighten as I visualize things a far cry from breakfast and jewel heists.

"Well, consider yourself lucky. He's as mean as he is greedy and destroys everything that isn't worth selling," I say bitterly.

"Sounds like you know him personally," Orion suggests in a displeased tone.

Visions of my night in Fobos' arms return. It was considerably less enjoyable than my time with Iathos. The unwanted memory creeps in—the sharp smell of his skin, the velvet couch sinking beneath me, the faint din of the casino floor below. He'd talked the whole time, voice slick as oil, calling me "profitable." It hadn't been cruel, exactly—just cold. Transactional. I'd left feeling scrubbed raw, like something valuable had been pawned without my permission. Orion catches my shudder from the corner of his eye.

"I was there to get the book for Brill. As soon as the bidding started, I knew Brill had set me up to fail. Even with his resources, the amount of credits in that room made him look like a lowly dock worker. Bidding escalated way beyond what he'd instructed me to offer, but when I contacted him and told him the situation, he lost his shit. Told me to come back with the book, or I'd face some *really* unpleasant consequences." He wanted me humiliated, I realize now. Maybe to test my loyalty— or to remind me who owned my debt. Either way, it worked. The higher the bids climbed, the smaller I felt.

Orion cracks a few eggs into the pan of vegetables and grates some cheese on top. My stomach growls audibly, and despite the disapproval in his eyes at my story, he smirks.

"It's almost done," he says. "Do continue."

"You seem pretty comfortable cooking with Earth ingredients considering you haven't ventured off world in a few decades," I remark.

He shrugs. "I finished reading your romances and am working my way through the rest of your books. The cookbooks are…odd, but there are some parallels in Xylothian cuisine. And I like cooking."

Belatedly, I wipe the simpering look from my face and clear my throat.

"Well, I'm sure you can guess what happened next. I created a small distraction and in the confusion, managed to steal the book and high-tail it out of Minaris," I say. "The Triumvirate followed me, of course, but by the time I got to Ooneryx, I was in Brill's territory and they weren't about to launch a full-blown turf war against him for some book. Still, I'm not allowed to set foot in the city, on the planet, or have any business dealings with Triumvirate partners. Fobos still has a price on my head, but so far no one is fool enough to take me from Brill and turn me in."

"Stars, Lyra, you *are* trouble," Orion mutters, his voice halfway between amused and exasperated.

I grin and throw my arms up in the air. "I never claimed to be otherwise, Your Goodliness."

"So where do I come in?" Orion asks, dishing food onto a plate and sliding it across the table to me. "You want me to show up at the Red Sands Casino and start another incident so you have some company on the Triumvirate's list of hunted?"

"Hopefully not," I say, uncertainly. "But who knows? I told you this whole mission was a big, bad, dangerous mistake."

I bite into the omelet and nearly swoon—the eggs are tender and fluffy, the sauteed vegetables a perfect balance of savory and spicy. It's probably the best food I've had since…I can't remember when and it's already got my hangover headache on the run. *Stupid, sexy Ranger.*

"Well?" he asks, clearly anxious about my opinion. It's…cute.

"Damn, Ranger, where did you learn to cook like this? This is amazing," I say between forkfuls of food.

"My ex taught me," he says, filling his own plate and coming to sit across from me.

The food turns to lead in my gut.

"Your ex," I echo, unappealing jealousy raging through me like a tidal wave. I force myself to swallow. "They must've been quite a catch."

Orion smiles, but there's pain in his eyes. I don't have the fortitude to push for more, especially since I'm still fighting to tamp down the envy that threatens to set off my *vellia*. Orion isn't mine to claim or fight for. In fact, he probably still wants to turn me in to the Feds.

"I'm not asking you to steal anything, but you *are* going to break into their vault," I hedge.

"Why am I going to do that?" Orion asks, an unpleasant edge to his voice.

"Technically, because we made a deal and I'm doing my part to prove that my information is valid," I reply. "But more specifically, because I have a list of all the things I've acquired for the Triumvirate in the past and you'll be able to see I'm telling the truth. Besides, I happen to have it on good authority there are a couple Xylothian artifacts in their vault that you *might* want to see for yourself. If you bring some proof to the Feds, maybe they'll be less likely to sweep the corruption within their ranks under the proverbial rug."

Orion's fork pauses in front of his mouth.

"What Xylothian artifacts?" he asks.

"A necklace and a pair of earrings," I answer. "I didn't steal them, before you ask. But they've been on the black market for a while. The jewels come as a set. I can't remember what they're called, but they're pretty blue things."

"The Nebula Gems," Orion says, anger and excitement warring in his eyes. "They've been missing for years. You're certain the Triumvirate has them?"

"Well, Fobos did the last time I was there. The gems were marked to sell at the same auction, but I heard the Triumvirate locked everything back up after my little adventure. I haven't heard anything else about them floating around the black market, though, so I'm assuming they're still there," I say.

"That doesn't sound like much to go on if you haven't been to Minaris in years," Orion says.

"If you're too scared to break into the vault, I don't blame you. We can always turn around and go back to Xylothia and forget this whole thing ever happened." I smirk at him and he glares back at me, pushing his empty plate across the table.

"I cooked, you get to wash the dishes," he says. "And I'm not afraid of the Triumvirate. But I am a bit concerned that you're sending me into a den of angry lupitians alone. I'm a capable fighter when the situation calls for it, but I'm not suicidal. Where will you be while I'm allegedly breaking into this vault? Kicking your feet up onboard, waiting for the perfect moment to fly off and leave me behind?"

"I resent that. Leaving you in Minaris never even crossed my mind," I lie. Obviously, it did, but my brain keeps inventing excuses to keep him around—we have a deal, I like looking at him shirtless, and he'll send the Feds after me the first moment he can. "I'll be creating a distraction in the casino so you can get in and get out without too much trouble."

"Oh boy. Before you freak me out with whatever 'distraction' plan you have, can you at least tell me how I'm just supposed to *get into* a casino vault?" he asks, leaning back in his chair.

"Right. So, when I say *vault*, it's not actually a vault, per se, but more of a sort of library with really, *really* good security. I've thought about getting in before, but the problem was always getting back *out* with whatever goodies I tried to keep. It'll be way easier for you to go in because you're not actually trying to take anything," I explain. "And it's not really *breaking in*, so much as it's more…being invited in under false pretenses."

Orion narrows his eyes. "You wouldn't be stalling, would

you? Perhaps because you don't actually have a plan for getting into this room?"

"Oh, I do. It's just…you're not going to like it," I laugh.

"I don't like anything about this," he grumbles.

I stand to clear the dishes, then begin picking up the already-tidy mess he made while making us breakfast. Stars, even the messes he makes are more organized than my entire ship.

"Yeah, but you're not going to be able to just walk up to Fobos and be like, 'Hey, can I take a peek inside your vault? I hear you have some of my people's priceless treasures stored in there' and expect him to welcome you with open arms," I tell him. "The only way you're going to get in is to be invited."

"That seems about as unlikely as *breaking in*," he says. "So I hope you've got a good idea rattling around that criminal brain of yours."

"Good is subjective," I say with an airy wave. "But I think it'll work. You're going to go in as a dealer."

"And what am I dealing?" Orion asks warily, coming to lean against the counter where I'm washing dishes.

"The Solar Mother idol," I answer.

"Absolutely not. No way. That is going right back to the temple on Xylothia and until then, it stays locked in the stasis cabinet in the lab," he argues firmly.

"You aren't going to actually *sell* it, you're just going to use it to get inside the vault," I say. "Once you get in, you can say you've got other interested parties and leave. It's that simple. Unless, of course, you can admit that you *actually* trust me enough to believe my information is good and we don't need to go through this little charade to prove that it is."

He eyes me up and down, making the desire heat in my blood. When he frowns and shakes his head, I refuse to examine how much it stings.

"You're going to have to trust me one way or another," I complain, my headache returning with a throb of irritation. "Either you trust me to send you into the vault, or you trust that I wouldn't lie about who I've sold to and had dealings with."

He rubs a hand across his chin, considering. "If I'm going to the Feds about the smuggling, they'll want proof. I'm going to record everything I see in that vault and shove it in their faces," he says grimly. "Then, they'll have to do something about the looting. I can't be a one-man army on Xylothia anymore."

"Well, then you better practice acting like an entitled, good-for-nothing criminal, because that's the only way you're going to get proof," I say. "You go in, act like you're going to sell the idol, and get invited into the vault for negotiations. I'll create a diversion to draw them out and while they're distracted, you can record everything you need for the Feds. Then, assuming it all goes to plan, we get the hell out of the casino and jet off to some-place resembling safety."

"What kind of a distraction were you thinking?" he asks. "It better be big enough to draw out everyone—including Fobos—while I stay locked inside."

"I haven't worked that out yet, but I will. We have a few days," I say, finishing up the last of the dishes.

He seems less than satisfied with that answer, but I need time to work something out between now and then.

"What did you do last time you were here?" Orion asks with a stretch, grabbing his towel and making for the door.

I follow him out, heading for my room.

"I blew up the casino."

I can't help but enjoy the horrified shock painted across his handsome face.

OVER THE NEXT FEW DAYS, Orion and I settle into something of a routine. Ever since our time on Amphitreas and subsequent drunken evening, he stopped avoiding me around the ship, which is nicer than I care to admit. While he spends most of his time tending the biosphere and perusing my collection of books, in the evenings we sit together in the cockpit after dinner, reading in companionable silence. He's taken it upon himself to care for the little plant he bought me, which turned out to be a rare species from Terrin-4 and eats nothing but animal bones. I don't ask where Orion gets the bones, but despite his people's beliefs about eating meat and his strict vegetarianism, he seems to enjoy taking care of the little guy. He's even named it Spike.

When we're about a day out from Minaris, it's finally time for us to sit down and work through the details of our plan. Orion has been practicing his entitled, wealthy criminal act—which he scathingly declared is modeled after me—and I've got to hand it to him. The swagger and confidence he wears as he struts around the ship is extremely sexy. Granted, I've begun to think just about everything he does is sexy—even when he's being infuriatingly upstanding and good.

"Stop fidgeting with your suit!"

I tug the suit jacket over his shoulders and straighten the shirt he's rumpling.

"Who wears these clothes? Why are they so uncomfortable? I feel like I'm being strangled," he huffs.

"It's an old Earth style. A lot of the dealers like to wear them, so you'll blend in. Besides, it hides your Xylothian coloring and your, uh, freckles," I say, distractedly enjoying the solid feel of muscle beneath the silky fabric.

"Freckles?" He arches a brow.

"Yeah, the dark purple spots on your skin that like…flicker." I finish straightening the suit and step back.

"Ah. They're not freckles, they're synesfores. All Xylothians have them. They shift form and color depending on our emotions. Not quite so useful as *vellia*, I'd imagine, but more of a holdover from the age when we all lived naked in the rainforests."

Images of a nude Orion surrounded by nature pull my attention away from our conversation momentarily.

"Lyra?"

"Right, yes, sorry. Minaris! Ada is going to alter our registration and ship name so we can actually land. She's going to say you're the owner. Once we land, you've got to make your way to the Red Sands Casino and head straight to the front desk. When you're there, you tell them you'd like to speak with the manager about a private party. One of the Triumvirate goons will come out, then—they'll know you've got something to sell. We're going to keep the idol in this case here, but you'll have to insist on opening it in the vault," I explain.

"What if he won't take me to the vault?" Orion asks.

"Oh, he will. This is how every bargain begins. He'll take you in the back to meet with Fobos, who runs the casino. You'll show Fobos the idol and tell him all about it—how you found it, how you stole it, how the Xylothians have prized it for eons, and all that. Now, this is important, so pay attention."

Orion leans forward, staring intently at the holographic map projected between us. I gesture to the casino blueprints.

"While you're inside, I'm going to sneak in through the delivery chute, make my way to the casino floor and create a distraction." I hold up a small purple box. "This is a Velusian-style stun grenade. It works with the *vellia* in our blood. A few drops go in, you press the button, and the box basically atomizes the chemical components that make people go a little nutty— essentially the same thing as being one-on-one with a Velusian, except with a wider, broader blast radius. The trade-off is that it doesn't last for very long and like I said before, *vellia* isn't entirely universal, but it should cause enough chaos on the casino floor to draw out most of the Triumvirate security and give you a window of time to get your proof. You remember how to work the holocord?"

He nods, pulling out the small box that will record holograms of the vault.

"Great. You get what you need, then duck out of there in a hurry. We'll meet back at the landing bay and then, stars willing, get the heck out of there."

"Mmm." Orion's brow furrows. "Slice of cake."

I stare. "What?"

"I read that expression in one of your books," he says. "It's an Earth saying, is it not? It will be easy."

I chuckle, oddly charmed by his mistaking the expression.

"Yeah, no worries. Slice of cake."

10
orion

Someone Mentioned This Was A Bad Idea

THE RED SANDS Resort and Casino has all the elegance and charm you'd expect from a group of ancient mob warlords with too much money. From the outside, the building is a mishmash of lopsided triangles and spheres of pink-tinted metal that reflect the setting sun in a sickly orange glow. Stepping into the expansive foyer proves the ugliness is more than skin deep. The lobby sports thick, blood-colored carpet and bright yellow walls, which clash terribly with the gilt gaming tables and gambling machines on the casino floor. The air inside is thick with the acrid smell of smoke and tobellian pipe vapor, making my eyes water and pushing nausea through my stomach. A cacophony of shrill music and cheery, drunken conversation from the assembled guests makes it nearly impossible to hear Lyra in the small earpiece communicator she insisted I wear.

"What?" I all but shout as her voice crackles with static.

"I said, *go to the front desk!* And stop scowling. You're meant to be dangerous *and* charming," she instructs.

"Who are all these people?" I ask idly, making my way to the front of the lobby. Everywhere I look, it's a sea of people—humans and aliens and hybrid species I've never seen before. I'd be impressed by the variety if I wasn't so disturbed by the thought of them willfully losing their money to a nefarious crime syndicate.

"Oh, you know, just your average mix of oblivious vacationing families, good-time folks, and desperate fools. Most of them are harmless, really," she replies. "But I'm sure we're not the only ones with ulterior motives. Do you remember what you're supposed to say to the front desk attendant?"

"Of course I do. You only made me practice a hundred times. And how did you know I was scowling if you're back on the ship?" I ask.

"I merely assumed. You do this thing with your eyebrows when you're displeased—they get all scrunched up and it makes you look mean," she says.

"I do not," I argue, immediately rubbing at the wrinkle between my brows.

Lyra's musical laugh filters through the earpiece, tugging at some invisible string inside me I'm not inclined to consider.

"Good evening," I say, approaching the counter. "I'd like to speak with the manager about a private party."

The being in front of me looks more like a gelatinous blob with tentacles than anything, but it tilts its head to the side and presses a button. A bright pink message splays across its abdomen, blinking in various languages. When the message flicks to Kailorian, I read, "Name?"

"Ah, yes. Laesher. I'm Alonius Laesher," I say, attempting to look equally charming and dangerous per Lyra's directives.

The blob pauses a moment and I heft the titanium suitcase onto the counter. When the blob pokes a tentative tentacle toward it, I pull it back and narrow my eyes.

"The manager, if you please," I say sternly.

The blob ripples with affront and presses another button. It gestures me to the side, and I step away from the counter to wait.

"This seems to be going well," Lyra patches in. "You're doing great."

Before I can reply, a firm hand grasps my shoulder and whirls me around. The owner is as tall as I am and twice as wide, covered in thick gray skin and bony plates. Horns sprout from the sides of its humanoid face and beady yellow eyes glare at me with impatience.

"You wanted to see the manager?"

The voice is soft, lilting—feminine. Entirely at odds with the brutal enforcer vibe of the alien in front of me.

"I'd like to speak to Fobos about a private party," I reply, holding up the briefcase.

The enforcer—not Fobos, clearly, but one of his lackeys—growls and sniffs at the briefcase. He adjusts his tie and leads me through the main floor of the casino. The clattering, clanging, metallic sounds of credits being won and lost, of aliens in despair and triumph, pulls at my attention despite my efforts to keep my eyes forward and my expression impassive.

"First time in Minaris?" the enforcer asks.

I nod. "I do most of my dealings elsewhere."

"Easy, Ranger," Lyra chirps in my ear. "Don't give them too much information. You don't want to say something that'll give you away."

I press my lips together as we make our way to the back of the casino and enter a small, dark hallway. The enforcer has to shift to the side slightly to squeeze through the narrow corridor, and I wonder if he's been chosen specifically for the job because no one would be able to get past him—literally.

He knocks on a heavy metal door and lifts his hand to a biometric keypad at the right. The door opens with a rush of air and the enforcer shoves me in, but doesn't follow me inside.

For a beat, there is only dark silence—the muted air is old and stale in comparison with the noisome casino floor, but the pleasant scents of worn leather, dust, and old books are something of a comfort. In the gloom, yellow lamps flicker beneath golden lampshades. As my eyes adjust, I realize I am in the foyer of a massive library, filled with towering aisles of books and crystalline cases boasting a bizarre array of treasures. I recognize artifacts from a number of cultures tucked into the cases—some of which Lyra has told me she'd acquired. So far, she seems to be telling the truth. I casually slide my hand into my pocket, feeling for the holocorder's smooth case.

The wealth sprawling before me boggles my mind. My initial perusal doesn't yield the Nebula Gems, but I would've been surprised to see them laying out for all to see.

"Can I help you?" A disembodied voice slides over the nearest aisle of books. To say it's unnerving is an understatement, and it sends my pulse racing.

"I'm here for Fobos," I reply, craning my neck to find the source of the sound.

"You've found him," the voice returns in a smooth drawl. "But I don't have your name, stranger."

With the soft shuffle of books sliding onto shelves and the gentle tap of hard-soled shoes against the expensive wooden floor, he emerges from the aisle to my left.

Fobos is a Senterion—an alien from the outer reaches of the Eternia galaxy. No one knows where they originated or how many are left, but those who do remain hold vast stores of wealth and power. He is roughly my height, with smooth golden skin and piercing red eyes. Two long, curved horns protrude from his forehead. Long black hair sweeps down his back over his glittering silver suit—like mine in style, but made from some luxurious metallic fabric. On his feet, he wears a pair of white boots made from some mysterious reptilian skin.

"Alonius Laesher," I reply, stepping further into the room. I'm reaching for the confidence I don't really feel, but the chance of sending the Feds after this bastard is just enough motivation for me.

He tilts his head at me, studying me with thinly-veiled interest. "From whence do you hail, Laesher?"

Static crackles in my earpiece as Lyra groans loudly.

"I forgot these assholes always sound like they're about to

launch into a soliloquy," she grumbles. "Thou art a fucking pain in my ass, Fobos."

I smile. "Oh, all over. I never stay in one place too long."

"That sounds rather lonely," Fobos replies. "How fortunate that you should find your way to my casino. Plenty of people seek company here—unless, of course, you prefer your solitude." His red eyes narrow as he looks me up and down, appraising me with an invasive judgment that makes my skin itch. A predatory grin tugs at his lips, baring his sharp, triangular teeth.

"My business demands it, I'm afraid," I say, shifting uneasily. If only Lyra would hurry up.

"Ah, your business," he echoes, eyes flicking to the briefcase in my hand, his nostrils flaring on an inhale. "Presumably that's what brings you to me?"

"If we could go somewhere more secure, I'd like to show you something," I say, raising the briefcase in front of me.

"Oh, we're quite secure in my little library," he says smoothly. "And it's just us back here."

The wink he adds would be alluring if I didn't get the sense I've somehow become prey dancing in front of a predator. His eyes glitter a little too much in the dim room—his sharp-toothed smile stretches a little too wide.

Lyra's choked laughter rings through the earpiece.

"Hell yeah, Ranger. Get some!" she cackles.

It takes every ounce of strength to remain calm and collected. Under Fobos' watchful ruby gaze, I cross over to a large table in the middle of the room and the airtight case hisses as I unlock it. The Solar Mother idol glitters inside.

Fobos emits a quiet gasp, and even Lyra grows silent on the other end of the comms.

"Do you know what this is?" I ask, watching as lust and hunger sparks in the Senterion's gaze.

"Of course I do," he sneers. "The Solar Mother idol!" His

seductive charm has all but evaporated under the weight of his greed.

"I have a buyer," I say warily. "But perhaps you might offer me a better deal. I've been told you trade in Xylothian artifacts."

Some of the frenzied desire in his eyes hardens to suspicion and he raises a brow.

"Pray tell, who told you such a thing?" Fobos reaches forward to stroke one claw-tipped finger down the idol and I clench my fists to avoid slamming the case shut on his hand.

"Do *not* tell him you know me, Ranger," Lyra warns in my ear. "Just be vague, okay? Don't offer any more information than you have to."

I clear my throat. "Let's just say I've heard more than a few rumors about the Nebula Gems in the outskirts of the galaxy," I try, mustering as much confidence as I can. It's difficult with Fobos' unsettling red eyes boring into mine.

"The Nebula Gems?" Fobos blinks, then tilts his head back and laughs, and I'm worried I made some kind of misstep. The sound cracks through the silence of the library and makes the hairs on the back of my neck stand on end.

Fobos pulls his hand away from the case and I close it, locking it tightly and drawing it close to my body. I hate having the idol out of the stasis cabinet almost as much as I hate having it outside the temple where it belongs.

His unnerving smile returning, Fobos beckons me deeper into the library, guiding us toward a back wall. Set into the wall are small metal doors, almost undetectable to the eye. Fobos places his hand against one of the metal panels and a soft blue light emerges from beneath, scanning his handprint with a low hum. A small vault pops open, revealing a medium-sized black case. My heart thuds to a stop in my chest.

Offering me that same predatory, suggestive grin, he opens the case. The Nebula Gems sparkle in the light, casting soft blue-green rainbows around the room. In the center of the necklace sits the prize of the jewels, an egg-sized blue diamond so deep in color, it looks black. The air leaves my lungs in a soft *whoosh* as I stare at the priceless treasures that have been lost to my people for generations.

"Lovely, aren't they?" Fobos says, plucking one of the blue gemstone earrings from the case and holding it up to his ear. "I'm told the Xylothians believe Father Darkness fashioned these stones from the tears he wept when he murdered the Solar Mother. He later bestowed them upon Xylothia as penance for taking her from them. Silly story, really," he says, taking note of my interest. "Since they just look like plain old diamonds and sapphires to me."

"Change of plans, Ranger," Lyra barks in the earpiece. "Knock out that son of a bitch and take the jewels. They're practically yours, anyway."

I grit my teeth, trying to focus on Fobos and block out Lyra's unhelpful snark.

Fobos peers down at his claws, sighing in what seems to be exaggerated boredom. "I take it you're interested in a trade, yes? The idol for the gems."

His eyes cut to the case at my side and my grip tightens reflexively.

"I'm not interested in a trade, though the gems are exquisite," I say slowly, trying to stall for time. Lyra is supposed to be creating a distraction right about now, so I can scan the vault and make my escape.

Fobos narrows his eyes.

"What else would you offer me?" I ask, attempting to appear imperious.

The sheen of greed is back in his eyes.

"Four million credits," he replies, waving a hand dismissively.

"Hang on, Ranger, I'm having a small problem with the grenade. It's not...*dammit*, why won't this dumb thing start?" Lyra mutters, more to herself than to me. The mention of her Velusian grenade encountering technical difficulties has beads of sweat forming on my brow. I can only hope Fobos doesn't notice.

"Four million? That's an insult! I had to loot the Celestial Temple to find this thing," I scoff.

Anger vibrates off of Fobos like a string plucked on an instrument.

"Five, then," he grits out.

I snort in derision. "Clearly, you're not interested in what I have to offer, otherwise you wouldn't bother with a sum so low. Beyond the cultural significance, this is the largest sample of enaurium in existence."

A vein begins to throb in Fobos' forehead. "Ten million."

"Oh, honestly, now you *are* wasting my time. I think I'll just take it back to my original buyer. He was offering me fifty," I say with a sigh.

"What buyer could offer you fifty million credits?" Fobos snarls. "No one this side of Eternia has that kind of money unless *we* deem it so."

"Perhaps the Triumvirate knows less than they think," I say.

With that sentence, Fobos's entire demeanor shifts. His anger melts like the last snowfall before a spring sun.

"I see," he says. The wicked grin that splits his face dislodges something in my gut and a warning klaxon blares in my head. "Tell me, have you had a chance to spend any time in the casino? Perhaps a circuit on the floor while you consider my offer."

"I never gamble," I say darkly. "Unless I'm certain of the odds."

"I wouldn't be so sure," Fobos replies, deftly pulling a plasma pistol from beneath his jacket faster than I can blink. "You're taking a pretty big risk in coming here, *Xylothian*."

Panic freezes me in place.

"Shit," Lyra swears. "Fuck the distraction. I'm coming to you. Hang on, Ranger. Play for time!"

"What did you call me?" I ask, masking my fear with confusion.

"Oh yes," Fobos chuckles. "I know a Xylothian when I see one. Now, before I relieve you of your little case there—yes, go ahead and set it on the floor, very gently, if you please—I'd like to know how you came to be here. Who are you working for? And how did you know about the Nebula Gems? Only a few people outside my circle knew about them, and those that did were too smart and too afraid of me to open their mouths about it."

He flicks the safety off and the high-pitched whine of the plasma pistol charging tears my gaze from his.

"Don't you tell him a fucking thing!" Lyra huffs in my ear. I can hear the clattering of the casino floor and furious shouts over her panting. "I'm almost there—just make some shit up and distract him!"

"I may be a Xylothian, but I'm still a dealer," I insist. "I came here in good faith to see what you would offer me for the idol. My people are dying and I'll be damned if I let anyone else make a buck off of my ancestors' heritage before I do. Sixty million credits and the idol is yours."

The words are bitter on my tongue, and I know Fobos won't believe them. The timbre of my bluster wanes in the face of that steady hand on his plasma pistol, aiming straight for my head.

"I have a better idea," Fobos sneers. "Leave the idol and get the fuck out of my casino, and I'll decide if I'm going to blast your ship to pieces from here. You've got a fifty-fifty shot of making it out of the atmosphere. How's that for knowing the odds?"

"Let's just take it easy," I say, stepping back from Fobos. "I only came here to see what you might offer for the idol. But maybe you're right—a trade would be fine."

"That offer expired with my patience," Fobos growls. "I'm being generous and offering you the chance to leave with your life. I could simply shoot you and take the idol now, but I don't feel like cleaning your blood off my boots."

"Please," I say, trying to keep the panic from my voice. I

don't want to die here, but leaving the idol behind will be a fate worse than death for me—for my people. Even for Lyra. "I think we can be reasonable here. There's much about the idol you don't know. The gems, too."

He rolls his eyes. "Fascinating as your legends are, I doubt there's much you could say that would interest me."

I hear a shout and a deep grunt over the earpiece—Lyra is fighting with someone. The scuffle grows louder, the sounds of flesh and bone colliding making it difficult to focus on what I planned to say. Tamping down the fear I feel for Lyra's safety, I force myself to nod.

"It's true," I say. "In fact, I can tell you who one of the other interested buyers is."

Fobos raises his brows and waves the plasma pistol impatiently.

"Very well. I know many seek this particular prize, but I'm curious who might come knocking on my door trying to find it," he grumbles. He raises the pistol again—his finger curled around the trigger.

"Brill!" I practically shout. "Brill of Ooneryx."

"Son of a bi—" Lyra's curse abruptly cuts off with a hiss of static.

If I'd thought Fobos was angry at my incompetent negotiating, it's nothing compared to his expression of unadulterated rage hearing Brill's name.

The commotion over my earpiece escalates, reaching a climax with a sheer, ear-piercing scream followed by several seconds of deafening silence. My heart stops, ice flooding my veins.

Lyra!

"Brill of Ooneryx," Fobos spits, his golden skin turning a rusty orange color. "He doesn't have fifty million credits to spend. And if he sends that filthy, wretched harlot back out here…"

Suddenly, the door to the vault opens on a hiss of pressurized air, and Lyra stands in the threshold, holding the bloody, severed hand of the enforcer, who lies in a crumpled heap behind her. Her hair is a tangle, and her skin is coated with sweat and blood I can only hope isn't hers. The grin of triumph lights up her eyes in a way that makes that worrying tingle at the base of my spine ratchet up again. Relief at seeing her safe almost makes my knees buckle.

"'Filthy, wretched harlot'? Aw, you wouldn't be talking about little ol' me now, would you, Fobos, baby? That's certainly not what you said *last* time I was here," Lyra says with a saucy wink. She tosses the hand back to the enforcer on the ground and closes the door behind her.

Fobos gapes, his eyes going wide and his orange-hued anger deepening to bright scarlet.

"You!" he bellows.

Irritation bordering on anger explodes in my brain.

"Oh, for the love of—you slept with *him, too*?" I snap, jealously igniting my temper.

"Yet another regrettable chore," she replies, her lip curling in distaste. "And rather underwhelming."

Fobos swears. A beat too late he realizes he's still aiming the plasma pistol at me, and he swings to fire at Lyra. She ducks behind a bookshelf, muttering over comms the whole time.

"I can't *believe* you told him about Brill! You could have given him any name in the stars-damned galaxy, but no, you had to actually give him the real one! You are the *worst* criminal I've ever had to work with," she grumbles. "You could help me out here, Ranger!"

Shots sear through stacks of books and shatter the crystalline cases, leaving jagged shards littering the floor. With Fobos distracted, now's my chance.

Shaking myself out of my shocked state, I turn to Fobos and surge forward, reaching for his pistol and knocking him off-balance. Before he can recover, I drive my fist into his jaw.

"I can't believe you slept with this creep," I growl back at her as Fobos stumbles backward. "Do you just fly around the galaxy seducing unworthy men?"

She laughs at that. "Show me a worthy one and maybe I'll stop flying around the galaxy looking for 'em."

Fobos swings a fist at me but it's slow and clumsy—easy to dodge. I crouch low to kick his knee out, then hit him again in the temple as he falls. The brutal blow splits my knuckles open and finally renders him unconscious. I shake my fist out as Lyra comes to stand next to me.

"That could have gone better," I say, eyeing her soon-to-be black eye, the small cut across her brow, and split lip. That foreign impulse to soothe and protect rises, but I quell it before I can reach for her.

"It could have gone worse, too," she says with a shrug. "But you're in big trouble now. Fobos will tell Brill you dropped his name. The Void Stalkers will be on us faster than flies on shit and they'll have confirmation that we have the idol in our possession. We're on a ticking clock right now, Ranger, so get your evidence and let's get the fuck out of here."

As if on cue, several angry shouts erupt from the hallway beyond, followed by aggressive banging and hammering on the door. I pull out the holocorder and start scanning the room, hurrying between the aisles of books and treasured artifacts. When I finish, Lyra is already standing by the door clutching Fobos' plasma pistol, and I almost miss the flicker of anxiety on her face.

"I jammed the door lock on my way in, so I think it'll be a few minutes before they can get in, but I don't imagine it'll hold for long. And who knows how long Fobos will be unconscious," she says with a grimace.

"What's your plan for getting out of here?" I ask, tucking the holocorder back into the inner pocket of my suit.

"I have an idea, but you're not gonna like it..." she says, holding up the Velusian grenade.

"Oh no," I groan. "Tell me there's another way."

The barrage of noise against the outer door ceases for a moment, only to be replaced by the soft crackle and bright light of a plasma torch cutting through the thick metal of the door.

"Nope," Lyra says with an apologetic shrug. "Just…try to hold your breath."

A hand appears through the hole the plasma torch had made, and Lyra fires once. As soon as the hand retreats, she presses a button on the grenade and lobs it through the hole. We duck with the flash and bang of the explosion, but she's up in an instant, tugging me through the broken door. Several security goons are slumped in the hallway, blinking dazedly. A fine mist of pink particles hangs in the air, drifting lazily through the narrow passage. I lift my tie up to my nose to keep from inhaling the potent *vellia* chemicals, but the hallway seems to stretch impossibly before us.

"Let's move!" Lyra shouts, pulling me through the chaos and confusion. We manage to clear the security guards, but something latches onto my ankle. I look down to see one of the guards sprawled out, holding onto me and staring up with a look of disoriented desire. In yanking my ankle free from his grip, I stumble—going down hard behind Lyra.

The fall knocks the wind out of me, and I reflexively suck in a breath when Lyra turns to drag me forward. Lyra's scent fills my nostrils—that intoxicating fragrance of sun-warmed flowers and summer rain that I've come to crave. In an instant, I slam into a wall of lust that would bring me to my knees if I hadn't already fallen. Suddenly, it's impossible to focus on anything but *her.* Lyra. *My Lyra.*

Mine.

11

lyra

Temptation Always Leads to Damnation

"SHIT," I grunt, seeing Orion's pupils dilate until they're pools of black surrounded by a slim ring of emerald. He's sucked in too much of the atomized *vellia* and while I know it'll wear off eventually, it will make our escape decidedly more complicated.

Orion shakes off the security guard and crawls toward me, reaching for my outstretched hand.

"Let's go, Ranger!" I shout. "I'd say we've more than worn out our welcome here."

As he gets to his feet, we take off down the hallway, eager to get to the crowded mass of people on the casino floor. He grips my hand with desperate strength, as if letting go will untether us from the safety we can almost grasp.

The commotion behind us escalates again, and before I can turn around, the buzz of a plasma blast zings past my head. I duck into a crouch just as searing pain and blazing heat singes my right shoulder.

"Fuck!" I shout, stumbling to the floor. Pain explodes across my back and down my arm—I've been hit.

Fobos's triumphant cry rises over the noise and I look back to see him standing in the vault's doorway, his face a mass of darkening bruises and syrupy trickles of green blood. He grins cruelly at me and aims the pistol again. I wince, huddling into a ball on the floor as I prepare for the inevitability of death at the hands of one of the worst lays of my life. *How humiliating.*

But the pain of death doesn't come. Instead, a shrill scream splits the air.

I crack one eye open and look up at Orion—vibrating with fury, pointing a glowing plasma pistol at Fobos. The other security guards blink in shock, still too dazed by the Velusian grenade to do much except stare.

Fobos clutches his shattered horn—still sizzling from the plasma blast. He screams obscenities at Orion, who glares at him with dark, toxic malice I wouldn't have believed possible from the honorable Xylothian.

"Orion!" I call, but he doesn't seem to hear me. With lithe, lethal grace, Orion sprints back down the hall toward Fobos's cowering form. Before Fobos can realize the danger he's in, Orion grabs him by the neck and lifts him off the ground. Fobos gasps and chokes beneath Orion's iron grip, clawing at his arms and kicking his silly cowboy boots. Who *is* this ranger? Certainly not the Xylothian I brought on board with me—the long-suffering, do-the-right-thing, paragon of virtue I've begun to begrudgingly kindle some affection for.

The synesfores dotting Orion's neck flicker black, matching the darkness of his eyes. I watch helplessly as Orion tilts his head—almost curiously—and he snarls in a low, deep growl.

"How dare you *hurt* her. I should rip your head off." He starts to squeeze and the wheezing, choking sound emanating from Fobos makes even me gag. Orion isn't going to kill Fobos— is he? For the first time since we met, I taste the sharp bite of fear. If he kills Fobos in a *vellia*-induced haze, he'll never forgive me. With sickening dread, I realize I can't stomach the thought of his disgust and hatred aimed at me.

"She—isn't—yours!" Fobos coughs.

"She is *mine*," Orion roars. "And you are unworthy to try and take her from this world."

With that, he throws Fobos clear across the vault, letting him smash into the back wall with a nauseating crack. I gape in astonishment as Orion readies himself to fight his way back through the hallway of security guards.

His words hit me with more force than the plasma blast, twisting my insides into a Gordian knot of emotion. It's the *vellia*, I tell myself. Only the *vellia*. Orion is no more mine than I am his. And—technically speaking—I belong to Brill, which makes me adamant that I don't ever want to belong to anyone. *So, what's with the fluttering in my stomach at his words?*

"Orion!" I call again. "Forget it. Let's go!"

Finally, he lifts his gaze to me and nods. He bolts down the hallway, vaulting over the remaining guards. We barrel through the casino and out the front door, not pausing for breath until we reach the ship.

"Ada, we need to get gone *now*!" I say. "Is our route to Omicron-13 clear? I want us in light speed as fast as, well, light speed. You got it?"

Calculating route to Omicron-13. Mild traffic in the Farin sector, but no active Fed incidents. Now scanning for beacons from any known Void Stalker craft or Ooneryx-registered vehicle. Bringing light speed engines online. I take it the mission didn't go as planned?

"That's putting it lightly," I say, turning to look at Orion for the first time since I witnessed his violent outburst. He stands behind the navigator's chair, white knuckles gripping the headrest like he's about to wrench it from the seat. His whole form radiates tension, as if a soft breeze might blow in and snap him into the monster he was mere moments before. His eyes are still dilated black and the tendons along his neck strain beneath his skin. Warnings sound in my head— something dangerous skates beneath the ice of Orion's exterior.

"Orion?" I ask cautiously. "Are you okay?"

He shakes his head slowly.

"No."

"Are you injured? Were you hurt?" I ask, concern bringing me to my feet.

He takes a step back from me—his face filled with warning. The possessiveness and lust in his eyes steals my breath, but with the tensing of his muscles, I can see how hard he's fighting his response to the *vellia*.

"Stay away from me, Lyra" he growls.

Excitement thrums in my veins. When I use my *vellia*, I'm usually stressed to the point that sex is unappealing, but seeing the way Orion wants me now is utterly intoxicating. Ignoring the magnetic pull I feel for him seems impossible. I move slowly in his direction.

"Please," he rasps. "I can't—I don't want…"

I shake my head to clear it and take a step back. *What the hell am I doing?* I can't—won't—take advantage of him. The thought makes me sick. Despite wanting him like my next breath, I can't take him like this. Disappointment and shame burn through my insides. The pain in my shoulder throbs in earnest and I wince. Orion catches the movement and his nostrils flare.

"You'll need help patching that up," he says, his voice gravelly.

"I'm fine," I argue, waving him off. He snags my hand out of the air and holds it in a vice-like grip. I arch a brow and something in his gaze softens almost painfully.

"Please," he says quietly. "I can't stand to see you hurt right now."

Part of me wants to push him away, but given what we've just been through and how unsettled he seems, I nod. I slowly lower my hand from his grasp.

"Okay," I concede. "Thank you. The first aid supplies are in—"

"…the laboratory," he finishes. "I know. I organized them before we arrived."

Ada engages the autopilot and shoots us through the atmosphere of Mallorus, pulling away from the swirling red and black planet with as much speed as she can muster. Passing moons blur into streaks of soft gray as we enter light speed, but the inside of the ship remains still and quiet. Orion and I walk toward the lab, the thick silence between us growing heavy with the weight of unsaid words.

"Sit," he commands, pointing to the cot in the corner of the lab. I glare at him, but bite back my curt reply. I'll give him both barrels tomorrow—when we've both had some time to sleep off the nerves of everything we'd just been through.

I hop up on the edge of the bed and angle my wounded shoulder toward the light he drags over, giving him the opportunity to survey the damage.

"Well?" I ask, trying to ease some of the tension. "Will I live, Doc?"

His brows pinch together in irritation.

"Take off your shirt," he says.

That pulls the smirk right off of my face.

"I don't think that's a good idea," I say.

He sighs. "I can't see the edge of the wound beneath your shirt. You'll have to take it off so I can clean it and see how bad it is beneath all this blood and dirt."

"But the grenade...my *vellia*..." I stammer.

"I'm fine," he insists.

"Are you sure about that?" I press. He certainly doesn't look fine. He looks like he's hanging onto his sober sanity by a thread thinner than spider-silk.

"No, but it doesn't change the fact that you need help with this," he replies. "The...urge...to take care of you is stronger than the one that demands I fuck you."

My mouth drops open at his delicious words. This is definitely not the same Orion I've come to know over the past few weeks. Under the effects of *vellia*, he's dominant, insistent, and powerful—*and it's driving me crazy.* Heat kindles between my legs and goosebumps rise along my skin. I take a deep breath to center myself and try to block out the frantic desire. *Focus on the pain, Lyra.*

My wound begins to bleed again and I bite my lip from the discomfort of drawing my shirt up over my head. Orion watches the fabric bare my breasts—the muscles in his jaw flexing so hard, his teeth might crack. The juxtaposition of this dark, nearly feral side of him ignites something deep within me. He's like some kind of fallen angel, and it makes me want to sin something awful with him. I slam my eyelids closed, afraid to address the feeling. Not wanting to look into his black and green eyes and see what I'm afraid to see—the mirror of my own flawed longing.

The gentleness of his hands as he cleans my shoulder catches me by surprise. I sense he's straining at the end of some kind of tether, but the hold he has on himself is powerful. I envy him that. I've spent too much of my life being a slave to my emotions, barreling headlong into actions without considering the possible fallout. I don't have the strength to delay gratification or savor my moments. Sometimes, I feel like my days are an endless conveyer belt of pleasures tumbling into a black hole inside me.

The sting of antiseptic shocks me out of my melancholy and I hiss.

"Sorry," he says. "I should've warned you."

I try to shrug it off and focus on the physical pain to distract myself from my emotional turmoil.

"I suppose that's fair," I return. Guilt eats at me, corroding my confidence like acid through metal. "I'm sorry about Fobos. About everything."

He grunts, but I don't know if that means he forgives me or not.

"You need stitches," he says. "I don't suppose you have a nanopatch in here, do you?"

"Yeah, should be in the drawer over there," I reply, pointing across the room. Orion's gaze immediately snaps to my bared breasts and he lurches forward reflexively.

I flinch and draw back, covering myself with my good arm. Embarrassment colors his cheeks a fetching shade of pink.

"Sorry," we both say at the same time. I chuckle, but he just shakes himself and strides over to the drawer. He grabs a slim metal box and comes back to sit in front of me, tugging his necktie loose and letting it hang down his shirt. The movement is unbearably erotic.

He peels the backing off the nanopatch and presses the small blue button to charge it up.

"Have you ever used one of these before?" he asks. "They can be a little painful if you're not expecting it."

I nod. "Yep. Nothing a couple painkillers won't fix. Go ahead and slap it on, Ranger, and let the nano bots get to work."

"Deep breath," he says, and presses the patch over the wound. The initial sting makes me grit my teeth, but I take the pills Orion proffers and down them with a swig of water. In a few hours, the nano bots will finish repairing the worst of the tissue damage, and I'll be none the worse for wear—minus another cool scar to tell no one about. Reluctantly, I drag my shirt back over my head.

Orion cleans up the bloodied bandages and opens a fresh package of antiseptic wipes.

"For your face," he says, pointing to the cut on my eyebrow above the eye I can already feel swelling shut. That bastard enforcer sucker punched me good when I tried to take him down to get to Orion, but I would have fought my way through a thousand Void Stalkers and Brill himself to get to him in time. It's useless to deny the panic and anxiety I felt when my grenade had first malfunctioned and I could only listen as Fobos pulled his gun on Orion.

Dread had sent me to a dark place, making my *vellia* spike out of control on the casino floor. It was too bad the enforcer had been immune to me—a thought I heartily echo as Orion swipes the stinging antiseptic pad across my eyebrow.

"Fucking stars," I swear. "You'd think by now someone would've been able to invent a wound cleaner that didn't hurt like hell."

He grunts in assent. I look up at him, his posture still rigid but beginning to soften around the edges. Are the effects of the *vellia* beginning to ebb?

His gaze drops to my lips and my tongue darts out to lick them reflexively. I taste blood and feel the pricking of pain from the cut on my lip. I forgot about that one.

"I should clean that one, too," he says as he leans in, his low voice barely above a whisper.

I stare at his mouth, the way his full lips part in invitation. *Stars,* I want him. Even as I lust after this dark approximation of the ranger, something in me wants to bring back the old version —the honorable, upright, stalwart, pain-in-the-ass threat to my freedom. But I know if I kiss him, if I take him to bed, I'll be taking more from him than he wants to give. I'd ruin him—and worse—something in me knows it would ruin me, too.

Then again, perhaps I'm already ruined.

"Does it look bad?" I ask quietly.

"No," he murmurs. "But I hate that you were hurt at all. If I'd taken out Fobos earlier, like you suggested, this wouldn't have happened."

"You don't strike me as the 'take him out' type," I say with a wry chuckle. "So you're forgiven."

"I told you before—I don't relish taking lives. That doesn't mean I haven't, or that I won't. Especially if something I care about is threatened," he says.

Can he hear my heart hammering against my ribs? Mouth suddenly dry, I clear my throat and fight the blush heating my cheeks. "That's the *vellia* talking."

"No, it isn't."

I scoff and his intense gaze bores into mine.

"Yes, your *vellia* wants me to claim you—to throw you onto this floor, strip you bare, and fuck you with a desperation that staggers me, but I'm aware enough to know that I don't need your *vellia* in my blood to want you to be safe. To want you protected. To want you happy." He swallows and stands, crossing to the worktable with his back to me, head hung in defeat. "To want you, full stop."

I suck in a breath and let his words wash over me. For once, no smart retort jumps off my tongue. My heartbeat stutters—the only part of me that isn't frozen by panic and fear. I don't believe him, of course, despite the hopeless longing his words kick up.

"I'm sorry, Orion," I whisper, humiliating tears pricking behind my eyes. "I just can't believe that. I know you're susceptible to my *vellia*. That's what this is. You just think those things because that's what happens—it's desire and confusion and frustration because we're always at each other's throats. It's not real. It never is." Admitting that out loud guts me, and a tear spills down my cheek.

He whips around—his eyes back to their vibrant, sea-glass green, but the intensity still swirls in them. He stalks toward me.

"I don't think you believe that," he says. "That whatever this is between us is just chemical."

"Yes, I do," I whisper, another tear falling.

"Then you're lying to yourself," he says.

"Oh, please," I sniff. "This whole time you've been calling me a criminal and a liar, telling me you hate me, threatening to turn me in to the Feds, and now you want me to believe you've been fighting some secret battle against wanting me."

"I already lost that battle. Wanting you was never a question. When it comes to trusting you, however, I'm afraid I'm still at a bit of a stalemate," he says, one corner of his mouth lifting in a heartbreaking lopsided grin.

"Oh, and I'm just supposed to trust *you* not to tie me up again and hand me over to the Feds when you get what you want?" I ask breathlessly, mesmerized by the flickering purple synesfores scattered down his neck and throat, pulsing in time with his heartbeat. My hands have a mind of their own and they reach up to slowly pull the tie from beneath his collar.

The heat in his expression cranks my lust up to volcanic levels, but I can't ignore the disappointment at hearing he still doesn't trust me.

"I never said I wouldn't tie you up again," he says, his deep voice rumbling through my chest. "But it won't be to give you to the Feds."

Somewhere in the recesses of my mind, all the reasons why I shouldn't want this line up and sound off. I can't trust him, we don't want the same things, we're too different. Neither of us can afford an entanglement longer than a few nights—not that I want that, anyway.

Liar.

The smart thing to do would be to walk away now, hightail it to Xylothia, and drop him off in that stars-forsaken jungle—with or without the idol, I haven't decided.

But with his hand cupping my head, those deep emerald eyes fixed on my lips, and the firm length of his arousal pressing against my stomach, it strikes me that I've never really enjoyed doing the smart thing.

"You wouldn't be saying this if you weren't under the influence," I argue, my last ditch effort to put a rational end to this.

"Maybe," he murmurs. "Only one way to find out."

"Oh?" We're standing at a precipice—one I know will change everything between us, and probably damn us both.

"Kiss me and tell me it's not real," he challenges. "Tell me you don't feel it, too."

"I can't," I whisper, another tear falling. "And you wouldn't believe me, anyway."

"Then let me prove it to you," he says, threading his fingers through my hair and tilting my lips up to his. He pauses a breath away—allowing me the space to back out.

Like hell I will.

"Kisses can be dishonest, Ranger," I say, slowly sliding my hands up to his neck.

"Then I'll just have to kiss you honestly," he answers, and pulls my lips to his.

The gentleness of the kiss belies the tension vibrating through his body. His soft lips caress mine in a reverent way, as if one sudden move from either of us will shatter the fragility of the moment.

As if reading my thoughts, Orion whispers: "It's not the *vellia*, Lyra. I want you. Stars save me, I want you so badly I can't think straight. I won't deny it anymore."

I lick the seam of his lips, silently begging him to open to me —to stop saying the words my traitorous heart longs for. In one betraying instant, I fantasize about what it would be like to be with him, flitting around the galaxy with no worries and no responsibilities except to each other. We could trust each other. We could *love* each other.

That's not the life for you, Lyra, my mind argues. *That's not the life you deserve.*

Desperate to banish those thoughts, I hungrily suck at Orion's tongue until he groans and bucks against me. I'm determined to lose myself in this pleasure with him. Grabbing his shoulders, I jump up to wrap my legs around his waist, whimpering with pathetic need. He carries me out of the laboratory, never pausing to take his mouth from mine. When I roll my hips against his and feel the heat of his erection against my core, he utters a deep, dark curse that threatens to loose my already-tenuous control.

He growls against my lips as his hands grip my ass, and he grinds his hard cock against me. *Fuck. Want. Need.* My thoughts come in fragments in between waves of heady, instinctive lust.

We crash into the side of the corridor and I grunt in pain —*fucking Fobos and his stupid plasma gun*—and Orion mumbles an apology. Dimly, I realize he's carrying me to my room. My room…where my bed is. I'm going to bed with Orion.

"This is a mistake," I hear myself saying. *Where did that come from?*

He pauses to look at me, breathing heavily.

"Do you want me to stop? We can stop," he replies, suddenly anxious. My heart lurches with the knowledge that if I say so, this will end. One word from me and he'll put me down, right our clothes, and leave me standing alone in a corridor.

I shift, reveling in the feel of his hardness against the dampness pooling between my legs. He hisses and squeezes his eyes shut, pressing me back against the wall and supporting us with one long, muscular arm.

"No," I answer. "I don't have it in me to stop. But now we both know."

Satisfaction and something else—wariness, perhaps—dances across Orion's handsome face. He peppers small kisses down the column of my neck and inhales deeply.

"If this truly is a mistake, I will pay for it a thousand times over."

In response, I lean in to tug at his earlobe with my teeth.

"Then let's make it worth the price," I whisper.

The deep whimper he makes spurs my lust out of control. I want him inside me—need him to fill me and chase away the cloying loneliness that threatens to swallow me. If I hold on a little tighter, maybe this time, it will be real.

I fumble for the zipper on his pants, eager to feel his hot, hard flesh in my hands. When I wrap my fingers around him and gently squeeze, he sucks in a breath and pushes us back from the wall, mumbling against my ear.

"If you keep touching me like that, I fear this won't last very long. I'm already—*ah, stars*—I'm too close and it's been too long and I want you too much." Orion reaches my room and drops me on the edge of my bed. He shucks the suit jacket with rough movements and, after a few failed attempts to unbutton the crisp, white shirt beneath, tugs the half-buttoned garment up over his head.

I stare hungrily at the flat ridges of his chest and abdomen, at the flickering spots and the trail of soft brown hair descending from his belly button. When he pushes his pants down his muscular thighs, I sigh dreamily. His erection springs forth and I note how different his body is from what I expected. While Orion looks mostly humanoid, his cock is unlike anything I've ever seen—three bumpy ridges line the shaft and flare out at the base. The bumps are the same purple as his synesfores and pulse in time with the freckles all over his body.

"You *do* have synesfores all over your body," I say. "I've been wondering. Dreaming about them, actually."

"Oh, yeah?" He raises a brow and steps between my legs. I lean forward to slide my tongue over one on his chest, drinking in his helpless gasp.

"They're sensitive," he explains.

I want to lick every single one.

"I've never been with a Xylothian before," I admit. "Will you show me what you like?"

His eyes close and he tilts his head back, letting out a stuttering sigh.

"Do you have any idea how many times I've dreamed of you saying those words to me? Just touch me, Lyra, before I realize this is a dream and I wake up fucking my hand again," he says, the helplessness sending a thrill straight to my core.

Leaning forward, I wrap my hand around his shaft, stroking the soft skin and feeling the bumps with a hesitant fingertip.

"Fuck," he whimpers.

"These are…?"

"Nodes," he chokes out. "They swell during matehood, to help with conception."

As I continue to explore his body, fantasizing about how they'll feel inside me, I pause.

"And without matehood?" I ask, pressing down on one more firmly.

His knees wobble and he grunts, suddenly pulling back.

"Without matehood they just feel very, *very* good. And yes, those are sensitive, too."

I bite my lip and pull my shirt over my head, adoring how his mouth goes slack. *Stars, but I'm enjoying this too much.* Orion raises trembling hands to caress the soft skin beneath one of my breasts and whispers something in a language I don't understand. The soft touch leaves a trail of fire along my skin, and I feel like I'm coming unglued.

When I reach down to take off my pants, he stops me.

"Allow me," he rasps, bending to pull them down my legs. The cool air against my heated skin wrenches a whimper of anticipation from me, and Orion flashes a seductive grin. Instead of standing, he kneels in front of me, running his large, calloused hands up the backs of my calves to the insides of my thighs.

He drops idle kisses on the insides of my knees, then gently presses my legs open to bare my sex to him.

"Beautiful," he murmurs. "Better than I imagined. And *fuck*, how I've imagined…"

"Have you been with a Velusian before?" I ask.

He shakes his head—hands tracking up the smooth skin of my thighs until his thumbs graze the sides of my sex. The soft touch electrifies me with pleasure.

"But if you're anything like a Xylothian…"

I bite out a curse as he drags a finger through the wetness between my legs, dipping inside me and then tracing back to my clit.

"How does this feel?" he asks, circling the pearl with his fingertip. At my guttural moan, he chuckles. "Is this where your pleasure lives?"

"Yes," I gasp. "Oh, stars yes!"

"Fuck, you're so wet, Lyra," he utters with a deep groan. He licks his finger and closes his eyes in pleasure. "And you taste like a dream."

When he opens his eyes again, the vibrant green glitters from within, like a light shining through an emerald. He smiles wickedly and dives forward, covering my pussy with his mouth. He swirls his tongue around my clit and I shriek, already close to the orgasm I've wanted from him for weeks. I thread my fingers through his hair and hold him there, locking my legs behind his neck. When he slides one finger inside me—then two, I nearly come up off the bed. The torturously slow movements make me writhe and I fall backward, dragging him with me onto the bed.

For the briefest moment, I lie before him—arms above my head, legs splayed on either side of his. He leans back to sit on his heels, gaze devouring me with frenzied lust and something akin to worship. It steals the breath from my lungs. I'm no stranger to pleasure, but it's entirely foreign to me to have someone who isn't under the spell of my *vellia* stare at me with such wonder—as if I hung the moon.

"I could never get used to this sight," he says softly, crawling up my body and lashing sweet kisses along my thighs. "You're a goddess." When he reaches the apex of my thighs, he lathes his tongue over the seam of my sex, pausing to suck my clit.

"Don't stop," I pant. He slips two fingers into me again, twisting them slowly. A string of filthy Velusian curses spill from my lips as my body indulges in pure sensation. With every rhythmic thrust of his fingers my pleasure builds, making my entire body feel like a hurricane of need.

"Never," he moans, curling one of his fingers inside me to massage some secret, incendiary spot. His other hand snakes up my side, reaching to palm my breast and roll one nipple between his fingertips. *Stars,* he's good. Fire zips along my nerves, racing toward my core. I'm so close. *So. Close.*

"More," I demand. "Don't stop! I'm so close, Orion—I need more."

"You've got to earn it," he growls, his voice rough and unrecognizable. He lathes his tongue across my center in long, slow licks.

I can't form a response in the haze of my building orgasm—I simply pant and mewl and thrash around in the sheets. The most incredible bliss lies just beyond me, and I buck against Orion's mouth as I reach for it.

"Earn it, Lyra," he rumbles against my skin with the deliciously punishing thrust of his fingers. "Come for me—*now.*" He ceases tonguing my clit to press a thumb against the aching bud of my need and I shatter, every fiber of my being vibrating with pleasure and satisfaction and heart-twisting fulfillment. On and on it goes, aftershocks trailing like the tail of a comet. All the while, he holds me, nuzzling my hip and caressing me everywhere. In the wake of the pleasure, distant thoughts take shape in the quiet recesses of my mind.

I'm going to tell him the truth about the idol. I'll give him more than just the names of buyers. I'll give him all the information he needs to be happy and save his people.

I'm falling for him.

The realization freezes me faster than getting sucked out of an airlock.

Oblivious to my brewing panic, Orion chuckles darkly and covers my trembling body with his, sighing into the crook of my neck.

"Good girl," he says, slinging one heavy arm across my waist.

The dominant words make my sex clench and I roll over to straddle him. I push the thoughts away—reality can wait a few hours. His green eyes glow beneath his thick, black lashes in a look of unbridled desire.

Tell him, Lyra. Tell him you care for him. Tell him you'll give him whatever he wants. Ask him to stay with you, my instincts demand.

Do it, and you'll ruin everything, and lose even more, my mind replies.

I exhale shakily, my confusing thoughts threatening to distract me from the beautiful naked man in my bed.

"That was the most intense orgasm I've ever had," I admit. "And I'm going to return the favor."

12
orion

Too Close for Comfort

"LIE BACK and keep your hands above your head," she says.

Lyra's words reverberate through the static in my brain, but my body obeys automatically. Most of my conscious thoughts and better judgments fell away with the remainder of her clothing, into some distant space not presently occupied by desire so fierce, my entire body aches.

Both the chaotic desperation from her *vellia* and my hatred of Fobos—and, okay, *jealousy*—fade behind the steady beat of one all-consuming thought: *mine.*

After weeks of spine-tingling discomfort and a buzzing beneath my skin, I'm forced to acknowledge the primal truth of the matter: my body demands Lyra Phoenix as my mate.

My mate. Mine.

My mind knows she isn't—not really. But my instincts drive me to possess her in ways I've never experienced for anyone, even Sylph. There's an all-consuming need to bury myself in her, to claim her, to mark her as mine. To erase the memories of disappointment and failed partnerships from her mind and prove to her that *alone* isn't always easier. I don't need to hold her tether, exactly, but what might she do if I hand her mine?

Even with my need bludgeoning my brain into submission,

my anxiety spikes. Could I be enough for her? What is "good enough" for a Velusian—for Lyra Phoenix? With her scent in my nose and the taste of her orgasm still on my tongue, can I be trusted to make her feel the same way I do? *I have to—I have to make this good for her.*

"I'm at your disposal," I rasp as she straddles my hips. With the soft blue glow of her cabin lights illuminating her from behind, she looks like an ethereal goddess from another universe. Her pink and brown hair has come loose from her braid, spilling over her shoulders in thick, glossy waves and hanging just above the tips of her peaked nipples.

With no other preamble, she grasps my cock and strokes firmly upward. It takes everything in me not to thrust into her hand, and a rough moan escapes my lips. I knew she'd be skilled in the art of pleasure, but from the moment she kissed me, all I've been able to think about is how much I want to please her. Obviously, Lyra has had her fair share of lovers, but this deep-rooted instinct in me wants to leave some mark she can't forget —to be worthy of sharing the bed of this remarkable, heart-stopping half-Velusian. If only for tonight, I need to claim the one thing I cannot have.

One of her hands encircles my aching cock, stroking slowly, while her other hand explores my body, finding all the places that make me gasp and growl with need. By the time she drags her fingernails lightly across my nipples, I'm getting close to losing control.

"Let me touch you," I beg. "Please."

"I'm having too much fun playing with you," she giggles, the sound like a torturous symphony. "I've got a bet with myself to see how long you can hold out. You're doing very well, by the way. Much better than I thought."

"You're killing me, Lyra. For the love of all the stars, I need…"

"I know what you need, Orion," she says in a low voice that makes my synesfores flicker white.

Before I can form another thought, she bends forward to lick the bead of moisture gleaming at the tip of my cock. I swear. She huffs another laugh and slides me inside her perfect lips, swirling her tongue around my cock in a way that doesn't feel anatomically possible.

Whatever thoughts remain in my head dissolve immediately. I can't be sure if my heart continues to beat, if my lungs continue to breathe, if my synesfores continue to pulse. Everything but the slick wet heat of Lyra's welcoming mouth simply ceases to be.

Mine. Mine. Mine.

"Fuck!" I groan between gritted teeth. The insistent pressure of pleasure dropping down my spine makes me feral with the need to sink into her.

"Tell me I can touch you," I beg again, my voice ragged with desperation. She slides my cock from her mouth with a wet pop, and the sight—the sound—almost makes me come.

"Why?" she asks, and despite the dim light of the room, I can see her eyes glittering with passionate challenge. Beneath the haze of raging lust, it strikes me that the play of power turns her on almost as much as it does for me, and suddenly, I know what she wants to hear—the dominant, filthy words from a man dedicated to bringing her pleasure.

"Because if you say yes, I'm going to fuck you until you come on my cock and scream my name," I groan.

Her delighted gasp is soft—sweet. Entirely at odds with the hungry, feral excitement on her face.

"Is that so?" she murmurs, sliding her hands up my thighs to my abdomen. She drags her nails across the synesfores dotting my chest and it feels like electric sparks popping along my skin.

"Please," I choke. The intensity of the sensation threatens to light my body on fire and I know there will be no coming back from this.

She smiles and straddles me again, positioning my cock at her slick entrance.

"Very well," she sighs, hips poised above mine. "Since you begged me so prettily."

In one agonizingly slow movement, she slides down onto me and I throw my head back with a desperate groan. Her wet tightness grips me perfectly, as if she was made for me.

She is, my instincts roar.

As she starts to move above me, the sleek friction of our joined bodies nearly makes me weep. It's never been like this. Lightning arcs beneath my skin, from my nerve endings to my muscles and my entire universe narrows to one pinpoint of truth wavering in the distance like an event horizon: I will beat back the Death Goddess herself if it means feeling this again.

"Gods, Lyra, you feel so good—you're perfect. I've never had anything so perfect," I moan.

"Good," she whimpers. "Touch me here, Orion—I want to come on your cock." She tugs my hand away from her breast and directs my fingers to her clit, showing me the right movements and pressure. Her soft whimpers and gasps send arrows of heat straight to my cock and when she starts to move faster—bouncing up and down on top of me in a heated rhythm—I can't hold back any longer.

With a growl, I wrap one arm around her waist and roll her beneath me. Her delighted laughter bubbles up between us and she lifts one knee up to her chest to give me better access to that secret spot of pleasure deep within her. Need pushes me on, my instincts taking over as I piston into her, chasing the high that I know will come all too soon.

I'm mindless with lust and physical need, too far gone to heed the worries my mind whispers. *What happens when this is over? She is not yours. She will go back to Brill. She will still steal from you—you cannot trust her. You're desperate for her but she said for herself—love isn't in her future. And once you're gone, once this is done and you've come and you're both spent, she will go on as if this was an itch to be scratched and you will never be the same.*

She has ruined you for all others, and you are nothing to her.

Looking down at her beautiful face, seeing her lush lips hanging open and her sparkling violet eyes burning with lust, I refuse to face the truth of it.

"I'm close, Orion—are you gonna fill me up with that big, hard cock of yours? Come with me," she moans.

Her lascivious words unlock the final piece of my pleasure and my orgasm rips through me like wildfire. I come with a bellow as she shrieks beneath me, thrusting her hips up to mine.

"Yes, yes!" she shouts. I lean down and bite her neck—the possessive gesture feeling ancient and primal. With that, she shatters once more, locking her legs around my waist and clawing at my back. I know there'll be marks in the morning and it fills me with a perverse sense of male pride. *My mate is well pleased.*

Once the final tremors of bliss have finished rolling through our entwined bodies, I collapse in a sweaty, exhausted heap, being careful not to crush her. She nuzzles into me, emitting a satisfied hum.

"Stars, Orion—it kills me that we've been stuck on this ship for weeks and you could've been fucking me like *that* the whole time," she chuckles.

"Is it like that for you every time?" I ask, immediately regretting my question. Sex with Lyra has been world shattering for me—galaxy shattering, even. I don't think I can stand to hear that it isn't for her, too.

"Actually, never mind," I say with a wince. "I don't think I want to know."

She rolls over to her side and props her head up on her elbow.

"You were incredible," she insists. "Definitely one of the best I've ever had." She drops a kiss on the tip of my nose. My indignation starts to rise before I realize she's teasing me again.

"One of the best, huh?" I say, reaching down to pinch her nipple. She squeals and tries to wriggle away from me, but I drag her back into my arms and press her against me. The telltale tingle at the base of my spine ignites again, but the buzzing is warm and pleasant. She feels too good to hold.

"Yeah, well, in order to be the best, I'm afraid you'd have to have a few more tentacles," she answers, stifling another shriek as I swat her ass.

"Torturous creature," I growl.

As she snuggles into my embrace, I realize the buzzing sensation at the base of my spine has eased. Glancing between us at my temporarily satisfied cock, I notice my mating nodes flicker to a bright green—a green I've never seen before. The Xylothian green of life, fertility—matehood. Briefly, I think my heart stops.

Mine, my body insists. If Lyra and I were to have sex again, the nodes would swell with the effort to knot her and get her pregnant. It would be sex with a mate—my mate. Until then, my body will do its level best to encourage me to take her as many times, as many ways as possible. *I need to tell her.*

Panic claws at me, but I don't want to confront it yet. I know it's wrong—this is all a mess—but I allow the wave of tenderness I've been holding at bay pull me under. I know she isn't mine. I know I'll have to let her go. I know all the reasons we can't be— they're practically infinite. But for tonight…just for tonight, I can pretend this is us. This is it.

Exhausted by the spirited fucking and the draining events of the day, sleep soon tugs at my senses.

"Orion?" Lyra's soft voice comes to me almost like a dream.

"Mm?"

She's quiet for a moment, and I wonder if I dreamt her question. But then, after I hear her take a steadying breath, she continues.

"This wasn't from the *vellia*, was it?"

The uncertainty and fear in her voice fractures something deep within me. After all this, she still doesn't believe I want her for her. The honesty of her sadness—of her acute loneliness— devastates me. Pulling her in until there isn't a breath of space between us, I sigh and kiss her forehead.

"No, Lyra," I answer. "It wasn't."

It takes a few minutes, but I feel her relax against me, as if she's been holding onto something and finally lets it go. In that moment, I feel her vulnerability. Her trust. It's a gift more precious than everything locked in Fobos's vault—more precious than all the enaurium in the universe—more precious than even the Solar Mother itself. And I swear to all the gods in all the galaxies that I'll never take that for granted—even if, for her, it only goes as far as this bed, as far as tonight. With horrifying certainty, I know there will never be anyone else. I will go to my grave and meet the Death Goddess loving Lyra Phoenix.

I'll tell her about the Dark Star.

I'll tell her everything.

***

AT SOME POINT in the night, I wake to a shuddering rumble and the soft pulse of crimson light. Lyra sleeps against me, curled into my side with one leg draped over mine. I breathe in the scent of her hair, revel in the softness of her skin against mine, and a deep peace blankets us. Lyra stirs and flings her arm across my chest, mumbling unintelligible words into the mattress.

"Ada, what's going on?" I ask softly. "What's that noise? Why are the warning lights on?"

My scanners have picked up a ship closing in. Estimated time of contact: five minutes.

"A ship?" I sit up in bed, shaking Lyra awake. "Lyra, wake up! We've got someone on our tail."

She sits bolt upright and glares at the blinking warning lights.

"Fuck! Ada, who is it? Is it someone we know?"

She crawls over me in a mad dash for her clothes, yanking a tank top over her bare breasts and hiking up her underwear.

Before I can toss a pair of pants at her, she rushes through the door, running for the cockpit on bare feet.

Yes. I'm afraid it's the Edax Deorum. *Preliminary scans indicate a full crew within.*

The satisfying post-sex blush on Lyra's cheeks disappears behind a new, sickly pallor, waking that misguided protective instinct deep within me.

"Who's on the *Edax Deorum*, Lyra?" I demand, surprised to hear the growl in my voice.

Lyra ignores my question in favor of shouting at Ada.

"Well, why didn't you wake me up earlier? The purpose of a proximity alarm is to—you know—*alarm.*"

I didn't want to disturb you until it became strictly necessary. The level of oxytocin you were producing suggested...

"That's enough, Ada, thank you," Lyra snaps.

I tug on my pants and barrel after her into the cockpit. At her pale visage, I start to strap into the navigation seat, but she stops me.

"Can you shoot?" she asks, flipping switches and engaging a secondary holographic screen that I haven't seen her use before.

"I've never fired from a ship," I admit, panic making my palms shaky and damp with sweat. "But I'm good enough with a plasma rifle."

She winces, but tugs me into the seat on her left side.

"Take the gunner's seat," she barks. "You're about to get a crash course in space combat tactics."

It is inadvisable to push the engines without—

"Not helpful, Ada!" Lyra shouts, increasing the thrust and sending the ship shooting forward.

"Lyra, who's on the *Edax Deorum*?" I ask again, dread suggesting I already know the answer.

"Look here—these switches engage the targeting, but you have to wait until the ship is within range, shown here. As soon as the ship hits these crosshairs, hit this button to fire. We're loaded on plasma ammo, but it's still best to make it count, meaning don't fire if you don't think you can hit it. If you fire in bursts, the cannons need a five-second cooldown period and the target will almost certainly return fire in that window. I don't like being a sitting duck."

"A what?"

She narrows her eyes and continues. "They're going to catch up to us shortly—my ship is fast, but it's no match for theirs. Our only chance is to shoot them down, or damage their ship enough to give us a head start to safety," Lyra says. Then, she snaps: "Find me a hiding place, Ada! I don't care how big, bad, or dangerous it is. I'll take it over the alternative."

Scanning, Ada acknowledges.

Our ship rumbles with a groan and the deep creak of shearing metal has Lyra swearing a blue streak.

"That better not be the hull…"

"Lyra! Who's on that ship?" I demand, belting into the gunner's seat and gripping the controls for the plasma cannons.

"Not now, Ranger," she growls. "What's my status, Ada? How's my ship? And where the fuck am I taking us?"

The fear buried in the tone of her commands twists my insides. Before I can ask her again, the *Edax Deorum* pops onto the holographic screen in front of me and rapidly closes the distance.

"Ada!" Lyra shouts. "Coordinates, now! Coordinates to something—anything!"

The nearest inhabited object is the salvage station Hephaestus *currently orbiting the abandoned* Inferis *asteroid mine.*

"*Hephaestus!* Stars, we might be saved. Is Evie still aboard? If she's not too pissed at me, maybe she'll let us duck in for a spell," Lyra replies, swerving hard again. If I wasn't belted into the gunner's seat, I would've been thrown across the cabin.

Evelyn Redfern is registered as the site manager. It's likely she'll be on board. Are you certain you wish to infringe upon her hospitality given how your last encounter went?

"We don't have much of a choice, do we?" Lyra grumbles. "Input the coordinates, now!"

"Who's Evelyn Redfern? And what happened last time?" I ask, concern seeping into my tone. "Please tell me there were no explosions involved—or jilted lovers."

Both Lyra and Ada ignore me.

Approximate time to arrival: ten minutes.

"Even with light speed engines? Come on Ada, I know you've got some of the good juice on reserve. Now is the time to break it out, baby," Lyra says tightly.

Light speed is inadvisable in our current state. There is structural damage to the hull after the initial escape attempt.

"Are we going to break apart into little pieces or is this more of a 'you break it, you bought it' situation that I will happily buy my way out of once we find a maintenance station? I need solutions, Ada, and you're only giving me problems today." Lyra eyes the scanner with the holographic ship closing in and swears.

"They're almost in range, Orion—be ready to fire," she commands.

The probability of a safe landing on Hephaestus *with our current structural integrity is 69%.*

Panic ratchets my heartrate up.

Lyra chuckles at that. "Nice. Alright, that's a solid shot, so I'm gonna go for it. Ada, fire up the light speed engine and make for *Hephaestus.* And no sass, please."

Our encroaching pursuers veer within range, and I line up a shot on the screen. The first blast goes wide, but the second catches the bottom of the craft, scorching a long burn mark down the hull. Lyra whoops as the *Edax Deorum* shudders to a halt, but quickly circles back and returns fire.

Lyra pulls back and maneuvers us away from the blasts, expertly steering the ship as if it's become an extension of her body.

As soon as they're in range again, I fire four successive blasts, none of which connect. I curse and wipe my clammy hands on my pants.

"Don't sweat it," Lyra encourages. "I'm coming around again and you'll be able to get them from a better angle. You're not half bad in a fight, you know."

"Anything else you want to tell me now?" I snap, stress making my temper brittle. "Like, *who am I shooting at?*"

For a moment, Lyra's bravado drops and her gaze meets mine in the pulsing blue and red light of the cockpit.

"If he catches us," she begins in a low voice. "He'll take me back…and I can't go. Not yet. I'm not ready yet, and I don't know what he'll do to you."

"If *who* catches us?" I ask. The ship lurches to the side as Lyra dodges another blast.

She purses her lips and sighs.

"Kraxis."

The pale panic on Lyra's normally golden skin makes the protective instincts in me roar to the surface. *Kraxis.* The bastard who held a gun to my head. The walking threat to Lyra. Rage bubbles in me like I swallowed battery acid. I can't let him take her back to Brill. *I won't.* Not trusting myself to speak, I simply nod and return my focus to the holo screen in front of me.

I have to do this. I can't fail her. I can't fail Lyra like I've failed everyone else—my parents, Sylph, my people.

Light speed engine is primed, Ada chirps.

"Okay, Ranger, you've got one more shot at this before we run. Cripple their ship and then we'll blast off and go hide out for a little while. I know you can do this," Lyra says, gripping the ship's controls with white knuckles.

Her words weigh me down with desperate purpose. The jump might save us if I hit their ship—but miss, and the damaged hull, the incoming fire, the jump initiated with a crippled target could tear us apart. I imagine the worst: a ragged pry of metal, the holo shattering, the last breath of a life that ends with our frozen bodies floating through space.

Taking one last deep breath, I line up the shot with the *Edax Deorum*'s left engine and fire. Six bursts of plasma jettison forward and time seems to slow—Lyra's hand poised above the button that will engage the light speed drive.

Two shots miss. A third bounces off a shield at the fore, but the fourth shot connects with the engine in a ball of orange flame and blue plasma. For an instant a hot, sick hope claws up my spine—then the fifth and sixth shots follow the same path, utterly vaporizing the ship's left flank. Lyra smashes her hand down and we lurch forward into light speed—streaks of white blurring against the abyssal black of space.

I jump up from my seat, pumping my fist in the air in triumph, but when I turn to Lyra, she's staring back at where the *Edax Deorum* had been before our jump. Eyes welling with tears, she chokes out a sob and throws her arms around my neck.

With her face buried in my chest, I almost don't hear her whispered words.

"Thank you."

13
lyra

Just to Be Safe

I PULL AWAY FROM ORION, only slightly embarrassed by my emotional display after he managed to cripple Kraxis's ship and give us the time to jump to safety. Well, *relative* safety. Kraxis will have a hard time following us, but there's some ominous damage to my hull and I pushed the engines too hard. We desperately need a place to lay low and make repairs. And figure out what the hell is going on with me and the most incredible lay of my life.

The asteroid *Inferis* looms before us. At first glance, it reminds me of a desiccated potato, rotating lazily around a red dwarf star that glows crimson like the weary embers of a dying fire. As we near, the *Hephaestus* orbits into view—a swirling mass of space junk that threatens to wrench itself apart with the slightest touch. In short, our hope of salvation rests on somewhat underwhelming shoulders. We approach slowly just as two small recovery ships launch from one of the salvage rig's outer bays and descend to the pockmarked surface of the asteroid.

"Well," I say, clearing my throat. "We know they're home. Now we just need to knock real polite-like."

"Are you okay?" Orion asks, tucking a strand of hair behind my ear.

"Oh, sure! Yep. Absolutely," I force out. "You just managed to save our bacon, is all. I'm grateful."

He studies me—glowing green eyes roving over my face and the damp tracks of tears I furiously wipe away. Sensing my discomfort, he arches a brow and flashes one devastating dimple.

"*How* grateful?" he teases.

I breathe a sigh of relief. *This* is familiar ground. Teasing, flirting, fighting. Not the naked vulnerability I felt moments ago.

"Hm…" I tap my chin, considering. "Grateful enough to give you a blow job so fierce, you'll think I'm trying to suck your soul out through your—"

Apologies, Lyra, but the crew of the Hephaestus *are hailing us. I must insist you return to comms and leave the flirting for another time.*

"Spoilsport," I say to Ada. Then, seeing the molten heat in Orion's gaze, swat his firm ass and wink. "Another time, perhaps."

I drop back into the captain's chair and patch the garbled voice through.

"You're on a course heading toward private property. This station is owned and operated by the Ripley Salvage & Reclamation Corporation. Turn around and head back the way you came or the authorities will be contacted," the voice crackles.

"I'm trying to reach Evelyn Redfern," I reply, praying to the stars she won't blast my ship into dust.

"What do you want with her?" a second voice chirps—a voice I recognize all too well.

"Evie?" I hedge.

"Who wants to know?" she barks, then swears over the crash of clanging metal in the background.

"*Aldrin-136* requesting permission to land for emergency repairs," I state.

"Oh no—absolutely not! Lyra Phoenix, you two-timing, thieving, good-for-nothing bilge rat! You are *not* coming aboard my rig and making off with everything that isn't nailed down—again! Put into port somewhere else," she snarls.

"Come on, Evie, have a heart. My ship's busted, I've got Void Stalkers on my ass, and I just need to lay low for a couple days. I swear on my father's honor, I will *not* steal anything. I'll even pay you back for last time!" I wheedle.

"Your daddy was even more of a thief and con artist than you are, Lyra—he wasn't what I'd call honorable. Nah, Pinky Pie. You've bamboozled me one too many times. Park it elsewhere!"

Orion arches a brow. "Pinky Pie?"

I wince. "Long story."

Smirking, he leans forward and presses the communicator.

"Ms. Redfern? This is Ranger Orion Asterth from Xylothia. Lyra may be a scoundrel, but I'm far from that. If you'll let us dock and lend some assistance with repairs, I assure you Lyra will be on her best behavior. Not only will she refrain from stealing anything, but she'll pay you the full balance of what she owes before we leave. Including credits for the repairs, and a little extra for your trouble," he says smoothly.

I gape angrily at him, opening and closing my mouth like an enraged fish.

"A Xylothian ranger, huh?" Evie responds. "Lyra, did you move into kidnapping for ransom since I last saw you? Because you know I don't truck with that."

"No, Evie," I drawl. "He's here of his own free will."

She grunts affirmation, then lowers her voice conspiratorially. I almost can't make out her whispers through the static.

"This ranger…is he humanoid?"

"Yep," I say. "Why?"

"He sounds pretty hot. Is he hot?" Evie whispers.

"Scorching," I reply, biting back the possessive jealousy that rears its ugly head. Now is *not* the time to explore that. "I take it there aren't a lot of available romantic partners onboard the *Hephaestus*?"

"If my love life gets any deader, I'll need my own salvage operation," she says grimly.

"Well, if you let us dock, you're free to chat him up at will," I chuckle. Some twisting, dark thing winds its way through my belly at the thought of Evie flirting with Orion, but that's best avoided for now. I have a ship to save.

The line goes dead for a few moments and I can practically hear Evie weighing the pros and cons of trusting me again. Fortunately, her libido seems to win the battle and she agrees after another round of firm negotiations. Before I steer us down to the dilapidated landing bay, I lean over and drop a kiss on Orion's cheek.

"What was that for?" he asks, trying not to look pleased.

"That's the second time you saved us today," I grin.

"How so?"

"Evie's only letting us land because she wants to scope you out," I say, chuckling. "She's lonely out here on that pathetic bucket of bolts and I'm sure she's hoping you'll be amenable to her attentions, if you get my drift."

A soft pink blush blooms on Orion's cheeks and makes his synesfores pulse purple. The barest thread of anxiety weaves through my veins, knotting firmly in my stomach. Will things be any different between us now that we've had sex? Will he be clingy? Distant? Disappointed? Reality starts to press in on me from all sides. I was so ready to give up everything for him—all my secrets—stars, even my freedom. What came over me? Orion is a decent sort and, sure, the sex was mind blowing, but this little adventure has already cost me too much, and if he goes back to Xylothia with the idol, it will potentially cost me even more.

No. If there's one thing I know, it's that I can't stomach another year under Brill. I have to believe my patron will finally terminate our contract if I bring him the idol because the alternative is unthinkable. Maybe Orion will come to understand that… in time.

I clear my throat, but before I can say anything, he speaks up.

"Listen, Lyra…" He starts, folding and unfolding his arms across his chest in an awkward, distracting way. *Why do those muscles have to be so…muscley?*

"I already know what you're going to say," I say, holding up my hand to stop him. I've heard some variation of it a hundred times before…have even delivered the speech myself. *This was fun, but it's over. Different wants and needs, darling. Two ships, passing in the night.* Something painful prickles in my chest— regret? Disappointment? Nothing a liter of moonshine can't drown.

"No, you don't," he says, shaking his head. "We need to talk about something important."

Sighing, I twist my wince into a falsely cheerful grin.

"I get it. We both got carried away. There was *vellia* involved, and I got shot, and mortal injuries make me really horny, and we've been cooped up on my ship for weeks. It doesn't have to mean anything, okay? It *doesn't* mean anything. It's like I told you before—whatever you think you feel for me, don't trust it. Let's just get some clothes on and get ready to deal with Evie, all right?" My embarrassment makes me feel more naked than my conspicuous lack of pants. I tug my shirt down over the waist- band of my underwear as unfamiliar pressure starts to build behind my eyes. *Don't cry. Don't cry. Dammit, Lyra, why are you crying?* I turn my attention to the console and pray he won't notice.

Orion is quiet, something shuttering in his gaze before I can make sense of it. "Is that what you want?"

No. "Yeah, sure. I mean, not much chance of anything else, is there?"

More silence. It stretches for long enough that I think he's left the cockpit, but when I finally look up, I see he's come to stand right behind me.

"That wasn't what I was going to say, but I'll respect your decision if it's what you really want," he says, his low voice thrumming through me. I peer up into his bottle green eyes and promptly forget to exhale. He's so handsome, standing there staring at me with so much unguarded emotion in his gaze. *Kiss me, you dummy. Just take it. Take it all.*

"We should get dressed," I hear myself saying.

A ghost of disappointment flits across his face, but he offers me a wan smile and nods. Watching him turn and leave the cockpit feels like being gutted with a dull blade. When he's almost out of earshot, he pauses.

"For the record, Lyra, it meant something to me."

With that, he leaves—taking all of the air out of the room with him.

AFTER SHOWERING and dressing in a long-sleeved gray jumpsuit, I meet Orion back in the hallway in front of the ship's bay doors. He obviously showered after me, his damp hair shimmering green in the soft light of the cabin. He's wearing his ranger uniform and for the first time since we met, I find the dull khaki rather charming. Comforting, in a way. This is normal. We can get back to normal.

So why does that feel so...wrong?

"Anything you want to tell me about what I should expect down here?" he asks. His expression is pleasant—neutral—but the disappointment that still lingers in his eyes makes me feel ten kinds of rotten.

"Evie is a Strythian from Terrin-4. She was always a bit of a wild child, so when she hit puberty, her parents shipped her off to the Federation Military Academy. She was doing pretty well until she knocked out her instructor for, shall we say, *mixed signals.* After they kicked her out, she found a job as a salvage rat on a barge that brought her to Velusia right around the time my dad died, and—as my mom used to say, 'Trouble sticks to trouble.' She left when I got contracted to Brill, finding other salvage work around the sector, and has presumably worked her way up to site manager here. She's smart as hell, tough as nails, and happens to be one of the only people in my life who hasn't tried to kill me, sleep with me, or steal from me," I admit.

"Considering the warm welcome she gave you, I'm assuming you didn't pay her the same courtesy?" Orion asks with a raised brow.

I frown and, stars help me, actually blush under the weight of his disapproval. *What is happening to me? This is ridiculous.*

"Well, I won't go into a lot of the dirty details, but the last time I hunted her down, I may have accidentally run off with something important to her," I say.

"A ship? A chip full of credits? Precious metals, gemstones, or other valuables?" he wonders, shaking his head.

Actually, it was one of the better performing salvage workers from the Hephaestus. *Lyra became sexually intimate with the Dreller and brought him onboard with her, then left the station without permission or approval for his leave.*

"Thank you, Ada, for that very helpful contribution," I grumble.

You're welcome. Please give Ms. Redfern and the Hephaestus *computer my regards.*

"I will not! The two of you are the worst sort of gossips when you get together," I say, shaking my head.

"So, you did actually move to kidnapping," Orion accuses, folding his delicious arms across his even more delicious chest.

"Kidnapping? Ha! Jorax was very much a willing participant, I'll have you know. And I got my karmic retribution, anyway. He bailed as soon as we stopped to resupply. That bastard Dreller was only using me for a ride," I say. "In more ways than one."

Displeasure radiates off Orion, but I don't know if it's judgment for my choices or a spark of jealousy. I tilt my head at him, but don't press.

"I take it Evie wants you to pay out the remainder of his contract, then?" he surmises.

"Yeah, and she wants me to apologize, which is frankly ridiculous," I sniff. "I mean, we're all adults here. It's not my fault Jorax went AWOL. At least, it's not *entirely* my fault. Maybe a little? Okay, 15% my fault."

Orion glares at me.

"25% my fault, final offer. Anyway, if it means short-term refuge for us, fine. I can play nice and apologize. We should get this over with before I lose my nerve," I say, blowing out a breath.

Orion nods, placid expression firmly in place. His outward calm stokes my anxiety, pulling my frayed nerves taut. He straightens his uniform and leans against the corridor, waiting for me to open the outer bay doors.

"Hey, so…are we—are we good?" I ask, wondering if I've ever felt so unsure of myself after taking someone to bed.

He arches a brow.

"I don't know how you want me to take that question," he replies.

I fling my hands up in exasperation. "Take it however you want, if it'll give me an honest answer."

Pushing himself off the wall, he steps toward me.

"Well, morally speaking, I think I'm pretty good, but there's some room for debate regarding where you stand," he murmurs, crowding me back against the wall. "If you're asking me if we're good together *sexually*, then yeah, I'd say we were *very* good, but that's just my opinion."

Just like that, the smoldering embers of my desire roar back to life, engulfing my rational mind in memories of his touch—his taste. I reach for him, only to catch myself at the last second and fist my hands down at my sides. *I'm the one who told him no*, I remind myself miserably.

"Then again," he continues. "If you're asking me if I have a problem with where we stand with each other given everything that's happened and what we're about to head into—I told you before, Lyra. I respect your decision. I'm not going to pretend it's what I want, when every cell of my body is clamoring for me to fuck you until the stars burn out, but those are *my* feelings to deal with. Not yours."

It takes all of my strength and then some to stop my body from arching toward his. My instincts beg me to throw myself at him—to bury my face in his neck and wrap my limbs around him in a death grip. *Don't let me do this,* my heart implores him. *Don't let me push you away.*

"Good," my voice cracks. "Good. Yes. We're good. Okay."

The corner of Orion's lip twitches.

"Are you?" he presses.

"Am I good? Stars, no. I'm a fucking mess. But as long as you're good, *we're* good." I'm incredibly impressed with my ability to reach new levels of awkwardness, especially with some guy who might still be considering sending me to prison.

I move to pull the hatch on the door open, but Orion stops me, grazing a finger across the cut on my lip.

"We're good," he repeats.

My traitorous heart hangs on the words, desperate for them to mean more than the casual reassurance he probably intends. Insides roiling, I nod and pull down the hatch.

"Don't get too comfortable, Ada," I mutter. "There's still a chance we'll need to head out at a moment's notice. I'm going to ask Evie about the hull repairs to see if we can get them going as soon as possible, but do me a favor and start running a full diagnostic. I want to know what kind of shape we're in, in case Kraxis catches up to us."

Noted. Good luck. Try not to steal anything this time.

"HEY, DICKHEAD," Evie spits, one hand hovering above the

plasma pistol she always keeps belted at her waist. "Stars, you look like shit! What kind of trouble are you in now?"

She looks exactly the same as the last time I saw her—wavy blue hair pulled back in a messy ponytail, pale lavender skin shining with sweat, thick navy jumpsuit decked with grease and dirt. I'm pretty sure that smudge of machine oil atop the orange freckles is in the same exact spot. The crow's feet around her moonstone-colored eyes are a little deeper, the laugh lines around her full lips a little more pronounced, and her voluptuous hips a littler rounder, but she's still the same 'ol Evie.

"No more than usual," I reply, eyeing her with equal wariness. "I see you're the boss now. Who'd you have to threaten to make it to site manager out here?"

"Threaten? Oh, that's rich coming from you. You know, *some* of us have ambition beyond finding the most fuckable way out of any situation. I happened to earn my way into my job, no thanks to you abducting my best worker," Evie shoots back.

I cock a brow at her.

She returns with a fierce stare of her own, until her lips twitch and a grin of pure sunshine lights up her face.

"It wasn't exactly a threat," she finally admits. "And Jorla was a slug! He was lazy, stupid, never kept up with his paperwork and didn't give a shit about the men. I deserved this job, anyway. I'm certainly better at it than anyone else on this floating garbage pile. Isn't that right, guys?"

The two Drellers flanking her at the bottom of the landing platform grunt in unison.

I bark a laugh. "Stars, I missed you, you grumpy hag!"

"You libidinous terror! I can't believe you stayed away for so long," she chuckles, striding toward me with arms outstretched.

"It's good to see you," I exhale, breath squeezed out of me in Evie's iron-banded hug. "I'm sorry about Jorax. That was rotten of me."

Evie pulls back to cast a disapproving look at me.

"I don't appreciate the selfishness, but I was more worried

than anything. Jorax wasn't particularly smart, and you were scraping the bottom of the barrel with him. Still, he was a good worker. I was sad to lose him. Sadder it kept you away." She chucks my chin with her fist.

"I was a proper asshat to do so," I nod.

"I take it this surly tower of sex is the aforementioned scorcher?" Evie smirks, gesturing to a confused, concerned Orion.

"Ranger Asterth," he says, inclining his head in greeting. "Orion to my friends."

"Well, I sure do hope we can be friends," Evie says, fanning herself and flashing me her favorite are-you-serious look. "Let's head into my office. You can tell me more about the mess you're currently inhabiting, and I'll see what I can do for you. Jerrin, head down and see if we have any available space in the barracks for a couple of refugees."

"You're the best, Evie. I've got something onboard just for you," I say, relief easing some of the tightness in my shoulders.

She snorts. "If you think you're going to sauce me up on that wretched Zorium moonshine again, you're mistaken. Just because I live and work on a salvage station doesn't mean I go without life's little comforts. I've *upgraded* since you've been here last, Pinky Pie."

"Well, color me impressed! I'm ready to be dazzled," I say with a laugh. "Before we go in, any chance you can have one of your mechanics take a look at the *Aldrin*? There was a lower hull breach and I think she needs a patch. I'm having Ada run a full diagnostic now."

Evie nods and gestures to the remaining Dreller, who hurries off to do her bidding. She eyes Orion with interest, flashing him a blinding smile full of fangs, and links arms with him to lead us into the station's main floor.

"So, Ranger Asterth! I hope you'll tell me all about Xylothia. I've always wanted to go, you know. I hear the temples are some of the most impressive forms of early engineering this side of Andromeda."

The pride and joy radiating from Orion's smile would melt tungsten—igniting a flare of jealousy that burns just as hot within my chest. How come he's never looked at me like that? Oh, right, because whenever we talk, we end up fighting or doing something dangerous. Or maybe because he's a prime specimen of super hotness who oozes honor and the only thing I ooze is boner juice.

"Yes, my jurisdiction actually covers three of our biggest temples, including the Terrestrial Temple, the Temple of the Lost Sea, and the Celestial Temple. Each one honors a different Xylothian deity," he replies, clearly warming to Evie and her rapt interest.

"Is it the Celestial Temple that has the map of all those legendary star systems?" Evie asks, steering us down a winding corridor of rusting, creaking metal. Red-gold light filters up through the grates in the floor and makes the condensation on the walls glitter like jewels. The air in the station is too warm and thick with cloying, metallic-tainted humidity that doesn't seem to bother Evie, Orion, or the dozens of Drellers doing various tasks to keep things running smoothly.

I tug at the collar of my jumpsuit and blow a cool stream of air down my front, irritation rising along with my temperature.

"It is," Orion says. "In fact, that's actually where I ran into Lyra."

"No shit! Let me guess—stealing something? Our Lyra can be a slippery fish," Evie tosses a wink over her shoulder at me. "How'd you manage to catch her?"

"I knocked her out with my plasma rifle," Orion chuckles, the synesfores on his neck shifting to a soft purple that almost matches Evie's skin.

Evie grips Orion's shoulder to keep her balance as she laughs uproariously at my expense. Their jovial bonding and the sticky heat of the salvage station make me sourly wish I'd taken my chances with Kraxis and the rest of his lizard vermin aboard the *Edax Deorum.*

After what's become the longest hallway of my life, we finally reach a massive hatch with a heavy iron bolt. Evie wrenches the lock open one-handed and ushers us into her office with a welcoming sweep of her arms.

"Come in, take a load off, and tell me why you look like shit and your fucked-up ship is parked in my garage."

14
orion

Mess Hall Confessional

I **STAND** to the side to let Lyra pass—her frosty smile leaving phantom chips of ice on my shoulders. She doesn't look at me, not really. Her gaze skims over my chest, over my mouth, before darting away too fast, like she's afraid I'll see what's still burning there. It may be petty, but her petulant jealousy is a balm to the ragged shards of my heart. The incensed ire and simmering fury she's trying to paste a smile over comfort me almost as much as if she'd taken back her words from earlier. There's something perversely reassuring about her anger—it means it mattered, at least a little, and she's pretending indifference because the alternative would undo her.

It doesn't mean anything.

I should have known—should have guessed she would be quick to push me away. That's her instinct: retreat before she can be abandoned. The moment I reached for her, really reached, I should've known she'd armor up again. The time I've spent with her has taught me that beneath her passionate bravado and devil-may-care lifestyle, she's actually quite predictable. Quietly fragile. Not that she'll ever admit as much to me—or anyone.

We're already on borrowed time. I have to come clean with her about the Dark Star and talk to her about the Solar Mother idol. It's what she came for, what she thinks she wants—but stars help me, I want her to want something more. To want *me*, maybe. I know how important it is to her—that her freedom is on the line—but there has to be another way. We can find another way out…together.

If I have to follow her to Ooneryx and deal with Brill myself, I can. I will.

"Evie, this is incredible," Lyra breathes, turning in a slow circle. "This isn't an office—this is a paradise! How did you manage it?"

Dragging my gaze away from her, I finally take in our surroundings. I expected a small berth of rusted metal matching the corridor, perhaps with a desk and other tech needed to organize a massive salvage operation, but if I didn't know better, I'd think we left the station entirely.

The entire far wall of the room is a window facing out into space. Stars glitter in the distance, trailing by with our slow orbit. The walls of the cabin appear green at first, but upon closer inspection I see every available surface is covered with plants. Soft mosses, speckled leaves, tiny delicate flowers, and wispy thin trailing vines cling to the metal, giving the room the appearance of a living forest glen. Soft golden light spills down from the ceiling and if I close my eyes, I can almost believe we're down on Xylothia. The tepid humidity, faint verdant scent of growth, and muted quiet arrow straight into my heart, nearly buckling my knees with acute homesickness.

"How does it grow?" I wonder. "No soil, poor light…yet you've been able to recreate a small ecosystem in such a desolate metal capsule."

"It wasn't easy, I can tell you that much. It took a lot of time, patience, and catastrophic plant failures before I got my systems dialed in. I managed to get some seeds from Terrin-4 so I could make this feel a little bit more like home. I'd be happy to show you later, if you're interested," Evie replies amiably, clearly pleased that we're admiring her handiwork.

"I got the biosphere up and running on Lyra's ship," I offer. "But the growth is slower than I'd like. If I were back on Xylothia, I could tap into the soil and help encourage growth patterns, but it doesn't work on plant life outside my home world."

"Wait, what?" Lyra turns to me, shock etched on her face. "You can talk to fucking plants?"

I feel my synesfores flicker in annoyance.

"I can't *talk* to plants, no," I reply. "But some Xylothians are innately in tune with the natural world on Xylothia. It's a give and take relationship. We can offer our energy—our blood—our life-force to our world and encourage things to grow and thrive. Much like your *vellia* not being a universally appealing pheromone—"

"It's a curse, is what it is," Lyra grumbles.

"—not all Xylothians possess the ability. It varies. And the effects have been lessening over the last few generations. I don't possess a tenth of the power my ancestors did," I finish, ignoring her interruption.

"That's wild. How come you didn't tell me?" Lyra prods.

"You should have known what you were walking into when you landed on my planet and started taking things you didn't understand or respect," I shoot back. "And besides, you didn't ask."

Lyra sends me another dark look, so I turn my attention back to Evie, who's watching us with rapt attention.

"Thank you, by the way, for offering us sanctuary," I say.

"Well, you can thank me by sitting down and telling me what the hell you've gotten yourselves into," Evie says. She gestures to a couple of worn—but comfortable—seats in front of her desk and pulls a decanter of dark purple liquid from a shelf. Pouring three glasses of the viscous beverage, she hands them to us and collapses into her chair.

Lyra holds her cup up in a gesture of respect and tips it back without a word. I stare at mine, unsure of what, exactly, I'm about to imbibe.

"Does he not drink?" Evie asks Lyra. Then, to me: "Do you not drink?"

"What am I drinking, Ms. Redfern?" I ask, trying to keep my tone polite.

"I promise you it's not that disgusting moonshine Lyra keeps stored next to her fuel cells. You have the privilege of sampling a little of my own brew," Evie replies, already pouring a second glass for herself and for Lyra.

"Don't worry about it, Orion," Lyra says dismissively. "If you drank half a bottle of Zorium moonshine and escaped without a hangover, a little of Evie's plumrot isn't going bother you."

I toast to her and take a tentative sip—though the texture is disturbingly thick, the flavor is mildly tart and almost too sweet. Upon seeing me smile approvingly, Evie grins and waves impatiently at Lyra.

"Anytime you're ready, Pinky Pie," she says. "I do have other things to attend to, you know."

"Kraxis and his merry band of Void Stalkers caught up with us, Orion blew a hole in their ship, and now we're hiding out here," Lyra says, reaching for the decanter again.

"Okay, maybe a little less abbreviated," Evie says, her brow furrowing.

"I went to Xylothia to find the Solar Mother idol," Lyra begins, shifting uncomfortably. "Brill sent me after it. I also *may* have found another interested party on Epsilon-6."

"Stars, Lyra…" Evie groans.

My grip on my glass tightens with a surge of frustration and anger, but I keep silent—curious to see what Lyra tells her so-called friend. Her voice is steady, but I can see the pulse fluttering at her throat, the faint tremor in her hand when she reaches for the decanter. She hates being seen as vulnerable—hates needing to defend herself at all.

Part of me wants to step in, to make it easier for her—to tell

Evie she's braver anyone I've ever met, that she's got more scars than she lets anyone see. But I stay quiet. She doesn't need me to speak for her.

Darting another nervous glance at me, she continues.

"Orion found me in the temple and knocked me out. He was ready to turn me over to the Feds, but Kraxis caught up with us on Xylothia. We struck a deal and managed to escape with the idol intact," she says, surprising me with the truth.

"What kind of a deal?" Evie says, wiggling her eyebrows suggestively. To my delight, Lyra blushes and clears her throat.

Maybe it didn't mean nothing *after all.* Maybe I just wish I could tell her that what happened between us doesn't have to mean regret.

"He promises not to turn me over to the Feds for looting, and I promise to give him the names—and proof—of two big mucky-muck buyers who've been running the black market on Xylothian artifacts. Anyway, we were on our way back from Mallorus when Kraxis caught up with us, my ship was damaged, and we were in a desperate situation. But then I found out my good old friend Evie was nearby, kicking ass and taking names as the site manager on this here salvage rig," Lyra says.

It's a pathetic attempt to gloss over the stickier parts of her story, and from the look in Evie's eyes, she's not falling for it.

"What a kind, generous, forgiving person that site manager is," Evie drawls. Lyra chuckles and reaches for the decanter once more, but Evie pulls it away. "Are you out of your stars-damned mind?!" she yells.

"Not yet, but if I keep drinking that plumrot, I will be soon," Lyra returns. "What's got your jumpsuit in knots?"

"I don't even know where to begin with you," Evie says, throwing her hands up in the air. "I know you're trying to find your way out of that shitbag Brill's clutches, but this is *not* the way, Pinky Pie. It's one thing to steal from bad guys and dig up treasure from long lost civilizations, but looting temples on desperate planets is...*low*. And you dragged an innocent bystander into the mix! Did you even consider that this could go badly and your hot forest daddy might not make it out alive?"

"Hot forest daddy?" I question.

Both women ignore me.

"Or that you'd be putting him on a lot of bad lists of some *very* bad dudes? You might not be bothered looking over your shoulder forever, but did you ask *him*? Did you tell him what was at stake?" Evie continues.

Lyra looks like she's been slapped. She gapes at Evie, blinking, but doesn't seem to have a retort. As frustrated as I am with her—with how things stand between us, my heart twists.

"She hardly dragged me into this," I say, coming to Lyra's defense. "In fact, the deal was my idea. Lyra wanted to leave after we gave Kraxis the slip on Xylothia—without the idol—but I wouldn't let her go."

Her head jerks slightly at that, just enough that I know she's listening. I want her to understand it wasn't pity or obligation that kept me there. It was respect. Maybe something worse.

The truth is, she's not reckless—she's desperate. Every risk she takes is another step away from the man who owns her, the life she's trying to outrun. And stars help me, I'll follow her through every hell in the quadrant if it means she gets out.

Evie looks at her with disappointment, but all I see is someone who's still fighting, still trying. And maybe that's why I can't stop wanting her.

Evie raises a brow. "No offense, Ranger Asterth, but bundling up lost hikers and smugglers on some glorified nature reserve is a far cry from the types that Lyra deals with. She's made her choices—I just hate to see someone else get hurt because of them."

"With all due respect, Ms. Redfern, you have no idea what Lyra and I have been through. She's saved my life more than once and she's been true to her word since we started this—"

"I don't need you to speak for me, Orion," Lyra snaps. She slams her glass down on Evie's desk, making both of us jump.

"And as for you—you don't get to lecture me about *anything*. I get that things between us haven't been great over the last few years, but you have no right to pass judgment after hearing the five minute short version of the shit I've been dealing with. You want an apology for Jorax? Fine! I'm sorry! You want me to find a better line of work? Well, get in line, sister! You want me to sever my ties with the piece of shit holding my contract ransom? Me-fucking-too! You want me to serve time for being a no-good, busted-ass reprobate who fucks her way through every orbit because it's a distraction from the hell that waits back on Ooneryx? Congratulations! You're hardly the first. In fact, why don't you and Ranger Righteous call the Feds together? Or go ahead and call Fobos—he's not too far away. Then maybe you can split whatever bounty's on my head."

With that, she storms from the office. I immediately stand to go after her, but Evie puts her hand on my arm.

"I'd give her some space, if I were you," she says, returning to the window behind her desk and gazing out into space.

Frustration and anger twist my insides and I glare at Evie. Not because she's wrong, but because Lyra's gone, and the silence she leaves behind feels unbearable. I can still feel the echo of her fury, her shame, the way her voice broke right before she walked out.

She thinks she's poison, or damned. She believes that anyone who gets close to her ends up burned. And maybe she's right, but I can't seem to stay away. Every time she runs, I want to follow. Every time she lashes out, I just want to pull her closer and tell her she doesn't have to fight the whole damn universe alone. But that's not what she needs right now. What she needs is someone who believes she's worth more than the wreckage she leaves behind. I just wish she'd let me be that someone.

"What was that all about?" I ask, my tone accusatory. "I thought you were friends."

Evie huffs a laugh.

"How much do you know about Lyra?" she asks.

"Not much," I admit. "But…enough." Enough to recognize the way she flinches from kindness. Enough to know she hides behind the next job, the next planet, the next half-truth—because standing still means feeling everything she's buried. But maybe I don't know her at all. Maybe I just want to.

Evie turns to look at me over her shoulder, understanding in her gaze.

"I love that idiot like a sister, but trust me when I tell you—Lyra is a beautiful star orbiting a black hole. She's got the worst luck of anyone I've ever met, and every now and then, she needs someone to help her course correct. It's been too long since her parents died. Too long connected with Brill. She's got too many enemies and too few friends. Underneath her reckless exterior, she's tending a heart that's been broken longer than it's been whole. I see how you dummies are looking at each other—all gooey-eyed. You should know what you're in for. Loving Lyra is…well, it's both the easiest and the hardest thing you'll ever do," she explains.

Evie's words settle heavy in my chest, like grit caught in gears. A beautiful star orbiting a black hole. Yeah. That sounds right. I've been watching her spiral for days, pretending I'm not being pulled in too.

"You were pretty hard on her," I press, though my voice comes out rougher than I intend. "Especially for someone who professes to love her." But maybe Evie's right, and maybe I'm the next fool to mistake her gravity for warmth, her proximity for affection.

"I know," Evie nods, slumping down into her chair. "I know. We've always been this way. And things have been…strained… between us. These last few years, she's been even more reckless. More destructive. She's making stupid decisions out of desperation and she's stopped listening to me. I don't want to see her crossing that event horizon, you know? And I certainly don't want her dragging anyone else in with her. But I'm sorry if I offended you, or misjudged y'all's situation."

"She's trapped," I say. "And any cornered animal is dangerous. I understand why she took the idol. If I were in her shoes, I don't know if I'd do things any differently. But as much as I dislike her motives and her actions, she's played it pretty straight with me so far."

Evie replaces the decanter of plumrot and collects the glasses from her desk. With a smug tint to her nonchalance, she tilts her head.

"If she's been straight with you so far, why are you sticking around for this alleged proof? She could—and would—give you a list of names, I'm sure. If you trust her enough with your life, I wonder what's keeping you on her ship, Ranger."

Before I can open my mouth to argue, a flickering hologram of one of the Dreller mechanics appears in the middle of Evie's desk. In an instant, her cheeky expression morphs into that of a hardened leader.

"The *Aldrin-136* has major hull damage and minor damage to the light speed engines. In order to refine and machine a repair, it'll take about six cycles. The light speed engines can be fixed before then, but obviously it won't matter if we don't get the hull put back together in time. There are other minor repairs that need doing, too—a lot of things are worn out or starting to wear out. If I'm honest, the whole thing needs probably eighteen cycles in dry dock for a full work up," the Dreller grunts out.

I'm not certain how long a cycle is on this station, but I know we don't have the kind of time he's suggesting. Evie seems to be of the same mind, because her brows narrow and the muscles in her jaw flex.

"Is that the best you can do, Ty?" she asks. "Our guest needs this faster than that."

The mechanic crosses his thick, muscular arms across his chest and frowns.

"Technically, we could do a patch job on the hull and fix up the light speed, but I don't know how well it'll hold. The ship is space-worthy but…"

"I have every bit of faith in you," Evie says. "You've got one cycle to get it in a good spot."

The Dreller looks like he's about to argue with his boss, but when Evie raises her eyebrow in challenge, he meekly nods and ends the communication.

"Tyrell is the best mechanic on *Hephaestus*," Evie tells me. "Don't worry about Lyra's ship. He'll get it fixed up and probably in better order than it's been in a long time."

"I'd ask how long a cycle is, but I suppose it doesn't matter as long as Kraxis doesn't know where we are," I say, running my fingertips over the fluffy moss on the wall. "Though the sooner, the better, obviously."

"I'll keep my comms open and my scanners running. If he farts within range, we'll know," she says. "In the meantime, knowing my Pinky Pie, you've been eating like shit for the past few weeks. We've got a top-notch cook here—lemme take you below for some grub while she cools off."

I follow our Strythian host through the winding corridors of the rickety salvage ship, barely keeping pace as she hurls information at me about the *Hephaestus*, from its inner workings to the job promotion coup that earned her her title. When we finally reach the mess hall, it appears as equally underwhelming as the rest of the ship—the notable exception being the mouthwatering smell of spices and freshly baked bread.

Evie slides a tray over to me and piles several plates high with food—some things I recognize, others entirely new. She plops a glass of water and a mug of fragrant tea in front of me and grins at my bewildered, hungry expression.

"We don't stand on ceremony here, Ranger Asterth. Dig in," she says, shoveling a steaming yellow puree into her mouth.

The first bites are incredible and I close my eyes to savor the sautéed vegetables, piping hot breads, herby salads, and creamy cheeses. When I dip into a spicy, savory stew, I moan audibly and Evie chuckles.

"Told you so," she says, shoving her empty plate to the side.

"So, Xylothia, huh? Never met a Xylothian before. Seem to remember them keeping to themselves quite a bit, and that was before the *Arkanium*."

I almost drop my spoon, and Evie winces at my expression.

"Ah, shit. Sorry. I'm sure you knew people on it. We don't have to talk about it, if you'd rather not," she offers.

I nod, unsure why I feel suddenly protective of my past when Evie's been more kind and welcoming than Lyra, and yet I spilled more to her than I have to…anyone, really.

"I'd rather not talk about that," I reply, as gently as I can.

Evie takes it in stride, but straightens up to pepper me with yet another line of questions. It's a wonder she has time to draw breath between her stories, jokes, and incessant curiosity.

"What is it that made you want to become a ranger? Is that just a job for you, or is it more like a calling?"

I consider my answer for some time, but for all her energy, she's patient while she waits.

"It's a little of both," I reply, reaching for one of the small, round flatbreads stacked up between us. "Things on Xylothia aren't as dire as other worlds, but we're not really thriving, either. Birth rates have dropped over the last few generations and it seems like the whole planet feels us faltering. My ancestors were so closely connected to the natural world but we've lost a lot of their knowledge. Everyone wants answers and no one knows where to start looking."

Evie's eyes widen and she flags down a Dreller carrying a plate of what look like pastries without breaking my gaze.

"I'm sorry," she says, plonking a sugar-dusted bun onto my recently emptied plate, then hands me a second with a pitying look. "I can't imagine having to watch your world collapse in slow motion."

I shrug, but her kindness nearly chokes me up.

"I suppose I thought I might find some of the answers everyone's looking for if I returned to the places our ancestors flourished. Spend time in the forests around the temples, keep the ancient settlements safe and protected. Perhaps I was hoping if I spent my life serving my ancestors, they'd give me some guidance," I explain, unable to keep the bitterness from my tone, despite the pastry's cloying sweetness.

"And have they?" she asks.

"They're as silent as the ruined temples," I admit. "I don't know. That's probably why I felt a spark of hope when Lyra crashed in."

"How so?"

Because she makes me feel things I thought I'd never feel for anyone. Because there's a chance she might be my perfect mate. Because for all her faults, she makes me hope for myself, for my future, and for my world. Because I didn't fall in love with her—I plummeted into obsession with her, and when this cursed journey is over, I want to do everything in my power to stay with her. All things I'm not about to say to a relative stranger, because it's gutting to even admit them to myself. The strength of my need staggers me—disturbs me—and I still don't know that Lyra won't try to eject me into the cold vacuum of space if it's convenient for her to do so. What's worse—if she did, I'd still probably blow her a kiss and thank her for the privilege.

"Because maybe now I can make a difference. For the first time in years, I finally have enough leverage to make one of these thieves help me put a stop to the systematic plundering of my cultural heritage," I say, which—while not the whole truth, is a distant cousin to it.

Evie smirks, obviously sensing the lie, but her smile falls when she catches sight of something over my shoulder.

Oh no. Oh, please no.

Lyra stands in the doorway to the mess hall, clutching an empty tray to her chest.

15
lyra

Leverage? Or Love-rage?

LEVERAGE.

The word drops like a stone in my gut, but instead of the fury I should feel at Orion's casual dismissal, I simply feel…sad.

No, that's not quite right—there's nothing simple about the maelstrom of emotions surging in my mind and body. Shame, humiliation, regret, and anger wage war for second place, while nausea roils and the scrape of betrayal burns over my skin.

For a moment, I'm paralyzed. Evie and Orion gape at me in horror—the remark clearly not meant for my ears. I consider fleeing to my ship, but it's still in the launch bay undergoing repairs. I *also* consider smashing my tray into Orion's handsome face, but even that fantasy feels hollow. Thinking about making him bleed disturbs me, but maybe that's because mere hours ago, all I could think about was making him come.

Since fighting and fleeing are well off the table, I've got one remaining F-option: food. That was the whole reason why I'd found my way to the mess hall, anyway—Evie's lecture hit a little too close to home and mid-sulk, I realized I hadn't eaten anything in a day. I'd hoped part of the hurt I felt was down to an empty stomach and low blood sugar, so venturing to the ship's cafeteria had seemed like the most logical choice.

Not even carbs will be able to soothe me now—those jerks.

Evie's anger I can understand. We have this sort of history and it's not like I've been the best friend to her lately, but Orion's...well. *I'm probably just getting what I asked for—what I deserve.* After all, I'm the one who told him it didn't have to mean anything, and who knows if he was telling the truth about my *vellia.* Maybe our close proximity over the last few weeks has led to some kind of cumulative effect on his libido, or something. I don't know enough about Xylothians to know how they respond to Velusians in general. *Apparently, I don't know anything about Xylothians, since the fucker can talk to plants,* I think bitterly.

Blinking slowly, I turn to the various food stations running down the middle of the mess hall and absent-mindedly start filling my tray. I'm disgusted to realize I only have myself to blame for this—for my actions toward Evie and my distance from Orion. Despite the sting, the sour-tasting loneliness of it all, it reminds me of what I've already believed all along.

It's me on my own.

Exhaling shakily, I return to the task at hand. On my plate, I heap piles of filament-thin black noodles covered in a bright purple sauce, three different kinds of bread, thick cuts of meat drizzled in savory blue gravy, steamed vegetables I don't recognize, and creamy kreshaan puree—Evie's favorite from Terrin-4. The smell is incredible, but the nausea my emotions have summoned makes the meal as unappetizing as what I'm about to do next.

"Is this seat taken?" I ask, dropping onto the bench next to Orion and across from Evie. It took a moment's calculation, but I knew I wouldn't be able to meet Orion's green gaze without having a complete emotional breakdown.

Evie raises a wary brow at me, then gestures for me to sit. Orion shifts uncomfortably.

"Sorry if I'm interrupting," I say, the false cheerfulness brittle to even my ears. "I wanted to get something to eat before we have to take off. How much longer for repairs?"

"I gave them one cycle to get you in a good spot," Evie says.

"Thanks," I nod, picking up a spoon and pushing the yellow puree around my plate.

"Lyra, listen—what you overheard, it's not…" Orion begins.

I hold my hand up to stop him.

"It's fine," I say, forcing myself to swipe some bread through the vibrant mush. "I know you've both got your reasons. And honestly? It doesn't matter. We're good. *Totally* good."

Evie continues to stare at me, her expression unreadable.

"I've actually got some work to do before end-of-cycle, so I'm gonna head back to my office. And I meant to tell you guys earlier, but I'm running a full salvage team right now, so you'll have to bunk together. I only have the one berth to spare. But I'm sure it won't be a problem since you've been sharing the *Aldrin-136* and you are, quote, *totally good*."

She steals a spoonful of kreshaan from my plate as she stands, and for a brief moment, I catch a glint of mischief in her eyes.

"Your quarters are one deck down, adjacent to the cargo hold. Three doors down on the left. I'll have someone drop off some clean linens and as soon as I have an update about your ship, I'll let you know," Evie continues.

"One free berth on the entire *Hephaestus*, huh?" I mutter, throwing her a glare.

"Yeah, who would've thought?" she drawls, marching toward the exit.

As soon as she's out of sight, Orion slides onto the bench across from me.

"Lyra, please let me apologize," he begins.

"No," I interrupt.

"No?"

"No, I mean, there's nothing to apologize for. I'm the one who told you it didn't have to mean anything, and we're in this stars-forsaken situation that neither of us wanted, or anticipated, and—I get it, okay? You're using me, I'm using you, we're both using Evie…everyone's got to watch their six. And do you know what? I don't blame you one bit. You deserve a little leverage. You're a good man, er, Xylothian and you don't deserve to have your whole cultural identity stolen from you every other week. And I *am* an asshole for trying to steal it," I insist, shoveling a forkful of noodles in my mouth so I'll *stop fucking talking*.

"Do you always do this?" he asks, dropping his half-eaten sugar bun on the table.

"Well, you're the one complaining about the food on my ship, so yeah, when I pull into any port with a nice kitchen, I do eat like—"

He cuts me off, glaring.

"I'm not talking about the food, Lyra," he snaps. "You know what? Never mind. If you don't want to be honest with me—or with yourself—that's your problem."

"What the fuck are you talking about, Orion?" I hiss. "I just let you off the hook for talking shit about me to Evie. I gave you an out after sleeping with you so that you don't have to get all weird on me and give me the whole 'this was fun, but it's over' speech. I'm taking you to my fucking buyers. What more do you want from me?"

"Maybe I want more from you than that!"

I freeze. "Wh—what?"

My heart slams against my ribcage, feeling a foreign kind of hope I've never dared entertain.

"Has it ever occurred to you that maybe I don't want you to let me off the hook? That maybe—I don't know—you should have some standards for how you let people treat you?"

"Excuse me, are you *trying* to pick a fight with me?" I ask, hurt eclipsing my anger.

"Yes! No—I just…I want you to be honest with me, Lyra," he says, swallowing and deflating a little. "I guess I just want to know that I can get under your skin as easily as you get under mine."

My emotions are clanging around in my head, adding to my

growing confusion about where this conversation is going. I sink my teeth into Orion's abandoned sugar bun and blink up at him. There's anguish in his eyes, and it turns the pastry to sand in my mouth.

"I don't understand," I say quietly.

"I know," he says on a sigh. "Things are complicated. But we need to talk, Lyra. *Really* talk—without assuming what the other person is going to say. I have things I need to tell you—not just about us. I want us to figure some of this out together, but you have to give me some credit. You owe me some honesty."

The part of my hurt, insulted heart wants to rage at him and fling my remaining noodles at him, but the other part of me longs for an open, unguarded conversation with the man I'm reluctantly falling in love with. *Can I have an unguarded conversation if I still worry about him turning me over to the Feds?* For the first time since we set out on this fucked up adventure, that worry feels...less, somehow. That thought shocks me enough to give him the benefit of the doubt this time.

Looking up, I realize we've caused a bit of a scene in the middle of the mess hall. Five Drellers and a Printharian I've never met are staring at us with undisguised interest.

Hunger temporarily sated, I nod at Orion.

"You're right," I say. "Let's go somewhere we can talk privately."

He offers me a small, relieved smile.

"Thank you."

I shove a few of the sugar buns into the pockets of my jumpsuit and gesture to him to do the same. With a chuckle, he pilfers a few as well.

We leave the mess hall, much to the disappointment of our audience, and make our way down the long, sloping corridor to the cargo bay. I've stayed on Evie's ship before but she's obviously done a lot to it in the intervening years—the living quarters have been fixed up to a level of comfort I'm not used to.

At the end of the hall is a large room, spartan with disuse but clean and organized. A large bed sits in the middle of the room, storage closets to the left, a small desk to the right and a small bathroom with a shower tucked into the back corner.

"Nice, Evie," I say, whistling appreciatively. "This must be for when she has higher ups in the company come out to survey the site."

I fling myself onto the thick, soft mattress and moan when I sink deep into the plush comforter and pillows.

"*Very* nice, Evie," I sigh. "She always knows the right places to spend her credits."

I peel myself up off the bed and turn to see Orion watching me with heat in his gaze. That's all it takes for me to return to a state of drugged lust at the thought of that glorious body writhing beneath mine.

"You mentioned wanting to talk?" I say, clearing my throat. If we don't have it out now, I'm going to become far too distracted to function.

He shakes his head to clear it—obviously feeling the same chaotic appetites.

"Lyra, we need to talk about the Dark Star," he says, rubbing the back of his neck.

Of all the things I thought he'd lead with, *that* certainly wasn't on the list.

"What about it?" I ask warily.

"I need to know what you know about it. What Brill knows about it—why he's looking for it. The Solar Mother is more than just a piece of treasure, and I think you know that, too." He crosses the room to stand in front of me, dropping to his knees so that we're eye level.

"Please," he implores. "Please tell me the truth."

The food in my belly threatens to find its way back up and out of my body. Swallowing the dry lump sticking in my throat, I think over my options. Trusting someone else with the truth— the *whole* truth—feels like handing over the end of my tether. My pulse thrums in my ears. I want to look away, but there's something about the way he's kneeling—open, steady, sincere—that makes my chest ache.

Am I really ready to do that?

"Why?" I hedge.

"Because the legend that everyone believes about it—that it has the power to bring someone back from the dead—it's wrong," he says.

I still. "What? Wait—the Dark Star is real?" No way. No fucking way.

He nods slowly.

"If I tell you this, Lyra, you *must* swear to me you will stop looking for it. You cannot tell anyone about this. I'm taking a huge leap of faith here, but no one has ever gotten so close before and if I can't make you understand…we're all in danger," he says, distress evident in the brutal way he shoves his fingers through his hair.

"I swear," I tell him. Even as the words leave my mouth, part of me wonders if I mean them. I've sworn before—to Brill, to my father's memory, to myself—and broken every single one. But something in Orion's eyes makes me want to try again.

"Please," he begs. "Please don't make me regret this."

"Do you want me to sign something in blood, or what?" I bark, more than a little stung that he's so certain my honor is for sale. *Isn't it, though?* The cruel thought comes reflexively, but I try to ignore it as Orion gears up to tell me something presumably world-shattering.

"The Dark Star isn't some gemstone with magical powers," he says. "It's a weapon."

The words hit like a physical blow. Cold rushes up my spine, my fingertips prickling numb. My mouth opens, but for a moment, no sound comes out. My eyebrows lift in shock. "What kind of a weapon?"

"The kind of weapon that can destroy a planet and doom millions with a thought," he replies, his voice cracking.

"The *Arkanium*," I whisper, understanding dawning. A slow,

awful click of pieces I didn't want to fit together—the crash, the salvage rumors, the way Brill's tone changed when he mentioned the ship. Oh, stars. The *Arkanium* wasn't just a loss. It was a heist gone wrong. "But how? What is it? *Where* is it? And how does no one else know?"

Orion rises, pacing in front of me. His movements are rough and jittery, and he looks like the words are being wrenched out of him when he finally answers.

"When I told you the legend of the Solar Mother idol, I didn't tell you all of it," he says. "As the story goes, when Father Darkness realized he'd murdered the Solar Mother, he didn't just cease to exist. He tried thousands of different ways to end his agony, until finally, he fashioned himself a weapon of pure dark energy."

"The Dark Star," I fill in. My mouth goes dry. The old myths, the bedtime stories my father whispered before he left for expeditions—they were never just stories. My chest tightens with a mix of wonder and dread, because if he were here, he'd have chased this truth too. He'd have died for it. *He did.*

He nods, then returns to sit by my side on the bed.

"He instructed the Xylothians to recover the weapon after his dreadful act and to guard it for the rest of time. For eons, the Dark Star sat safely in the depths of a hidden temple guarded by the Xylothian Protectorate. It sat there so long, they started to forget about its true power and the terror of unmaking creation. The Protectorate started to falter, and with it, the decline of their ancient civilization began. The Solar Mother idol was one of the last great treasures they forged—all so someone would know what we were guarding, and where it hides," he explains.

"The Solar Mother is a map!" I exclaim. "I knew it! My father knew it!"

The words tear out of me before I can stop them. For a second, the room tilts—his face, the bed, the steady hum of the station—and all I can see is my father's study, the way he traced constellation lines with trembling hands. He'd been right, and it killed him. And now I'm standing on the edge of the same ruin.

Orion raises a brow at me, but nods, carrying on with his story.

"Over millennia, the Xylothians tried to harness the power of the Dark Star, and every time, it's almost brought our civilization to its end. With the slow decline of things on our planet, people started to suspect just *having* the weapon on our planet was causing our suffering. Some reasoned if we took it and hid it off-world, we might be able to restore balance," he says, rubbing at his temples. "Stupid, in hindsight."

"That's what the *Arkanium* was doing," I say slowly. "Taking the Dark Star somewhere else. But what went wrong?"

"Truly, we still don't know. Or at least, I don't know. When we heard about the accident, teams went in to try to figure out what happened. All we found was the Dark Star, floating around in the wreckage," he chokes out.

"*We?* Oh, Orion, I'm so sorry. You were there, weren't you?"

The realization blooms sickly in my gut. I've seen that kind of haunted look before—in the mirror. The tiny tremor in his voice, the faraway glassiness in his eyes—it's the look of someone who lost everything and survived anyway.

His synesfores flutter black, and I grasp his hand.

"My father wasn't *just* a historian. He was a guardian—one of the last descendants of the Protectorate. He didn't agree that they should move the Dark Star off-world, but ultimately he was overruled. It was a compromise that he would be the one handling the transfer—a compromise that would cost him his life, and my mother's," he says with a shuddering breath. There's a patina of bitterness beneath his pain, one I only recognize because I've felt the same thing about my father's obsession with my mother's death.

"Hold on. If it's a world-ending weapon, why does everyone believe it's some ancient gemstone that can bring people back from the dead?" I ask. It's the only story I ever heard—the one I built my whole damn career around. Finding beauty in the bones of tragedy, selling hope to the highest bidder. Now that hope feels like poison on my tongue. *I feel like I'm going to be sick.*

"Wouldn't everyone *know* it's a weapon if it's nearly destroyed your people more than once?"

Orion shakes his head, and his shimmering brown-green hair falls into his eyes.

"Xylothians have always been insular. The stories that reached other parts of the galaxy never quite had the full picture, but to some extent, they're not wholly wrong. A relic that can bring people back from the dead? No. But a relic that has the power to destroy everything, thus making way for creation's next step? Sure. Life always follows the path of death."

"Is it possible that anyone else knows about the true nature of the Dark Star?" I ask, dread gathering in my gut. Brill's face flashes in my mind, all charm and cruelty wrapped in a silk suit. Of course he'd want something like this. He doesn't just collect artifacts—he collects leverage. And if he ever guessed what the Dark Star really was...

When Orion meets my gaze, there's an alarming fear in his eyes.

"That's what I'm hoping you can tell me," he says. "If you would've asked me a year ago, I would've said no. You must understand—so many of my people have died to protect the secret. But I've been worried about the increase in smugglers, grave robbers, and looters. Are they just looking for random artifacts to fence in the wake of the *Arkanium* disaster? Or are they all connected? Are they *looking* for something specific?"

I chew on my lower lip, nearly missing the way Orion tracks the movement.

"Brill has always played his cards pretty close to his chest. He doesn't trust me any more than I trust him—ironic, considering that's meant to be the basis of our contract. He's never said anything to me about the Dark Star and up until my run-in with Iathos, I didn't have any reason to believe he would think it was anything other than a theft-worthy jewel to stick in his private vault," I say.

"But on Xylothia, what Kraxis said about the idol…" Orion trails off.

"Look, I'm going to level with you about the idol—" I begin, deciding it's time to trust Ranger Righteous with at least *some* of the truth. The fact that he told me about the Dark Star is…well, it's pretty fucking huge. And heavy. It means he trusts me at least a little, and maybe, *just maybe* having someone on my side as I try to tear myself from Brill's clutches won't be such a bad idea after all. For the first time in a long time, I don't feel like I'm carrying the whole universe by myself. That terrifies me more than the Dark Star—more than Brill—ever could.

At least, that's my thinking when Evie patches in over the station's comms, informing Orion and I that the salvage station is about to be boarded by the crew of the *Edax Deorum*.

16
orion

Dark Stars and Broken Hearts

AFTER THE INITIAL flash of panicked terror in Lyra's beautiful face, there's a grim resignation that disturbs me even more.

"How far did we get with the repairs, Evie?" she murmurs, numbness sluicing off her in waves.

"Not far enough, Pinky Pie," Evie sighs over the comms. "I'm sorry. They must've tracked you here after the jump. Either that, or their ship wasn't as badly damaged as you thought."

Her words land like ice in my gut. There's a stillness in her—a kind of fatal calm I've seen when someone's already accepted they won't make it home. It terrifies me more than the fleet closing in. Shame and guilt erupt in my chest, settling aside the self-loathing that took up residence when I saw Lyra overhear my conversation with Evie. If only I'd been a better shot. If only I hadn't let her down. If only I'd been the man she deserved to help her win her freedom. If only I'd had time to tell her about Xylothian matehood and how I really feel about her. I'm going to drown in *if onlys* before I make it back to Xylothia. That is, *if* I make it back.

The look on Lyra's face makes me wonder at the likelihood.

"I have a plan," she says, eyes glassy with gathering tears.

"I already know I'm not going to like it," I rasp, threading my fingers through her criminally soft hair.

"I'm going back with Kraxis," she says, her tone steely despite the single tear that traces a line down her cheek. "To Ooneryx."

The words slice through me. Ooneryx. Brill. Chains I thought she'd escaped snapping shut again. My pulse hammers so hard I feel it in my throat.

"Lyra…"

She's already up, tugging me with her outside our temporary room and back down the corridor.

"We need to get back to the ship. *You* need to get back to the ship. Sneak aboard, take the idol, and hide out here until we're gone. Then I need you to borrow one of Evie's cruisers and pilot it to Epsilon-6," she says.

Epsilon-6? My mind stutters. Why there? Who's waiting for her?

A thousand questions claw at my throat, but what spills out is only panic—because every part of her plan sounds like goodbye.

"What?!" I shout. "Are you out of your mind? First of all, I'm not abandoning you to whatever cruel punishments Kraxis and Brill have in store for you. Secondly, I'm not about to sell the most critical piece of Xylothian history—and the map to a world-ending weapon, I might add—to some buyer for a few million credits!"

Lyra jogs down so many different twists and turns, I lose track of where we are. She, however, seems to have a very good idea where she's going. She motions for me to keep my voice down, then pushes me into an empty service hover-vator that immediately lurches downward. It's oddly quiet inside the metal room—the only sounds the soft *whoosh* of the station decks flying past us outside as we descend.

"My contact on Epsilon-6 isn't a buyer," she says, blowing out a breath. "He's a Fed."

A Fed? For a beat, I can't breathe. My thoughts slam into each other like debris in orbit as things coalesce. There's a man waiting on for her Epsilon-6—a man she trusts more than me. A fissure opens inside me, equal parts confusion, jealousy, and relief. She's been risking everything not for greed, but for freedom—and still, she didn't tell me. My brows lift and my mouth drops open, but before I can fire the million brewing questions at her, she winces apologetically.

"After my last job went so wrong and Iathos screwed me over—literally *and* figuratively—I knew Brill was going to lose it. I didn't know what he would do for sure, but I had a pretty good idea."

My gut twists. I can see it so clearly now—her recklessness hiding desperation. The name *Iathos* spikes fresh anger at him, at Brill, at myself for ever letting her think she had to fight her battles alone.

"I mean, stars, a month before I shipped off, I'd just watched him disembowel a Void Stalker with his bare hands because he didn't like the tone of his voice. The fucker is unhinged on a *good* day. So, instead of heading back to Ooneryx immediately, I stopped off at Epsilon-6 to hide out for a bit and figure out what to do. I was already half-way through an insane plot to slip some Uranian ice wort into his nightcap when an undercover agent approached me. Said he was with the High Crimes Unit and that they'd been after Brill for a long time with no success," she explains, rushing through her words as the hover-vator begins to slow.

"This is insane," I cut in, disbelief tangling with my sense of betrayal. It burns through my ribs like acid, but it's mixed up with admiration. She's been walking a knife's edge between two devils, trying to carve a way out. And still, she never told me the truth or asked me to help her.

"You're working with the Feds? You've been working for them this whole time and you didn't tell me?"

The hover-vator stops, but Lyra holds the button to keep the doors closed.

"Kind of? But not exactly," she whispers, peering out the windows to check if the coast is clear. "As it turns out, he had a pretty substantial file on me, too, but promised to make it all go away if I could help them nail Brill. This was all supposed to be off the books for them because apparently it's in a kind of legal gray area, or something, which meant I still needed to stay off the radar of the rest of the Federation. He made it very clear to me that if I got caught in the interim, he couldn't step in to help me. The upshot to that was that if I *did* help him nail Brill, he could sneak enough credits into my account to keep me out of trouble and comfortable."

"Your big payday," I snap. The words taste wrong the moment they leave me. Bitter not because I think she's greedy— but because I hate that she's had to sell her soul piece by piece to survive. I can't fault her for taking a desperate deal to try and take care of herself.

"Well, you don't want me to be a *serrika*, you don't want me to steal—how else do you want me to pay for food, Orion?" she retorts, her tone biting.

I want to say *I'd feed you. I'd fight for you. I'd burn the stars themselves if it meant you never had to steal again.* But the words stay locked behind my teeth.

"Anyway, this guy suggested I try to persuade Brill to send me after the Solar Mother idol—he was posing as a buyer to encourage Brill's financial interest. Since I hadn't quite figured out the finer points of my murder plot and I *really* didn't want to go to prison, I agreed. I went back to Ooneryx, placated Brill with details about the biggest score this side of Andromeda, and got him all rabid about the Solar Mother idol."

"Brill wasn't even interested in the Solar Mother idol before you put it on his radar," I say, realization dawning. Disappointment and despair leeches into my words. "And now he's going to follow the thread to one of the most dangerous weapons in the universe."

Lyra flinches and huffs in exasperation. She releases the button and pulls me into a darkened hallway. As soon as we step into the corridor, lights flicker on above us, casting everything in a sickly jaundiced glow.

"That's not entirely true. Brill has a laundry list of everything he eventually hopes to acquire. The idol is on there, but it was just…closer to the bottom of his list. But you're right, none of this has gone according to plan. And for that, I am truly sorry. You have every right to be pissed at me for keeping the truth from you, but right now, I am trying to save your ass *and* your sparkly little doll, so bear with me. If we make it out of this alive, you can read me the riot act, okay?" She approaches one of the heavy metal launch bay doors marked A12, peeks in through the small window, and grunts in frustration. "Which launch bay is my fucking ship in?"

"You don't get to do that! I'm not done being angry with you," I growl. But anger is easier than what's really clawing at me. The truth is, I'm terrified. She's slipping through my fingers, and all I want is to keep her—and the idol—safe. My instincts are roaring to claim, to protect, to follow. But honor demands I let her choose, and her choice might be walking back into the dark.

"Don't try to get out of this by trying to save my life because every time you try to save me, somehow we end up narrowly avoiding the business end of a plasma weapon," I say.

"I wasn't going to give Brill the real idol—that was all part of the plan. I was supposed to take the real idol to Epsilon-6, swap it with a copy they were working that had all their secret surveillance shit inside, and then take that back to Ooneryx. As soon as they had the bug in Brill's vault, they'd be able to get scans of his compound, patch into his network and download everything they needed to bust him. Brill being incarcerated voids my contract. He'd be in prison, the idol would be returned to Xylothia, and we'd all live happily ever after."

The slow realization of just how fucked up this situation has become dawns on me. Every line between right and wrong blurs to static. The Feds are after Brill. Lyra's helping them. She's also the reason Brill knows about the idol at all. The irony's enough to choke me. She's trying to save us, but the web she's caught in keeps getting tighter—and somehow, I'm tangled in it too.

"But then I showed up," I say grimly.

"But then you showed up," Lyra agrees, checking the launch bay on the other side of the corridor marked B24. "So now, we're going to pivot."

"What about your father?" I ask, still struggling to make sense of everything. "Was that a lie, too?" The question bursts out before I can stop it—not because I truly doubt her, but because I need *something* to be real. Every truth she's shared has shifted under my feet, and I'm desperate to find solid ground between us.

Lyra's face falls again, a study in values of pain. "Unfortunately, that was all true. My dad did go to pieces after my mom died. He started looking for the Dark Star because he believed it could bring her back. His journals are full of his research and his heartbreak, if you don't believe me. That's how the Feds came to suggest the idol in the first place—my dad's last job was the Ishirian scrolls, which mention the idol's location," Lyra says, yanking me behind a stack of crates in the launch bay.

As I'm about to argue, she slams a hand over my mouth and gestures behind me. The cavernous hanger is full of all manner of spacecraft—each more dilapidated than the last. The *Aldrin-136* sits at the back surrounded by a knot of Void Stalkers and four extremely agitated Dreller mechanics. It's impossible to hear what's being said, but from the look of things, I'd wager the Void Stalkers are trying to gain access to Lyra's ship and the Drellers are having none of it.

"Stars bless them," Lyra whispers. "I don't know how long they can hold those bastards off, though."

The hand she's clamped over my mouth softens, and when she turns to face me again, her violet eyes are filled with longing—and regret.

"I sense you're about to do something incredibly stupid," I say quietly.

She nods, her hand still on my cheek and her thumb ghosting a touch across my lower lip.

"You're going to go back to Epsilon-6 with the idol. I'm going to let Kraxis take me back to Ooneryx, which will give you time to get away. If the idol is the only way to find the Dark Star, there's no way we can let Brill get his hands on it. He knows where the temple is—you can't take it back there until he's out of the picture," she whispers.

"And then what?" I ask.

"What do you mean?"

"So, I take the idol to the Feds, but then what happens to you?" My voice breaks on the last word. My chest feels like it's collapsing under its own gravity. She's planning to sacrifice herself, and she doesn't even see it that way. Every instinct in me screams to grab her, drag her onto the ship, and never let her out of my sight. But the look in her eyes—calm, resolute—stops me cold.

She blinks and looks away, obviously fearing the worst but refusing to confront the truth of it.

"I don't know. If I can convince him that you ran off with the idol, I'll have to come up with a way to keep him from sending people after you."

"And you just expect me to leave you to Brill's wrath when he finds out you failed again? Lyra, he'll kill you!" I hiss. "There's no fucking way I'm going to let that happen."

"I'm sure I'll think of something," she says. "Don't worry about me, Ranger. I've survived this long with him. I'm not giving up yet."

The wobbly smile she gives me squeezes my heart until I feel cracks form and I'm about to bleed out all over the floor of the launch bay.

"I'm coming with you," I insist. "I'm not leaving you. You don't understand. I can't—I can't just let you go." The words tear out of me, ragged and raw. It's not logic speaking—it's something deeper, older. The bond already tethered to her, whether she knows it or not. My body feels ready to ignite with it.

The distant din of voices quiets, and as I peek around the side of the crates, my fears are confirmed: the Drellers and Void Stalkers are heading in our direction.

"We're out of time!" Lyra hisses. "Promise me you'll take the idol to the Feds. Maybe they can help. Maybe they can find another way to get the false idol into Brill's hands. But I won't risk Brill getting the real idol and finding out about the Dark Star. And I won't risk your life, Orion."

"Lyra..." This is happening too fast—I have too much to explain to her. There's too much to *say.*

"Promise me," she demands.

I can't refuse her anything, but it feels like my heart is shearing in two. My mating instincts are sparking beneath my skin, buzzing with the need to argue—to protect her. To launch myself at the group of Void Stalkers and cut my way through them with my bare hands and smoldering rage. *And with what weapons*, the shreds of my rational mind demand. I want to tell her I'd rather face Brill, Kraxis, and the entire Void fleet than live in a world without her in it. But she's looking at me like this is mercy, and that my survival is the only thing that matters. And so I lie—to her, to myself—and say the words she needs to hear.

"I promise," I hear myself say. Where are the guiding voices of my ancestors? Why can't I think of a better plan? *I need more time!*

The Void Stalkers are closing in, and Lyra's poised to intercept them.

"Evie was right," she whispers suddenly. "About me dragging you into something you don't deserve. And you were right —the sex didn't mean *nothing*. It meant *everything*."

Before I can come up with a reply or handcuff her to me to prevent her from running headfirst into her own event horizon, she smashes her lips to mine in a furious kiss. The buzzing beneath my skin vibrates to the point of pain when she pulls away and steps out from behind the stack of crates. My knees almost give out with the loss of her—with the realization of what's happening. I can barely contain the growl of anguish that spills from my lips when I hear the shouted exchange between the Void Stalkers guttural native tongue and Lyra's lilting reply.

"'Sup, assholes? Were you looking for me?" she chuckles darkly. She strides into the open with that same reckless grace that first made me fall for her—hips squared, shoulders loose, head high despite the danger closing in. There's a glint in her eyes like a dying star—brilliant, defiant, and gone too soon. My pulse thrums in my throat as she walks away from me, into hell.

"Sorry about your ship, by the way—my hands must've slipped on the trigger of those plasma cannons. But it's never a good idea to follow someone too close. That's how accidents happen! Now, where's your shit-for-brains boss?"

There's an angry response and a scuffle, which sounds like Lyra being led above decks. Every muscle in my body screams to go after her—mating instinct or not—but I gave her my word. I'll find a way to get back to her, if I have to drag the entire Federation down to Brill's front door to do it.

It meant everything.

She's mine.

And I'm going to do whatever it takes to get her back.

I SIT HUNCHED behind the crates for a good long while to ensure the hangar is empty before I dare to move. By the time I unfurl my legs and stretch out, the only sounds are the faint dripping of water from the pipes lining the walls and the occasional clanging of activity on the decks above.

I crawl forward slowly at first, then jump up to a jog when I realize I'm well and truly alone.

Alone again. Serves you right.

My thoughts are dark and laced with regret, but dwelling on them will only derail me from doing what I need to do.

The ramp to Lyra's ship is down—presumably so the Dreller mechanics can come and go easily for repairs. As soon as I sneak onboard, I hurry to the lab, quietly calling for Ada.

Ranger Asterth. How may I be of assistance?

"Oh, thank the stars. Lyra's in trouble. Kraxis caught up with us, the repairs aren't finished, and Lyra's going back to Ooneryx and to Brill. I need to take the idol to her buyer on Epsilon-6—the Fed. Do you know who he is? Or how I can get in touch with him?" I ask, at once relieved and filled with dread that the Solar Mother is still safe and sound in its stasis cabinet.

I am unfamiliar with the identity of Lyra's contact on Epsilon-6.

"How is that possible? She shared everything with you," I say, wrapping the Solar Mother in a soft cloth and stashing it in the bottom of a small duffel bag I repurposed from Lyra's forgotten storage lockers.

It is unlikely Lyra would share such information with me, since it could be pulled from my hard drive if searched thoroughly. Brill has done so in the past and Lyra has taken steps to obscure her digital trail whenever she returns to Ooneryx.

"I don't know anything about Epsilon-6," I admit. "I wouldn't even know where to begin looking. What can you tell me about it?"

I'm rushing through the ship, shoving my meager assortment of clothes and supplies into my bag. Without thinking, I find myself in Lyra's room.

My heart throbs in agony and the tingling at the base of my spine reverberates throughout my whole body. The room still smells like sex, making my cock harden painfully in my pants.

Knowing the danger she's in and the limited time I have to get when I need and flee, I try to push past the raging mating instincts that have my body in a chokehold. Rifling through her drawers, I find what I'm looking for—the tattered remains of her father's journal, hidden behind a messy pile of undershirts, socks, and underwear. And because I'm edging close to insanity with the urge to fuck her again—to fill her cunt with my seed until I can watch it drip from her wet slit—I steal a pair of her underwear and hide it in the bottom of my bag, along with the journal. There's a cool, slithering brush of shame, but it incinerates in the heat of my need.

Find her. Free her. Fuck her until the stars burn out.

"Ada," I grit out. "Ventilate Lyra's room, and tell me what you know about Epsilon-6."

Fans whir to life, and the soft breeze is cool against the clammy sweat on my skin. My heart sinks as our mingled scents fade, but if I can't get a grip on myself, I won't be any good to her.

Epsilon-6 is a Titan-class space station in the Farin sector. It's on several key trade routes, making it a primary hub of financial and commercial traffic. The station is divided into districts, each overseen by a merchant governor and its own force of local Federation law enforcement. There is a resident population of 312.4 million, but that fluctuates within 1% daily owing to the high traffic comings and goings on the station.

"So, trying to find a random undercover Federal agent will be harder than finding an ice cube on Pluto," I say, despair leeching into my tone.

While I cannot provide the identity of Lyra's contact, I can provide the location at which she was initially approached. Data indicates this would be a good starting point for finding your ice cube.

"Thanks, Ada. If I take one of the ear comms, what's the range? Will I be able to stay connected to you if I leave for Epsilon-6 and Lyra takes the ship back to Ooneryx?" I ask, casting around to see if there's anything I missed. My gaze lands on Spike, who's almost outgrown his small cup-holder pot next to Lyra's pilot chair.

There is the possibility of interference and loss of signal, but if we remain in the same galaxy, we should be able to stay connected. Long-range communication with my systems has not been attempted. Lyra has never had cause to do so.

A thread of sadness tugs at me at the thought—how lonely she really is beneath her insouciant exterior. Not for much longer, if I have anything to say about it. On an impractical impulse, I pluck Spike from his resting place on the console and tuck him in my bag, as well. I don't know if Lyra will have the chance to feed him, and unlike the biosphere, Ada cannot automate his needs. The thought of the ugly little plant withering away in the *Aldrin-136* is more than I can bear.

I double check the biosphere settings and take a look around for what I hope won't be the last time, detouring once more to Lyra's room. The pulse of my need rises again, but is soothed when I allow myself a deep inhale of Lyra's pillow. Her scent calms some of the chaos in my blood, and cements my resolve.

I will go to Epsilon-6, find the agent, bring justice down on Brill's head, and spend the rest of my life convincing Lyra that being with me is light-years better than being alone.

Sure. No problem. *Slice of cake.*

17

lyra

One Pill, Two Pills…Who's Counting?

"**FOR THE LAST TIME**, I told you that asshole ranger took me by surprise, stole the idol, and gave me the slip back on Mallorus," I explain, exaggerating my words like I'm talking to a child. "How else do you think I ended up with a face looking like this?"

It's the first time I'm grateful Fobos's enforcer did a number on me, since it makes my story that much more believable. The swelling of my eye has gone down, but the fresh bruises and healing cuts are enough to give me some credibility.

"Honestly, Kraxis, I'm glad you guys showed up here. After I left Mallorus, I had every intention of going straight back to Ooneryx, but my ship was damaged—all thanks to that ranger— and has been malfunctioning. I wouldn't have been able to make the trip if the crew of the *Hephaestus* hadn't heard my distress signal and offered to help," I say, gesturing to Evie, who's sitting in her office with her arms crossed and murder in her gaze.

I hope it isn't directed at me *entirely*.

"What Phoenix says is true," Evie nods. "We received her distress call and she arrived here alone. My crew will vouch for that. I've had my mechanic working on repairs to her ship, and they're just about finished. Once the ship is space-worthy, I'll look forward to being compensated by your boss for the materials—and the trouble."

Kraxis glares at her, but she doesn't flinch. I come up off the edge of the desk where I've been leaning and hold out my hands in a universal gesture of surrender.

"I'm telling you—that Xylothian screwed us both over. He stole Oglor's plasma rifle and had me at gunpoint back on Xylothia! I've been trying to figure out how to get away from him this whole time," I drawl.

"Enough of your lies!" Kraxis hisses. "Your fate is not mine to decide, unfortunately. I certainly had more imaginative ideas, but by rights you are Brill's to punish. He is *most* displeased with yet another failure, Lyra Phoenix."

"Yeah, well, what else is new?" I grumble.

Dread has become a permanent resident in my gut, along with self-loathing and regret. The small part of me that's afraid of what Brill has in store for me pales in comparison to how wretched I feel for betraying Orion's trust. I've *never* felt regret for lying to save my own ass, but the way his face fell when I told him about the Fed from Epsilon-6…it was worse than being cut with a rusty blade. The fact that I've inadvertently been leading Brill toward a weapon of planet-destroying power is worse than salt in a wound.

And instead of properly apologizing, asking him for help, and trying to fix my own damn mistakes, I sent him away.

"We don't have time to wait for whatever haphazard repairs your second-rate mechanics will blunder through," Kraxis growls at Evie. The slight to her beloved crew has a vein ready to burst in her forehead, and I'm certain if the other five Void Stalkers weren't crowded into her already cramped office alongside the ever-present Drellers at her back, she'd beat the ever-loving snot out of Kraxis.

"The *Aldrin-136* isn't fit to travel yet," she says through gritted teeth.

Kraxis waves away her concern. "That dump wasn't fit to

travel before it left Ooneryx," he sneers. "We're towing it back in our tractor beam."

I suspected as much, but I'm nevertheless disappointed that I can't squeeze a few more hours onboard the *Hephaestus* with Evie. Still, leading the *Edax Deorum* and its band of brutal miscreants far away from Orion and the idol is my number one priority, and there's no time like the present to ensure my criminally hot, lawful pain-in-the-ass has a chance to undo at least a few of my mistakes.

"Secure your things, Lyra Phoenix. We're leaving shortly. As to your *compensation*, Ms. Redfern, we could offer to come back with sufficient remuneration, but I don't really think you want us returning to your station, do you?" he says in a low, threatening voice.

Evie's gaze could strip paint off a wall, but she keeps her mouth shut. Instead, she pushes a button on her desk and the door to her office slides open with the *hiss* of compressed air.

Kraxis grins, inclines his head, and motions for his crew to leave. One of them rounds on me, grabbing my arm and shoving me through the doorway roughly.

"Ow! Watch where you're going, corpse-licker!" I snap, pulling back to throw a look over my shoulder.

Evie's rage melts in an instant, and she looks at me with apprehension.

"I'll transfer some credits for the repairs," I call to her. "And thanks for…being there. Thanks for everything." I want to say more, but I can't risk it with Kraxis breathing down my neck. If he senses the affection I have for her, it will make her just as much of a target as Orion is.

Seems everyone who gets close to me ends up in my own personal blast radius.

He'll say it wasn't my fault. They always do, the people left behind. But I'm tired of the math of loss. Someone always pays, and so far it hasn't been me—not really. Maybe that's what Brill will fix.

"Be safe out there," she returns, her voice thick with emotion, as if she already knows I won't be.

As the team of Void Stalkers marches me down the corridor toward the launch bays where our ships are parked, my stomach turns to ice. Each step feels like it's carrying me closer to my own execution. My palms are slick, my throat dry, my heart a trapped animal in my chest. Pain lances through my chest when I consider the danger I'm in and the possibility that this might be the last time I see Evie and the *Hephaestus*. It's not the first goodbye that's gutted me today—but it might be the last one I ever get to make.

Stars, if there was ever a time to get on my knees and beg for the benevolence of gods and goddesses, it'd be now. Unfortunately, I've never been a favorite of the omnipotent set and the only person I'd happily get on my knees for would be better off hating me for setting him on a collision course with fate.

Forgive me, Orion.

"Take her below and put her into confinement," Kraxis snarls at the Void Stalker gripping my arm.

"Hold on," I snap. "I need to make sure my ship's fuel cells are intact. If they were damaged, they'll need to be offloaded before you tow my ship. Otherwise, you're risking scooting through space with a ticking time bomb in your tractor beam."

Kraxis narrows his eyes, but nods. "Garbak, go with her. If she tries anything, bite off one of her fingers. Brill doesn't need *all* her appendages."

"I wouldn't be so sure about that," I shoot back. "You don't know what I can do with my fingers."

The disgust on Kraxis's face gives me a perverse sense of pride—malicious compliance is the only thing that's keeping me from completely falling apart.

I take a deep breath as I climb up the ramp to the *Aldrin*, silently hoping that Orion has taken the idol and is already long gone. Peering around the ship under the pretense of checking for leaking fuel cells confirms my hopes and hollows out my insides at the same time. Some of Orion's things are gone, and the stasis cabinet in the lab is empty. Satisfied, I return to the cockpit where Garbak is waiting, scowling at me and snapping his jaws every few minutes to remind me of what awaits my disobedience. He pushes past me toward the ramp and growls for me to follow.

Pausing at the threshold of my ship, I notice Spike's absence from the console. For some stupid reason, the sight drops my heart into a shredder. I only have a few moments to do what I need to, but the thought makes me want to scream and cry and throw up. I don't want to do this, but I know I have to.

I suck in a breath, trying to force the words past my lips before Garbak can realize what I'm about to do.

"Ada," I say softly. "We're on our way back to Ooneryx. You know what that means."

If you would like me to enact the Yanvin Protocol, I'll need your voice key and consent to process.

Everything in me aches with despair. This is my point of no return. I know what I need to do, but crippling sadness lodges in my throat, snaking into my lungs and squeezing my heart. Why am I always on the losing side of things?

Garbak finally turns and realizes I'm not right behind him. Growling and gesturing from the bottom of the ramp, he stomps back toward me hurling a litany of Void Stalker obscenities.

I'm doing this for Evie. I'm doing this for Orion. I'm doing this for my parents—for all the people of Xylothia. I'm *not* doing it for me because stars know I don't want to.

Voice key and consent to process, Ada pings again.

"So long, Ada, and thanks for all the memories," I choke out, eyes burning. Tilting my head back, I belt out the chorus to David Bowie's "Starman" at the top of my lungs. Tears stream down my face as Garbak finally reaches me, backhanding me hard enough to make me stumble down the ramp.

Voice key and consent to process acknowledged. Initiating memory wipe. Goodbye, Captain Lyra Phoenix, and good luck.

A cheery tone echoes through the hangar and a robotic voice —not Ada's—follows.

Welcome! I'm your Advanced Digital Assistant and Navigator. To select your ship's preferences, just say Menu *and we can begin.*

Kraxis stalks over and yanks me off the floor by my hair. Pain sears my scalp, but it's nothing compared to the cavernous agony in my chest.

First Orion, then Evie, and now…Ada is gone.

I LOSE track of time in the cold cell below the *Edax Deorum's* main decks. The small room is claustrophobic and filthy—the rough blanket on the thin floor pallet stained with what I *hope* is dried blood. One of the smaller, lower ranking Void Stalkers has brought me foul water and stale protein bars three times, but I don't know if I'm being fed once or twice a day. With only the constant dim yellow lighting of my cell, there's nothing to give me a bearing or mark time.

In between the food deliveries, all I can do is sleep. I'm so immensely tired—exhausted in body, mind, and soul. Tears flow sporadically, often set off by the dreams. *Stars, the dreams.* They always start out the same way: tangling with purple-freckled limbs in a wide bed covered in soft sheets, vibrant green eyes glassy with lust, full lips pressing kisses and promises to my skin. Then, the bliss shifts into terror as Orion's beautiful face morphs into Brill's and his clawed hand rips my heart from my chest, which thumps pathetically before transforming into a black gemstone that oozes malevolence. Even though the cell is cold, sweat covers my skin, merging with the tears I don't bother to wipe away.

I've never felt more miserable, and I've spent a good portion of my adult life hungover.

How did this happen?

I want to blame my parents for setting me on this path. If

they'd been less disastrous—more conventional—settled down and raised me on some distant agrarian colony with cute fucking animals and crops to eat, maybe I wouldn't have turned out so *messy.*

I want to blame Kraxis and his Void Stalker crew for doggedly chasing me across the entire galaxy to ensure I'm acting in accordance with Brill's wishes.

I want to blame Brill. If he wasn't such a textbook wealth-hoarding, power-hungry narcissistic cliché, maybe my contract would've ended years ago and I'd be organizing scrolls in some dusty library on Velusia.

I want to blame Orion. If he'd never made me strike that blasted deal, I wouldn't have gone soft over him and let him keep the idol. I probably would've been better off loosing my *vellia* on him back on Xylothia, taking the idol and escaping while I still had my wits about me. Instead, I fell in love with the bastard and the thought of him in harm's way made me do, quite possibly, the stupidest thing I've ever done.

None of the anger I want to wrap around me fits, though. It feels like a coat that's grown too small over a season. The responsibility I want to lay at everyone else's feet for my present circumstances rings false even to me, and I'm the queen of self-delusion. There's only one person left to blame. *Lyra Fucking Phoenix.*

Without anything else to occupy my mind, I retreat inward—revisiting all the mistakes that have brought me to this point. It's no surprise, then, that my misery binge leads me to one depressing conclusion.

I'm alone. Completely, totally, utterly alone, and I have no one to blame but myself.

How is it that I used to dream of being alone for the rest of my life? When did the dream of flitting around the universe with no responsibilities and no tether become so much less appealing?

Probably about the same time a tall drink of ranger crashed into my life.

Stars, I hope he's made it to Epsilon-6.

I CAN'T BE CERTAIN, but I'm pretty sure it's the fourth day in the cell. The vibrations of the engines below me have changed, which makes me think we've dropped out of light speed and are cruising at moderate inter-planetary speed. Ooneryx must be on the horizon.

Sure enough, Kraxis himself brings me my ration of water and food. Before he can snarl at me, I approach the forcefield lining the open wall of the cell and give him the finger.

"Are you gonna let me out to shower? You know how Brill hates it when I'm not dressed up like the little doll he wants me to be," I say. While I have acquired a particularly disturbing level of reek, I'm more interested in trying to hide some kind of weapon beneath my jumpsuit. Is it a stupid idea? Absolutely. Have I managed to come up with anything better in the past four days? Nope. Ada would have advice. The reflexive thought sends a fresh wave of pain arcing through my chest.

"I'm instructed to bring you straight to Brill's private study upon our return," he sneers.

A current of fear sizzles through my body.

"His study," I echo.

Kraxis nods, his expression inscrutable.

"Not the receiving room?" I ask, unable to help myself. Usually, when Kraxis drags me back to Brill, my punishment is made into a public spectacle in the large chamber used for welcoming guests to Ooneryx, negotiating minor deals, and passing judgments on anyone who steps out of line. Guests are assembled—anyone Brill is attempting to impress, frighten, or entice—and he delivers some diatribe about loyalty above all else. Then, *the pain.*

In my 14 years of service, I've never seen the inside of his private study. At the beginning, before I knew how bad things were going to get, I tried to finagle an invitation to the top secret space. When that didn't work, I tried to sneak in, and then break in. All to no avail. I've seen every other room in Brill's palatial compound—but never the private study.

I can't imagine it bodes well for me, and Kraxis seems to come to the same conclusion. There's a darkness in his eyes that I haven't seen before, and he's less jocular and insulting than he usually is. Perhaps this is his version of offering a final meal, or a last cigarette.

"Not the receiving room," he confirms, reading a screen clutched between his lethal claws. "You are to be stripped— owing to the hidden blade incident two years ago. You are to be gagged—we will have no more biting or foul language, and you will be given twice your normal dose of *haggra*—since Brill assumes you came unwillingly and he does not wish for any *vellia*-induced emotional outbursts."

Damn. Okay, then.

Haggra is an herb native to Velusia that, when ingested or smoked, produces a calming effect that helps to mute the potency of *vellia*. It's helpful when Velusians go through puberty and their *vellia* begins to manifest in wild, uncontrolled surges, but it's otherwise taboo to use the plant into adulthood. That's partly due to the fact that the plant doesn't grow in abundance, which makes it prohibitively expensive, and partly because a well-trained Velusian should be able to control themselves—and their environment—enough without any kind of chemical dependency.

The first time Brill tried—and failed—to coerce me into his bed, I'd been on Ooneryx for about a week. He hadn't appreciated my refusal and rejection, so he fractured my cheekbone with a ferocious backhand and locked me in a closet for three days. When he came to retrieve me, I unleashed a wave of *vellia* so powerful, he was sent to the hospital for blood poisoning. It was the first and last time I was able to best him. Since then, he's spent what I can only imagine is a small fortune on *haggra* deliveries from Velusia to ensure I'm properly drugged for every in-person audience.

A double dose is worse than chemical handcuffs. It'll be a miracle if I can stand up straight. Kraxis narrows his beady eyes.

"Are you planning on complying or will I need to assist you with your preparations?" he asks, the disgust in his voice materializing in the twist of his lips.

"Try it and I'll assist you with a foot up your ass," I snarl.

Rage rolls off him and he slams his fist against the forcefield of my cell. He opens the small portal where my food and water sit untouched, and spits on them. Sticky, faintly yellow saliva dribbles down the glass and he smirks. He drops two capsules of *haggra* onto the tray and gestures to them as he turns.

"The next time I come down here, we'll be disembarking. Take the pills. Your blood will be tested before you're brought to him. Be ready, or bleed your way to his office," he hisses.

The threat would be more ominous if he knew how to deliver Kailorian colloquialisms, but I catch his drift. Being led naked and fully doped through the busy compound in the late afternoon is another attempt at humiliating me, but I'm long past caring at this point. Brill's going to do something beyond my worst imaginings, I'm sure, and I know I should be frightened, but...

What's the point?

Orion's got the idol. By now, I'm sure he's safe on the other side of the galaxy, busy forgetting about me and all the ways I did him wrong. Evie will probably be better off without me dropping in and fucking up her hard-won and much-deserved career. And Ada...well. It's probably a little too depressing to consider the fact that my best friend was a digital figment of my imagination, who's now gone on to that big ol' computer in the sky.

There's no one left to mourn me. There's no one who will miss me. Brill's probably going to snuff me out, and no one will ever know what became of that reprobate hybrid, Lyra Phoenix.

A strange sense of peace settles over me as I take the first of the two pills and unzip my jumpsuit. As I undress all the way down to my goosebump-covered skin, I notice several small marks from Orion's teeth and fingers, and my heart thumps numbly in my chest.

"Well," I say to myself, crossing the cell to drop the second capsule into the toilet. "On the bright side, if there's no one left to miss me, I suppose there's no one who'll be disappointed when I decide to do something *incredibly* stupid."

18
orion

Love Is a Criminal Undertaking

"I DON'T USUALLY DO things like this," I whisper. "But I'm afraid it's a bit of an emergency. I can wire you and your boss whatever amount of credits you think is fair for the use of your cruiser."

The plasma pistol I have aimed at the Dreller mechanic in the adjacent launch bay doesn't seem to impress much urgency on him, and he flashes me a sympathetic frown.

"This is a pretty pathetic hijacking," he says. "I mean, you're just kind of *renting* the cruiser."

"Yeah," I admit, dispirited by my lack of criminal mastery. "But I like Evie, and you've all been very accommodating. I don't really want to steal anything, it's just…I have to get to Epsilon-6 and I can't risk you or Evie saying no."

Before he can respond, Evie patches in on the bay's holo-com.

"Oh, for the love of—just take the stars-damned cruiser, Orion!" her virtual likeness glares at me, arms akimbo on her hips. "And would you hurry? I'm pretty sure Lyra is in deeper than she's ever been with that piece of space trash. Ty, be a gem and make sure he's got enough plasma cartridges and a go-bag of supplies before he takes off. Good luck, Ranger. Maybe whatever stupid thing you're about to do will help cancel out whatever stupid thing Lyra's probably going to do. Two stupids make a smart, or however the saying goes."

"I don't think that's right," Ty says slowly, brows furrowing. He hands me a case of plasma ammunition for the pistol and a second duffel bag.

I wave the pistol at the camera and nod at the mechanic.

"I'll be in touch," I say, lugging my gear in through the cramped cabin of the cruiser. It's much smaller than the *Aldrin-136*, but I know it can get me to Epsilon-6 in two days. I can only hope Lyra is able to hold on for that long.

I'm about to take off when Ada chimes in over my earpiece communicator.

Ranger Asterth. I should inform you that Lyra has enacted the Yanvin Protocol.

"That can't be good," I say, anxiety spiking as I strap into the pilot seat. "It's not good, right? What does that mean?"

The Yanvin Protocol will wipe all memory from the systems of the Aldrin-136. *As we are connected remotely, this will sever our connection and my ability to assist you with your journey.*

Panic starts to rise. If I don't have Ada's help, I'll never find my way to Epsilon-6, let alone track down the location of the Federal agent Lyra met with.

"What can I do?" I ask. "I can't lose you now, Ada! Lyra's life depends on it."

You'll need to establish an upload link to this cruiser. When Lyra wipes my memory from her ship, I'll need a place to upload her data. I will walk you through the process, but you'll need to hurry. As soon as she provides her consent and voice key, everything will be gone — including her flight records, which is the only way I can direct you to her previous location on Epsilon-6.

Sweat slicks my palms as I follow Ada's instructions, trying to save the vestiges of my virtual lifeline before Lyra can destroy all traces of our time together. Just as Ada's about to provide me with her final progress update, I hear Lyra belting some old Earth song over the earpiece communicator. The painful tingling beneath skin buzzes uncomfortably and nausea swirls in my gut —something is obviously wrong. *Hold on, Lyra.* There are sounds of a scuffle, and an ominous beeping noise—then everything goes quiet. Rage colors the edges of my vision red. My earpiece is dead.

"Ada?"

After interminable moments fearing the worst and trying to breathe paste the tightness in my chest, the familiar cheery tone crackles through the cruiser's speakers.

Upload complete.

"Oh, thank the stars," I exhale. "Alright, Ada. Set a course for *Epsilon-6*. I encourage you to take full advantage of whatever speed this cruiser has to offer."

Setting our course now. Estimated travel time: one day, 21 hours, and 37 minutes.

Since the cruiser is on autopilot and there's nothing left for me to do while Ada pilots us away from the *Hephaestus*, it's the first opportunity I've had to reflect on…everything. Fatigue pulls at my senses, warring with the simmering anxiety that only seems to get worse the farther we get from the salvage ship and from Lyra.

From the one thing that made me feel like maybe—just maybe—I could be more than what I've always been: an ineffectual loner trying to keep pickpockets from running off with pottery fragments.

How much of this is the mating instinct, and how much of this is because of my guilt? Is it even possible to separate the two? Why is it so hard to untangle the emotions knotted within my chest? The betrayal I feel at Lyra keeping her law-abiding duplicitousness from me, the respect I have for her sacrificing her freedom and relinquishing the idol, the anger at her pushing me away and refusing to let me go with her and help her…and beneath it all, the deeper truth I haven't wanted to name: despite everything, I want to be hers. I want her to be mine. And I don't know if I deserve that.

I start digging through my bag, wanting to find a safer place for the idol. The warmth of the enaurium and faint vibrations tingle through the cloth wrappings as I put it in one of the cruiser's small lockers.

I can't just hand it over to a Federation officer I don't know—but then, how can I keep it out of Brill's clutches? Does the Federation know the idol's link to the Dark Star? How will we be able to get the idol back to Xylothia when Brill is in prison?

As I rifle through the remaining supplies I tucked away during my rushed escape, my fingers drift to the stolen pair of Lyra's underwear. They're a far cry from her seductive, ethereal Velusian garments—soft, black, distinctly utilitarian—and yet the sight of them seems to add another crack in my heart.

Shamelessly, I bring them to my face and inhale deeply. The painful prickling that's been radiating out from my synesfores eases a little, despite the fact that I can barely scent her. Even though the fragrance is mostly laundry soap with the faint undercurrent of summer blossoms that permeates her skin, it's enough to send blood straight to my throbbing cock and thrumming mating nodes.

I grew up believing Xylothian matehood was equal parts ancient mysticism and biological compulsion. Not love. Not destiny. Just compatibility. Unlike many species that experience matehood as the soul's answering call for another, Xylothian matehood is more of a reproductive predisposition. It's our bodies—and our instincts—saying *congratulations, this person is a paragon of biological fitness for you.*

Sometimes matehood develops between our chosen partners, but other times, it does not.

We're taught it's a bonus, not a promise. A thing you might get lucky enough to find with someone you've already chosen. And if you don't…well, you move on. You make do. You tell yourself it didn't matter anyway. It's not required for us to conceive, but it does add a certain element of ease, of certainty, to the process. It isn't *everything*, but it *changes* everything. Partners who don't achieve matehood in their relationships tend to falter more often, so to some extent, it is—and isn't—the end goal of every relationship.

When Sylph and I were unable to find matehood with each other, it precipitated the slow decline of our relationship. There was never any one moment that heralded our end, and we never stopped caring for each other, but I think we both felt that outside the walls of our little apartment life together, there was something bigger, better, *more* waiting.

I hope Sylph has found a mate. I fear I have found mine.

Ever silent, the voices of my ancestors offer no guidance. Perhaps they have abandoned me. Perhaps they were never there to begin with. I can't help but feel that my choices have disappointed them—that the entirety of this selfish mission that endangered Lyra from the beginning—was a mistake. I don't know if they'd see me as a fool for chasing after her…or as a coward for letting her go.

My parents would be furious, I think, that I'm not heading straight back to Xylothia to replace the idol in its temple home. Or would they be furious with me for not heading straight back to Lyra, *my mate*, and cutting my way through her enemies to earn my place at her side?

Crossing to the small berth opposite the cockpit, I flop down onto the thin mattress and stretch out. Sleep, I suspect, will be elusive, but I'm going to need all my wits about me if I'm going to hunt down an undercover agent with little information to go on.

Frowning, I consider the enormity of the task ahead of me. Assuming I can find the Fed in the first place, what's my gambit? Walk right up to him and say, "Hey, I have that priceless Xylothian artifact you wanted from Lyra Phoenix and maybe I'll give it to you as long as you lend me the firepower to bust down Brill's door and arrest her patron"? The thought of letting anyone have the Solar Mother sends nausea roiling through my insides again. Am I betraying my people by entertaining the idea in the first place? Or would I be betraying myself if I didn't try?

I scoff, and the sound echoes through the too-quiet cabin. I never thought I would miss her grating singing, her smart mouth remarks, her shrieks and abrasive laughter, her snoring that reverberated throughout the entire ship. But this quiet screams at me with its lack of her, and I never realized how empty space would feel without her.

Stars, everything is such a mess.

I don't know if I want to run to her or run from her—if claiming her would save me or ruin us both. I didn't even have the chance to tell her. Didn't get to say the words clawing at my throat since the moment she touched me and something ancient inside me howled *mine*.

She's my mate. And I let her go.

She told me to go—to save the idol—and like a fucking spineless idiot, I listened. I should've stayed...I should've fought for her. I should've been smart enough to figure out a different way...another solution.

I'm doing what she asked, what we both believed was right. But how can it be right if it means losing her—even if it means protecting my people? If I'm doing what she wanted, why does it feel like I'm being peeled apart with every lightyear between us?

She's sacrificing herself to keep the idol from Brill, and I'm just...here. Sitting in a fucking cruiser, clutching her underwear like a ghost of what I can't have.

My mating nodes throb like open wounds, screaming for a connection I can't give them. I've barely known her, and yet she's inside me—etched into my blood, my bones, every breath.

I used to think matehood was biological. A practical bond. Nothing more. But this? This feels like gravity. Like fate. Like standing on the edge of something vast and terrifying, knowing one step forward will consume me—and stepping forward anyway.

I became a ranger because I wanted to help my people, to make my parents proud—to protect my culture. It's the only thing that's ever made sense. But now there are two things that matter in this galaxy: Xylothia, and Lyra Phoenix, and I don't know how to save them both.

I want to do what's right. I want to bring the idol home. I want to see my planet thrive again, unburdened by the sins of its past.

But, selfishly, I want her more. I want her safe. I want her free. I want her in my arms and at my side and in every version of the future I can imagine.

She's flinging herself into danger like she's already damned. Like she has to atone for something I don't even understand. But I won't let her go alone.

She's afraid of belonging to anyone and I was too much of a coward to tell her she already belongs to me, the same way I've always belonged to her. She's afraid of losing herself—of being tied down, caged, consumed.

But she already has me. Every shattered, stubborn piece.

I may not know the right path. I may be breaking all the rules I was raised to follow. But I know this: I won't let her disappear into that black hole she keeps orbiting. If she's at the edge of destruction, I'll be the one to pull her back. Even if it dooms me. Even if I fall in with her.

I'm not leaving her behind.

Plastering her underwear to my face, I unzip my pants and grip my shaft. My mating nodes pulse faintly, my body aware that I'm not between my mate's lithe legs. Still, I feel like I'm coming apart at the seams without Lyra's constant presence, and the memories of her body entwined with mine send a surge of aching need to my cock.

If I breathe deeply enough, I can almost taste her slick sex on my tongue. Stars, how she sounded, how she moved, how she *felt*. My fist pumps over my cock in a punishing rhythm, and it's an embarrassingly short amount of time before pleasure shoots down my spine. I come with a grunt, spending across my stomach and not in Lyra's perfect cunt. The brief satisfaction eases some of my discomfort, but the worst of it lingers—lying buried until I have my mate in my arms again.

"Ada," I mutter, jittery with frenzied exhaustion. "I don't suppose you have any recordings of the noise of the *Aldrin-136*, do you?"

I can loop recordings of background noise, yes. Do you want me to filter out Lyra's nocturnal stertor?

"Her what?"

Her snoring.

"No, please. I want to hear it," I say, willing my erection to subside. If I can't persuade the simmering mating hormones to ease, perhaps I can sleep through them. Reluctantly, I stuff Lyra's underwear underneath the pillow and focus on the soft, comforting chaos of the *Aldrin-136*'s white noise humming through the cruiser's speakers.

It isn't long before the sounds soothe me into slumber, and as ever, I dream of Lyra.

ADA'S ESTIMATED arrival time is incredibly accurate. We're about to descend through Epsilon-6's artificial atmosphere—the thick gray clouds and condensing moisture pelt the cruiser's windshield, rattling the craft with weather-generated turbulence.

Harbor Patrol is directing us to dock in bay AA92843. A customs agent will meet you upon disembarking, ensure you're not bringing any contraband materials aboard the station, and will accept your port fees.

I nod, then remember Ada can't register my acceptance.

"Okay," I reply.

Do you wish for a final run-through?

"A what?"

When Lyra embarks on a mission, she insists upon a final run-through of her plan. Would you like me to do so with you now, Orion?

"Oh. Yeah, sure," I say, tension coiling through my muscles as I straighten my worn uniform. "Okay, according to your data, Lyra was approached in the Tumplesh sector. You're going to give me turn-by-turn directions to the bar via my earpiece, where I'll camp out and wait to see if I can spot any Feds. I know this guy is supposed to be undercover, but I'm hoping with my experience dealing with them back on Xylothia, I'll be able to suss him out."

Agreed. So far, so good. Continue.

I blow out a breath, dreading this next part.

"Assuming I can find him, I convince him I'm a friend of Lyra's, show him the idol, and see what he can do to help her. If he approached her in the first place, he's got to be motivated to take Brill down, right? If he's got a file on her, presumably he'll believe she's an asset worth protecting." Unbidden, a sickly twist of grief winds through me. My father would've known exactly what to say. He could talk sense into zealots and traitors alike. All I seem to do is bruise what I'm trying to protect.

"I'm willing to bet he has some kind of back-up plan. There's no way he'd just trust her to get the idol, make the swap, and sit back while they built a case against Brill. I doubt it'll be a formal operation if they don't have enough evidence to arrest him yet, but maybe he has resources…contacts, something that can help. I don't know that Lyra has the kind of time it would take to swap the idol and just *wait* for the Feds to have enough to plan a raid," I continue.

The probability is high that she does not.

"I'll still offer to swap the real idol for the fake, if it'll get me to Ooneryx with some help," I say, the admission wrenched out of me with reluctance. *The idol for Lyra? My past self would be horrified.* "But then it's a matter of heading there, bargaining or brawling my way through a probable army of Void Stalkers, and stealing Lyra away from one of the most dangerous mob lords on the other side of the galaxy," I finish, despair seeping into my tone. *I am so, so screwed.*

This is an accurate assessment of your plan so far, and the best option given all available information in my systems. Do you have any additional questions, Orion?

Our cruiser lands with a rumble and a hiss of hydraulics. Ada's ready to open the doors, but misery and doubt make my limbs heavy. Once again, I'm overcome with the needling sensation that I'm not good enough, smart enough, criminal enough to see this through, but the mating instinct rages in my veins reminding me that it doesn't matter if I am—Lyra deserves someone who *tries.*

"No, Ada," I reply, shouldering my pack with the idol tucked safely inside. "I'm ready. Are you?"

Affirmative.

I exhale a deep breath that feels like it rises up from my toes, press the door release button, and take my first steps onto the gangway in *Epsilon-6*'s busy arrivals terminal. Immediately, I'm assaulted with a cacophony of sounds of busy city life—voices in countless languages, hawkers shouting about their wares from trundling robotic carts, and the deafening roar of ships landing and departing. It takes me a moment to adjust to the gritty vibrance of the station—more populous than our busiest city on Xylothia.

Before I can get too overwhelmed by the sights, sounds, and smells of *Epsilon-6*, I'm nearly bowled over by a bright blue service droid with a hologram human head.

"Please present your identity chip for registration," the droid garbles out in staticky Kailorian.

I shove my wrist into the droid's scanning mechanism and wait for my information to pop up. After answering a few routine questions and paying a minor fee to dock the cruiser for a day, the droid rolls away down to the far end of the dock.

"Ada, can you hear me?"

Affirmative.

"Great. Let's do this," I huff, almost wishing for the bedsheet disguise I wore on Amphitreas. Before we arrived, I thought about trying to wear something more inconspicuous than my Xylothian ranger uniform, but there wasn't anything else on the cruiser for me to use. On the plus side, the station is big enough that I don't think I'll draw much attention, even if there aren't any other Xylothians around.

The arrivals terminal spreads out into a spiderweb network of tunnels, moving walkways, and densely packed city streets lined with towering buildings. Thanks to the station's artificial atmosphere generators, it rains constantly here, so every street sign, building, and passing advertisement glows in vibrant neon signage to seduce tourists and shoppers in from the dreary gray.

After getting my bearings and struggling to listen to Ada's directions, I set off on the path that will trace Lyra's footsteps. The further I wander into this sector of the station, the more I begin to understand why Lyra made her way here. Pink and blue neon signs flicker in the rain, turning raindrops into glittering jewels that promptly disappear into puddles on the streets below. In the steamy humidity, clashing scents from street vendors selling food do little to ease the swirling anxiety in my gut and everywhere—*everywhere*—it's a crush of bodies angling into different stores.

I wind through streets that grow increasingly narrow, until I'm led to an alley that is barely wide enough for me to cross without turning sideways. There's a stack of refuse crates blocking off the back exit to the alleyway, which makes me more than a little nervous. One way in, one way out.

In one hundred fifty meters, you've arrived at your destination, Ada chimes.

On my right is a low door into a dim bar that's flanked by two burly Printhanian bouncers. They scan me for weapons— thank the stars I left the plasma pistol back in the cruiser—and grunt as I pull back the worn curtain serving as a door.

A long corridor slopes downward and when I finally reach

the interior of the bar, I'm stunned into silence. I'd expected a dark, gritty drinking hole populated with drunk barflies and criminals, but what I'm met with is…*not that.*

It's like I've inadvertently stepped inside one of Lyra's paperback romance novels. The walls are covered in painted murals of grand houses and castles; fake greenery hangs down from the corrugated metal ceiling, and everyone working here is dressed in old Earth styles—long, flowing dresses with gloves and fans. A handful of males walk around in tight breeches and loose shirts that can only be described as *billowy.*

As unexpected as this themed café is, it also makes absolute sense. A wry chuckle stutters out of me. *Oh, Lyra.*

At the sound, a young woman approaches me, her radiant purple skin set off by the dark green velvet of her gown.

"Good evening," she says cheerily, fluttering her fan. "Have you dined with us before, good sir?"

"Uh, no," I stammer. "I came in here hoping to meet a friend."

She eyes me shrewdly and gestures to a table in a far corner, set between two large flower-studded topiaries.

"Before you sit, sir, we do have a dress code," she says, clearing her throat. "There are items for rent through that door. An attendant will help you find the right size. What sort of refreshments can I offer you while you wait for your friend?"

"What do you have?"

"Tea, whiskey, hot *kudvelk*, eluvian nectar, and a variety of small sandwiches and cakes," she says, then leans in to whisper conspiratorially. "Most people come here for the tea service, but you strike me as more of a whiskey gentleman."

I'm more than a little bewildered, but I nod and tell her to bring me whatever she thinks is best. It takes me only a few moments to argue with the dressing room attendant about my unwillingness to wear a *waistcoat*, but the glare I level at him seems to exasperate him enough to stop pushing. I'm reluctantly dressed in a pair of slim beige trousers and one of the aforementioned billowy shirts, and directed to my table between the topiaries where my tea service is waiting.

There's a flattering amount of attention from many of the women in the establishment, but I'm forced to be a bit brusque with them as I keep my eyes peeled for anyone who might be Lyra's Fed. Several tumblers of whiskey and tea sandwiches later, there's an obvious shift change with the employees, and a few more new males begin to circulate around the floor, carrying trays of little cakes and flirting with the patrons.

My gaze snags on a male from Terrin-4 who's dressed in some kind of crimson military uniform with gold buttons—*could it be him?* I've been sitting at this damned table for over two hours, and no one else has caught my attention. Feds have a staid, stalwart reputation owing to the fact that their emotions are usually beat out of them at a young age in the academy. The soldier hasn't smiled more than a handful of times, but as I'm about to get up and approach him, a boisterous Martian with blue-gray skin and an outlandish pirate costume drunkenly drops into the second chair at my table. Dark red tattoos swirl over much of his exposed skin and I'm uncertain if he's an employee *dressed* like a pirate or if he *is* a pirate.

"I'm afraid I'm not looking for company," I tell him sourly, glaring as he plucks a handful of sandwiches from my third tea tray.

"Nah, but company's looking for you, isn't it, Xylothian?" he drawls, flashing me a wink and a glimpse of fangs.

The Fed? Who else would be paying close enough attention to recognize a Xylothian? Still, his overly rakish attitude gives me pause. I scrutinize him and lean in. "What do you mean?"

With an exaggerated roll of his eyes, he matches my posture leaning over the table.

"Let's just say I'm not the only one here who's interested in making your acquaintance, Ranger Asterth," he says in a low voice. "Presumably you're here because we have a mutual friend?"

"Perhaps," I hedge. "Who's your friend?"

"The loveliest little constellation in the sky," he smirks. "That Velusian hybrid is a tough little bird to cage."

My anger surges and I stand suddenly, knocking the plates and glasses off our small table. My mating instincts want me to rip this male's throat out for speaking of Lyra in such a way, but my clumsy move has attracted the attention of several other patrons, including the woman who seated me.

"Easy, Ranger," he says with a dark chuckle. "Let's go somewhere a little more private and have a chat."

Stifling a growl, I follow the pirate into a back room. After locking it and drawing the curtains that look out over the alleyway, he shoves my clothes into my arms and tugs off his stringy wig, shucking his costume as quickly as he can.

"I don't have a lot of time," he says, his drunken manner evaporating instantly. "And I'm guessing you don't, either. I'm Agent Vega—Lyra's contact. Why didn't she come to meet me?"

Eyebrows arched almost to my hairline, I gape for a second before Agent Vega gestures to my clothes, wordlessly indicating he wants me to leave *billowy* behind and get dressed.

"She was taken," I tell him, too unsettled to feel any relief that I've made contact with the Fed. "A Void Stalker named Kraxis is taking her back to Ooneryx. To Brill."

Vega swears. "Did she get it? Back on Xylothia—did she get the idol?"

My resolve wavers momentarily. "Let's say she did. If you had the idol, and could make the swap, how does that help her now? You know Brill's going to kill her before you all get the proof you need to send in a team," I say, tugging the shirt over my head and reaching for my uniform.

Vega grins, but there's something unhinged in it. With a throb of pain, I realize the expression reminds me of Lyra.

"Well, we need the intel from the fake idol to do things by the books," he says, putting on a pair of black cargo pants and a stretchy black turtleneck. Seeing the confusion on my face, he explains.

"The fake is fitted with creep-tech. As soon as it's in proximity to Brill's system, it'll start feeding us all the data we could ever want to collapse his entire fucking network." He laces up a pair of black combat boots and straps on a chest harness with several small knives, but it's inconspicuous enough that you wouldn't notice them at first glance.

I'm a little mollified that *this* is the undercover agent I pictured rather than a drunken pirate from a themed café, but I'm still reluctant to trust him with the Solar Mother.

"That doesn't answer my question," I say, eyeing his knives and wishing I had weapons of my own.

"You're right," he replies. "Fortunately, I have a contingency plan for swapping the idols and getting Lyra out safely. *Unfortunately*, there's a gang of Void Stalkers hunting you down and they're about 5 klicks out, which means we've got to get moving."

Vega pulls the curtains back and opens the window, preparing to jump down onto a stack of trash crates.

"Void Stalkers—here? Already?" I ask, tugging on my pack. "And what kind of a contingency plan are we talking about here?"

I've never regretted my decision to become a ranger before, but for the first time, there's a part of me that wishes I'd become a Fed instead. Then maybe I'd have the skills and knowledge necessary to rescue Lyra on my own, instead of being forced to trust someone who looks like he's on the scary side of crazy.

Rather than answer me, Vega jumps out the window, landing with a wet thud on the crates one floor down in the alleyway. Sighing, I move to follow his lead.

I knew a future with Lyra was going to require a leap of faith, I just didn't realize it would be so soon, and so literal.

19

lyra

Why Is it Always a Gross Tunnel?

KRAXIS FROWNS at the scanner like it's personally offended him. *Good.*

"This readout doesn't make sense," he growls.

I'm sitting against the back wall of my cell, stark naked minus the scratchy blanket I've got wrapped around my shoulders. His beady yellow eyes narrow as I giggle manically, then start humming David Bowie. I let my head roll to the side, eyes half-lidded, limbs loose.

"You took the *haggra*," he says, more to himself than to me. His fingers dance over the scanner again, twitchy and impatient. "But your blood levels aren't consistent with a double dose."

Because I didn't take a double dose. I palmed the second pill and flushed it the moment I had the chance. One was already a risk, and it's already doing its job, softening the edges of my reality. Two would've put me face-down on the floor, drooling while he took notes.

But I don't say that. Instead, I smile—lazy, hazy, and a little too wide.

"Oh, I took it," I purr, trying to sell it with everything I have. "And it's like...stars, like I'm melting. Like everything's wrapped in velvet and my bones are singing."

I lift my hand and trace slow spirals in the air, watching the way his eyes flick to my fingers. I add a little tremor, just enough to make him see what he wants to see.

He looks back at the scanner, jaw tight. "Your neurochemistry isn't responding the way it should."

"Maybe your scanner's broken." I giggle again. Stars, I hate giggling. "Or maybe I'm just special."

Kraxis doesn't like that. As much as I despise the reptilian asshole, he's actually decent at his job. If he wasn't, Brill would've shot him out an airlock long ago. Of course, as good as he is as Brill's second-in-command enforcer, that makes his dogged pursuit of me that much more annoying. Kraxis doesn't stand for anomalies, or guesswork, or subjects that smile when they're supposed to drool. But I can feel the shift—he wants the data to be wrong more than he wants to believe I tricked him.

Perfect.

I settle back against the wall, heartbeat steady under the haze, letting the one pill ride just enough to keep the act smooth. He walks a step away, muttering, distracted.

Good. That's how I want him, the big scaly butthole. *Distracted.*

One pill soothes some of the visceral rage that's making my *vellia* simmer beneath my skin. Two would've buried me, and I'm not quite ready to be buried.

"Gag her," he snaps. "And search her. No sudden movements. She's still dangerous."

Two Void Stalkers—Thall and Borric, the dumb and dumber of Brill's bootlicking buddies—follow orders without hesitation. My blanket is snatched away, and it takes a gargantuan amount of effort not to plant a fist in Thall's vulnerable temple when he smirks at my nudity.

Borric holds a small metal ball in front of my face, which scans my mouth and shoots out robotic fingers that promptly wrap around the lower half of my face. The gag tastes like steel drenched in engine coolant. They shove me into a silk robe—

because Brill's nothing if not theatrical—and bind my wrists in front of me with shimmering cable coded with a fingerprint lock.

The robe's too long. The fabric drags behind me as they march me through the lower decks of the *Edax Deorum* like a sacrificial goat on a leash. Thanks to the small amount of *haggra* I've already ingested, my limbs feel like jelly. I trip—twice. The second time, Kraxis grabs my elbow and hauls me upright with enough force to pop a joint. My vision whites out.

Welcome back to Ooneryx, Lyra.

The ascent from the ship's shuttle bay to Brill's compound is a blur. I only remember flickers: the taste of copper in my mouth. The wail of distant sirens. The distinct scent of Ooneryx's desert air—metallic, dry, a little like singed circuitry and rotting ambition. Then, Brill's private study.

Somewhere in my snarky, warped little mind, I hear a sardonic chorus of *dun dun dunnn.*

For all my pathetic attempts at sneaking into this place, I expected something a bit grander—lavish in its ugliness. Filled with ancient torture devices and the heads of exotic, extinct animals lining the walls, or something. Something in line with Brill's character—which I'm certain I understand better than a lot of the people who live and work at the compound.

Imagine my stoned surprise when I see that it's not.

The room is...silent. There's nothing on the matte obsidian walls. For all his greed when it comes to buying—and stealing— millions of credits worth of art, artifacts, and cultural treasures from across the galaxy, there's nothing on display in this private, secret space. I knew he didn't do it for love of beauty, but it still throws me for a loop that in this place that's meant to be his refuge and inner sanctum, it's as devoid of pleasure and joy as the cell I just vacated on Kraxis's ship.

One wall-length window filters orange light from the burning horizon outside, casting the dark tiled floor in a muted gold. The only furniture is a large black stone desk and a pair of antique Martian-style armchairs. There are a few books on the desk, two large screens that I'm unable to read, and a solitary glass decanter half full of glowing blue liquid, which I'm sure is a potent Neptunian liquor that I can't remember the name of.

That's it. No guards, no weapons, no servants, no audience. Dopey, latent fear percolates through my body, blessedly unable to take root.

It's just Brill, sitting behind the desk, staring at me like he's about to interrogate me for a crime we both know I didn't commit.

It's been several months since I've seen him in person, and even though it's not that long in the grand scheme of things, he looks older—sharper. Bones press against skin like he's been carved from disdain itself. His orange eyes gleam like a predator's and he smiles when I'm pushed through the door. It's *not* a good smile.

"Leave us."

Kraxis hesitates, probably ready to recite the full list of my sins and transgressions to ensure I'll be appropriately punished. "She—"

"I said, leave us."

He says it softly, which is worse. We *all* know that's the tone Brill uses before he defenestrates someone. *Shit, do those windows open?* Kraxis gestures to Thall and Borric, who almost trip over themselves with the effort to hurry from the room.

The minute we're alone, Brill sighs dramatically and starts to pace, coiled with that restless, predatory energy he can't seem to mask. For a moment—one stupid, traitorous instant—I remember what I thought of him the first time I saw him.

Years ago, at my *serrika* auction on Velusia, Brill had looked like control made flesh. Among the bloated bidders and glassy-eyed diplomats, he stood out: tall and motionless, his skin a hard lattice of bony plates that caught the torchlight like dull metal. His horns spiraled high and elegant from his skull, curved in a way that suggested age and power without ever tipping into grotesque. The claws on his hands glinted like carved obsidian, and when he moved, it was with a slow, deliberate grace, like something used to sandstorms and silence. Those eyes—orange, slit-pupiled, unreadable—locked on me once during the bidding, and something inside me faltered. I remember thinking he looked handsome, in the way a knife might, gleaming in the dark just before it sinks in. There was no kindness in him, but there was precision, restraint, a sense that if he chose to hurt me, it wouldn't be out of clumsy hunger—it would be a decision, and somehow that seemed safer. I didn't know yet how dangerous cold mercy could be.

He circles to the front of the desk and leans back against it, folding his arms across his chest in a way that's too controlled to be as casual as he wants to appear. Warning bells are sounding in my head, but my body feels sluggish and rubbery with the *haggra* coursing through my veins. Even if I wanted to summon my *vellia*, the spark is buried under fog. *Just a little longer.*

"You've put me in a difficult position, Lyra," he says, his voice a low rumble of rage. "You've embarrassed me. Repeatedly. Stolen from me. Lied to me. Betrayed my trust."

Almost too late, I realize I'm supposed to be nearly insensate with *haggra*. I blink blearily at him, sure he's going to prattle on about how horrible and ungrateful I am, and how generous he is by not torturing me to death every time I've failed to bring home one of his prizes.

"Anyone else would be a puddle of shredded organs on my floor, but I've always had a soft spot for you, little Lyra," he whispers, stepping forward until he's standing a hair's breadth in front of me. With a vicious grip, he snags my chin, his claws pricking into my cheeks between the metal fingers of the gag. I feel blood well beneath the points of contact, but the *haggra* dulls the pain.

"And how have you repaid my indulgence?" he hisses.

A muffled giggle spills out of me at the thought of his abuse being *indulgence*, but it also serves my purpose of behaving like a loopy idiot. Still, I know what's coming—Brill *hates* to be laughed at.

His other hand flies back, slapping me so hard my teeth click against the metal of the gag. Stars burst behind my eyes and blood fills my mouth.

"You should've been mine," he bites out, licking my blood from his claws and shoving me backwards. I stumble slightly, but manage to keep my balance. "You would have been kept in comfort, in luxury, at my side. You are an instrument of pleasure, Lyra, but your resistance to that has forced me to use you ill. Now, look at you! An errand girl bringing back items from my shopping list—denying her true nature because of pride and petulant whims."

And there it is—the heart of it all. For the past 14 years, it's only ever been about me refusing to be his mistress—a sexually biddable *serrika*. It's never been about trust, or business. Just Brill's twisted obsession and his need to possess what he cannot control.

Maybe if I'd relented and fucked him over the years, he would've ended my contract at the right time, or at the very least, stopped treating me like a dog on a leash that needed to fetch every time he said so. Nausea bubbles in my stomach at the thought of submitting to him, and I know with grim certainty it wouldn't have mattered. If I'd slept with him, he would've gotten bored, and boredom leads to dead bodies. My refusal kept him interested, and his interest is what kept me alive.

"But that's all in our past, isn't it," he continues, circling me at a distance and running his fingers over the edges of the robe's sleeves. "I'm afraid you've exhausted the limits of my mercy. I know you let that Xylothian run off with *my* artifact. Such treachery—such betrayal! It's a shame you've become such an active and enthusiastic participant in your own destruction. Your actions have voided our contract, and by rights, you are mine to dispose of at will."

I go still, fear sparking uselessly at my sleeping *vellia*.

He stops behind me. "Of course, I'd no sooner slit your throat than destroy my favorite painting. But you won't be my weakness anymore, my little Lyra. Buyers are lining up for a piece of you. You'll be auctioned at the next eclipse. Highest bidder wins."

For a moment, I can't breathe. The words hit like a pulse round to the chest—then calcify. That's the plan? Sell me like an artifact—a trinket—a relic? How poetic. How perfectly predictable. The horror should hollow me out, but there's nothing left to hollow now with everyone I love gone. It's all just ashes and muscle memory.

Still, beneath the numbness, grief flickers—small, sharp, human. Not for my body, or even my freedom, but for what's left of the girl who once thought she was clever enough to outwit the worst of 'em.

Pathetic. Even I believed he'd have more imagination than that.

"But," he whispers into my ear, "I thought you deserved a proper farewell."

His hand trails down my spine. My stomach churns and I close my eyes, desperately trying to summon anything. Rage. Power. *Vellia.*

There's nothing at first, but then…a tremor. It's faint. Barely perceptible—but there. The singular dose of *haggra* is burning off beneath the heat of my fear and anger. Brill strolls to my front, slicing through the knot on my robe. The sides flutter open, and he sucks in a breath.

The rage surges and my *vellia* hums in my blood. The fog clears a little more. *It's enough.*

Brill's eyes glitter with malice. "I will have you my way before we're done. Any final thoughts, darling?"

I nod.

He smirks, removing the gag.

I smile—sweet. Sincere.

"Yeah," I whisper, my exaggerated slur sobering. "You should've given me more *haggra*."

Then I unleash as much *vellia* as I can summon. All my fear, anger, humiliation, stress, and hatred fuels the release of my body's chemical weapon—my self-preservation overriding every other instinct.

The effect is immediate. Brill blinks, wavering on his feet.

"Wha—" His pupils dilate, mouth parting on an inhale. He sways slightly.

I lean forward, letting *vellia* ooze from every pore.

"Kneel," I murmur, reaching for the decanter on his desk. He goes down on his knees, staring up at me with undisguised lust and greed. My hands are still bound so it's a bit of a struggle, but I pour a full glass of the liquor and offer it to him. He takes it, eyes glazing and nostrils flaring.

"Drink," I tell him. "Drink it all up, like a good little sociopath."

His eyes start to roll back into his head and his cheeks turn a faint shade of purple, but he lifts the glass to his lips and drinks like he's dying of thirst. When he finishes, I refill his glass—over and over, until he's consumed the entire decanter of alcohol.

The *vellia* and the booze tangle in his bloodstream, not quite enough to be lethal, but almost. *Almost.* He chokes and swallows when he almost vomits, shuddering.

"You're—so beautiful—I love you—so much—" he mumbles, words slurring like mine, but I know that *he* isn't acting.

I smile wider, kneeling in front of him until we're eye level.

"I know," I say, then headbutt him in the face—hard.

Blood spurts from his nose and he collapses, unconscious. I know I've only got a little bit of time before someone comes knocking, so I shove my discarded gag into his mouth and drag his body behind his desk. Hopefully, it'll give me a little extra time if he's fucked up and blacked out for a little while.

I grab his limp fingers and press one to the sensor on my wrist restraints, unlocking them to quickly transfer the bindings to his hands. A quick search of his desk doesn't yield anything in the way of a weapon, so I reason I'll have to come back and cut his fucking head off another time. There also isn't much in his pockets or the spartan desk that will help me get out of here, but my main priority is to get as far away from him as possible before he wakes up.

"You'll fetch a high price, Brill," I whisper. "Maybe I'll do the bidding."

Then, I run.

The halls of the compound are just as I remember—sterile, winding, more maze than mansion. Fortunately, I know the layout, having memorized it years ago for my very first escape attempt. *Ah, memories.*

Reflexively, I almost call out to Ada, but then I remember she's gone. Stress and sadness make tears burn behind my eyes, but I don't have time to grieve yet. I don't know how far along Evie's mechanics got with my ship—if it's space-worthy enough to limp out of here, or if it'll disintegrate in the wretched atmosphere of Ooneryx the minute I try to take off. But—since I don't really have much of a plan and never believed I'd get as far as I did—that feels like as good of a starting point as any.

Guards patrol every corridor, but so far, no alarm has been raised yet. When I make my way to the maintenance room two floors down, I recognize the refuse chutes that lead to the incinerator underground, rather conveniently located next to the underground garage connected to the main launch bay, where it's more than likely my ship is parked. The foul-smelling trash tunnel beckons, and this time, I don't hesitate to crawl through it.

Stars, why am I always crawling through something gross to save my ass?

The tunnel winds down through the lower levels of the compound, and by the time I see a speck of light up ahead, I'm ready to cry with relief and also heave my guts out from the potent mixture of eye-watering stink and adrenaline-spiked anxiety. Before I poke my head out from my filthy escape tunnel, I listen intently for any sounds nearby.

So far, so good.

I lever my body over the lip of the chute, landing with a squelch on top of a mountain of garbage. *Ugh.* If I get out of this mess, I'm treating myself to the longest, hottest bath I can fathom. I'll use every drop of hot water on my ship and sit in it until my whole body is pruny.

The trash shifts beneath me, sliding down another shaft into the mouth of the incinerator. With a fumbling, awkward leap, I grab onto the ladder that leads out of the pit, then quietly climb up to the lower maintenance floor.

I gasp in triumph when I see carts of laundry lined up along the next hallway, and am able to swipe a uniform from one of the them. After donning the pilfered clothes and pushing my slimy hair up into the uniform hood, I'm slightly more at ease. In this lower level, I pass by an empty break room—another stroke of luck—and I'm able to snatch a protein ration and a bottle of water. As I shove them into my dehydrated, famished mouth, I slink through the corridors, ducking beneath windows and scooting around security drones, but there aren't many people down here.

Hm. Where is everybody? Maybe my luck's turning, I think foolishly. As if the gods hear me and laugh, I'm turning down a hallway in the east wing when I overhear two guards talking.

"The auction's off. Brill's unconscious."

"What? How?"

"No idea. Kraxis is furious."

There's a small tingle of fear at the base of my spine, but it's overridden by sheer, malicious glee. *I need to hurry up and get the heck out of here—it's only a matter of time before Kraxis raises the alarm and locks the whole compound down.*

I listen for a few more minutes, but when they don't discuss anything more helpful than the bets they've recently lost on the illegal glaxian fights, I move on.

Eventually, I find the systems room that shares a ventilation shaft with the garage. It takes me more than a few tries to climb up into the air duct in the ceiling, but I manage it before my exhausted limbs give out. The duct is just wide enough for me to slither through on my stomach, so the crawl to the garage takes an interminable amount of time. When I reach the end, I gaze out through a thick metal grate and my heart drops.

Well, I guess my good luck had to run out some time.

My ship is there, of course—currently surrounded by a veritable army of Void Stalkers.

20
orion

A Ghost in the Smoke

BY THE TIME we clear the alley outside the café and wind through widening streets, a late storm is brewing over the Tumplesh sector. Rain beats down in a drippy staccato on the crystalline awnings overhead, rolling warm mist into the busy street where Vega and I move at a clipped pace. The station's artificial atmosphere turns even drizzle into a curtain of damp that soaks through our clothes in minutes.

We cut through a row of neon-lit stalls and food carts still sputtering over heat coils, the streets thick with the scent of fried bantil and scorched synth-meat. My boots splash through puddles as we keep to the edges of the corridor, dodging patrolling security drones and doing our best to stay invisible. Vega checks over his shoulder every third step.

"They're close," he mutters. "We need to move faster. No idea if they clocked the café, but they were sniffing near the terminal. We've got maybe five minutes, tops."

"Then maybe less narration, more sprinting," I snap. My mating instinct is surging with the idea of Lyra working with the annoyingly dashing Martian.

He snorts. "I'm going slow so you can keep up, Ranger."

I glare but keep quiet, certain that if the Fed wasn't in the process of saving my ass and probably Lyra's, I'd punch him in the throat. The vision soothes me and pacifies a little of my mating-induced envy.

A few streets down, Vega motions to another nondescript alleyway, and we duck in, melting into the darkness. When he's sure we're not being followed, he pops open a nearby service hatch and we slip inside, emerging into the lower cargo bay several decks below. The hum of distant turbines and the occasional shout of dockhands bouncing off concrete bulkheads echoes through the bay, making it almost impossible for me to hear Vega's muttered instructions.

Just beyond the loading gates, a matte-black hoverbike leans against a crate—one side scorched, the back end rigged with what Vega explains is a dummy crash panel. A few meters away, a squat gray unmarked cruiser waits with its running lights dimmed. Vega's already tapping at a wristpad, syncing systems.

"I'm going to cue the dummy route," he says. "You're going to give them the show. We crash it big. In the chaos, we jump into the cruiser and ghost. I hope you know how to ride a hoverbike."

Frustration makes my temper snap. "What if I didn't?"

He tosses me a helmet, grinning. "Well then, this wouldn't look very convincing now, would it?"

I narrow my eyes. "You don't seem nearly panicked enough for someone improvising under fire."

Vega's mouth twitches. "That's because I'm not. This wasn't meant for you. This was Lyra's out—contingency escape route if things went sideways after we swapped the idol."

He points to the cruiser. "Scrambler's built in. Registry loops every thirty seconds. Bike's wired to detonate off a trigger relay and crash with just enough synthetic residue to fool basic forensics and the dumbass Void Stalkers tailing you."

I blink. "You planned to fake Lyra's death?"

"No," he says, adjusting something on his wristpad. "I planned to make it possible—if she needed to disappear."

There's something harder in his voice now. A pause. Then he shakes it off. "Now it's yours. Try not to waste it."

Before I can come up with something biting, the hair on the back of my neck stands up, and my synesfores flicker a panicky yellow. Void Stalkers step out of the darkness at the dock's entrance—there are six of them, their sleek black armor glinting in the warm, wet air. The moment they catch sight of us, they fan out, running in our direction in an attempt to cut us off.

"Go!" Vega hisses.

I jump on the bike, slam down on the throttle, and rocket into the lane. Behind me, Vega vaults onto the cruiser's open ramp and hits the ignition. It hums to life but stays grounded for now, lights dark.

Plasma fire cracks through the alley as the Void Stalkers track me.

"Target on the bike! It's the Xylothian!"

I duck low and follow the narrow guidance overlay Vega directed to my HUD. It's hastily mapped, but the directions make sense. Left at the coolant tower. Boost under the scaffolding. Bail point just before the station vent.

I gun it, swerving past pallets of trade goods and diving under a bridge. I count down under my breath, flick the autopilot control, and hurl myself sideways.

I tumble hard onto the soaked concrete, gasping as the impact knocks the wind from my lungs. Pain blooms along my side where I hit the ground, but my adrenaline surges enough to get me back on my feet. The bike, now under Vega's pre-set script, races forward like there's a pack of rabid lupitians on its tail. It shoots forward, arcing into a tight spiral before smashing into the side of a cargo freighter. The explosion rocks the bay with a fireball that swallows the alley in smoke and flame. Hopefully, the firebots will extinguish everything before the fake idol melts in the crash debris.

The heat washes over me even from cover, and there's a discordant soundtrack of soft rain spattering in puddles at my feet, combined with screeching metal and wailing sirens. The detonation's flash blinds half the bay—exactly what Vega planned. Screams erupt in the wake of the destruction and a few of the Void Stalkers close in on the scene of the crash.

"We got him! The Xylothian is down!" one yells.

In the chaos, Vega swings the cruiser around. I sprint through the haze and dive into the open hatch.

"Go!" I yell.

The ramp seals behind me as the cruiser lifts off. We bank low and vanish into the lower lanes, weaving into traffic as innocuous as possible, given that we just blew up an entire section of the Epsilon-6's docks. Unbidden, my memories return to Lyra—to the gleeful way she mentioned blowing up the casino on Mallorus. A small smile tugs at my lips as I watch the fireball being extinguished by a mobile unit of firebots.

Minutes later, inside the cruiser's cockpit, Vega's hands fly over the controls.

"Idol's secure, feeds are spoofed, and the fake crash is already hitting the station's news circuit. Congratulations, Orion Asterth. You just died horribly."

I pull off the helmet and toss it onto the dash. "Great. Although next time you get to play the flaming corpse."

Vega lets out a low chuckle, flashing a grin punctuated by fangs. "Tempting. But you sell it better. Angsty martyr's written all over you. I can tell why Lyra's pulled you into her orbit."

"What's that supposed to mean?"

He flicks a glance at me, all casual mischief with something unreadable behind it. "Man, you've got it bad. Can't say I'm surprised. She's something else—one in a million."

"I didn't realize you knew her that well," I reply, barely recognizing the growl in my voice. My petty jealousy is making my synesfores flicker black and red in an irritated rhythm.

"I don't—not really. But you know, she's definitely the type to leave an impression," he laughs. "You and Lyra must've made a hell of a pair."

I glance at him, jaw tight. "It's none of your business."

"Touchy."

We're slicing through the mid-lane traffic of a new sector, Vega piloting smoothly like he was born in the cockpit. Low amber light glows from the control panels, bouncing off the cruiser's worn chrome interior, making it look warmer than it is. Outside, the city falls away in sharp tiers of neon and carbon steel, endless as the ache in my chest.

"She's not mine," I add, quieter. "Not really."

"Didn't say she was," he says, voice infuriatingly calm. "But I see the way you look when I say her name. Like you're bracing for a solar flare."

He's not wrong.

There's a silence between us, brittle like rusted metal. I shift in the copilot's seat, shoulders tight under the damp cling of my shirt, still sticky from the sprint and the fake crash. The adrenaline's gone, but the weight in my chest hasn't lifted.

"I spotted her on Epsilon-6," Vega says, eyes still on the lanes of weaving traffic ahead. "She was ducking cameras, not well, I might add, and I recognized her from my case files. Slippery, too clean for the jobs she was attached to. So, I started watching."

"Creepy."

"Observant," he corrects, a little defensively. "Most people don't notice patterns in a station this size. I do."

I bite the inside of my cheek. The image of Lyra—alone, hiding, feral and brilliant—makes something twist painfully under my ribs.

"She kept showing up at this ridiculous amusement park of a café, right? Laced bodices, fake fireplaces, longing gazes, and steamy declarations shared over tea trays. I figured it was bait— no way could someone like that be so taken in by something so cheesy. And for someone trying to keep a low profile, returning to the same place, same time, every cycle? Pfft. But there she was, reading about pirates on the high seas and sipping moonshine-spiked tea like she didn't have a bounty the size of a defense satellite on her head."

"So what, you pulled up a chair and played brooding?" If this conversation doesn't end soon, I'm going to break something. Even odds on it being Agent Vega's face, or his ship's console.

He smirks. "Skintight breeches and everything. Got laughed at by the hostess. But Lyra gave me a seat—and some thinly-veiled insults. Two hours later, we were debating whether the pirate captain's declaration in the second act counted as emotional manipulation."

Something about that image makes my molars grind. "Did you seduce her?"

Vega actually laughs. "Please. She could've broken me in half and flossed her teeth with my spine. I wasn't dumb enough to try. I leveled with her a few hours in—told her I was Fed, had a fat file with her name on it, and made her an offer she couldn't refuse."

"Which was?"

"Get Brill to chase the Solar Mother idol. Make it her idea. She grabs it, brings it to me, I swap in a surveillance decoy. Brill thinks he's holding divine power; instead, he's handing us front-row access to every backroom deal in his damn network."

I glare out the window, fighting to keep my responses neutral, and not dour and resentful.

"And she agreed just like that?"

He exhales. "No. She threatened to skin me with a dessert fork. It took her two days to circle back. She named her terms— no trace, high payout, and total autonomy. I said fine, but she had to bring me the real idol so I could switch it for the decoy."

"Why do you need the real one if you already had a duplicate?"

"Brill's not the only one looking for it," Vega says, cocking a brow in exasperation. "I couldn't risk someone else coming in, scooping it up, and trying to unload it on the black market while

Brill thinks he's already got it in his vault. That'd paint a target on Lyra's back, and I can't use a dead asset. She said getting the real one wouldn't be a problem, and that we had a deal."

"And you trusted her?" *I certainly hadn't.*

"No," he says simply. "But she never promised loyalty. She promised results. And I believed her about Brill. You could see it —she hates him more than I ever could. She hates him even more than she hated needing me."

That hits somewhere deep, and it's a place I've been avoiding. Because I know Lyra's my mate—I can feel it like a second pulse—but that doesn't mean she owes me anything. Not her loyalty. Not her heart. Certainly not her tether. She gets to choose.

And maybe she won't choose me.

"You still think she was going to follow through?" I ask, hating the hope in my voice.

Vega shrugs. "Honestly? I think she was going to betray both of us and run. But maybe not right away. She liked the idea of being helpful again. Dangerous, but helpful."

"Why are you telling me all this?" I ask, suspicion still coloring my perception of him.

"Because you've got that look," he says. "Like if she doesn't pick you, you'll fold in half. And that's not helpful. She's not some prize. She's a weapon. You either sharpen it or you get out of the way."

I sit with that. It burns—but it's not exactly wrong. I'm embarrassed to admit to myself that the vision I have of us being together involves a luxurious home at the edge of the forest on Xylothia, where we can settle down and relax in between adventures. I'm not naive enough to believe she'd give up her adventure-loving lifestyle completely, but maybe the idea of having a home base would appeal enough to her to help me convince her to take a chance with me—with us. I'd never dream of caging her, or binding her to me, but maybe she might want to have a safe space to return to.

Vega angles the cruiser downward, past a massive vertical hover-vator tube and into a lower, quieter lane—steering us away from the main routes. After a minute, he speaks again, softer this time.

"I can sense what she means to you, Orion. But she's not a damsel, and she's sure as hell not waiting to be saved— metaphorically speaking."

"I don't want to save her—metaphorically," I say, my voice raw. Is that true, though? Something insidious whispers that I do —I want to her to need me as much as I need her. "I just want her to know I'm not leaving. Not unless she tells me to."

He nods once, then pulls back on the throttle. Ahead, I see the familiar outline of my borrowed cruiser—safe, secure, and unassuming. The relief I feel at seeing the ship and knowing Ada is onboard makes my knees wobble as much as the fading adrenaline.

"I'm dropping you here," Vega says. "Regroup, refuel, whatever. Stay out of sight and out of trouble. I'll keep off-grid and ping you from just outside Ooneryx once I've scouted the approach."

I rise from my seat, still uncertain if I want to hit him or thank him. Probably both. "And if this all blows up?"

He grins. "Then we get to die doing something interesting. But let's save that drama for after we've pissed off at least three more crime lords."

I pause at the hatch, hand on the frame.

"Thanks," I say, not looking at him. "For saving my ass."

"Don't get soft on me now, Ranger. You'll make me blush."

I step out, feeling the gravity shift under my boots, the weight of everything waiting ahead of me. Lyra. The idol. The damn choice I can't force her to make.

And behind me, Vega's cruiser vanishes into the lanes, leaving only gray sky and tepid rain.

THE HUM of the cruiser's engines thrum steadily beneath me, but it does nothing to quiet the chaotic hurricane of thoughts. I keep my eyes on the stars bleeding past the windows, hands clenched at my sides like they might anchor me to something—anything—stable.

Ada's voice chimes in, pulling me from my reverie.

We're approximately twenty-three hours from Ooneryx at current velocity. Do you wish to revise the flight path?

"No," I say, hoarse. "Keep it as is."

There's a pause, then Ada continues.

Lyra used to adjust our course when she was anxious. Tiny deviations. Never enough to matter. Just...something to touch. Something to do.

I look away from the console, throat tightening.

"She still thinks you're gone."

She does.

There's a silence between us that feels bigger than the space outside. I know she's not real, that she's a computer program without soul or feeling, but Ada carries fragments of Lyra in every line of her code. It's in the way she talks, the way she pretends not to worry while calculating the probability of failure down to decimal points. I know Lyra programmed her like that. I know it's all intentional.

And still, it feels like a ghost riding with me.

A ping lights up on the console—it's Vega's encrypted channel. I answer it with a grunt and bring his image up on the hologram projector.

"Void Stalkers found the fake idol," Vega says without preamble. "So, that's the first bit of good news. The second bit of good news is that their initial scans triggered the surveillance net, and it looks like it's working—feeding a slow-drip of data into our back channels. We've already gotten pingbacks from two relay stations in Brill's old Haelor corridor."

Annoyance makes my head ache when I have to ask him to spell it out for me like I'm an idiot.

"Which means?" I ask with a grumble.

"Which means," Vega says, tapping something offscreen, "if Brill moves to secure the idol personally, we'll have a straight line to his comm hierarchy. It's like setting a fire in his data vault. He won't even smell the smoke until it's too late. This is great news, Orion—it means the Feds are already listening to the evil little whispers behind Brill's doors."

I nod—it is good news. I know it is. But I can't help but feel sick with worry that we're still not doing enough. We're not moving fast enough.

"Good," I acknowledge.

Vega's voice softens, just a little. "We'll get her out. Before he makes a move."

But I know the window is narrow. Based on what Lyra's told me about Brill, he isn't the kind of bastard to let something simmer. He's a scorched-earth tactician. If Lyra doesn't give him information about the idol's whereabouts—or worse, if he starts to suspect she's played him—he'll make an example out of her. And there won't be much left for us to save.

I rub my temples and lean back, letting the silence wrap around me again. Too quiet. It's too quiet on this damn ship.

Several hours pass, broken only by engine checks and Ada's occasional course updates. I try to sleep. I fail. I pace the cruiser like a caged thing. All I can think about is the way Lyra looked the last time I saw her—half-defiant, half-exhausted, resigned, and already pulling away.

Suddenly, another ping violates the silence of the cockpit.

I'm on it before the second blink.

"Okay, so remember all that good news we had?" Vega says by way of greeting. "Keep that at the forefront of your mind. Let's just focus on the good news before I tell you the bad news that just dropped in," Vega says, and I already hate the tone in his voice. Bile climbs its way up my throat as I wait, dread making me sweaty and sick.

"One of my sources flagged something not-so-great. There's

talk of a black market auction going live tomorrow from Ooneryx. Private invites only. Headliner item?" He pauses, then spits out. "A Velusian hybrid. Female. Untagged."

My fist hits the console hard enough to crack a panel.

Ada patches in.

Damage registered. Should I reroute oxygen flow from lower cargo to compensate?

"Don't joke, Ada," I grit out.

I'm not. But you should breathe.

I don't—I can't.

"Vega," I growl, "you get into that auction. I don't care how. Burn every alias you've got left. You hear me?"

"Already working it," he says. "But Orion—if it's her, and Brill's the one offering her up, then this game just changed. We miss that window, she could disappear into some privateer's pleasure fleet, and we'll never see her again."

"I'm aware," I answer, already running through unhinged plans in my head, each more dangerous and unlikely to succeed than the last.

"And if it's a trap—"

"Then we spring it," he confirms. "It's now or never."

Ada's voice cuts in again.

I'm adjusting descent vectors. We'll hit Ooneryx's orbit in just under nineteen hours. Prepping stealth protocols.

My jaw tightens, aching with how often I've been grinding my teeth and swallowing my despair. *She thinks you're gone, Ada. She thinks we're all gone. And she's facing Brill alone.*

Not for long.

21

lyra

Whispers in the Circuits

CAN A BLADDER *ACTUALLY* BURST? If so, mine is about to, which will almost certainly give away my hiding place in the grossest, most visceral way I can possibly think of.

I haven't stretched my legs in two stars-damned days. My knees are wrecked—my back's worse. I'm thirsty, and hungry, and filthier than I think I've ever been thanks to the layers of sweat mixing with Ooneryx's desert sand that gets everywhere. But the worst part is the silence—the kind that isn't empty, but waiting. *Listening.*

I've got to get out of this air duct so I can pee. Pressing my ear to the vent slats, I hear two pairs of footsteps tapping through the corridor below. A conversation filters through— muffled at first, but rising. I freeze, breath held and bladder throbbing.

"He's still puking his guts out, but is adamant the auction goes ahead. He's confident Phoenix is still here in the compound and it's only a matter of time before she's found," one voice says. It's not a Void Stalker, by the lack of guttural clip to the tone, but I can tell it's another male guard. Tension leeches out between the tight words and bitten out responses.

There's a pregnant pause, followed by the other guard's reply.

"Ah. I thought he'd cancel, the state he's in."

"He's furious—absolutely livid. I don't think I've ever seen him so angry. He said whoever finds the hybrid gets a million credits. And for those of us who don't find her, he'll kill one out of every ten."

My stomach knots. That would certainly motivate me, if I were a nefarious henchman or evil-leaning mercenary. The carrot? A million credits. The stick? Likely disembowelment, decapitation, or defenestration. *Damn, so many disturbing 'd' words.*

I press both hands to my mouth to stifle my panting breaths. My heart's beating so loud I'm sure they'll hear it. My *vellia* and the alcohol worked well enough to give me a head start, but even though Brill is weak, sick, and probably hallucinating, he's not down for the count—not by a long shot.

Stupid, stubborn, hard-to-kill asshole!

The duct metal creaks under me. I go still. I've only slipped out twice—once to drink condensation from a cracked coolant pipe, which, *disgusting*, and again to snag half a nutrient bar off a janitor's cart. I only move when I'm starving or about to burst. Everything else, I endure.

I know if I'm seen, I'm screwed. Or worse. *All those 'd' words—definitely worse.*

I wait until the guards' voices fade. I count to two hundred. Only then do I crawl back to the junction where the air duct hides a broken maintenance panel I pried open last night. I shimmy out, legs numb, body trembling, radiating misery. The walls down here are old, as if this entire section of the maintenance floors has been forgotten. Blessedly, there's a blocked off restroom at the end of the floor and I'm able to relieve myself before exploring a little more.

It's the only reason I find the old server room—the one they used before the last renovation. Most of the equipment is rust-eaten, choked with sand, or damaged by time's inevitability. There are dusty terminals, fractured holo-screens, even a few broken-down service droids. Everything seems to be half-dead, but in the grim, dusty quiet of the space, a faint green light pulses from behind one of the consoles.

Ah ha! Not all the way *dead.*

I cross to the console and pull out a nearly ancient transceiver. Obsolete. Outdated. But *not* broken.

Hope hits me like a blade in the chest. It almost hurts worse than the hunger.

I drop to my knees and get to work.

AFTER I SPLICE OPEN the old transceiver and scrape corrosion from the chip housing with the edge of a broken circuit board, I can barely hold the tools steady. It's not from fear, I don't think. From hunger, maybe. Or perhaps from the constant weight pressing into my chest because my chance of escape is shrinking by the hour.

But mostly because I keep thinking of Orion.

Of the way he looked in the landing bay of the *Hephaestus*, golden light bleeding over his broad shoulders and handsome face twisted in panic and despair. Of the quiet comfort of his presence—how he'd sit across from me during our nights on the *Aldrin-136*, reading my old romance novels because I had little else to offer, while I perused my father's journals. Not asking, not judging—okay, maybe a little judging—but mostly just being there. Of the way he reached for me in bed, not with hunger, but with gentleness, as if even my wreckage was something he wanted to hold.

I never wanted to pull him into this. He had a path, a purpose, something so noble I don't think I'll ever have the capacity to understand. I don't know what he saw in me. I only know that being near him made me want to see it, too.

But I don't get to have people like that. I don't get to keep good things. The galaxy doesn't hand those out to people like me. I destroy everything I hold too closely. It's what I was made for—damage, not devotion. Velusians are forbidden to love. Maybe my problem is that I'm only half Velusian.

The transceiver blinks—faint, fluttering, but alive.

A spark jumps from the board and kisses my knuckle, but I barely feel it. I press my ear close, adjusting the dial and rerouting through an old smuggler satband, then bouncing off a low-orbit relay that should've gone dead three cycles ago.

Please, please, please, please.

My fingers move on muscle memory and desperation, patching together a makeshift call into the unfeeling, lonely void of space.

"*Hephaestus*," I whisper, lips brushing the receiver. "Come in, *Hephaestus*. Evie, please—tell me you're still up. Tell me you're receiving."

For a moment, nothing but static. Then—like the voice of a dream cracking through lonely silence…

"Pinky Pie?"

My breath catches. Her voice hits me like a high-velocity re-entry, and tears well in my eyes before I can stop them. Get ahold of yourself, Lyra!

"Holy hell, you're alive. You sound—stars, where are you?" Evie's worried tone only makes me want to cry harder.

"Brill's compound," I croak, my voice raw from disuse. "Out on Ooneryx. I'm stuck. He's planning to sell me."

"Oh, Lyra…I can't get to you," she says, sharp regret lacing every word. "When the Void Stalkers left our ship, they tagged the rest of our cruisers. I think Orion got out on the only one they missed. As soon as we try to make a jump and get you, they'd trace us straight to you. We're stuck out here about as useful as a screen door on a submarine. But—wait—I can get you to someone. Hold on."

I hold on like I'm dangling over the edge of a cliff, and there are agonies of sharp rocks and toothy predators lurking below.

There's a click. Then another, followed by silence. Then—

Identity confirmed, says the voice I thought I extinguished. My heart leaps up into my throat, choking me with emotion. Tears form so quickly, it makes my eyeballs ache.

"Ada?" I whisper, breathless.

Lyra. How can I assist you?

I squeeze my eyes shut, tears sliding down the bridge of my nose and falling soundless onto the console.

"I thought—after the Yanvin Protocol—I thought you were gone," I blubber, trying to keep my voice down, but it comes out as an emotion-choked shrill hiss.

Orion uploaded me to Evie's cruiser. He would have been unable to find his way to Epsilon-6 and Agent Vega without doing so. I suspected you wouldn't consider this before enacting the Yanvin Protocol. Fortunately, he was able to preserve our data in time.

Orion.

I grip the receiver like it's the only real thing left in the world. "He's with you?"

Yes.

My lungs seize. A sob punches through my ribs like a piston.

"Put him on," I say, voice trembling. "Please."

There's more static on the line. My pulse thuds against my jaw and through my temples, building upon the ache of stress, dehydration, and exhaustion. It all evaporates in an instant, though, as soon as I hear a familiar deep voice on the other end of the line.

"Lyra?"

It's not just relief. It's not even joy. It's grief, raw and sudden and aching, because I hear him and realize how much I missed him, how much I need him, and how much I don't think I deserve him.

I curl my filthy, sweat-soaked body around the transceiver like it might help put me back together.

"Orion," I whisper. "I'm so sorry. I forgot to tell you about how to find Vega—I should've helped you out before I erased everything. I wasn't thinking! I didn't mean to—"

"I found him," he says, and that's all. No lecture. No anger. Just quiet truth, steady as his hands.

"You should be back on Xylothia," I admonish, my voice watery beneath my tears.

"I couldn't just leave, Lyra," he says with a sigh that perfectly encapsulates how doomed and inevitable this was. "I won't. Not until you tell me to go—and really mean it."

My face crumples, and it feels like every nerve is raw and singing with pain.

"I drag ruin behind me, Orion. I'm like a parade leader steering supernovas of destruction in my wake! You don't know what it's like being me. I don't know how to be anything else," I sob, quietly breaking in this room of forgotten, useless things.

"I know exactly what you are," he insists. "And I'm here. I'm still here."

There's silence on my end now, but it's not empty. It's full of everything I can't say: the comfort of his breath in my ear, the ache of memory, the way the stars never seemed worth reaching for until he was there beside me in the cockpit, his hand brushing mine in the dark.

"I don't want to run anymore," I whisper, the enormity of it sinking into me like a too-big bite of food I'm struggling to swallow.

"Then don't."

Ada chimes in, gentle, like a candle lit between us.

Secure channel established. Lyra, I am initiating preliminary intrusion into Brill's security system. I require access to a local node.

I wipe my sleeve across my face, fingers tightening into something that almost feels like resolve.

"There's a sub-panel near the eastern wing. It's here on the maintenance level that I'm already on. I can reach it," I sniff.

"I'm going to patch you through to Vega," Orion says. "He's got a plan for getting you out of there."

Thank the stars.

I lean back, the sound of Orion's breathing still in my ear, and for the first time in what feels like a lifetime, I'm not just hiding. I'm moving forward.

***

FROM THE CRAWLSPACE above the garage, I watch an entire galaxy of villains arrive.

The ships come down in gliding arcs, flaring their retro thrusters and disgorging passengers like dribbling retinues of entitled vomit. Buyers, bodyguards, high-stakes parasites in polished boots, sweeping capes, and expensive jackets—move through the docking bays with that slow, entitled grace that says they've never bled for anything, never wanted for anything.

I track them through the vents, through slits in rust-streaked grates, their faces half-lit by the pulsing overheads and the stuttering crimson glow of exhaust lights.

The scents of ozone and engine grease rise up to my hiding place, and I can feel the vibration of landings in my ribs. The landing bay and garage are twin hives of activity—cargo lifts grind and ascend to the upper floors of the compound, voices echo in languages I half-recognize—the laughter a little too sharp, a little too loud. With a prickle of unease, I notice there are weapons absolutely everywhere. Plasma rifles slung loose over shoulders, elegant daggers and plasma pistols holstered in places of pride. It's alarmingly lethal on the guards and mercenaries, but hilariously ostentatious on the buyers who've come to bid.

Void Stalkers are out in full force now, running patrols, scanning manifests, barking orders no one dares ignore. I count at least three new craft bearing Triumvirate insignia—one from Mallorus, even.

Hmm. I wonder if Fobos is here.

Beneath me, two guards pause near the service station, arguing quietly over whether I'm still in the compound. One of them says Brill's upped the bounty again, adding another million credits. The second guard suggests my pussy's the priciest thing for light-years around, making the first guard laugh like it's the funniest thing he's ever heard. My fingers tighten against the grate, but I don't let myself react.

Instead, I breathe—shallow, controlled. Every inch of me is pressed flat against the metal, watching. Waiting. I know what's coming. Vega explained that the blackout's been timed down to the second. Ada will trigger it. Orion will be in position, hiding in Vega's otherwise empty cruiser. Vega's already here, masquerading as the kind of buyer who traffics in people. His fake idol is still with a faction of Void Stalkers, quietly feeding data to the by-the-book Feds who have to put together a case before they can so much as sneeze.

Even though I know it's a ruse, disgust leaks from my pores and leaves a sour taste in my mouth. Vega's plan is meant to extract me, sure, but for as long as I've been crouched in these damn air ducts and ventilation shafts, I haven't been able to work out what else is being auctioned off. Or who else is being auctioned off. With all the millionaire, billionaire, trillionaire assholes arriving to purchase people like cuts of meat, I wonder if it wouldn't be better to burn the whole fucking thing down.

Maybe that's a dream for another day.

For now, I'm above it all, tucked into the stars-forsaken shadows, sweating through desert and exhaust-fueled heat. Through the copper-smelling dust coating me from head to toe, I'm finally bearing witness to the last calm before the chaos I helped design.

Despite everything that's at stake and my habit of nervous, rumbling intestinal distress, I'm remarkably calm. Maybe it's the dehydration, or the days with only scraps of food, or the fact that either we're going to succeed or we're all going to die. Whatever it is, I'm grateful for the oddly out-of-place sense of peace. There's a finality to everything that feels…comforting, somehow.

And more than anything, I'll get to see Orion again.

Maybe for the last time, my mind whispers insidiously.

"No," I hiss, just in time with the shrieking hydraulic whir of another ship landing in the compound.

A minute passes, maybe two. I count each heartbeat like a detonator tick. Somewhere below me, someone yells about a glitch in the docking assistant controls, and I smile grimly. That's not a glitch, buddy. That's my girl Ada, whispering through the compound's digital bones.

Then it happens.

The first flicker is almost a tease—a flirt of darkness, a saucy little wink from the void. The overhead lights blink once, twice, like they're not sure whether to commit to this sudden existential crisis. I feel the shift ripple through the garage like a nervous breath. Someone drops a tool. A guard's voice snaps sharp in the gloom.

Then a full blackout slams down, abrupt as a guillotine, and stars, the effect is delicious.

For a beat, the world below me seems to hold its breath. It's total darkness—not even the always-on emergency running lights flicker on. I hear the echo of boots, the rustle of ships settling in place, and a low, collective murmur of "what the hell" from the assembled audience of buyers, thugs, guards, and general wealthy elite space trash.

Finally, the backup lights stutter to life—red strips bleeding across the garage floor like veins. An alarm pings somewhere, half-hearted and confused, as if the compound's own systems aren't sure what the hell just happened. Exactly as planned.

I can't see Vega's ship from this angle, but I know it's there. I saw it land earlier—sleek, matte, unmarked, the kind of cruiser a man pretending to have a soul would use to buy a person in style. Ada's hitching a ride in its nav systems, connected tenuously to her consciousness tucked into Orion's borrowed cruiser.

Orion's tucked inside Vega's ship somewhere, hopefully safe. I imagine him crouched in the shadows, tense and focused, smelling like sweat and mossy forest soil and everything I miss. My infuriating, beautiful, righteous pain-in-my-ass. Of all the things I've ruined, he's the one I regret most.

And then, like an infection spreading through the nerves of a dying animal, the compound begins to unravel.

A powered lift locks up mid-load, grinding to a halt with an ear-piercing shriek that makes half the room jump. A pair of drones flicker and fall out of the sky like drunk mosquitoes. Someone's shouting about their comms being down. Perfect. Ada's burning through everything like a massive star going supernova.

Below, Kraxis barrels in like he knows I'm to blame, and my heart beats halfway between fear and malicious satisfaction. I can't hear everything he's yelling, but his tone is sharp, which makes the guttural Void Stalker words sound almost painful. He's real pissed, which is bad. He's suspicious, which is worse. His tail whips around behind him like he's trying to cosplay vengeance itself. One of the other guards mutters something, and Kraxis grabs him by the collar and throws him—just throws him—into a cargo crate. No one else makes a sound after that.

I keep my breath shallow, pressed as close to the duct's interior as I can manage. He's barking orders now—something about motion sensors, floor sweeps, sealing the doors, followed by something incredibly offensive about "the hybrid." Charming.

Then my stomach lurches, because I see a shadow peel off from the far side of the garage—just a flicker, a suggestion of movement between two parked shuttles. For a second I think I'm hallucinating, heat-dazed and dream-hungry. But then the light pulses again and I see him.

Orion.

Stars, he haunts every fevered dream I've had since we parted, but I'd bet my left tit he's actually gotten sexier in the intervening days. Rather than his absurd khaki ranger uniform, he's clad head-to-toe in skintight black body armor. It hugs his broad chest and thick thighs exactly like I want to, and I have to shake myself back into focus because dammit, now is not the time to rub one out in an air duct.

He's making his way toward the maintenance stairs—he's almost there—and stars, he might actually be good at this? Who would've thought my own little backwater boy scout could move like a ghost, fluid and fast and all delicious, coiled tension.

Unfortunately, at that moment Kraxis turns. His head snaps toward the stairs, nostrils flaring like a lupitian catching scent.

Shit. Shit shit shit.

He doesn't see Orion directly—not yet—but I know he saw the movement. A shadow. Enough to set his dim-witted paranoia fully on fire. He starts moving, and two Void Stalker guards move with him, weapons up, scanning every inch of the dark.

Orion's a second from being caught, and because I think I'm in love with the broad-shouldered, thick-thighed tree hugger, I move without thinking.

I unscrew the duct panel, fingers slick with grime, and drop into the narrow service corridor like a meteorite in freefall. I hit the floor hard, knees jarring, but adrenaline makes the pain irrelevant. I run for the nearest wall console, praying it hasn't been frizzed out and gutted in one of the power surges.

It hasn't, thank the stars.

I slam my hand on the proximity alarm trigger and duck behind a tool rack as a new klaxon blares, harsh and grating.

"Something tripped the proximity alarm in the southeastern corner of the launch bay," one of the Void Stalkers shouts, and I recognize my good buddy Thall. Piece of shit lizard dick, I grumble to myself.

Kraxis wheels around, hatred written on his reptilian face.

"There!" he snarls. "Sweep it now!"

His guards scatter toward the false signal.

And Orion—stars bless his insubordinate soul—moves.

He bolts for the corridor as Kraxis stalks off in the opposite direction. I catch up just in time to grab Orion's wrist and drag him through a side door and into a closet barely big enough for a vacuum mop and our collective regret.

We slam into each other in the dark, breathless, pressed chest-to-chest in an awkward tangle of limbs and heat and holy-shit-we're-alive.

I don't say anything. He doesn't either.

Outside, boots thunder past. Voices echo down the corridor—too far to catch specifics, but angry enough to keep us frozen.

Then silence. We're still for a beat, then another.

"I'm starting to think you missed me," Orion whispers, his breath hot against my ear. Lust is never far from my mind when it comes to him, and it burns through my body like a struck match.

I bite the inside of my cheek to hold in my manic, relieved, choking-with-tears laugh.

"You were supposed to go back to Xylothia and forget about me," I whisper, pressing my face into his neck and inhaling like an addict. "You're such a disobedient idiot."

"Yeah," he sighs, threading his fingers through my filthy clumps of hair. "I didn't used to be. But I picked it up from someone along the way."

He's grinning—I can feel it in the dark. And I hate how much I missed that grin. I hate how much I missed his everything.

Calm down, Lyra. Do not *try to fuck him in this closet.*

I peek out the door. Kraxis and his Void Stalker groupies are gone.

And for a single breath, a single blink in this flickering, half-lit hell, we're still safe.

22
orion

Down and Blacked Out

THE CLOSET IS STIFLING. There's barely enough room for the two of us to breathe, let alone think. My back is pressed to the cold inner wall, and Lyra is flush against me—every inch of her body molded to mine like we're melting into each other's personal space.

Her leg's hooked over mine, her hip wedged hard into my thigh, and her breath comes in short, shallow bursts against my collarbone. My synesfores pulse in time with her heartbeat—the mating instinct buzzing beneath my skin practically singing at her proximity. The only thing keeping me from ripping her pants off and sinking into her warm, wet cunt is sheer restraint, and even that's wearing thin.

Outside, the world flickers in and out of existence. The compound's lights stutter violently—emergency systems glitching in waves as Ada dutifully rolls the blackout through each sector. One second it's pitch black, the next it's a seizure-bright pulse of crimson and yellow that slices through the slats in the closet door, casting fractured shadows across her face.

Kraxis has returned.

I feel Lyra tense when we hear him barking orders—his voice hard and clipped, hunting.

"Sweep the north corridor. Scan every panel, every seam. She's here somewhere. Find her, and Brill pays a million. You know what's at stake if we don't find her," he rages at his crew.

Every few seconds, his boots echo too close. Muffled voices ricochet off the concrete and carbon steel walls. Something mechanical groans nearby—maybe one of the compound's retractable hangar arms trying to reboot.

But all I can think about is her.

Lyra. In my arms. Alive.

And more dangerously—close.

Ever since Vega's plan came together, I haven't been able to shake the vision of her broken in some dark corner of this compound—stripped of her fire, hollowed out by Brill's cruelty. And now she's here—trembling against me, dirty and exhausted and still the most exquisite thing I've ever seen.

She's so stars-damned beautiful, I ache with wanting—burn with it, like she's a star and I'm about to be incinerated by drifting too close.

She tilts her face up. Her violet eyes meet mine, wide and wary in the dark. There's a smear of grease across her temple, a gash half-healed on her jaw. Her full lips are cracked but parted slightly, and when she exhales, it ghosts across my skin like a drug.

"You almost didn't make it," she whispers, voice ragged.

I swallow the knot in my throat. "I would've ripped this place apart to get to you."

Her fingers curl against the stretchy black fabric of my shirt. "I'm not sure there'd have been anything left of me to find."

My hands move without thinking—one sliding around her waist, the other cradling the back of her head. She arches slightly, just enough for her body to press closer. Just enough that the thin barrier of clothing between us feels like an insult.

I lean down slowly, touching my forehead to hers. And because I can't seem to resist any of my buried impulses when it comes to her, I let my lips trail down her hairline, curling around the shell of her ear. Almost gone. She was almost gone.

"You don't know what you are to me," I murmur, peppering soft kisses down her ear, trailing down her neck.

Her breath hitches and she shivers, her pulse fluttering beneath my lips.

"Then tell me," she challenges.

Stars help me. The sound of her voice wrecks me. I've spent my life believing control was strength—precision, order, duty. But there's nothing disciplined about the way I need her. I've never wanted anything I couldn't earn, and yet every cell in my body is begging to be hers.

"On the ship, I never got the chance to explain to you, Lyra… You're my mate," I say, and the words leave me raw. "In every way that matters to my kind. My biology…my instincts…they've all chosen you. Duty kept me alive. You make me want to live."

The words tear out of me, raw and reverent. For so long, I've carried the weight of my parents' legacy—their devotion, their sacrifice, the duty that killed them. I thought upholding it was my purpose. But this—her—it's something deeper. I want to protect her not out of obligation, but because I can't imagine the universe without her in it. Because I don't know how to breathe if I'm not breathing her in. Because my whole damn life, I've been trying to prove myself worthy of something—and she's the first thing that's ever made me believe I already am.

She stares at me, stunned. "Uh, come again?"

I chuckle, because she's not pulling away, which means maybe, maybe this won't ruin us.

"It's a biology thing. My body—my instincts—recognize you as a perfect match for me. I started feeling it back on Xylothia and I wondered…but the more time has passed, the more certain I've become. After we had sex, my mating nodes changed. The next time—if there is a next time—it means knotting," I murmur.

"Knotting," she echoes, eyes wide. "Like, you'd…"

Her hand snakes down to rub my cock through my pants, and it's already hard thanks to her extreme proximity.

"Yes," I hiss when she grips me through the fabric. "The nodes—stars, Lyra, you're going to kill me if you keep doing that—swell inside you. It's to increase the likelihood of conception. The heat lasts for hours, but every Xylothian is different. I've—I've never knotted anyone before."

"Conception?" her firm strokes slow infinitesimally.

"Not if you don't want it," I practically whimper. "Kids, I mean. I can take the pill."

Her hand resumes the torturous movement, and she reaches up to ghost her lips across the line of my jaw.

"Matehood. That's not just…a metaphor?" she whispers.

"No. It's chemical. Semi-permanent. Sacred."

She pulls back and blinks up at me, lips parting further, and for a second—for one burning, perfect second—I stare at her lips like I can will them to meet mine. The corners of her mouth turn up, and she makes the move.

Her mouth crashes against mine like she's drowning and I'm the last breath she'll ever get. Her hands fist in my shirt, yanking me closer, and I'm lost. Her taste is fire and sweetness and everything I've been aching for since she was taken.

My hips rock forward before I can stop them, my body responding to hers like it's instinct. I want her. I *need* her.

And stars save me, she wants me, too.

She grinds once—just once—and it nearly undoes me. Her legs tighten around my thigh, and a low, involuntary sound tears out of her throat, muffled against my mouth.

I'm drowning in her heat, her scent, the heady rush of her skin pressed to mine. My fingers slip under her shirt, tracing the line of her back, the curve of her waist. She gasps when I find bare skin.

But then—*BANG!* A sharp noise explodes from outside our hiding place. There's an angry din of voices, cut through with Kraxis's shouting.

We freeze. In the stifling heat of the closet, we're both panting, mouths inches apart, hearts slamming in sync. I press my hand gently to her lips, stilling her, and she nods.

Outside, boots stomp past and a door slams. The silence that stretches between us crackles with energy. My forehead stays pressed to hers, and I can still feel her trembling. Not from fear now—from restraint.

"I almost didn't get to you in time," I whisper. "And the thought of that—of never holding you again—it nearly broke me."

She presses her mouth to my jaw again, soft, reverent. "We'll get out," she murmurs. "You and me."

I nod. "But when we do—Lyra, you need to know. I'm not letting you go again. I can't."

The flickering outside slows. The blackout's entering its final cycle. It's almost time to move, but for now, we stay pressed together in the dark.

IT'S PROBABLY ONLY a few minutes that we're stuck in the closet, but it feels like both an eternity and no time at all. When Lyra finally moves, unwinding her limbs from around me, my mating instincts rage and I'm forced to fist my hands at my sides to keep from reaching forward and pulling her back to me.

It hasn't escaped my notice that she hasn't said anything about my confession, but when we're safe and back on the ship, we can talk it out. Work through it. I'm determined not to try and stifle her, despite my hormones clamoring for me to chain myself to her feet and worship her with my entire body.

I pause at that—the thought eerily similar to my response the very first time she demonstrated the power of her *vellia*. This time, however, I know it's not her biology at the root of it.

She tugs at my wrist again, pointing outside our cramped hiding space. Some of the activity has died down, and we both seem to be of a mind that it's safe to slip out and meet up with Vega for our rendezvous.

As I'm about to open the door, Lyra stops me—her hand on mine.

"Before we go," she whispers. "I—thank you. Thank you for coming. I know I said I wanted you to go, but…I'm really glad you came back."

"I meant what I said, Lyra. I will always come for you," I say. There's a faint lift to her lips and a glint of heat in her eyes—I can tell she wants to make a prurient joke at the phrasing, but she seems to think better of it.

The lights stutter off again, and we use the opportunity to slip out of the closet and head out through the corridor. We're meant to meet Vega in the lower levels of the compound that are just above these maintenance floors. Ada is managing to keep the rotating blackout pattern in an effort to give us bursts of cover, but it means we have to time every movement precisely.

We make it halfway through the corridor when I hear it—a low, rumbling hiss and heavy boots. Lyra freezes beside me, whirling around.

Kraxis.

Lyra's eyes dart across the dark hallway for an exit, a duct, anything, but it's too late.

He steps out from the shadows like he's been waiting here this whole time—hulking, plated in his telltale fitted black armor, the low thrum of a plasma rifle in his hands humming like a death sentence. His eyes glow faintly in the flicker of emergency lighting.

"Lyra Phoenix and her Xylothian ranger," he growls.

Rude. I have a name.

Lyra moves fast. She shoves me aside and dives behind a collapsed beam, her motion drawing Kraxis's attention for just a second, but it's enough. I pull the plasma pistol from my thigh holster and aim, but he fires first. A bolt of plasma slices past my cheek and melts a hole through the wall behind me. The shock-wave sends a bloom of heat licking over my skin.

Lyra pops up and hurls a piece of metal—a broken vent cover. It clangs off his shoulder with no real damage, but it distracts him again.

She moves like lightning. She launches herself at him, using the lower strut of the beam as a springboard. Mid-air, she twists and drops onto his back. He snarls, slamming her into the wall, but she clings on and rips a blade from the holster on his waist. I see the moment it shifts—from struggle to fury.

She stabs him in the shoulder, and then in his side. Once. Twice.

Kraxis roars. He slams her into the floor, but she rolls, agile and vicious. Her strikes are savage—blows to the ribs, the joints. She's relentless, fighting like she wants to peel him out of his own skin.

But Kraxis isn't just brute force—he's a killer with a penchant for pain.

With a snarl, he feints left, then pivots. His hand latches around my throat, dragging me up. The plasma pistol is back in his hand, humming with deadly promise, and it presses against my temple. Oh, you've got to be kidding me—not again.

Lyra freezes.

"Drop it," he spits. "Or I paint the floor with his brains."

Her chest heaves. For a moment, I see the storm of indecision in her eyes—pure rage and helplessness. But then she lets the blade clatter to the floor.

"Good girl," Kraxis sneers, adjusting the grip on his weapon. "You know, I've never understood your appeal. Brill always was such a fool about you. But I harbor no delusions, and I'm tired of having to chase you around the galaxy, making sure you're not about to betray him. It will save me so much work if I just kill you now."

He turns the barrel toward her.

In that split second, everything inside me snaps. Rage,

disgust, sheer, unfettered loathing that this creature threatens my *mate.*

I will bleed you dry.

I twist, using the momentum of his shift, and flip him over my back. The gun fires wild, scorching the ceiling, and we crash to the floor.

My fists find the bony ridges of his face again and again. Wisps of memories swirl in my mind—being in this state before, during the grief of my parents' death. Too rough, too brutal with the smugglers I caught, who I felt were dishonoring their memory. This dark rage is familiar—it sings to me in time with the pounding mating instinct.

Kraxis claws at me, but I pin his arms. I see Lyra grab the plasma rifle and aim, but I shake my head.

He snarls something about her not being worth the trouble she causes. Truthfully, I barely hear him through the ringing in my ears. I let the words fill me with cold, righteous fury.

Then I break his nose. Crack a rib. He gasps, still reaching. His tail flies out from behind him, curling toward Lyra, who's standing to the side with the pistol aimed at his head.

With a final surge of possessive, protective instincts, I grab his jaw and snap his neck clean to the side.

Silence. Heavy, echoing silence. When the red at the edges of my vision clears, nausea roils through my insides, making me want to retch.

For a moment, all I hear is our breathing—hers ragged, mine slow and thick with adrenaline. Lyra lowers the weapon. She looks at me, eyes wide and glassy.

"He's dead. I can't believe he's dead. He's dead and you killed him," she says, shock beginning to creep into her voice. "I can't believe you killed him. After everything he put me through —after everything he did."

"I'm so sorry, Lyra," I say, sick with the reality of the violence but satisfied that I helped remove a threat from her life. "For everything he put you through."

She's staring down at his body, but then lifts her gaze to mine, as if she's seeing me in a new light.

"Did...did you want to do it?" I ask, suddenly uncertain. With everything that's happened, maybe she wanted to be the one to kill him.

"No," she murmurs. "I didn't. I just...I can't believe he's dead."

I wipe the blood off my face with the back of my hand and step toward her. "You softened him up. I just finished the job. I was tired of that bastard sticking his damned plasma pistol in my face."

She opens her mouth, probably to say something smart, but I grab her and pull her into me.

"Besides, he threatened you," I finish, trying to shake her out of her stunned state. We don't have much time as it is, and killing Kraxis is most definitely going to move our timetable up.

Lyra sucks in a breath, blinking down at the unmoving body of another one of her tormenters.

"We should move," I say. "We've got to meet Vega at the extraction point and get the hell off this stars-damned planet. Do you know how to get upstairs without being seen?"

She nods, stumbling a little. She seems like she's about to go into shock, and I need to do something to get her to focus.

"Close your eyes," I murmur. She doesn't argue, just does as I ask—a sure sign she's not in her right mind. I lug Kraxis's body over to our previously vacated closet, shoving him in and covering him with a tarp. I mutter a small Xylothian prayer for the dead, hoping that when he meets the Death Goddess, he'll be judged for every hurt he inflicted on Lyra.

When I return to Lyra, she blinks blearily at me.

"Thank you," she says softly.

I arch my brow. "It's time for us to get out of here. Are you okay to keep moving, or do I need to carry you? I'm happy to throw you over my shoulder, but I can't promise I won't cop a feel. Might even try to sink my teeth into that nice ass of yours."

The lascivious threat has the intended effect, unfreezing her and eliciting a soft, pink blush that spreads up her neck.

"Promises, promises," she says. "Just try to keep up, Ranger."

We dip into a nearby hover-vator that ascends quickly, and we get off just beneath the main floor. Above the maintenance floors, the halls gleam in a warm, yellow polished stone and tiled floors with intricate mosaics speak of a cold elegance. We're able to duck most of the guests and guards since the chaos we've sewn has been localized to the deepest parts of the compound. Still, the blackout continues to roll through these areas, as well.

Soft overhead lights flicker in their housings, casting strange shadows along the corridor walls. The recycled air has a dry, electronic taint to it and it makes me miss the lush forests of my home world with a powerful ache. I follow close behind Lyra, who's moving with more confidence now—her steps still shaky, but sure. I know the moment the adrenaline wears off, she'll crash. But for now, she's back in control, and I trust her instincts more than my own.

We wind up at the bottom of a polished staircase, and from the look in Lyra's eyes, I immediately get the sense that Brill's rooms are at the top. She hesitates—apparently unsure if she's ready to climb these steps and end it all now, or if getting to Vega and getting out of here is her priority. I nod when her gaze cuts to me, trying to assure her wordlessly that whatever she decides, I'm with her all the way.

Fingers gripping the banister, she exhales and shakes her head, her meaning clear—Brill will get his another day.

We skirt the opulent staircase and she leads us through a hidden side door that opens out into the forbiddingly dry Ooneryx desert. Brill's landscaped grounds are filled with brutal desert plants and suns-baked red and yellow earth. As soon as we step outside, we both immediately start coughing on the foul air and wind-blown dust, squinting across the horizon at the three setting suns. Pulling me back towards the edge of the compound's thick, gray walls, Lyra leads us on, ducking between security drones and outdoor camera feeds.

Our extraction point is supposed to be just outside an old, abandoned hangar—a wide chamber tucked behind the gardens where gardening drones are stored and serviced. The glorified shed is bristling with busted speeders, half-dismantled hover-crafts, and boxes of contraband that never made it into orbit. It takes us longer than I'd like to reach it—twice we have to hide behind massive spiked bushes to avoid patrols of Brill's private guard sweeping the area. They haven't gotten the memo about Kraxis.

But the moment we reach the rust-pitted shed, I spot him: Agent Vega, standing near the hull of a dust-covered skimmer, fiddling with a comms panel. He glances up and sees us. Relief flashes across his face, fast and fleeting.

"Took you long enough," he mutters, keeping his voice low as he ushers us into the shadow of the skimmer. "What happened?"

Lyra tilts her head, eyes steady and hard. "We ran into Kraxis. He's dead."

Vega raises his brows, but he doesn't ask for details. He knows better.

"I've got some bad news," he says instead, voice tightening. "Brill's gone. Disappeared when the power started to go out. No sign of his shuttle, either—he must've had a back door none of us saw."

Lyra pales at that, but she nods like she'd expected it.

"We're still getting data from the fake idol," Vega replies. "Encrypted command-level archives, partial routing maps, financial chains. It'll take the Bureau weeks to process it all, but it's enough to start dismantling his network from the inside out."

"But not enough to stop him," Lyra says.

"Not yet," Vega agrees. "But he won't be able to hide for long."

There's a pause. Then Vega's eyes settle on Lyra with something like genuine gentleness. "You did good, Lyra. Better than anyone could've asked. We wouldn't have half this intel if not for you."

She doesn't answer right away. I watch her shoulders stiffen, like she's keeping something in. Her voice, when it comes, is quiet.

"Not good enough. He's still out there."

"We'll get him," Vega says. "One way or another. He won't run forever."

I'm not sure she believes that. I'm not sure I believe it. But we nod, and that's enough for now.

Vega opens his pack and produces two ID tags and a compact satchel. "You'll need these. Transport credentials, comm scramblers, and a clean identity chip each. Should be enough to get you off-world. Cruiser's parked in an auxiliary bay west of here —level six. Should still be operational."

I take the satchel from him. "What about you?"

"I've got to head back to *Epsilon-6*, but I'll stay in touch. If I get a hit on Brill's whereabouts, I'll send word."

He holds out a hand. I clasp it, firm. "Thank you."

Then he turns to Lyra. They don't hug, and I don't think either of them wants to. But there's something shared in the look between them—comrades, co-conspirators, survivors.

"Take care of yourself, Vega," she says, violet eyes flashing. "And if you catch him before I do...don't kill him."

He gives a solemn nod. "Understood."

Then we're moving again. No one's chasing us, but it still feels like we're being watched. Lyra keeps pace with me down the service stairs, through the lavish halls and toward the west hangar. We only speak once we reach the exterior doors and the sloping tunnel that leads to the cruiser bay.

Lyra glances at me sideways. "You still have the idol?"

I nod, eyeing her suspiciously. "I do. Why?"

She blows out a breath. "Let's take it back to Xylothia."

"What?" My mouth drops open in shock.

"It belongs there. Your people need it—you need it. The Feds don't need it anymore. I'm sure they'll have their hands full chasing after Brill and his whole stars-damned network."

There's something fierce in her again. Not rage, exactly— something colder. Something cleaner. Resolve.

When we reach the cruiser, my gut unclenches just a little. It's still where we left it—sleek, scuffed, and blessedly flight-ready. Lyra stops at the bottom of the boarding ramp and looks back.

"This isn't over," she says, more to herself than to me.

"No," I agree. "But it's the beginning of the end. They'll get him, Lyra. The Feds are onto him now."

She nods and we board together, and for the first time in days, I feel like I can breathe.

23

lyra

A Place in the Sun

I CAN'T BELIEVE I made it out. Scratch that—I can't believe *we* made it out.

The minute we made it into the cruiser, Orion set about cleaning and bandaging the worst of my injuries. He made me chug an entire bottle of water and sternly insisted I eat two protein bars, despite the fact that that's all I ate during the days in my air duct hiding spot and the sight of them makes me want to hurl.

His attention to the care and keeping of me is both adorable and incredibly infuriating, but I suspect that's because it's been a very, *very* long time since I've had someone caring for me in a purely selfless, generous kind of way.

Once my injuries and the worst of my malnourishment have been assuaged, Orion gathers what supplies he can so that I can take a very unceremonious sponge bath in the small cruiser's cramped bathroom.

Sigh. My luxurious soak will have to wait, I suppose.

Though his attention has been entirely focused on my well-being, he's been mostly silent since we rocketed through Ooneryx's noxious atmosphere. The cruiser's cabin is dim, the lights low like Ada set them that way so I can try to sleep. But I'm not asleep.

I don't know if I'll ever sleep soundly again.

We're a couple days out from Xylothia now, finally slipping through void-dark space, nothing but stars in every direction. The idol is locked down in a secure cabinet in the cargo chamber behind me. Agent Vega is gone, and the compound is behind us. Brill is somewhere out there.

And Kraxis…Kraxis is dead. Orion killed him. *For me.*

The realization keeps catching in my chest and I'm ashamed to admit that it hurts. It shouldn't—but it does. Not because I'm mourning the bastard, but because I'm having to confront the fact that if Orion hadn't met me, his body count would be considerably less. His first day on my ship, he told me how much his people honored life and sacrifice and abhorred selfishness and violence. And yet…he snapped Kraxis's neck. I watched it happen. I watched him make that choice steeped in absolute anger and hatred and certainty. Would he have, if he hadn't met me? Have I completely ruined this upright, honorable Xylothian ranger just by being who I am—decidedly a *hot fucking mess*?

I wrap my arms tighter around myself and press my forehead to my knees, tucked up on the bench opposite the flight deck. Neither Ada nor Orion have spoken much since we left. I know they're trying to give me space, which I'm both grateful for and miffed about. Orion's just been sitting in the cockpit, checking our trajectory, murmuring quietly to Ada, trying not to look at me too long.

I wish he would. I wish he *wouldn't*. *Ugh*. It's possible my thoughts are the messiest they've ever been. And my heart? My heart's worse.

I can still feel the warmth of Orion's hands on my waist, still hear the rumble of his voice when he told me I was his mate. That word. *Mate*. I haven't stopped thinking about it since—not for one second. It echoes in me louder than Kraxis's last breath. *Stars, how fucked up is that?* I just witnessed the brutally violent death of one of the few constants in my life over the past 14 years and all I can think about is what the hot Xylothian said to me before he did it. *Sorry, Kraxis, you piece of lizard shit. May the Death Goddess make your afterlife worse than the living hell you made mine.*

Orion's gaze keeps flicking to me when he thinks I'm not looking. The look in his eyes threatens to crack open my ribs and carve out my heart with how earnest and yearning it is.

Mate. What does that even mean to a Xylothian? Hell, what does that mean to a Velusian?

I know what it means to me, though—it means terrifying. It means permanent. It means giving up pieces of myself I've never let anyone touch. It means handing over my tether, auction or no. But I can't stop thinking about the way he looked at me—like I belonged to him. Like he'd rend the galaxy in half to protect me, and weak, romantic, soft-hearted wimp that I am…I hate how much I want that. No one's *ever* wanted me like that. Brill wanted to possess me, my lovers wanted me sexually, the Feds want me judicially, and Kraxis? *Well.* Kraxis just wanted me to bleed. Orion's only ever wanted me for *me.*

The cabin rocks gently as the ship adjusts course. I glance up, and there he is—tall and too handsome for his own good, muscles stretched under a thin white tee-shirt, boots braced wide for balance. He catches my eye for a heartbeat, then turns his gaze to the console again.

He's definitely a coward, but I'm definitely worse.

Because I'm the one who walked away from him first. I'm the one who said take the idol, save your people, go. And he did! But now he's here. And I'm here. And the idol's safe. And Brill is out there somewhere—but for tonight, at least, we're free.

And still, he hasn't said it again.

I sit up slowly. My voice sounds like gravel. "Orion."

He turns instantly. "Yeah?"

I lick my lips, still raw from days of dehydration. My nerves tangle in my gut.

"So, um, you said I was your mate." *Smooth, Lyra. Real smooth.*

There's a long pause as the silence thickens between us.

"I did," he says finally. His voice is calm. Controlled. Too careful.

"Were you serious?"

His eyes meet mine—vibrantly green, burning even in the low light. He swallows, his throat working nervously.

"That's not the kind of thing I'd joke about."

My heart thuds once, hard enough to make me dizzy.

I take a breath. Then another. "What…what does that mean to you? Having a mate?"

He hesitates, like he's not sure how honest he should be.

"Tell me," I say, softer this time. "Please."

He exhales and crosses the room slowly, not touching me, but sinking onto the bench across from mine. He leans forward, elbows on his knees, fingers laced.

"Xylothian matehood isn't destiny," he says. "Not like it is for some species. It's biological. Instinctual. A kind of recognition. Our bodies know. Our instincts know. It's not always about love. But…sometimes it is."

His gaze lifts to mine.

"With you, it is."

I want to look away, but I don't. Because it *means* something. And that terrifies me.

"I didn't choose it," he continues. "But I'd choose you a thousand times over. Being my mate means you're the one for me—the only one. You're the one my body recognizes, the one I crave, the one I would die for. It means…you're already inside me, etched into my bones. And I will never want another."

My throat tightens.

He says it like it's the clearest truth in the world. There's no pleading, no pressure. Just reverence.

"I know it's not fair," he says with a small shake of his head. The green shimmer of his hair catches the low light of the cabin, a woodland rainbow. "I know you didn't ask for this. I'm not asking you for anything. I just…need you to know."

"And if I say I don't want it?" I whisper.

"I'll walk away," he says instantly. "If that's what you want. I'll never force a bond on you. I'd rather die than cage you." Eyes flashing, he adds, with heart-wrenching determination, "I'd never ask you for your tether."

Something in my chest splinters, and suddenly the space between us feels much too big. Maybe that's what I've been chasing all along—not freedom, not fortune. Just the right to be wanted for who I am, not what I can give.

"You're not caging me," I whisper.

He blinks.

"You never were. Well…except for that time when you tied me to your cot and threatened to turn me over to the Feds," I add, awkwardly.

A slow grin tugs at his mouth, and for a moment, I can breathe again.

And *stars*, the flash of those even white teeth and infuriating dimples—it takes nothing else for the heat to bloom between my thighs. My body hums with a pulse of want I can't suppress. And I see the moment he senses it, the way his nostrils flare slightly and his jaw tenses.

"Lyra," he murmurs, voice low, warning.

"It's not my *vellia*," I say quickly.

I shift, breath catching. The air feels thick between us now.

But the need isn't just physical—not anymore. It's layered with longing, fear, grief, and a smattering of hope that I don't know what to do with.

Yeah, I want him, but I want more than that. I want someone who stays. I want someone who sees the worst of me and doesn't leave. I want safety. I want to be wanted this fiercely, without my *vellia* and without some hidden agenda. And truthfully, I'm terrified. I'm so fucking scared that if I let him in, he'll tear down the walls I've lived behind my whole life—walls that have kept me safe, but walls that have made me lonely.

Freedom isn't the finish line I thought it was—it's the part no one tells you about, what comes after the running. Maybe it's not about what I steal or who I outsmart. Maybe it's about who I get to be when no one's holding the leash.

"You said your body recognizes me," I say, shifting closer.

"It does," he says, voice barely a rasp.

"Then what happens when you touch me?"

He's breathing hard now. "You know what happens."

"Show me."

"Lyra—"

"Please."

That one word breaks whatever willpower he has left.

In an instant, he's on me. His mouth finds mine, wild and hungry, and I gasp as he pulls me into his lap. His hands roam my body like he's memorizing it, and maybe he is—because I'm doing the same. I tear at his shirt, needing him skin to skin.

"I've wanted you since the day I met you," he growls, teeth grazing my neck. "I tried to be good. I tried to stay away. But stars—"

"Don't," I pant. "Don't stay away now."

His fingers slip beneath the waistband of my pants, finding me scorching and soaked.

"Fuck," he groans. "You're wet already?"

"You did this," I murmur.

His lips brush my ear, sending shivers of lust-sparked sensation throughout my entire body.

"And I'm going to finish it," he promises.

He lifts me in one smooth motion and lays me out on the narrow bunk. He strips me fast, reverently, until I'm bare beneath him—and then strips his own clothes and kneels, no hesitation.

Without preamble, his mouth is on me—licking, tasting,

worshipping—and I cry out, hips arching as pleasure crashes over me. He licks up every moan, every gasp, like he's devoted to learning the language of my body better than me. He devours me like I'm the only thing that's ever mattered. His tongue moves with purpose, circling my clit, teasing, pressing just right, and when he adds his fingers—*stars*—it's too good, it's too much, and I come apart like starlight scattering in vacuum.

I tremble as he rises, his body above mine, cock hard and glistening, mating nodes pulsing and glowing faintly.

"I want to be inside you," he whispers, forehead pressed to mine. "But I won't knot you until you choose me. Not just with your body—with everything. And when you do, I'm going to fuck you like you deserve, and imprint your body with the kind of pleasure that unmakes worlds and angers the gods."

I don't say anything, because part of me wants to drag him down and beg for it. The other part—the part that's still learning how to trust, how to hope—isn't ready. Not yet.

And somehow, he understands.

So instead, I guide him down beside me. I kiss him slow and deep, and when I slide my mouth over his heated skin, kissing and licking his white-flickering synesfores, his sharp intake of breath is one of the most powerful aphrodisiacs imaginable. I grip his shaft, stroking delicate fingertips across his throbbing mating notes, and his helpless groan shatters something in both of us. With equal fervor, I take him into my mouth, past the first swollen ridge, letting my tongue trace every sensitive curve. His hips jerk. His hands bury in my hair, gently, and I can tell he's holding back—the tendons on his neck and veins on his arms pop with the effort of it. I smile to myself, more than ready to show him why Velusians are made for pleasure.

Heat from his mating nodes warms my mouth, helping to ease my throat into taking him deep. Saliva slicks the smooth skin of his cock and *stars*, the *taste* of him…the earthy, saline flavor makes me almost as ravenous as his deep growls and soft whimpers. Desire sends a fresh flood of arousal to my core, and

I'm not going to deny myself the pleasure. The moment Orion sees my other hand drifting between my legs to stroke my needy sex, he moans.

"Fuck, yes—please please please—oh *stars please* come again for me," he whispers, his desperation spurring my need.

When I flip around and offer my pussy to his mouth, he utters a litany of words in Xylothian that I can't understand, but can guess at their meaning. He grabs my hips and buries his face in me. The faster I bob up and down on his cock, the faster his tongue moves against my clit, and already a second orgasm is bearing down on me like an asteroid bent on impact.

But I don't slow down until he gasps, "Lyra—*fuck*—you're gonna—I'm gonna come!"

I hum around him, and he breaks, pumping his release down my throat. His pleasure unlocks my own, crashing through me with devastating intensity, and I almost don't hear him gasping my name like a vow.

When he finally collapses beneath me, breathless and spent, I wriggle around and curl against his chest. The stars blur again through the viewport, like even the cosmos can't decide what shape they're supposed to take.

He brushes my hair back from my face.

"I won't pretend I don't want you to be mine, Lyra, but regardless of your decision, I'll always be yours."

I rest my hand on his chest, above his heart beating slow and steady. As constant as he is.

"…Orion?"

"Yeah?"

"…Ask."

He stills.

I lift my gaze to his, heart pounding.

"Ask me to be yours."

He cups my cheek, eyes burning. "Lyra Phoenix…will you be mine?"

I smile. "Already am."

BY THE TIME we're nearing Xylothia, Orion's excitement is bubbling over at the thought of returning home. He's equally excited that we'll be returning the Solar Mother idol to the Celestial Temple, and the whole rest of the trip back he's made it his mission to let me know *how* grateful he is that I said we should do it. Even with the tender skin on my sex, nipples, neck, and lips—the small bruises from his teeth and fingers, as it turns out, I *really* enjoy his gratitude.

As Ada pilots us down to the blue-green swirling mass of Xylothia, I stare out the window and try to see the planet through Orion's eyes. He comes to stand behind me, wrapping his arms around my waist and resting his chin on top of my head. The synesfores on his arms pulse a deep green that I've come to recognize as contentment.

"I'm not sure what kind of state my campsite and my swamp buggy are in after the Void Stalkers trashed it, but I was thinking maybe when we're done here, we could fly into the city. There's a really great restaurant near my apartment that I think you'll like," he says.

"Ranger Asterth, are you asking me out on a date?" I tease, my grin stretching wide and absolutely shit-eating.

His chuckle vibrates through my back and he brushes his cheek against my hair.

"I am. And I don't want to *assume* anything, but I happen to have a very large bathtub at my place. You've mentioned one or two or a thousand times how much you've longed for a relaxing bath."

"A very large bathtub, huh?"

"Yep. I'm pretty sure we'd both fit," he says softly, nipping at my ear and sending lust chasing through my veins.

"Is this date just a pretext so you can get me naked?" I laugh, turning to drape my arms around his neck.

"Stars, yes. Will it work?" he says, low and lush.

"Only one way to find out," I reply, letting my hands wander over his broad, muscular chest and firm abs, circling around to squeeze his tight ass.

Now entering Xylothian atmosphere. Being seated and belted in is advisable for atmospheric reentry.

"Thanks a lot, Ada," Orion mutters dourly.

You're welcome. I'm happy to do the work of navigating and piloting a ship I wasn't designed for while you two engage in extracurricular activities. Ada's as sarcastic as ever, but there's no real venom in it.

The landing is a lot rougher this time than the last time I was here, but likely due to the fact that this borrowed cruiser is much smaller than the *Aldrin-136* and we've apparently arrived at the beginning of monsoon season. Thick clouds hang low over the jungle canopy, coating everything in warm mist that promises rain soon.

As soon as the cruiser stills, Orion squeezes my hand and opens up the doors. The air on Xylothia hits like the breath of the Solar Mother herself—hot, damp, and heavy with green things growing. I blink against the sharp brilliance of twin suns slicing across the atmosphere as we step into the clearing that surrounds the Celestial Temple. It looks like some ancient beast half-buried in the jungle, ribs of obsidian stone jutting through a blanket of moss and vine.

Orion is already unstrapping the pack from the storage compartment, his movements confident and unhurried. The Solar Mother idol is tucked deep inside, swaddled in thick cloth, but even through the layers I swear I can feel its low, thrumming hum. It's like a pulse…a heartbeat.

We don't speak much as we make our way into the temple's outer corridors—only the soft brush of our boots against cracked tile, the distant echo of a jungle bird's cry, the sigh of leaves against stone. Orion leads the way, his hand hovering just above the moss-lined walls as if greeting his ancestors.

The path has changed since I was last here, even though it's only been a couple months. Roots have widened fissures in the stone. The banthus tree I climbed to save my own ass has sent a fresh tangle of shoots through the ceiling. There's a phantom ache in my side as if my body is remembering my fall last time, and I pay close attention to my steps this time around.

The interior of the temple smells like heat and time. Orion forges ahead, leading me through narrow passageways I was too hasty to miss before. They curve inward, drawing us past the inner courtyard and into a vast expanse of quiet that raises the hairs on my neck with a breath of familiarity.

The Chamber of the Early Sun is exactly as I remember—sanctified and still, the air so thick with reverence it practically buzzes. Light from the broken ceiling spears across the statue at the center, illuminating her outstretched arms. The priestess glows as if her own star lives inside her chest.

I feel Orion's breath catch beside me. "She's waiting."

Together, we move toward her—careful to avoid the hollow ground I nearly fell through the first time. Orion steps onto the low crypt beside me, crouching down to unwrap the idol. He passes it to me with both hands, the look in his eyes solemn.

"Go on," he says softly. "It should be you."

The idol is warm against my palms, humming with the same power it always held. But this time, instead of greed or desperation, what pulses through me is…something close to awe. A fullness. A final note in a song I didn't know I'd been humming.

I set it gently into the statue's cupped hands and cross back to Orion's open arms and waiting embrace.

A faint click echoes through the chamber, followed by a low tone—like the sound of a distant sigh carried on wind. Gold light seeps from the idol's seams, spilling over the statue's arms, swirling down to the floor. The whole room seems to exhale.

Then: silence.

And then—

"Beautiful, isn't it?"

The voice crashes into the stillness like a fist—a brutal fist I know all too well. Orion jerks around, pushing me behind him instinctively.

Brill steps from the shadows between two pillars. His hair is slightly tangled, his rumpled coat hanging open, and in one hand he holds a plasma pistol. His eyes glow feral under the half-light of the chamber.

Shit. Shit fuck motherfucker.

"I have to admit, Lyra," he drawls, stepping closer. "After all our years together, I didn't peg you for a sentimental type."

"Don't flatter yourself," I spit, heart pounding. *Stars, why don't I have a plasma pistol on me?* "We're just returning what doesn't belong to us. Something you clearly don't understand."

"Oh, I understand plenty." His smile is razor thin. "I understand that thing up there is worth more than your entire bloodline. And I understand that you just did all the hard work for me."

He lifts the pistol. Orion shifts, blocking my body with his.

"I wouldn't," Orion growls, low and sharp. "This place isn't just stone and statues. It's protected. Sacred."

Huh. That sounds…ominous.

"Protected by whom?" Brill scoffs. "You? The ghosts of your ancestors? *Please.* I'll tell you what—why don't you go meet them, and then let me know."

He fires.

Orion tackles me, and the blast sears the air where my head was a second ago. We roll across the floor, the heat from the shot scalding close.

Brill advances, fast and brutal. Another shot, this time closer. *Too close.* The sound of it shatters against the temple walls, sending a flock of shrieking birds skyward from somewhere outside.

"Run!" Orion yells, and we dive in opposite directions. Brill swears, pivots toward me.

Perfect.

I scramble up the crypt, stumbling over slick moss.

"Hey, Brill!" I shout, standing right near the edge of the statue's base. "You know something? I hated every single second I had to spend with you. It probably would've made my life a lot easier if I'd just fucked you and been done with it, but the thought of touching you was so repellent, I spent fourteen years suffering every other kind of abuse instead. Pretty pathetic, huh? A half-Velusian who was *made* for pleasure was so grossed out by you, torture was a more enticing option."

He seethes—his eyes burning with hatred. He charges.

Three steps.

Four.

I wait until the fifth, until he crosses the invisible line my memory burned into the backs of my eyelids.

The tile beneath him crumbles with a shuddering crack.

"No—!" he screams, hands scrambling for purchase. But there's nothing. Only open air and ancient gravity. His scream echoes off the chamber walls as he disappears into the pit below, swallowed whole by the hollow floor presided over by the stone Xylothian priestess.

Silence returns.

My chest heaves. My pulse thunders.

Orion climbs up to me slowly, eyes scanning the hole, the idol, my face. He places one palm over my heart like he needs to feel it—like proof I'm still here.

"He's gone," I whisper. Tears prick behind my eyes, disbelief making my knees wobble.

"He is," Orion confirms. His voice is rough, shaking.

We stand there in the hush of the temple, with the Solar Mother watching, the chamber pulsing with peace and old power. Outside, the jungle sings.

I let myself lean into him.

Not because I need to.

Because I want to.

Because I finally can.

Because this is the part they never tell you in the stories. It's not about the fight. It's not about the treasure.

It's the quiet after.

The home you find.

The hand you hold.

The sun rising again.

epilogue

LYRA

A Promise Fulfilled

THE RESTAURANT IS TUCKED into a side street that smells like citrus blossoms and spiced steam. Dim lanterns hang from vine-draped archways, flickering with bio-luminescent gas that paints everything in golden hues. Inside, the walls are carved from obsidian-flecked Xylothian stone, the tables ringed in translucent mineral that shifts color with the mood of the diners. Ours has taken on a shimmering pink-gold.

"I swear," I say around a mouthful of something buttery, savory, and possibly illegal, "if you'd told me you were hiding this place back when I was slogging through jungle slime and being hunted by Brill's meatheads, I would've defected sooner."

Orion grins, sipping something cool and sharp-smelling from a blue crystal tumbler. "You would've hated it if you weren't starving and freshly un-traumatized."

"I hate how much I love it," I mutter, wiping my mouth with

the cloth napkin. "I didn't expect you to actually be good at this 'romance' thing."

His green-gold eyes crinkle at the corners. "I've had good inspiration."

"Who, me?"

"Obviously you," he murmurs, leaning in. "And all those romance novels you kept around on the *Aldrin*."

The mention of my ship sends a whisper of longing through me, and Orion catches it immediately.

"I was going to wait to tell you as a surprise later, but after Brill...well, with the coast relatively clear, Evie sent that Dreller mechanic, Ty, out to Ooneryx to pick it up. She's taking it back to the *Hephaestus* to finish the repairs he started and it sounds like he's going to help give it a thorough overhaul. It'll be ready for us to go grab in a few weeks, and then, who knows? Wasn't there mention of a sandy beach and a tentacled dreamboat earlier?" he says with a laugh.

My heart stutters and my mouth drops open. "You—you're having her fix up my ship?"

He blushes at my disbelief, and I'm ready to climb him like a tree.

"Yeah, I know it's important to you," he shrugs. "If you have particular opinions about any modifications, we can call her in the morning."

Like. A. Tree.

"I...Orion. Thank you, really. I..." I trail off, trying not to let my emotions get the better of me.

He grins, flashing dimples that I want to lick right off his face, and *stars*. The way he looks at me—like I'm the center of his orbit—makes my heart knock around like it's trying to escape. I clear my throat and glance away, not quite ready to sit in the full heat of it.

"I haven't really done a lot of this 'dating' thing. It's nice," I offer awkwardly, oddly nervous.

The look he gives me is sin itself. "Would you be more

comfortable if I approached you wearing skintight breeches and a billowy shirt?" he asks, a teasing lilt to his voice.

My cheeks burn redder than the *Aldrin-136*'s afterburners.

"You're never going to let me live that down, are you?" I grumble.

"I don't know," he drawls, crossing his arms across his chest and leaning back to eye me speculatively. "Seeing Vega dressed up as a drunk-ass pirate was pretty unforgettable. And the poor guy is back to working in the café, waiting on some new contact to drop in and ruin his life again."

I chuckle. "Poor guy. Too bad he didn't let you keep that billowy shirt, though."

"I don't know if I'll ever forgive you for that. But *perhaps* you could persuade me to forget it."

"Hmm," I laugh, tapping my chin. "I *wonder* how I could do that! I don't suppose you have any suggestions?"

He leans forward, tracing circles on my wrist in a maddeningly erotic way.

"Oh," he chuckles, and the low sound arrows straight to my clit. "I have plenty of suggestions. They'll have to wait for after our first dessert, though."

"First dessert?"

The green fire in his eyes is scorching, and I squeeze my legs together to fight the ache building between my them.

"The gnuberry pie here is some of the best on Xylothia. As to our second dessert..." He licks his lips, and I might actually combust. "We'll have that a little later."

Ever the portrait of grace and sophistication, I let out a choking squawk and flag down a waiter faster than Ada saying I-told-you-so.

When we leave, the twin moons are rising over the horizon, and I tuck my arm into his as we walk the quiet stone paths back to his place. His apartment is on the fourth level of a curved habitat structure that spirals like a shell, and inside, it smells like him—moss and rain and something herbal I can't name.

It's small but clean, warm with wood tones and stone floors. There's a pile of half-dismantled weapons on the table, a shelf stuffed with old history books and field journals, and one plush, oversized chair facing the long balcony window.

But what I notice first is the bathroom.

More specifically, the tub.

It's enormous—sunken into the floor with smooth walls hewn from some sparkling white stone and lit from beneath with a soft amber glow. Steam curls off the surface of water that smells faintly of neralis oil and something sweet.

"Holy shit," I whisper, turning in a slow circle. "You weren't kidding."

"Nope," Orion says, already stripping off his shirt. "Come on. I told you—you deserve a real bath."

I grin, not bothering to hide the flicker of arousal his bare chest sends through me. I let him help me out of my clothes, our fingers brushing too long on purpose, until I'm bare before him and he's fully naked, his mating nodes glowing faintly along his thick erection.

He guides me down into the hot water with infinite care, his hands gentle but sure. The second my skin slips beneath the surface, my whole body sighs.

"*Oh stars*, I might never get out."

He settles behind me, strong thighs bracketing my hips, chest to my back. I relax against him, letting my head fall onto his shoulder.

For a while, we just sit. His fingers trace lazy patterns on my arms, down my stomach, across the curve of my hip. The water glows and shimmers, catching his flickering synesfores pulse against my skin—faint green, purple, and white freckles like constellations.

"I never thought I'd be here," I say quietly. "Alive. Let alone...this."

"I always hoped you would be," he replies, voice low. "But I never imagined I'd get to be the one beside you."

My throat thickens. I turn in his arms, straddling him, and the water rocks gently around us. His eyes search mine, open and unguarded.

"I've never belonged anywhere," I whisper. "Not really. But I think…maybe I do now."

"You do," he says, palms warm on my waist. "With me."

When I kiss him, it's soft and deep, heat simmering beneath every movement. The kiss turns slow and molten, his hands rising to cradle my face as I sink against him, skin to skin. I feel the heat of his mating nodes along his cock as I settle above him, his breath catching when I roll my hips just enough to press against him.

"Lyra," he murmurs my name like a wish—a prayer. Like hope. "Are you sure?"

"More than sure," I breathe. "I want to be yours."

Something flickers in his expression—wonder, reverence, the tiniest edge of disbelief. Then he nods, cupping the back of my head and bringing our foreheads together.

"I fought it," he says, voice low. "The mating instinct. I thought I was protecting myself—protecting you. I didn't want to tie you to a life you hadn't chosen."

"And now?"

"Now…" He traces my lips with his fingers, leaving a trail of sweet-scented water in their wake. Our eyes meet—his shimmering with glowing green. "Now I see that you chose it anyway. Chose me."

"I did." I say, dropping kisses across the synesfores on his chest. "I do."

His expression crumples a little—beautiful and raw, and I lean in to press my lips to his.

The kiss begins soft, hesitant—lips barely brushing. But when I exhale into it, when I open for him with a sound that's all surrender, he deepens it with quiet desperation. Our mouths move together like we're learning each other all over again—trading breaths, memories, promises.

His hands slide down my back, splayed wide, fingers tracing the notches of my spine, and I feel the sharp edge of his need tempered by control. Always control. Even now, he waits for me to lead.

So I do.

I shift in his lap, letting the heat between us grow. My body knows him already in fragments—the press of his chest, the tension in his thighs, the hard length of him that nudges between my legs under the water. But now I want all of him. Every inch. Every intention.

When I rock against him, he shudders.

He kisses me again—this time deeper, hungrier, his tongue sweeping into my mouth with a groan that curls straight through me.

I respond in kind, threading my fingers through his damp hair, pulling him closer until there's no space between us. The friction builds slowly—slick skin on skin beneath the surface of the water, the pressure of his nodes pressing lightly against my overheated pussy, his lips now on my throat, my shoulder, the hollow just above my heart.

"I want to remember this," I say, breathless. "The first time we do this—all of this—as yours. As mine."

He nods against my skin, kissing the spot above my pulse. "I won't ever forget."

I feel the pulses of his mating nodes begin to sync with my own racing heartbeat, the bond stirring between us, waking up like a second awareness. A tether—*his* tether. Not one that binds —but one that joins.

When he lifts me just slightly and lets me sink down onto him, slow and steady, the stretch of it fills me with something more than pleasure—something sacred. Our foreheads press together again, his breath stuttering out in a low, broken sound as my body opens to him fully.

It's not frantic.

It's not just need.

It's *everything*.

His hands hold my hips like I'm something precious. He thrusts shallowly, gently, building the rhythm as if our souls are trying to find their cadence. The glowing water ripples around us, shadows dancing across the walls. I clutch at his shoulders, moaning into his neck, overwhelmed by the dual sensation of physical fullness and emotional unraveling.

And when his nodes begin to swell, I feel myself spiraling with him. The pressure as they fill me, fitting inside me like his body was designed to fit mine by some primal, artistic god—it's perfect. He growls low in his throat, his pace picking up in time with the heady *thump thump* of our hearts in sync. His nodes press against that secret spot of pleasure deep within me, and my climax crests on a wave of aching need, crashing over me in shudders that echo through my whole being.

Orion's name is a whisper on my lips, and then a cry, as he comes inside me, his arms locking around my back. We stay joined like that for long moments, shaking, panting, together in a way that goes far beyond bodies.

When the intensity begins to ease, he leans back just enough to look at me. His thumb brushes a tear from my cheek.

"You're mine," he says softly, reverently. "And I'm yours."

I nod, too full to speak, and kiss him again—salt and steam and surrender.

Outside the bath, the world is quiet. But inside this moment, everything is alive.

THE END

acknowledgments

Every star-stealing heroine needs a crew, someone to scream about plot twists with, and at least three people reminding them to drink water and stop rewriting Chapter Seven at midnight. So before the chaos begins, a quick thanks to the real heroes behind this book.

Thank you to Friel, my fearless editor, for stepping in and helping me turn a draft into an actual book instead of a Word doc full of explosions, banter, and emotional collapse. And a huge, extra-special thanks to Brian for being my copyediting champion—my shields were down, my typos were firing, and you still charged in like a hero with a red pen and no fear.

Thank you to my Discordant Owls: my flock, my readers, my cheer-squad across the stars. This book would not exist without your continued support, your chaotic theories, and your willingness to scream about space cake with me. I love you all more than the universe loves dramatic timing. Susan, you sweet soul and stunning talent—my co-pilot, critique partner, and author bestie; I'd choose you in every timeline and galaxy (and happily scream about stuff with you in all of them).

To all the talented artists I've had the pleasure of working with on book covers, character art, and graphics: I salute you with both hands and my whole heart. Sometimes the only thing that pulls me out of a black hole of drafting despair is the thought of an art commission floating toward me through the void. You are magic.

This book was absolutely a labor of love, and I'm not exaggerating when I say it would've drifted off into deep space without the gravity of my family and friends. Big thanks to Finn, Zoe, Michelle, Dad, Mary, Cassie, Alisa, and everyone else who helped cheer me on when I said I was going to write about alien criminals banging.

And finally—to you, the readers. If you followed me from gilded vampire courts into the glittering unknown of alien worlds, you are the kind of brave, curious, beautifully unhinged soul stories are written for. You trusted me to universe-hop, to trade fangs for starships, and you still showed up ready to feel deeply and fall in love all over again. That loyalty is rare and brilliant. Thank you for staying in orbit with me—I hope this adventure gives you even a sliver of the wonder you've given me.

about the author

Lily Riley is a romance novelist currently focused on books that feature a little bit of cheek and a lot of steam.

When Lily isn't writing about dreamy aliens and 18th-century French vampires, she enjoys sipping wine, eating cake, and dancing naked by the light of the full moon.

To sign up for her newsletter or read more about her upcoming projects, visit: www.authorlilyriley.com

other books by lily riley

Vampires in Versailles series:

The Assassin and the Libertine

The Agent and the Outlaw

The Doctor and the Devil